THE GREAT URGE
DOWNWARD

Also from Alyson by Gordon Merrick

The Lord Won't Mind
One for the Gods
Forth Into Light
Now Let's Talk About Music
An Idol for Others
The Good Life (written with Charles G. Hulse)
The Quirk
Perfect Freedom

THE GREAT URGE DOWNWARD

GORDON MERRICK

alyson books
los angeles | new york

MANUFACTURED IN THE UNITED STATES OF AMERICA

THIS TRADE PAPERBACK IS PUBLISHED BY ALYSON BOOKS,
P.O. BOX 4371, LOS ANGELES, CA 90078-4371.
DISTRIBUTION IN THE UNITED KINGDOM BY
TURNAROUND PUBLISHER SERVICES LTD.,
UNIT 3 OLYMPIA TRADING ESTATE, COBURG ROAD, WOOD GREEN,
LONDON N22 6TZ ENGLAND.

FIRST EDITION PUBLISHED BY AVON BOOKS: 1984
FIRST ALYSON EDITION: OCTOBER 2000

   01 02 03 04 ▇ 10 9 8 7 6 5 4 3 2

ISBN 1-55583-296-2
(PREVIOUSLY PUBLISHED WITH ISBN 0-380-88971-X BY AVON BOOKS)

COVER PHOTOGRAPHY BY MICK HICKS.

AUTHOR'S NOTE

This novel—like *Perfect Freedom,* which preceded it, where Robbie Cosling also figures—had its origins in long ago, long out-of-print work. In both cases I have dealt with characters and themes that I was unable or unwilling to explore thoroughly at the time. Over the years they remained naggingly in my mind like unfinished business or an unpaid debt. In this case, so little remains of the earlier work—a setting, a family background, the partial outline of a plot—that it's worth noting only for the sake of an occasional reader with the gift of total recall who might be afflicted at moments with a sense of *déjà vu. The Great Urge Downward* is an original publication of Avon Books. It has never before appeared in book form.

G. M

"WHAT DO people *do* down here?" Lance demanded, his manner successfully concealing the hopelessness that swept over him as he phrased the question.

He stood with his hands resting lightly on his hips, wobbling his knees in and out so that, except for the fact that he didn't move his feet, he looked rather as if he were doing a tap dance. The hotel clerk to whom he had addressed his question sat motionless behind the cement reception desk of the enormous dusty lobby with his arms folded across his chest. He spoke good English, for which Lance would have been grateful if he'd had any desire for communication.

"You mean the tourists?" the clerk asked through scarcely moving lips.

"Yes, I guess so. Is there anything I should see or anything?" He wasn't interested in sights; he hoped only that he wouldn't become one. The one and only, the amazing Lance Vanderholden. He continued to jiggle his knees without being aware of what he was doing. The slight exertion made sweat break out on his body in the thick, airless heat of the hotel lobby. His legs ached. He had had quite a walk the day before.

"You are not a friend of Mrs. Rawls?" the hotel clerk asked, looking at his guest and thinking, Oh, what a life I would have if I looked like that. Oh, the girls!

"Mrs....?" Lance began, not quite following the conversation.

"Mrs. Rawls. You don't know her? So." The clerk moved his shoulders slightly as if everything had been

1

explained. Lance glanced at the big, rumpled, fleshy man leaning against the far end of the reception desk who appeared to be concentrating on the blindingly bright square outside the entrance.

"Mrs. Rawls, you say? Who is she?" He stopped jiggling, hoping for information that would give his mind something outside himself to hang on to.

"She's an American. She is perhaps peculiar but she has done much for Puerto Veragua. We are grateful to her."

"She lives here?"

"Indeed, yes. She lives on the Hill, where all the foreigners live. *That* is something you can do. Go to the beach at the Hill. On the other side of the bay. All the foreigners go there."

"Are there many foreigners in Puerto Veragua?" Lance asked, congratulating himself for keeping this pointless conversation going. He stood with his hips thrust a little forward, his blond head up, lithe, graceful, full of unconscious power, wondering why the clerk was staring so intently at him. Had there been pictures in the papers even down here?

"There are more every year," the clerk said. "Mostly, the people who come here are friends of Mrs. Rawls. She has many friends."

"I might as well go down and look things over. Do they have someplace where I can change?" Lance looked down at his shirt and his dusty linen slacks.

"About that, you can do as you wish. We don't encourage nakedness but I believe Mrs. Rawls and her friends are careless about clothes."

Lance looked at the clerk for a moment with a ghost of a smile hovering on his wide mobile mouth.

"Oh, man," Lance said lightly, using his voice to load the exclamation with irony. The clerk had noticed the voice already; it flowed deeply, avoiding the flat, domineering note he associated with North Americans. Lance forced a chuckle, picked up the suitcase he had just fetched from the bus station, and headed off toward his room.

The big man who had hitherto remained silent heaved himself around with a windy sigh and leaned his stomach against the desk. He pushed his face into his hands so that it became a grotesque assortment of lumps and rolls of flesh.

"Interesting. Interesting," he said, looking at the clerk sleepily. "The rich are always interesting."

"Why do you insist he's rich?" the clerk demanded, gazing off after his departed guest. "If you'd seen him arrive yesterday, you wouldn't have thought so. He was carrying his shoes in his hands, like a peasant. I almost asked him to pay in advance."

"I understand the bus broke down again," the big man said. His name was Ramiriz and he was the chief of police.

"Yes, but that's no reason to walk seven kilometers in the afternoon sun. The rich never walk. He must be mad."

"He is handsome," Ramiriz mused.

"Handsome? *Ai!*" the clerk protested. "I didn't know a man could be so handsome. What success he must have with the women!"

As he considered this, the police chief hoisted himself around so that he was leaning sideways against the desk and put one hand on his massive hip. He looked out at the tattered palm trees and the hard-packed dust of the square and grunted. "Yes, life is apparently lively where he is," he said thoughtfully. "I wonder why he comes here."

Some half an hour later, the subject of this conversation was stretched out on the beach indicated by the hotel clerk. Prepared for something lurid, he found only a pretty, sheltered stretch of sand on the seaward side of the peninsula, populated by dark, silent children and a few middle-aged, adequately covered people whose features marked them as foreigners but who were all burned a native shade of brown. Lance felt pale and conspicuous. He lay on the sand and felt the sun sting into him. Now, if he could just keep his mind from wandering. The immediate present was the thing to think about. New surroundings must bring new thoughts. Otherwise, what would be the point of being here? Was it enough that in this remote corner of Central America he could hope that nobody knew who he was? After the last few weeks, it was a great deal to hope for.

3

Yesterday, passing over the crest of the coastal hills, he had been quite impressed by the panorama spread before him: the narrow plain confined between sea and hills, the ridged peninsula that flung a protective arm around the quiet bay, the pure white curve of the beach fringed with nodding palms. Even the village of tiled roofs huddled at the head of the bay had looked inviting from a distance.

"Why don't you go to Puerto Veragua?" Andy had suggested the other day—Andy who had managed everything, without whom he could never have left New York and found some measure of forgetfulness in traveling. "D. H. Lawrence or somebody once lived there. It'd give you something to do while I'm sweating through these contracts."

Because Lance was afraid of being a burden to his friend, who, after all, had work to do in the capital and couldn't play nursemaid indefinitely, he had acted on the suggestion.

His thoughts hung in his mind limply, blending into each other in the merciless heat of the sun. He rolled over onto his stomach and couched his head in his arms. If only he could get rid of the feeling of guilt that seemed to have entered into his skin, making his body tight and sensitive. He might eventually come to terms with the loneliness and the sense of irreparable loss, but the guilt would gnaw on relentlessly—guilt now for being stretched out luxuriously in the sun, guilt for not knowing anything better to do, guilt for having run away.

The four years since the end of the war—all he could consider his adult life—was a record of failure. There was no running away from that: a wrecked marriage, the brilliant beginning of a career he had voluntarily abandoned, and now, finally, the disaster that had brought him here. He was oppressed by a sense of some obstacle in himself, some obstacle that hid him from himself. Everything he did seemed to turn him into something he wasn't.

He jumped slightly when he heard a voice close to him say, "Aren't you an American?"

He turned over and sat up, shielding his eyes from the sun with one hand. Squinting, he saw a trimly built middle-aged woman standing beside him. Her hair was gray and smartly arranged. A bold attempt had been

4

made to compensate for age with cosmetics. A wide expanse of sagging, heavily tanned flesh separated the two pieces of her bathing suit. Her features were sharp and firm. As he looked up she smiled and cocked her head slightly on one side in a way that was utterly charming—intimate, coquettish.

"Yes, I am," Lance said, warming to her with his quick friendliness, and almost simultaneously checking himself. He didn't want to get involved with people, especially Americans.

"I thought so." Her voice was soft but persistent. As she went on, she seemed to install herself without changing her position. "I noticed you when you walked down the beach. Something about the way you moved reminded me a little of Jack Barrymore. He was a dear friend of mine when I lived in Hollywood. Before the war, of course. I'm Flip Rawls. I usually know everybody who comes here. I've made a sort of hobby of Puerto Veragua." Lance had risen and now he offered the woman a sandy hand.

"My name is Lance Vanderholden," he said, slurring over it and watching her closely. She seemed to take it in her stride. She enclosed his hand in both of hers and looked up at him with her shyly childlike, irresistibly winning smile.

"How nice to meet you. Of course, I should've known."

Lance's hopes fled. The name demanded obeisance. If his family wasn't the richest in America, it was certainly *one* of the richest, and this detail was insignificant in view of its age and prestige. One could follow the Vanderholdens back through generations, active, prolific, unexpectedly Roman Catholic, across an ocean to an exotic burst of minor titles, back to where history became obscure. Lance slowly brushed sand off his behind, wondering how much she knew, or rather, how much she thought she knew. Her smile didn't change but her manner somehow sharpened and her voice became more assertive.

"Of course, I know all your family. The Junius Vanderholdens. Let me think. Lance. That's right, you must be Marcus."

"I was until I decided it didn't sound like me. Sort of Roman and imperial. I prefer Lance."

"Your Uncle Somers was a true friend of mine. *He*

5

was a great friend of the Roosevelts. We had wonderful times together. Albany. The Governor's Mansion. Franklin was governor then. I remember there was that English writer—not Huxley. I've never liked Huxley. He behaved so ridiculously because I wouldn't receive him when I was living in London... What was I telling you?"

"About the *other* English writer," Lance prompted hastily, scarcely daring to hope that his family had been so quickly bypassed. He smiled encouragingly.

"What lovely teeth you have. So important." Mrs. Rawls leaned forward slightly as if to get a better look at them and then went on. "Yes, he wrote some terribly clever books. I don't know what ever became of him. I'm sure you'd know him. I'm so terribly out of things down here. My friends don't understand it—they think I should go back to London or Paris or New York, where my life has always been, you know. But it isn't time yet. A place has a cycle in one's life, don't you think? You mustn't break it. I'll know when the time comes." She pronounced the last with such conviction that even she seemed startled. She glanced around vaguely and then motioned graciously to the sand. "Sit down, Mr. Vanderholden, sit down. I didn't mean to interrupt your sunbath. Tell me what brought you to Puerto Veragua." Lance sat as he was told, like a guest in her drawing room. She remained standing.

"Oh, well..." he began with a shrug.

"It's a fascinating place," Flip Rawls continued, as if he had answered her question satisfactorily. "You'll love it. Of course, you really have to become part of the native life. But that's true anywhere, don't you think? You must become part of the native life. Have you been in the water?"

"No, I haven't. It looks—"

"It's marvelous. It's the only place in the world I can really swim. The Mediterranean doesn't compare to it. You can stay in for hours. Do you like to swim?"

"Yes. Very much. I'm—"

"I thought so. You've got a swimmer's build. Good heavens, your body is stunning. It's so important—a good body. That's one thing I don't like about the States. They don't pay enough attention to the body." She regarded his with frank appreciation. It had been admired

6

by others, but since he had made no effort over it, it seemed as alien to him as the rest of his discarded heritage. He would just as soon have been a hunch-backed dwarf.

There was an instant's silence and then she lifted her hand to her hair, drawing her own body up, and chuckled youthfully. "Isn't it dreadful we all have to get old? Of course, you wouldn't know about that. Still— the *Junius* Vanderholdens. How old *are* you? Twenty-six or -seven?"

"Almost twenty-eight," he put in, but she scarcely skipped a beat in her conversational flow.

"It's never too soon to start taking care. I really think the Starnovsky method is the solution. Do you know it? I've made a study of it. Fascinating. I'll have to teach you. Why don't you have lunch with me? There's nobody there so it won't be very exciting but I find it's such a relief to be alone for a change, don't you? For me, it's a real need—a spiritual need. Of course, I've had hordes of people in the house for months and more coming next week. I suppose I shouldn't let them but I've never known how to refuse. I've always given so much of myself. Join me when you've had your swim. I'm over there at that blue cabana. This is really my working time. I'm doing a book on China and one simply must stick to a sched-ule. You'll find that yourself. There's no hurry. I don't lunch till three." She smiled her shy little smile and bowed graciously and was off down the beach before Lance could struggle to his feet.

He watched her until she was at a safe distance and then flopped back on the sand, stretched out full length, and laughed—really laughed, fully and satisfyingly, for the first time in weeks. It came from deep in his throat, thick and rich, so that one could almost hear in it the swelling of his neck muscles.

"You crazy lady," he muttered. Then he realized he'd let himself in for a lunch party and the laughter died in him. He didn't want to see people, especially here, especially someone who knew his family. All he wanted was a few days alone, a few days to get used to the idea of being alone again; then he would go back. It did no good to dwell on the fact that he had nothing to go back to.

The sun fell on him like some great weight. He felt

7

as if his body were being pressed into the sand with the force of it. It drained him of all sense of identity, whoever he was. He wished he could lie here forever.

When he joined Flip Rawls, he found her sitting at a table under a blue tent, like a general conducting a desert campaign, confronted by a mass of untidy manuscript. She greeted him with disjointed delight.

"Come in. I'm so glad you could come. Oh—how silly of me. I get so absorbed I forget where I am. Carried right out of myself. Just let me finish this paragraph. The publishers have been after me to do this book for years and I've finally found time. It's fascinating material. I'm just whipping it into shape." She bent over her dog-eared papers once more, scratching at them distractedly with a pencil.

Lance stood in front of her, his legs spread and his toes dug into the hot sand and his arms folded across his chest, watching, feeling that it was all unreal— himself, his being here, this woman writing a book about China on a tropical beach, everything. After a few minutes, she put down her pencil and looked up at him as happily as a child being released from lessons.

"There. Now I think it's time for a drink." She began to gather up her things, handing odds and ends to Lance, retrieving them, replacing them with others.

Finally everything was packed up and she led him to the road, where a casually dressed young Indian was waiting beside a large, aging Buick. Dark, almost naked children materialized around her and she stopped, opened her bag, searched it elaborately with one eye on the watchful children, deliberately creating suspense, and then handed around coins with lingering solicitous attention to each recipient.

The great lady succoring her poor, Lance thought. An instant antagonism toward Mrs. Rawls tightened his muscles.

As he was following her reluctantly into the car, he hesitated, suddenly aware of his costume. Acting on the clerk's words, he had changed into his brief swimming trunks at the hotel and had nothing else with him.

"Damn," he exclaimed, not quite convincingly, for he was thinking now of escaping from her. "I haven't got anything to wear."

8

"Oh, get in, get in. It doesn't matter in the least. I'll give you something. Or you can go naked if you like. In Africa I got so used to seeing people wander around with nothing on that I don't even notice it anymore. Nudism is so healthy, don't you think? Except that most people are sinfully ugly. I once spent a weekend in a nudist colony in Germany but that was very different. Beautiful people. Beautiful. Like gods. All Nazis, I suppose, but they couldn't help that. It gave me a completely new feeling about the human race."

They drove up a winding road on the side of the Hill while Flip Rawls chatted on about China, India, Capri, with passing references to Noël Coward, Lady Mendl, Somerset Maugham, and a great many others whose names she couldn't remember. It sounded to Lance terribly outmoded and prewar. Suddenly his loneliness became a new and piercing agony. As tears burned behind his eyes, he struggled to whip his attention back to the smooth flow of Flip Rawls's self-congratulatory reminiscences.

In a few minutes they drew up in front of a blue wooden door set in a mud-colored wall.

"Here we are," she said complacently. "It's a funny sort of house but I think it's rather exciting. I designed it myself and practically had to build it, too. It cost a perfect fortune but I don't regret a penny. That big architectural magazine—*Architectural Something-or-Other*—you know, it's absolutely tops—they sent people down to take pictures of it. They said it was the finest example of tropical building they'd ever seen."

On the other side of the blue door, they descended through a series of terraces of orange trees and great cacti and strange tropical plants. At every turn of the path there were vistas of sea with blue hills beyond, framed in fantastic patterns of myrtle and oleander and towering century plants. The air was heavy with the hot scent of flowers and herbs.

"This is the guest house," Flip Rawls explained as they came upon a low pavilion around a bend in the path. "Use this first room. You'll find plenty to wear— sarongs, fishermen's things from St. Tropez, heaven knows what all. I really must go over these things someday. Some of them are priceless." She flung open closets and drawers overflowing with brightly colored fabrics.

"When you're ready just follow this path down as far as it will take you. I'll have a drink ready for you."

Alone, Lance was tempted to look through the exotic clothes surrounding him but couldn't dispel his mood, and kicking off his wet trunks, he snatched up the first thing that came to hand, a blue sarong shot with silver threads, and wrapped it awkwardly around himself.

He found his hostess mixing drinks on a long, curving, covered terrace that resembled the promenade deck of an ocean liner, an effect heightened by its being built on the edge of a sheer drop to the sea: all that was visible from its parapet was a limitless expanse of sky and water. It was strewn with low tables and over-stuffed bamboo chaises longues.

"Perfect," she announced, surveying him as she handed him a drink with the winning little tilt of her head. "You picked just the right one. I can see you have an eye for color. You must keep it. Here, I'll show you how to wrap it."

Before Lance could explain that he had nothing on under it, she had whipped it off and given it a vigorous shake. He had no time to react, however, for her hands were deftly adjusting the fabric around his waist, like a mother dressing her child, and for a moment he felt himself enveloped in a disarming human warmth.

"There. That makes all the difference," she said, standing back from him and giving no sign that she had been aware of his nakedness. "You don't want it all bunchy in the middle."

They had several drinks and a meal of exotic dishes accompanied by appropriate French wines.

"How long are you staying in Puerto Veragua, Mr. Vanderholden?" she asked over coffee.

"Oh, just a day or two. I've—"

"Why so quick? You should stay. I'll tell you what. You take the guest house for as long as you want it. I have some charming boys coming next week but I can just as well put them here. I have lots of room. That way, you'll have it all to yourself. I feel you're depressed and nervous. Have you suffered some unhappiness recently? I can tell those things. India, you know. I lived there several years. Uncanny. What was I saying?"

Lance's heavy lids had dropped slightly, and the corner of his wide mouth twitched.

10

"You were talking about my staying here," he said quietly. "It's very kind—"

"Nonsense. It would give me pleasure. Of course, you might prefer to rent but there simply isn't anything here. You can't stay in that awful hotel. It's no place for a person who's been through a bad time."

"No, really. I haven't planned—"

"Well, there's literally nothing else here," she said with odd vehemence. "Anyway, they demand outrageous rents. Your name and being an American and all. You might not mind but it's the natives I'm thinking about. So bad for them. I've really discouraged any sort of real-estate development here. If there were houses for rent, it would turn into just another resort."

Her insistence intrigued him. Perversely, it occurred to him that it might make sense to take a house for a week or two, just to be completely on his own for a bit. The sun and the swim this morning had steadied his nerves, but he had no intention of being Flip Rawls's houseguest and did his best to make this politely clear to her.

"Well, if you should change your mind—somehow I think you *should*—just bring your things out whenever you like," she said in parting.

When her chauffeur had deposited him back in the village, he put on some clothes and wandered around looking for something to send her. He gave all his attention to the quest, eager to find something that would please her.

As he wandered, he came across a real-estate agent's office and acting on the impulse Flip Rawls had inspired, he went in. Houses? Why, Puerto Veragua was famous for the number and desirability of its houses. Beautiful houses, all practically being given away. The agent spoke in Spanish and scrappy English, helped along by the few words of Spanish Lance was able to contribute. Before he could think of the words to excuse himself, he was being bundled into a car and driven back along the road he had just traveled, past Flip Rawls's blue door, and half a mile farther to a house not unlike hers on a miniature scale—two rooms and a kitchen built along a partly covered terrace with the same immense view of the sea. Its water supply was a

11

well and there was no electricity. Lance was ready to admit that perhaps Flip Rawls had been right.

Didn't he think it was beautiful? At least, that's what he understood the agent to ask him and he agreed that it was *muy bueno*. They drove back, the agent wreathed in smiles. When Lance was thanking him and taking his leave, it appeared that there had been a misunderstanding. Much Spanish, obviously angry, while Lance looked on helplessly. At last, he gathered that the agent considered the house rented. He protested. The agent insisted. Lance had apparently said something that closed the deal. Incapable of creating bad feeling where money was concerned, he gave in and asked the price. It was ludicrously low and included a servant. Lance paid the month's rent demanded of him. He didn't care how he spent the little money he had left, so long as he kept enough to get home. What the hell. He would stay for a week. Maybe Andy would come down for the weekend and they could go back together.

He wrote that evening to his friend in the capital:

Dearest Andy Bear—I made it, whatever "it" is. I've just been conned into taking a house for a month, which is about 25 days longer than I wanted. Don't worry. It doesn't cost anything. I don't like beds you haven't slept in, so please come and get my new one warm for me. It's about 110 in the shade here so you don't have to take that literally. If you have to go back to NY suddenly like you said, just leave my bags with the hotel or, if you think it's safer, send them down here. Try to get down. I won't go on saying thank you but I'll never stop saying I love you.

Sir Lancelot

(I happen to be writing on a round table.)

He moved in the following morning. The place was deserted but there were signs of somebody's having been there since the day before—fresh mosquito netting over the big beds in the two rooms, some cheap garden furniture scattered about the terrace. He dropped his bag in one of the rooms and went out to the edge of the terrace.

Silence. Silence and heat and the sun turning the sea into a blinding sheet of light. He squinted and lifted his hand and slowly began to twist his long fingers through his thick blond hair. Far off to the left he could see a big clump of foliage and a bit of tiled roof that he supposed must be Flip Rawls's place. He pulled off his shirt and dropped it on the terrace wall and ran his hands over his muscular arms and torso, wiping away the sweat. He looked down at himself and slowly, with infinite care, plucked one stray hair from his smooth chest. It was so still that he fancied he could hear the hair give way. He lifted it between thumb and forefinger, scrutinized it to see if it had come out whole, and blew it away. He absently rubbed his chest where the hair had been and the corner of his mouth twitched. Loneliness grew in him, threatening to break his controls. This is the way it's going to be from now on, he told himself. Where in hell was the servant the agent had promised? he wondered impatiently, seizing on any pretext to take his mind off himself.

He looked down across rocky, precipitous ground to the sea. He couldn't even get down to take a swim. Down maybe, but it would be hell getting up again. Well, that was something to do to pass the time. He could hack out some steps down to the sea. A private beach. His mother would approve. The Vanderholdens liked to feel they owned things that were generally considered part of the public domain, like the sea or a city park. He turned abruptly and went back to a bedroom to unpack his bag. The effort of hanging up his light summer clothes brought sweat streaming from him and he took off his trousers. Even in jockey shorts, he felt heavily dressed. He had begun to gather up his shirts when he heard a light step behind him. He turned, crouching on the floor over his bag. A girl was standing in the door.

The sun was bright behind her, so he couldn't see her face clearly but he saw that she was wearing a white blouse and a long full skirt that fell almost to the ground.

They remained motionless a moment, staring at each other like two startled young animals. Then Lance sprang up, snatching his dressing gown off the floor and pulling it around him.

"What is it?" he demanded, surprise making his voice harsh.

13

The girl took a timid step back into the light. He saw that she had a flat face, like the faces he had seen in Balinese drawings, round with great, wide-apart, almond eyes and a soft mouth whose lower lip was almost the same size and shape as the upper. Her black hair was drawn straight back and wound in plaits on the back of her head. She was not tall and her body, though not heavy, looked capable of hard work. She stood with her hands at her sides gazing at him steadily with wide eyes.

"What do you want?" he asked more mildly. *"Yo no hablo español."*

She spoke rapidly in Spanish and, seeing his look of blank incomprehension, beckoned him out onto the terrace and indicated a basket of provisions. She picked it up and led him into the kitchen where she set it down and spoke again. All her movements were slow and without sharp definition, as if she were saving her strength.

"Usted..." Lance pointed at her and performed a complicated pantomime that included sweeping the floor, bending over the stove, and washing dishes. When he was finished he had created a meal, complete with messy pots.

She watched him with the simple wonder of a child and finally she laughed with a restraint that matched her movements. Her body didn't sway or contract. She uttered a series of high fluty sounds and then nodded, smiling at him, and said, *"Sí."* She looked awfully young to be a servant.

He wanted to say something friendly in welcome but he could think of no words, so he made a frustrated gesture and smiled.

"I can see it's going to be very stimulating, from a conversational point of view," he said. "I'll go finish unpacking." She received this information with unblinking attention and remained standing beside her basket of provisions until he had gone. He returned to his suitcase feeling a little less lost.

His unpacking completed, he returned to the terrace wrapped in Flip Rawls's sarong. He sat on the parapet, his knees up, clasped in his arms, his chin resting on them, watching the kitchen door like some odd, passionate, brooding god. Whenever a pot clattered or fat hissed over the fire, a reluctant smile played across his lips at the thought of the child performing her grown-up chores. Eventually she emerged bearing a steaming dish. Lance sprang up and stood over her as she set it down on the table where a place had been set for one.

"Adonde usted comida?" he asked, looking around for the Spanish phrase book he had brought with him. She looked up at him as blankly as if he had spoken an unknown tongue and after a moment's hesitation started back to the kitchen without speaking. He followed her and found her own place laid on the kitchen table. He gathered up plate, knife, and fork and carried them back to his table. She trailed after him. He drew up another chair opposite his and gestured to it. She sat down obediently.

"Comida con migo," he said. He was watching her for signs of embarrassment or uneasiness but she seemed to be taking it placidly as part of her job. Their eyes met and he rewarded her with a dazzling smile. For the second time since he'd been here, his rich laughter burst from him at the way she sat, prim and self-contained and terribly young.

"Well, this is great," he said. "What have we got here?" He served them what appeared to be fish buried under a scarlet sauce and she began to eat with her head bowed over her plate. He continued to watch her.

"You're very pretty," he said with his mouth full and laughed again as she looked up with a polite attention that suggested she would be delighted to speak to him if she could. "What's your name?" He put down his knife and fork and leafed through the phrase book. Growing impatient, he put it aside and branched out on his own. *"Usted. Nomme. Nomme usted."*

She uttered her careful laughter and spoke at some length during which he heard *Luisa* repeated several times.

"Usted...Luisa?" he asked.

"Si." She nodded.

"Yo...Lance." He pronounced the *e* as a separate syllable to make it easier for her.

"Señor Lance," she repeated gravely, turning the *c* into a soft *ch* and the *e* closer to *o,* as in *Sancho.*

"No. No *señor.* Lance. *Es todo.* Lance."

"Si, señor," she agreed.

15

"Lance," he insisted.

"Lance," she whispered at last with the reluctance of a child who is encouraged to do something she knows is wrong. They ate. She served several more dishes deep in fiery sauces. Every time she leaned across the table, her loose blouse fell away from her shoulders revealing her round childlike breasts. It was a pleasant sight and Lance wasn't insensible to it, although he felt himself forever beyond the reach of physical sensation, past wanting or caring.

When the meal was over, he withdrew to a deck chair at the end of the terrace to give Luisa working room, but he found himself watching her as she moved around the table, studying the slow-motion movements of her legs under the long skirt, observing the way her bare feet seemed to grip the ground. When she went to draw water from the well, he jumped up to help but she shook her head vigorously. It was good having somebody moving around the house. It created a homely atmosphere but it was a bit of a nuisance, too. He would have liked to stretch out naked in the sun, but the place was so small that there was no corner where she mightn't stumble on him. Finally, he went to his room and took a nap.

When he awoke, the sun was setting with the unleashed splendor he was learning was characteristic of Puerto Veragua. He went to the edge of the terrace and stood between sea and sky, looking down at the waves rippling into the rocky cove below and up at the glory of the passing day. It began at the top of the sky in piled-up castles of pink cloud. Below were the foundations of color on which they rested, like the strata of the earth, orange and bloodred and purple. Slowly they shifted into the deep velvet tones of night. The sky was filled with the announcement of night and the sea grew still at the wonder of it. What could one do with a day to justify the majesty of such an ending? Lance wondered with uneasy awe.

His contemplation was interrupted by the arrival of Luisa around the corner of the house, carrying a hissing lamp that gave off a bright white light and had the effect of banishing the twilight, so that the day was turned abruptly to night. They ate a light supper together, engaging in fragmentary conversation as at lunch. When she left him, vanishing into the night, he wanted to call her back. As he sat in the bright pool of light shed by the lamp, the night drew in, whispering secretly, until it seemed to tower just outside the circle of light, threatening in its immensity.

He had the whole long evening ahead of him, alone. He should have asked the girl to stay with him a little longer. What had ever possessed him to move to this desolate house? He stared broodingly into the night and cursed the habit of money that had made him rent it so casually. When he thought of the way he had lived these last few days, letting himself drift, lolling in the sun, he felt the quick stirring of anger with himself. He felt his mind drifting back into the past and he fought against it. It was too painful and it couldn't tell him anything anyway, except that he had struggled to find his own place in the world—his own place, not that provided by the accident of birth—and that every time he thought he had succeeded, everything had gone terribly wrong.

Sitting alone, with the night so close that it seemed he might touch it, the future seemed a dark void. He would stay here long enough to get his nerves straightened out and then he would go back—to work, to achieve something, even though there was no longer any hope of reward. His savings were almost gone. There was that to look forward to—the force of necessity, the relief of no longer being able to choose.

He awoke the next morning to find Luisa already there. She presented him with a breakfast of beans and chili sauce topped by a fried egg, which after a moment's hesitation he downed without protest. Her presence made the place seem bearable once more and in turn charged him with energy. After breakfast he set off down the road in the blazing morning sun to pay his respects to Flip Rawls and to deliver the bit of native pottery that was all he had been able to find for her in the local market. He also hoped he might borrow some tools to create his private beach.

He found her on her terrace having breakfast, a very different affair from his, all silver pots and dainty slices of toast. The *New York Times* was folded beside her. He doubted that there had been anything about him in it for more than a week. In view of her strong stand on

17

the housing situation, he was a little embarrassed about telling her what he'd done but she was unruffled by his news.

"I'm so pleased," she purred with the delightful tilt of her head. "I didn't dare suggest it myself—one never knows with people—but I hoped—I had a *feeling* you might come to it. Those things are in our destinies."

Lance felt as if she had tricked him somehow. She showered him with invitations—for lunch, for dinner, for lunch the next day—all of which he refused in order to hold his own against her. Eventually he made off with a pick and shovel and trudged back along the dusty road, indulging himself by imagining that he was a real workman with a real job for which he would be paid. He had always enjoyed things that were supposed to be disagreeable, like selling his possessions during the brief period when he had had the exhilarating experience of being broke. He had been fascinated by pawnshops; necessity was a tonic.

He attacked his self-imposed task vigorously. He liked the feel of his muscles straining and he liked the sting of sweat in his eyes and the sun burning into his body. He liked in a perverse way the searing sting in the palms of his hands as the tools raised blisters on them. By noon he had hacked tenable footholds out of the rocky ground all the way down to the cove and when he reached the bottom he let himself fall into the sea with an enormous splash, still wearing shorts and sandals.

He worked his way out of them in the water and swam around naked for half an hour, diving and splashing and feeling surprisingly pleased with himself. Occasionally he looked up at the little house, where a flitting shadow told him reassuringly that Luisa was in competent charge. When he climbed back up in his dripping clothes, she indicated to him that lunch was ready.

After lunch, he decided to settle the question of his privacy once and for all. He dragged a deck chair to the farthest corner of the terrace and called Luisa to him. He wanted to explain that while he was in the chair he might be naked and in any case was not to be approached. Luisa stood beside him with the patient attentiveness that was becoming familiar to him.

18

"I like to take sunbaths without any clothes on," he explained in English. He made gestures of removing his sarong and stretched himself out in the deck chair. He rose and pointed at her and made forbidding signs that were supposed to indicate that she was to keep her distance. He went through the motions of removing his sarong once again. Not convinced that he had made his point clear, he stretched out in the chair again and closed his eyes and gestured the sarong away.

"*Si*," she said.

He heard her moving beside him and then his sarong was unfastened and hands were on his cock. He let out a yelp and shot up into a sitting position as if a gun had gone off behind him. She was kneeling beside him and her blouse was gone. Her firm young breasts pressed against his thigh as she leaned down to him and ran her lips and tongue lightly over him. He was too astonished to do anything but enjoy it. His cock sprang up to welcome her attentions. He guessed that she couldn't be more than sixteen but she was doing everything with assurance and composure and great skill. Perhaps it was a local custom.

She hoped that the way her father had taught her to do it would also please a foreigner. Her brothers liked it. She was the only female in the household and it was a great honor for her to be allowed to pay homage to this sacred part of a man. Her father had taught her that it was a sin only if she allowed it to be put into her, as many fathers did with their daughters. He had taught her to remove her blouse because playing with her breasts added to the pleasure. The foreigner had made it clear that he wanted to be naked. She had been sent away from her last work because she hadn't understood her duties and she didn't want to risk its happening again.

The *señor*'s prong was much bigger than the ones she was accustomed to and she wasn't able to put much of it into her mouth. She hoped that she could please him with her hands. She loved holding it. At first it had been as soft and tender as some small wild creature. Now it was big and hard and mighty, as if it were about to release its juice. For the first time, she didn't want a quick ending. She loved having it in her mouth and feeling it and looking at its beautiful color, pink and golden. If all men looked like this, it would be very difficult to resist the great sin of letting them be inside her. She had never before been tempted but she longed to let this one into her.

Recovering from his astonishment, Lance drew her up and put his mouth on her adorable breast and nibbled a nipple. She felt him get very hard when he did this and she uttered little cries of delight, knowing that she pleased him. He lowered his hands to the waistband of her skirt, trying to find out how to unfasten it. She pushed his hands away and pulled back and shook her head and spoke at some length. Was she telling him that she was a virgin and that their pleasure must be restricted? He couldn't think of anything else she would have to say under the circumstances.

He smiled and nodded and let her continue the service that she performed as if she were proud of her accomplishment. She brought him easily to a wrenching orgasm, ending his long celibacy. When the spasms had subsided, he took a deep breath and rose and pulled her gently to her feet. Her small breasts lifted to him with the firm buoyancy of youth. She looked more than ever like a Balinese drawing. The problem of naked sunbathing had been solved.

Her blouse was lying where she had dropped it and he picked it up and held it in front of her. She reached for it but he shook his head and smiled. "No shirt," he said in Spanish. "Never here. Beautiful like that." He let it fall on his sarong and took her hand and led her to the bedroom. He wasn't going to try to seduce a child but she had released his carefully disciplined sexual needs and he wanted to find out how far she was willing to go. He wished he could explain that she could be safely naked with him; they could give each other much pleasure without his entering her.

He held her in front of him beside the bed and cradled her breasts in his hands. He stooped to kiss them and straightened and drew her closer so that he could feel them lifting against his chest. He leaned to her and took her mouth in an exploratory kiss. She seemed to expect and welcome it. Her hands moved over him and dropped to his cock and stroked it. He drew back and smiled into her eyes as she revived his erection. She obviously liked it that way.

She released him and unfastened her skirt. His heart gave a little leap of excitement but subsided as she dropped it and he saw the white petticoat under it. She made no move to remove it but took a tentative step toward the bed and looked at him questioningly. He nodded and they stretched out together and he held her sweet brown body lightly in his arms.

"Here tonight?" he asked in Spanish. "All night?"

"*Si.*"

He kissed her again, fondling her breasts while her hands stroked his erection. He reached down to lift the petticoat to test his understanding of the rules. She seized his hand quickly and fell back, her breasts quivering with her rapid breathing. If she let him touch her there she wouldn't be able to resist him. It was too great a sin to commit until she knew more about him. She saw that the tip of his beautiful pink and golden prong touched the little hole of his birth and her body seemed to turn all liquid as she thought of it inside her.

When he woke up he was sprawled out alone in the bed, still with a hard-on, his body heavy with heat and sleep and satisfaction; he stretched lazily, a smile playing around his lips, and called her name. After a moment, he gathered himself together and leaped out of bed and went to the terrace. She was nowhere about and he stood irresolutely, wondering about her. Was she available to everybody who took this house? Had it been a momentary folly that she had immediately regretted? With the memory of her lovemaking fresh in his mind, he didn't believe either possibility.

He felt himself stiffening with desire and took a few paces around the terrace. He had needed a girl. It changed everything. For the first time in weeks he found himself thinking ahead to an hour from now, to tomorrow, without the awful sinking emptiness in the pit of his stomach.

He went in and took a leisurely sponge bath from the pitcher of water on the washstand. He dressed in shorts and shirt, considering a walk into town to look for her if she didn't come back soon.

He was spared the trip. She returned just as color was beginning to flow into the sky. He was at the table trying to make time pass with a Spanish lesson when he heard her footsteps stop at the end of the terrace.

21

He looked up and saw her standing there holding a little bundle at her side. They stared at each other for a moment and then he jumped up and went to her. When he reached her, he looked down into her eyes and they exchanged a questioning look. He leaned over and kissed her, reaching for the intimacy that had been interrupted by his falling to sleep. She accepted his kiss and lifted her bundle and explained slowly in simple words that she had brought some things so that she could stay.

So that's all right, he thought, and smiled and nodded his approval.

She looked up at him with little expression in her almond eyes and round, smooth, untroubled face. She was thinking that he was splendid with his fine, big body and his rosy skin. Her eyes slid from his immaculate linen to the golden hair curling close around his head. Most splendid, and smelling so good. She thought he must be very rich to smell so good.

He saw her eyes widen in a way that made him laugh softly from deep inside him. Taking the bundle from her and putting it down, he reached around behind her and unfastened her blouse and removed it. "No shirt here, you understand?" he insisted.

He shed his clothes and put her hands on his cock. It was erect by the time he drew her to him to feel her nipples hardening against his chest. Sex might partially restore him to life, but he was glad that she had imposed limits. What she permitted, although surprisingly sophisticated, was like children playing together. If she had allowed him to take her, there would have been the risk of a commitment he wasn't ready for, might never be ready for again. He didn't know how much was left of him that could be deeply touched and he was afraid to find out. Thought exposed feelings that were still raw and bleeding. He welcomed the mindless pleasure of his body, her breasts pressed gently to him, her hand holding his cock as he turned back toward the bedroom.

That evening over their simple meal, the phrase book at hand, he told her that he was married and had two children but that he hadn't seen any of his family for more than a year. In fact, he hadn't ever seen his second child but that was too complicated to explain.

22

She accepted his information with equanimity. She was accustomed to living each day as if it were all of life and the fact that he was learning to speak to her so gently and kindly was more real to her than any shadowy wife he had left behind. Surely he wouldn't bother to learn words if he wasn't going to stay with her awhile. She would serve him and give him pleasure. That was all a man could want of a woman. When he told her that he didn't know how long he would be staying in Puerto Veragua, he put into words her own simple knowledge that no one knew what the next day would bring. He hadn't said that he was going. She would watch for signs that he considered the place his home, at least for a little while, and then she might commit the great sin, even if it gave her a baby. Her father and brothers would know what to do about that. She had a friend who had had a baby without being married and her family had immediately found her a husband, an ugly old man whose wife was dead. She wouldn't mind being given a husband if first she could sin with this beautiful foreigner.

He tried to tell her about the world he had left behind but all she really grasped was what she had already suspected—that he was very rich, beyond her capacity to understand riches. This was just the contrary of the impression he was trying to convey but his vocabulary was too limited to make her understand what it meant to be disinherited. There was so much to explain, so much that he didn't completely understand himself.

"Grande. Muy grande," he said with an expansive gesture, caught up in his memories of the marble house on Fifth Avenue where he had passed his youth, the house where he was no longer welcome.

He could see by her expression that Luisa was forming a vague picture of something vast and glittering like places she had seen in movies with rows of girls dancing in them. He saw the massive dark reality: the glass and wrought-iron portal, the bleak marble entrance hall; the silent, black-clad figure of Morris, the footman, holding open the elevator door; the curtained opulence of drawing room, dining room, music room, and library; the more cheerful comfort of his mother's study, the vast, rarely used ballroom, the bedrooms above where everybody could at least escape one an-

23

other; and the distant shadowy regions behind closed doors where the servants lived and worked, the forbidden region that had excited Lance's curiosity simply by being forbidden. Closed doors, the life outside the limits fixed by family tradition, had exerted a powerful tug on his imagination from the beginning.

He was the repository of the glorious tradition. His mother had instilled in him, a fatherless child, the sense of being the fruit of an immaculate conception, wholly hers. The atmosphere he breathed was almost too rarefied to support human life. He felt at times that he would suffocate if he didn't throw open the doors that enclosed him but as he grew up he had given her nothing specific to complain of. Everybody agreed that his manners were exquisite. He never raised his voice or laughed immoderately. He deferred to the opinions of his elders. He was able to satisfy her that he had learned that most essential element in a gentleman's equipment, self-control.

But little things he was scarcely aware of revealed an unspoken tension. He sometimes failed to answer when he was spoken to, lost in absorbing thoughts of his own. He had developed a slight twitch in the corner of his mouth and he had a nervous mannerism of combing his yellow hair with his big-knuckled fingers. A cousin at a family gathering told him that when his heavy lids were lowered over his very blue eyes, his face acquired a strange, hooded look, almost like a mask. "Restless and dangerous," the girl had called him, to Lance's delight. Had his mother noticed that look? She had apparently been better prepared for his rebellion than he.

A rebellion against nothingness. The world of the Vanderholdens—no joy, no tragedy, no uncurbed passion, no creativity, no ambition, no adventure—was built on negatives. There was something in the air that supported his rebellion. The world outside was changing. The fighting men had returned to civilian life, claiming their rewards for killing. Class and social distinctions were blurring. The sense of immutable order that he remembered from his prewar childhood and early youth was gone. He had the feeling that the Vanderholdens were obsolete, that he was an anachronism.

24

Once his mother had issued her edict, barring her door to him and cutting him off without a penny, he had had no choice but to rebel, although he found it difficult at first to put rebellion into practice. He learned eventually that he could at least be a sexual rebel; he had had plenty of shackles to cast off in that respect.

Both he and Pam had been virgins when they went to their marriage bed and it hadn't occurred to him that a well-bred woman, a lady, would find any pleasure in the sight of a naked man. His sexual initiation had embarrassed him so deeply that he had suffered a momentary failure, and after that the dread of being impotent had led him to hurry through the act so that there would be no risk of his not being able to carry it to a conclusion. He told himself that a "nice girl" like Pam wouldn't want him to elaborate or prolong it. Except for the professional expediency of his affair with his Broadway costar, he had been faithful (husbands and wives were *always* faithful) and he had remained so until his spectacular success on the stage had permitted him to send Pam and the baby to the country for the summer while he led a bachelor life during the week. Before he knew it, he had abandoned himself to a life of joyful promiscuity, discovering that lots of women, even "nice" ones, liked looking at naked men.

He was first taken over by three women from the show who lived together, and they spent many inventive days and nights discovering everything that three women and a man could possibly want to do together. A procession of women followed. Sex was a wonderful, new, narcotic world and he plunged into it wholeheartedly, sensing that he had finally found himself. It was another break with the rigid conformity of his past, just as deciding to be an actor had been, and confirmed his growing awareness that his whole life was going to have to be a constant breaking away, a remodeling of everything he had been trained to be.

He meant nobody any harm and because his sexual partners were experienced there were only occasional tears and heartbreak. For the most part, that summer had been a composite of hot, sleepy afternoons and cool, promising dawns, lying in darkened rooms with the sound of muted laughter in his ears, his nostrils full of heady, female smells—perfume and flesh and secret essences.

One of the few disciplines he had imposed on himself during Pam's absence was regular attendance at an athletic club for a workout and massage, not out of vanity but because his role in the show was physically demanding and he had to keep trim as an antidote to women and late hours. He found one day that old Mac, the regular masseur, had been replaced by a youngish guy who introduced himself as Jim. He was probably in his mid-thirties, with a powerful bodybuilder's physique and an open, amiable, all-American face.

He had a light but manly scattering of hair on his chest that Lance envied. Women sometimes called him a sissy for being so hairless. When Lance lay down on the table with a towel draped loosely over his middle as usual, Jim told him that he could work better without it and Lance pushed it off indifferently.

After a few minutes, he began to wonder if he should have hung on to it. There was an insistent caress in the skillful professional hands that he felt sure must be intentional and caused a surprisingly pleasant fluttering in his groin. If a guy could make him feel this good, he shouldn't complain, but it raised unexpected questions. The oil Jim was using doubtless had something to do with it but that was a technicality. He hoped that what he was feeling wasn't visible yet.

Unless he misinterpreted the hands' intentions, he was confronted at last with forbidden sex. He had heard endless joking references to cocksucking and buggery, especially during his stint in the navy, but he had never quite believed in homosexuality. School was the place where boys were supposed to play with each other, but except for a friend who had declared his love amid tears on the day before their graduation, he had never seen anything of it.

He had begun to see quite a lot of it in the theater but it still seemed to be considered rather a joke. There were several effeminate boys in the show who flirted with him unabashedly but even they didn't seem to take it seriously. As he went about his business in the theatrical district, he was aware of guys who looked at him in a particular way but in their case it was more frightening than funny. They looked like trouble. He was

26

committed to opening all the doors that had been closed to him, to casting off whatever shackles remained, but he reluctantly admitted to himself that he might not be ready to plumb all the depths.

As the massage progressed from neck to shoulders to arms and chest, there ceased to be any doubt; this big muscular guy was a pansy. The way the hands moved in his armpits and over his nipples was less massage than a search for erotically sensitive areas. Lance's cock lay between his legs but its stirrings grew more pronounced. He had never felt so naked in his life. He didn't care if the masseur thought he was a pansy, too, but feeling himself on the verge of erection raised doubts about his equipment. He had never seen a guy with a hard-on so he had no way of knowing how his measured up. He wasn't attracted to Jim in any way that he recognized as attraction but he couldn't deny that the guy was making him feel sexy; and if it showed, he wanted it to be worth looking at. He hadn't had any complaints, but women probably weren't reliable judges.

He felt a growing purposefulness in the way Jim lifted one of his legs, bending it at the knee, and held it against his chest while he went to work on the inside of his thigh. His hands swept down over it so that they brushed against his cock. Lance's breath caught as it swelled lethargically and began to stiffen. There was no doubt of its showing now. An explicit forbidden move might still shock him into calling a halt but so far he felt no inclination to interfere.

The masseur moved Lance's foot down to the end of the table to straighten his leg. His cock rolled up and lay on his belly. His cheeks burned with shame but he made no move to hide it. An involuntary moan escaped him as a hand stroked it to complete his erection. Jim put it in his mouth. Lance's body leaped and he uttered a cry of astonishment or protest and then lay back and was still, acquiescing.

He couldn't stop him without making a scene. He had a hard-on. Jim wanted it. Lance admired people who knew what they wanted and took it without apologies, regardless of consequences. He was having his cock sucked by an expert. Sex was sex, even with a guy. Another door had opened.

Jim's mouth was much bigger than a woman's; he

27

felt as if his cock were being swallowed. He closed his eyes and abandoned himself to pleasure. He was being brought to a climax with startling rapidity. He made small, murmuring warning sounds and to his dismay, Jim desisted. He gave Lance's shoulder a tug in a way that told him to roll over and Lance held his cock and placed it under him as he did so. Lance remained frustratingly close to orgasm and wondered if he was expected to reciprocate in some way. He had let the guy give him a hard-on, for God's sake. What more did he want?

Jim trailed a hand over his body as he moved down to the foot of the table. Lance heard unidentifiable sounds and then his legs were parted and Jim clambered up onto the table between them. He didn't need encouragement, after all. The masseur kneeled over him and dropped forward with his hands on his shoulders. With long sweeping gestures, he began to apply oil to his body from shoulders to buttocks and down between his thighs, fondling his balls.

Lance felt indecently exposed but congratulated himself for allowing his body to be handled in this way. The novelty of it excited him, resistance to being wanted by a guy sharpening his appetite for the unknown. He lifted his hips slightly to ease the pressure on his cock. Jim made a sound like a grunt of satisfaction and slid his hand under his balls and stroked his erection. He lifted his hips higher to allow the hand free play. Both hands became active on him, kneading his thighs, squeezing his cock, parting his buttocks. A finger was inserted between them and exerted electrifying pressures within him. He gasped as he was brought still closer to orgasm. He started to twist his hips away but the imminence of climax paralyzed his will. He apparently could be made to come this way.

Jim ran his oiled hands up over his body again and slipped them under his chest. He folded himself over him and drew him in against him. Panic struck as Lance realized that his partner was no longer wearing shorts. A man's nakedness was pressed to his. He felt the hard thrust of his erection against his balls. His heart pounded. There was a strange drumming in his veins. He began to tremble so violently that he lost control of his body. Jim drew back and gripped his hips and drove into him.

"No!" Lance shouted as everything in him was abruptly wrenched into a knot of outraged protest. His body was being brutalized, every shred of decency in him violated. He writhed and bucked as he struggled to free himself but the grip on his hips was implacable and the invasion slowly deepened, growing enormous, too great for him to contain. It was tearing him apart. Pain sharpened outrage. He was being fucked.

The word splintered his mind. A man was in him, finding loathsome satisfaction in him, indifferent to his consent. His instinct to protect himself wavered as a deeper urge came boiling to the surface, an urge to participate in his own debasement. He was being dragged down into the filth of life, being compelled to face for the first time his common humanity. He claimed no special rights or dispensations. Resistance was shattered. He was overwhelmed by his will to surrender. Tension drained from his body. The pain was gone. Hard flesh moved smoothly in him, asserting its mastery of him.

He began to move to Jim's rhythm. His erection had wilted under the initial assault but he became incredulously aware that it was reviving. He was being taken, possessed, enslaved. The fastidious Lance Vanderholden was nothing but a body being used for a man's pleasure. He exulted in his degradation. He wanted to be fucked.

Their bodies were in tune for the approaching climax. They grunted and cried out and Lance shouted with triumph as they had simultaneous orgasms. He welcomed the full weight of the powerful body that collapsed on his back in tribute to his ability to serve another's desire. His chest was heaving but he was scarcely aware of having had a sexual experience. He retained no sense of pleasure or lust satisfied. It had been a psychological shock, a radical realignment of his whole personality. He felt as if he had taken a first faltering step in learning who he was. He was lying under a man who was still in him, defiling him, retaining his claim to him. Lance belonged to him more than he belonged to anybody else in the world.

He uttered an audible gasp as Jim withdrew from

29

him. He lifted himself off the table and Lance watched the strong back disappear into another room. He still hadn't seen the instrument that had forced his surrender. He lay numb and motionless, soiled by his own sperm, amazed and appalled. There was an emptiness in him that he had never felt before, an emptiness that could be filled only by a powerful man seizing him, brutalizing him, bending him to his will. He couldn't think clearly about what it meant. He was seething with outrage and revulsion and an exultant sense of having triumphed over his carefully cultivated sensibilities.

Jim returned and stopped near him. "You can go clean up if you want," he said in a quiet, pleasant voice, the accent softer than a New Yorker's.

Lance was aware that Jim was wearing his shorts again but he couldn't look at him. How could he face a guy who had fucked him? Jim turned away and Lance quickly pulled himself up from his mess and hurried to a small bathroom. He took a healing shower, assessing the damages. He was sore but seemed unharmed. Trailing a towel at his side, he returned to the massage room. Jim was standing at a trolley-table arranging tubes and bottles on it. Lance forced himself to look at him as he approached. He saw no conqueror's gleam of triumph in his eyes, only stolid amiability. Jim's apparent indifference was more humiliating than letting himself be had. He wanted him to pull off his shorts and take him again. Still unsure that his cock was big enough to offer for inspection, he lifted the towel over it while it burgeoned startlingly.

"I've never been fucked before," he said.

"That so? Don't let it throw you. Lots of guys don't know they want it until it happens. You sure as hell wanted it. God, what a body. Having my cock up Lance Vanderholden's ass made me feel like God Almighty."

The crude words thrilled him; they stripped him of all pretensions. "You know me?" he asked.

"Doesn't everybody? Mac told me you were one of his regulars."

"How did you know I'd let you?"

A small grin appeared on Jim's friendly face. "It was obvious. You were hot for it. I don't go in for rape. If

30

you want to make a definite date for next time, I'll be sure to be free for you. We can have some extra time."

"Tomorrow," Lance said, amazed by his unhesitating shamelessness. "Four o'clock."

"Okay. Try not to be late."

It sounded like a parental admonition. Lance had always wondered what it would be like to have a father. Jim's authority over him was absolute by right of possession. He couldn't imagine refusing another session. He dropped the towel to his side, revealing what had happened while he stood in front of him, waiting to be sure that he was still going to be dismissed.

"Okay. I've seen your cock," Jim said, smiling comfortably. "It's a beauty. Beat it before I start thinking I'm Superman."

"Is yours much bigger?"

"Bigger than that thing? No such luck. You'll see tomorrow."

"It felt huge."

"Look, cocks are like clothes marked Small, Medium and Large. Guys who take Large aren't all the same size. I might be a Large but you're bigger. Why should I have to tell you? Don't you suck?"

"No."

"Famous last words. See you tomorrow."

Lance thought of him during the rest of the day and first thing when he woke up with a girl at noon the next morning. He was coming to terms with the experience. The moment when he had resisted, the moment when Jim had taken him by force, was seared on his memory. He had felt a sense of atonement not unlike, he thought unexpectedly, what he imagined he was supposed to feel when his mother sent him to confession. As he entered adult life, he had begun to be aware of sins of which no priest could absolve him— the sin of being spoiled and pampered and protected, of being suffocated by privilege. Jim's merciless cock had been an instrument of absolution. He was learning to atone for his heritage. His humiliation had given him a glimpse of genuine humility.

Somehow, he didn't think it had anything to do with discovering that he was queer. Atonement wasn't supposed to be a pleasure. Nobody had ever made demands on him the way Jim had. Regardless of shame or suffering, he was eager to offer himself for his satisfaction.

When he went to his appointment that afternoon, he had a hard-on almost before he had closed the door of the massage room. He discarded his towel. Jim looked up with his small grin from the trolley-table.

"Well, hi there," he greeted him. "Thanks. That's very flattering." He peeled off his shorts and sauntered over to him. Lance's eyes were fixed on an erection for the first time in his life. It looked muscular somehow, like the rest of Jim's body, knotted and aggressive and bigger than he expected a cock to be. Something in him instinctively recoiled from it. He glanced down at them both and saw that his own was undeniably bigger. He felt a small lift of pride as Jim put his hands on him appraisingly, looking down at it.

"I've seen bigger. You should be thankful it stopped there. I know a kid with a twelve-incher. He has a terrible time, poor guy. Nobody can figure out what to do with it."

Jim put his arms around him and pulled him in against his powerful body. His tongue was aggressive when it entered Lance's mouth. Lance hadn't known that guys kissed each other. It seemed a bizarre dislocation of the natural order and he responded avidly. Their whiskers scraped against each other.

Jim released him and pulled a wrestling mat out from a wall and threw towels and a bottle onto it and pulled Lance down to it. He kneeled over him, his hands on his hips, his knotted erection thrust out with crude command. "Okay. Let's see Lance Vanderholden suck cock."

Tears of shame stung the back of Lance's eyes as he moved to obey. He could feel Jim observing him as he opened his mouth wide to receive him. His craving for self-abasement provided an illusion of eagerness to his performance. His own erection grew painfully rigid. The hard flesh in his mouth felt like some strange rubberized manufactured product, unlike anything his lips had ever touched. It stretched his jaws uncomfortably. It didn't satisfy any of the senses. He couldn't feel the pleasure he was presumably giving, as he could when his mouth was joined to a mouth. He supposed that the reward might come with orgasm but hoped that it

32

wouldn't reach that point. He was grateful when Jim pulled back.

"That does it. I don't want to come," he said.

"Don't I do it right?"

"Beautifully. You're going to be an ace cocksucker but I've just got started on you. We're in no rush." His expert hands took charge. Struggling against shame, surrendering self-respect, Lance felt as if his body were being reinvented. It assumed positions at the slightest bidding of the hands, legs sprawled out wantonly or lifted in the air, kneeling with his body flung out backwards on the support of Jim's arm so that his cock soared into his mouth. He masturbated when directed to do so and his ejaculation was flung out between them, soiling them both.

"Fuck me," Lance blurted, swept by a fierce exhilaration at acknowledging his abject lust for punishment. He cried out as a blinding flash of pain struck him. He choked on a sob. Tears welled up in his eyes. Jim knew that he didn't want to be spared.

The next few days dulled the edge of Lance's ecstatic submission to the masseur's will. He lost the exciting feeling of being brutalized. His body had adapted. He had learned how to serve Jim's depraved demands. That thrill remained but what they actually did, their unorthodox acts, became a banal catalogue of sexual license. He had grown accustomed to the feel of a man's body, but caressing a cock or a hairy chest appealed to him less than caressing a girl's soft body. He felt in closer contact to ugly reality but he was sure there was a world of depravity that remained closed to him. He kept hoping that Jim would impose on him some ultimate degradation beyond which there could be no further atonement. The thought of it kept his cock hard for his partner.

When he went for his usual appointment after a Sunday break in the country with Pam, he found old Mac, the regular, back at his accustomed post. Lance didn't ask any questions. He assumed that Jim must have been a temporary replacement. They had never talked about anything except sex. Jim hadn't felt it worth mentioning that they wouldn't be seeing each other again. Maybe Mac had returned unexpectedly.

He was left with the feeling of emptiness but supposed it was time to stop before he went too far. Whatever cravings remained in him were too daunting to be explored except under duress. Shackles still confined him. The looks he encountered from guys in the street no longer frightened him but he didn't see anybody he felt like taking on. He doubted if many queers could match the masseur's brutal authority. He couldn't imagine choosing to go to bed with a guy simply for peaceful pleasure.

He had been booked with Geraldine Fleet, his costar, to make a publicity appearance in Chicago on the following Sunday, flying out after the show on Saturday night, and he had checked to make sure that they would get back early enough on Monday to see Jim before the evening performance. He wouldn't have to worry about that anymore.

Waiting at the airport for the plane to load, he left his star sitting with their luggage and wandered off to a newsstand on an island in the middle of the lounge. As he browsed, his attention was caught by a pretty girl similarly occupied on the other side of the stand. He gazed at her across a stack of newsprint. She looked very young and her short brown hair was boyishly tousled. All he could see of what she was wearing was the top of an open-necked man's shirt; a view of her breasts was cut off by magazines. She looked up and their eyes met. Despite her youth, hers immediately filled with such explicit, knowing sexuality that he began to get an erection. He had never known a girl to make it so clear so quickly that she wanted him.

She lowered her eyes while his mind searched frantically for something he could do with her. There was only half an hour before his scheduled departure. An airport offered no shelter for eager lovers. He hadn't ever picked up a girl and this seemed hardly the time to try.

She looked up again and their eyes locked into each other. The desire in hers was almost palpable, like hands caressing him. She seemed to take it for granted that they were going to make love. Her lips parted and he saw the tip of her tongue between them. His heart accelerated. He was struck by something undefinably odd and ambiguous about her, suggesting that sex with her would be different from anything he had ever experienced. She inclined her head as if to beckon him and turned and strolled away.

He was immediately in motion. As he rounded the newsstand, he got his first full-length look at her and, with a shock that almost brought him to a halt, he realized that she was unmistakably a boy, wearing sports shirt and slacks. The momentum of pursuit carried him on while his mind raced to adjust to facts. He was being led to a door marked MEN. He had heard of things happening in men's rooms that sounded pretty disgusting but his tastes had lost a good deal of their refinement in the last few weeks. His erection was straining to be let out.

The door the boy had been heading for closed behind him. Following him into the big antiseptic room, Lance couldn't deny that he found it a bit alarming. Danger lured him on, not any danger in the pretty youth but the danger of discovery. A man was standing at the end of a long line of urinals. The boy had stationed himself at the opposite end but others might move in closer to him. Lance knew that his erection was too big to produce in front of a urinal without everybody seeing it. He would be committing a public indecency. Crossing the few yards that separated him from the act, he felt an army of Vanderholdens watching him, wailing and rending their garments and sprinkling ashes on their heads with shame at his descent into further depravity.

When he reached his destination, the boy eased himself over toward him so that their shoulders touched. It took Lance an incredulous moment to accept the fact that his companion was unabashedly, if discreetly, masturbating; the motion of his hand was imperceptible except from Lance's vantage point. The instrument he was manipulating was startingly substantial for such a feminine kid, bigger than Jim's. Maybe Jim had filled him with misplaced pride about his own. It was too late now to avoid finding out.

He struggled with a tangle of shirttails and shorts, and produced the evidence. He took a small backward step to avoid contact with porcelain and edged around toward the boy so that his back was partially turned to the other urinals. He felt reasonably safe from observation although his position might look odd for the ostensible purpose of his being here. The boy made a

35

murmur of admiration. Lance saw that he had nothing to fear from comparison. An impulse to thrust it forward to touch the other was abruptly curbed by his catching movement out of the corner of his eye. The man at the other end was going through the motions of completing his business. Lance dropped his hands to shield his nakedness and prepared for an outraged denunciation.

His heart was racing as the danger passed. He heard footsteps receding and the sound of the door opening and closing. A hand pushed his hand out of the way and moved on his erection, taking bold, expert possession of it. His orgasm was instantaneous and his knees buckled as his ejaculation splashed out into the urinal. A hand moved purposefully beside him and another ejaculation jetted into the air in front of them. It was followed by the sound of the door opening and closing again and approaching footsteps.

With panicked haste, Lance wiped himself with his handkerchief and bundled himself back into his trousers. The boy's composure seemed unshaken as he unhurriedly followed suit.

"Going to Chicago?" the girlish stranger asked. The hum of ventilators and the rush of water made private conversation possible. The new arrival stationed himself halfway along the row of urinals.

"Yeah," Lance said.

"I'll see you on the plane. Be sure to get a seat by yourself. First class?"

"I think I'm supposed to have some sort of compartment."

"Perfect. My God, Lance. Your cock. I'll give you the best blow-job you've ever had."

With that blithe boast, the boy turned and moved toward the door with graceful assurance. He had said his name. People had recognized him long before he had set foot on a stage, so it gave him no satisfaction. It simply added to the danger. He was courting blackmail. He felt very daring, beyond any hope of rejoining the ranks of the privileged few. He was sinking deeper into the mass of corrupt humanity. Lance followed the boy slowly, letting the distance grow between them. By the time he was out, his astonishing partner had disappeared among the loitering passengers.

When the flight was called, an escort presented himself to usher them on board, followed by a uniformed attendant carrying their belongings. His mother would have approved but Lance found it irksome. He felt as if he were being isolated from the contamination of his fellow passengers. He didn't see his pretty playmate and wondered if the ostentatious VIP treatment would scare him off. He should have expected difficulties when he was in the mood to open more doors.

Makeshift compartments had been rigged up for them at opposite ends of the first-class cabin. They had each been allotted two seats with the arms removed and curtains hung around them, so they had adequate beds and a degree of privacy, but the accommodations weren't suitable for the athletic display Gerry expected of sex so Lance was able to give her a quick good-night kiss without fear of reproach and went a few rows forward to his curtained space.

An attractive stewardess was waiting to get him settled. His attempts at a flirtation were repulsed by smooth professional cordiality. He dropped into a seat across the aisle from his improvised compartment; there was no need to make himself difficult to find. The stewardess told him that there would be only five or six first-class passengers, so he could take all the room he wanted.

Once airborne, he read *Variety* until box-office figures began to make him sleepy. The handful of first-class passengers snapped off lights and retired for the night. He rose and stretched, stepping across the aisle to his compartment. He experimented with the curtains for privacy. They closed around him adequately, although anybody brushing against them might open gaps through which he could be seen.

His seats had been made up like a bed, with sheets. It looked inviting. He wanted to take his clothes off. He had never heard of anybody getting undressed on a plane but he couldn't see any reason not to. He would be more comfortable—and more easily available to a visitor.

He was beginning to wonder whether either of them would dare act on the boy's brash offer. It would be even more dangerous than what they'd done in the men's room. The stewardess might pop her head through the curtains at any moment to see if he were comfortable. Was he ready to let her find him naked with a pretty boy on his knees in front of him? He could see the headline in some tabloid: VANDERHOLDEN NABBED ON PLANE FOR HOMO OFFENSE.

He stripped to the waist, opened his traveling case, and pulled out a sheer silk dressing gown. Throwing it over his shoulders, he wormed his way out of the rest of his clothes. Being naked in these odd surroundings completed his erection. If Pam ever stopped making him feel that it shocked her, he might get over his impulse to produce it for anybody who seemed interested.

He turned out all the lights within his control except for the pinpoint reading light and stretched out on top of the sheet with his dressing gown on but unfastened and carelessly draped over his midsection. Returning to *Variety* to check the fortunes of people he knew in out-of-town shows, his attention was caught after a few minutes by something displacing his curtains from the outside. They billowed slightly as if someone were feeling for the opening. His grip tightened on the newspaper while his eyes followed the movement of the curtains. His heart was beating rapidly with apprehension; they were running an insane risk. The curtains parted. The pretty boy slipped between them and closed them behind him. Nothing had deterred him.

Lance didn't have time to notice what he was wearing before he was wearing nothing at all. A slim, willowy body was outlined in dim light. Lance started up with a residual instinct to resist but made amends by running his tongue along the considerable length of the erection that swung against his face in the cramped space. The boy uttered a little yelp as Lance let his dressing gown fall off to free his arms. He lifted them to encircle a slender waist and sank back, bringing the boy down on top of him. The insubstantial body lay on him lightly and went limp with a sigh of surrender. Soft yielding lips were pressed to his. His experience with Jim provided little for him to draw on now.

He opened his mouth to a skillfully provocative tongue. Making love with him was almost the same as making love with a girl. His hands strayed over smooth delectable flesh, soft and with no pronounced muscles or hair. The slim but somehow voluptuous body coiled around him with knowing eroticism. The chest pressed to his wasn't much flatter than one or two women he

38

had known. His hands moved down and found richly curving buttocks. He stroked them with pleasure. He was doing nothing that he mightn't do with a woman, only he was doing it with a boy.

The boy drew back with lingering little flicks of his tongue, a rapturous smile on his soft lips. "Oh, God, I wish we really could," he whispered. "Your cock, darling. Utter bliss." It was obvious what he wanted and Lance was glad that circumstances forbade it.

The boy snaked his way down over him, worshiping his body with his mouth as he went, and slid to the floor to make good his boast.

Lance sat up, the ardent worshiper at his feet. He shifted so that the pinpoint of light picked out the contortions of the lips that felt so eager for him. The boy's face looked rapt and ecstatic. He couldn't imagine a cock inspiring such adoration in himself.

His eyes moved to the flimsy barrier that hid them. Through a gap in the curtains he saw a light in the ceiling of the cabin outside. Thinking of how easily they could be observed set off the strange drumming in his veins. He was naked and visible to anybody who passed, having his cock sucked by a naked boy. An immediate orgasm shook him, the convulsions of his hips a tribute to the voracious mouth. His ejaculation was eagerly received and swallowed. Jim had never carried it this far. Neither had women. It was amazingly satisfying. He saw that the boy was providing his own satisfaction, holding a towel in front of himself.

Lance shook off a postcoital lethargy. He couldn't accept pleasure without attempting to reciprocate. He pulled the slim body up onto the improvised bed and slid down and took the boy's place on the floor. He moved the big cock to catch the light. It looked gentle, prettily formed and somehow effeminate. Lance was reminded that until he was almost fifteen he'd thought that women had them too. If they did, he wouldn't hesitate to make love to them.

He opened his mouth and directed the cock into it and used his lips and tongue to simulate welcome as he had learned to do with Jim. He rolled his eyes up and saw the glitter of ecstatic eyes gloating down at him. He saw himself as he'd seen his partner, his mouth stretched to receive him, prostrate in abject worship.

He cringed from the gloating eyes and his stomach knotted in protest as he steeled himself for the dreaded conclusion that he'd been spared so far.

Violence seethed in him. He wanted to sink his teeth into the hard flesh that was sliding into his mouth again. He dug his fingernails into quivering thighs and raked the boy's chest and flanks with them. The slight body swayed and lurched, buffeted by ecstasy. Lance's mind exploded with half-formed images of tumultuous bodies, priapic and dangerous, clamoring for satisfaction, himself in the center of them being taunted and tormented. He caught an intimation of the absolution he craved.

He realized that he was erect again. He heard muted cries above him and his mouth was flooded with thick pungent fluid. He forced himself to swallow it. His stomach turned over in rebellion and settled. It was disgusting but he'd done it. He was an ace cocksucker. He was always surprised to discover that he was good at anything.

Lance returned to New York with his name, Bryan Singleton, and his Chicago telephone number, and a tendency to take second looks at the effeminate boys who had been flirting with him. If any of them had been as pretty as Bryan, he might have welcomed the opportunity to find out if a boy could make a satisfactory substitute for a woman. Bryan had left him wondering what it would be like if he could ever bring himself to take one as Jim had taken him.

He made the most of the last few weeks of his summer freedom. Once Pam and the baby returned to the city, he was planning to become a model husband again.

He said a dutiful farewell to his latest girl friend the night before Pam was due back. No more dates. No more parties without his wife. Probably no more boys, although it seemed less important to make hard-and-fast rules about them since a boy would hardly be a threat to a marriage.

Pam returned full of plans for another baby although in bed she continued to act as if she would just as soon know as little as possible about how it was to be accomplished. He loved having little Angela back and looked forward to having another one, maybe a son. That might give a whole new interest to life.

His good intentions persisted mostly because the resumption of a normal married life kept him too busy to make straying easy. The casual women he'd been having weren't worth the trouble of a complicated double life. If he was occasionally tempted by a guy, circumstances were never right for him to do anything about it. Fragmentary fantasies haunted him from time to time but fantasies weren't for real life. The door Jim and Bryan had opened for him threatened to lead to a radical confrontation with some new appalling reality. Despite his determination to reject everything he'd been taught and accept the promptings of his nature, he couldn't accept being a faggot and, except for some dimly remembered moments with Bryan, he had no reason to think he was one. He had just barely come to terms with the profound changes in his life and wasn't ready to face so soon another reassessment of his place in the world.

He still had so little to hold on to. His theatrical success had been too easy to have any real substance or provide a sense of direction. He looked back on the first months of his marriage as the most exciting of his life, unexpectedly faced with poverty, living from hand to mouth in a tiny apartment, losing himself in an anonymous crowd of young hopefuls. When the show closed, he might once more be one of the unemployed, forced back into a couple of cheap rooms with the burden of babies, but the show gave no signs of closing. He had a strong feeling that he was waiting for something.

When he met Scot he discovered what he was waiting for. He was waiting for love, for a grand passion with its discipline of dedication and self-sacrifice. Everything about him was wrong for Scot. She hated his background, his flashy celebrity, the triviality of his work. She was tough-minded and realistic and against her coolly rational better judgment, she fell helplessly in love with him. He didn't leave Pam for her for the simple reason that Pam had already gone. Luck left him free to give himself to the joy and heartbreak of the most crucial experience of his life.

Beginning to be able to talk to Luisa, rather than simply enjoy their childlike sex play, brought it all back

41

to him more painfully than he wanted. The agony of the last weeks had locked him into himself in a way that blocked self-examination. He had been paralyzed, an inert tangle of incommunicable suffering. His faltering but increasing ability to explain himself to Luisa made things flow in him again.

When Luisa asked if she could keep a couple of chickens, he leaped at the small challenge. He set to work constructing housing for them with bamboo and rushes, determined to prove that he wasn't completely helpless. She watched his efforts with a good deal of astonishment and dismay. She didn't want to become a nuisance by asking him to do chores.

"It's only for chickens," she pointed out.

"Yes, but if chickens not happy, they no make eggs," Lance said in his erratic new tongue.

"Perhaps in North America," she conceded, "but here they lay eggs anyway."

"Yes, but more happy, more eggs," Lance insisted and Luisa didn't argue because he gave her the impression that he was enjoying himself. He was so pleased with his success at binding bamboo into mats that he built a palisade of bamboo around the outhouse to give it a tropical look. He started digging up a plot for vegetables.

"There is no use doing that," Luisa told him, convinced that this was something no one could enjoy, not even an unpredictable foreigner.

"Why not?"

"Because you can't make any money farming here."

"I have no hope for money."

"Then why do you do it?"

"Because—" It took him a moment to select his words whenever he tried to express an idea. "It is good the ground make things."

"But if you want vegetables, why not hire somebody to work for you? There are men here who will work for very little."

"No, no. It is good to put things in the ground yourself and then they grow. It is good to eat things that you put in the ground with your hands. It is an idea."

"It's a difficult idea to understand—to work if it isn't necessary."

"But it is good work. You will see." He was surprised

at such a sophisticated attitude toward work but supposed that it was due to his inability to express himself adequately. If there was anything good here it was that his day was regulated by the rising and setting of the sun, that he could work with his hands plunged into the earth or wander around almost naked under a huge straw hat, exposing his body to the sun and air.

Working with his hands was a revelation. He had discovered that he liked to make things, build things. He hadn't felt so close to finding an identity since the opening night of his show. Then, it hadn't lasted for more than a few minutes. It was when the curtain fell on the final scene and rose again to thunderous applause that he had believed that he finally knew who he was.

As he stepped forward to take his bow, press photographers crowded down to the orchestra pit and the theater exploded with flashbulbs. The pictures would show him standing alone, tall, blond, a faint, incredulous smile on his lips, his eyes shining with a dedicated light. A thousand voices proclaimed their approbation. The tremendous moment had been recorded for history.

The next day as he looked at the pictures, doubts had already begun to undermine his proud confidence. The captions told the same old story: it mattered very much what his name was. The news wasn't that the theater had acquired a bright new talent but that a Vanderholden had done something unexpected. He should have changed his name. He had wanted to be listed as Lance Holden in the program but nobody had paid any attention to him.

Lance Holden would have had a marvelous time. Life burst like a rocket into such an array of dazzling particles—interviews, lunch parties, cocktail parties, supper parties, radio appearances, stunts arranged by the press agent to keep his picture constantly before the public eye—that for a long time he was able to dodge the fact that he had achieved very little that wouldn't have been his by birth—a grand apartment, servants, celebrity, entrée to the city's most glamorous social life.

The working part, the part he was paid for, became pure drudgery within weeks. He liked having to report for work daily at the same place and hour, and he liked payday, because all that proved that he was a working man like everybody else, but when he found himself on stage repeating words and gestures that had ceased to have any meaning for him, he was depressed by the monotony of it.

To keep boredom at bay, he reminded himself of the difficult months that had preceded his success, but he soon found himself looking back on the period with fond nostalgia. The break with his mother, the initial, essential break, had abruptly and thrillingly changed all the rules of life. He had neither sought it nor expected it, but she had announced that she would no longer consider him her son if he persisted in becoming an actor. From one day to the next, he found himself literally in the street, with a bride and no idea how to turn his improbable fantasy into reality. It took more than saying you were going to be an actor to become one.

Overnight, the world became a fascinating novelty shop. There was the novelty of replacing the elaborate establishment his mother had been setting up for him with a cheap place of his own. There was the novelty of learning how much things cost and that some shops were cheaper than the ones he had always heard of. There was the enormous novelty of discovering that there were places where he could pawn or sell his valuable possessions. Over Pam's tearful protests, he began to get rid of their superfluous wedding presents, including a car and his own jewelry.

Through people he had spent a few months with in summer theater, he met other struggling actors and writers and assorted artists, including Phil Boetz, a struggling writer who was fascinated by Lance as a case study. There was the novelty of making friends with people who talked about their mothers' cooking and their fathers' Saturday-night binges and their own experiences of farm or slum life.

No one knew how to achieve the ambitions they were all struggling for, least of all the actors. It was apparently a question of being in the right office at the right moment when somebody might be casting a part that you looked right for. They all eked out a living with haphazard jobs, but Lance's attempts at finding even the most menial work came to nothing. As soon as people found out who he was, they laughed at him, thinking it was some sort of joke.

When Pam announced that she was pregnant, the struggle took on ominous overtones. They still had things they could sell but babies seemed to be expensive. The thought of throwing himself on his mother's mercy fanned his ambition to white heat, but it was difficult to entirely exclude the possibility from his mind.

After a grim Christmas, the theater district was buzzing with gossip about Bernard Hoffman's new production. The star, Geraldine Fleet, had been signed but the male lead called for a special type—a boy on the threshold of manhood with poetic good looks who could project enough intelligence to be convincing as a writer of budding genius. There was a dream sequence, so they said, in which he appeared almost naked and performed some sort of dance, so a presentable body was essential too. Word was out that unknowns were being considered. It was going to be one of the first big postwar productions so everybody wanted to be in it.

Lance was prepared to lay siege to Bernard Hoffman's office but when he gave his name to a receptionist he was ushered past a horde of waiting youths into a large office where people were sitting around a desk. He recognized two of them as Hoffman himself and Geraldine Fleet. He was to learn eventually that the others were the director, the producer, and a production manager of some sort. He noticed glances being exchanged as his name was mentioned and passed around the desk. He was asked to read from a script. He was told to stand and walk around the room. Additional glances were exchanged before Bernard Hoffman uttered one of his historic pronouncements: "You're it."

His engagement was treated like a press event, complete with photographers. He got a taste of the future when his picture appeared on the front page of all the tabloids the next day. He hoped somebody would have the courage to show them to his mother. He got another taste of the future after the first few days of rehearsal when Bernard Hoffman drew him aside for some professional advice.

"How are you faring with our Geraldine?" he asked. He was a heavily built man with striking Semitic features and had adopted an expensive East-Coast executive style. He was unlike anybody Lance had known and he was proud that the playwright seemed to like him.

"Miss Fleet? We get along fine, as far as I know."

"Ah yes, *Miss* Fleet. I'm sure you're going to have a most beneficial effect on our manners." Lance blushed and resolved to call her Gerry at the first opportunity. "Miss Fleet is inclined to get a bit overexcited in the presence of handsome young men. I must say, for the son of railroad barons and real-estate tycoons, you're quite a dish. I don't know how that old battle-ax, your esteemed mother, managed to produce you."

Lance threw his head back and let out a whoop of laughter, more scandalized than he wanted to admit. He had never heard his mother spoken of with disrespect. She was, after all, a distinguished leader of the social and cultural community. She would consider this slick Broadway playwright beneath her notice.

Hoffman waved a jeweled hand. "We mustn't lose the thread in hilarity and mirth. Gerry can make your position in our little production quite untenable. She's already hinted that all your best scenes should be cut. I would suggest a warmer personal approach to her. Have you thought of fucking her? I understand it's rather like going over Niagara Falls in a barrel but you appear to be a sturdy lad."

Lance covered his shock and embarrassment with laughter. "Are you serious? Do you think she'd let me?"

"Why don't you ask her and find out?"

He thought of Pam and tried to quell his scruples. Gerry simplified matters by showing him her remarkably well preserved breasts in her dressing room while he was attempting a tentative approach that evening. It would have been rude not to display some appreciation of them. He showed her his erect cock. The Pandora's box of his carefully disciplined sexuality had been opened.

It was the following summer when Lance's restlessness prompted his sexual rebellion. The show became a tiresome interruption to more pleasurable pursuits. In the fall a fat Hollywood offer gave him something new to think about. The usual post–New Year slump came around and the show finally faltered: word spread that it wouldn't make it through another summer. Lance was elated. He would be free at last to work and learn his craft if he managed to stay out of two-year runs. He turned down the Hollywood offer. New York was home, the theater the only challenge he knew. Friends confirmed his decision about Hollywood; success could bring money but no sense of achievement for an actor. He was offered a starring job in summer stock and Bernie told him he would undoubtedly be free to take it.

Pam's second baby was due just before the summer season started. Lance proposed drastic retrenchment. Out with the cook, out with the maid, out with Nanny as soon as Pam was well enough to take care of two babies. When they returned from the summer theater, they would move into a small apartment.

Pam received these proposals with stricken outrage. What about all the Hollywood money? Any real actor with a career to consider would have leaped at the offer. She wasn't going to slave in the kitchen just because of his whims. She wasn't going to raise a family in pointless poverty.

It was a real blowup of a sort that nothing in Lance's background had taught him to deal with. Civilized people didn't shout at each other. He went out to cool off and thought of all the money he planned to save. If the show ran for three more months, he could put away enough of his salary to see them through six or eight months of unemployment. When he went home after his performance, Pam and the baby were gone.

With the help of the servants the next morning, Lance got a fairly clear picture of what had happened. Pam had made a pretext of her condition to ask his mother for asylum. Mrs. Vanderholden had swooped down on the apartment and carried her off with Angela, to the impregnable fortress on Fifth Avenue. When he called, Pam wouldn't speak to him. His mother would, but he hung up. What was the point? If she wanted to resume relations, she knew where to find him.

The point was, Pam had left home. She had only to come back where she belonged for them to carry the row to some conclusion. If she thought her departure would make him change his mind about the Hollywood offer, she was mistaken. He hadn't surrendered to his mother's ultimatum. He had no intention of surrendering to Pam's. He couldn't pretend that she was in-

47

dispensable to his life. He couldn't quite remember why he'd married her although they usually had pleasant times together and were too busy to be seriously dissatisfied with each other. Little Angela delighted him when Nanny allowed him to play with her and he was looking forward to the new child. He was used to being married but habits were easy to change. He knew that Pam hadn't intended to end their marriage but understood how easily she could get trapped in something she didn't know how to handle. Heaven knew what plots his mother was hatching, all with a view to bringing her rebellious son to heel. It was funny when he thought how powerless she was; she had used up all her ammunition in the first round.

He entered a limbo period, waiting for the show to close, waiting for the summer theater job to begin, waiting to find out one way or the other if he should include his family in his plans, and, above all, saving money. He was amazed how much he could save, once the cook and the maid were gone. He saw no reason to pay Nanny's wages or Pam's expenses so long as his mother was running the show. Money in the bank—his very own. He loved it.

He slowly dropped out of the city's party life and made contact again with friends from the early days, among them Phil Boetz. Phil approved of the way Lance was handling current developments.

"Stick to it," he said, sucking on his pipe. "Hollywood you don't need. You married Pam under false pretenses. She thought she was getting a Vanderholden, poor girl. Maybe you'll find you don't even need the theater."

"I'd quit it in a minute if I could think of something else."

"Coal mining, spot welding, repairing telephones, to name a few of the more glamorous possibilities. I'll bet they *do* sound glamorous to you. Nobody but you would think of quitting after the success you've had. Most people would want to hang on to it for dear life. What can fame and fortune mean to a Vanderholden? You think it would be exciting to disappear into the downtrodden masses. There's a girl I want you to meet. You're getting so close to being a human being that a lot of people probably can't tell the difference."

48

Phil introduced him to Scot. From then on, being with Scot was what life was all about.

He told his building's agent that he was leaving. Legal steps could be taken to seize the contents of the apartment for nonpayment of rent or, perhaps more reasonably, his wife could be contacted in care of his mother. He felt sure that the balance of the rent would be paid and the place emptied in the normal way. The agent clearly wanted no trouble with the Vanderholdens although he reminded Lance of what the papers would make of the story if he were forced to carry out a legal eviction.

Lance packed his opulent wardrobe and moved out. He had notified the summer theater that he was turning down their offer. He didn't know what he was going to do. He knew only that he had to be with Scot and Scot didn't take actors seriously.

The uneventful peace of Puerto Veragua didn't drive away the nightmares about Scot. He would wake up in a panic, his heart pounding, stomach leaden but protesting. He was never going to see Scot again. He whimpered, half-asleep, shifting his limbs about to ease the weight of dread in them. He knew that the sleeping girl beside him was Luisa. He knew where he was. His half-waking thoughts scattered and his heart steadied. Only half-formed words remained, and the guilt for being who and what he was, guilt for not being what Scot needed, guilt for the moments of contentment, the glimpses of accomplishment he was beginning to experience in Puerto Veragua without her.

As Luisa and the sun and sea and his odd jobs all conspired to give him a sense of a new life beginning, he resisted the message of hope that stirred in him. It was all too easy, too exotic, too escapist. The days passed under the burning vault of the sky; at night, the little house on the hill was cut adrift from the world, lapped by the infinite silver sea. He was simply there, every day marking a postponement of his departure. He told himself that he was waiting to hear from Andy. Andy had expected his work in the capital to take about a month. He might turn up any minute if he found some free time over a weekend. If anybody could, Andy might help him see some sense in what he was doing, give him a feeling of life continuing rather than being cruelly cut in two. At least Luisa was saving him from the madness of loneliness he had brought with him.

Unknown to him, she was acquiring a sense of the future. She found herself wondering, to her own surprise, if there was anything more she could do to keep him with her. She had never thought in this way, as if she could exercise some control over life. She reminded herself that he was a rich foreigner, she was his servant. Yet he made her feel somehow that there was more to it than that.

As she watched his activities around the place, she was almost convinced that this was sign enough that he was staying. Nobody planted vegetables without intending to eat them and it took time for vegetables to grow. She wondered if committing the sin she was so eager to commit would help to keep him or if, as many older women had warned her, a man lost interest in a girl after he had put his prong inside her. She didn't think he was that kind of man. If he were, he would have done it when he was lying so beautifully naked beside her, whether or not she wished it, and gone out to look for a new girl. He was waiting for a sign, just as she was. Perhaps they would recognize it together when it came.

To find some sense of conflict in the soothing passage of tropical days, Lance chose Flip Rawls as an antagonist. From the day he had moved into the house she had pelted him—it was the word he chose to describe the mild annoyance of her chauffeur's constant appearances—with reminders of her presence as a neighbor.

Invitations, bottles of wine, another sarong, exotic plants were delivered regularly by her emissary. Lance refused the invitations, first because he had no taste for the sort of social life she represented and then because he chose to make it a battle of wills. When simply refusing began to pall, he decided to test to what extent Mrs. Rawls believed in becoming a part of the native life. He wrote a note explaining that he was sorry to have refused her previous invitations but that he had a friend, a local girl, staying with him and didn't feel he could accept for himself alone. He was sure Mrs.

Rawls already knew about his living arrangements. He was interested to see how she would sidestep the issue.

When he told Luisa what he'd done, she was terrified. "But you don't expect Señora Rawls to invite me too!" she cried.

"But of course," he said, smiling down at her as they stood together on the terrace. "We are together. It is natural to invite you."

"Do the North Americans always invite their friends' servants?" she asked slowly. The words were a shock to him. No matter how slight his emotional commitment to her, he certainly didn't regard her as a servant, and he was shocked that he hadn't made her feel it. He put his hand under her chin and lifted her face and looked into her eyes.

"You are not my servant," he said gravely. "You are— You are—" What could he say that wasn't too much or too little? He shouldn't have used Luisa to make his point with Flip Rawls. He dropped his hand and turned from Luisa abruptly and stood looking down at the rocky cove, realizing that he had already stayed too long to be able to leave without marking her in some way. He had been thinking only of himself, of finding something good here for himself. Could he stay on without its becoming too important to her and a responsibility for him that he was in no position to undertake?

"You don't understand," Luisa was explaining steadfastly behind him. "Even if I were your wife, the wife of a great man, I wouldn't go. Here, women don't go out with men. It is not expected."

"It's no matter," Lance muttered. "We will not go."

"Oh, but you must go," she said, realizing with a thrill of pride that she was speaking to him as an equal. She had dared compare herself to a wife to make her point clear. "Señora Rawls is very important here." Lance turned back and took her hand and gave it a squeeze without looking at her.

"To me, you are more important than Señora Rawls," he said before striding off down the terrace toward the vegetable garden. He had to close the incident before his uncertainty with the language led him to say more than he intended.

Luisa stood looking after him even when he was out

51

of sight. As her first alarm at being invited by Señora Rawls passed, she was aware that something had happened between them that required understanding. She had to think of each moment one by one in order to take it in. He hadn't ordered her to go to the party. When he knew that she didn't want to go, he had been willing not to go himself. It was the first time anybody had considered her wishes to this extent and it gave her an odd feeling, almost like being lost and alone and having to choose between two paths, but it made her chest swell with pride, too. Best of all was what he hadn't said. There were so many things he didn't know the words for but she knew from the way he had looked at her, from the way he had spoken, that he was trying to say something that would have pleased her very much. It made her feel that her time might be coming.

Flip Rawls's reply to Lance's note was prompt and unequivocal. The chauffeur returned with it tucked into an enormous cardboard box. Of course he must bring his friend, she wrote. She was dying to meet her. Meanwhile here were some things that might please her. He was pleasantly impressed. The box contained several brilliantly colored robes heavy with gold and silver thread which to Lance looked vaguely Oriental. Luisa stood at his elbow while he shook them out.

"What are they for?" she asked wonderingly.

"For you. To wear, I think. But not for every day." They laughed together at the thought. She was puzzled by the savagery of their colors and decorations. She would have preferred the much plainer sort of dress the film stars wore. Of course, she knew Señora Rawls hadn't really sent them to her—he must be very important indeed to receive such attentions—but it was an additional source of pride that she should even be mentioned by the great lady.

"I think now we go," he told her. "I ask her invite you. She invites. Rude if you not go. These not your people. Foreign husbands and wives go together. You with me, you do the same as foreigners."

Her eyes widened as she looked up at him, and the place between her legs seemed to melt. He was telling her that he thought of her as his wife.

"I will go if you wish it. I will go and thank the *señora* for her gift. Must I stay and talk to many people? They do not speak my language. To them I am your servant. It's not suitable."

He put a hand on her bare breast. Mrs. Rawls's reply eliminated her as an antagonist and brought him a step closer to thinking of Puerto Veragua as a possible solution to the immediate future. His growing affection for Luisa was beginning to provide a sort of center to life and couldn't do either of them any harm so long as they observed her sexual restraints. She was gently submissive but had a mind of her own. It wasn't fair to ask her to go through a whole evening in a situation where she would feel totally lost. "Then it is like that," he said. "You stay how long you want. Thank you."

No one had ever thanked her for saying what she thought. Her chest swelled with pride again. A great deal was happening that she would have to think about carefully and try to understand. "What will I wear?" she asked.

He caressed her breasts and made her nipples stand up. "So pretty like this. We get a dress."

The invitation was for the following evening. They walked into town the next morning and Luisa picked out a frilly little American-style day dress. She looked sadly commonplace when she tried it on but she seemed very pleased with it. She asked timidly if she could have shoes and picked out some cheap-looking pumps.

That evening Luisa was greeted by their hostess as if the party were especially for her. Mrs. Rawls clasped her to her bosom and told her that she was *adorable,* pronouncing it in French. Luisa made a polite little speech in Spanish. Mrs. Rawls turned to Lance, looking bewildered. "She has a rather odd accent. I get all my languages so terribly mixed up. Does she—"

"She can't stay. She wanted to come to thank you for the things you sent and for inviting her."

"She's delicious. I know her, of course. I know all the natives. They're my children." She turned to Luisa. "Forgive me for giving you such short notice," she said in English in a loud firm voice. "Next time, you must stay all evening."

Lance gave Luisa a rough idea of what had been said, pleased that he could already act as an interpreter. He squeezed her hand and nodded in reply to the question in her eyes about leaving. "Me home not late," he assured her.

Flip Rawls took his hand in both of hers when she was gone and leaned back, looking up at him with a winsome tilt of her head. "Dear Lance. I feel as if I'd known you for years. I'm going to call you Lance. I'm Flip. How superb you're looking. Your tan is very becoming. The sun is turning your hair quite golden. If you hadn't come, my evening would have been a disaster. My guest of honor couldn't make it. He won't be here for another week or two. I've been saving him as a beautiful surprise for you. Robbie Cosling. Do you know him? The famous painter who calls himself Robi. One of my dearest friends. His father is Lord— Oh, you know the one. The richest man in Canada. He hasn't been a lord very long. When I last saw him he was plain Stuart Cosling, although there was nothing plain about him."

"I've heard of Barry Cosling. He's Lord Barstlow, isn't he?"

"Was. You've got it exactly. I knew you would. Robbie's grandfather. Now his *father* is Lord Barstlow. Of course, Robbie's a celebrity in his own right."

"Are you talking about Robi, the painter?" he asked with interest, snatching a nugget from the conversational torrent.

"Yes. Isn't that right? I'm sure it is. He's brilliant. You have so much in common. I don't know which of you is the better-looking. Robbie lived for years with a charming man who was recently killed in a plane crash. Such a waste. You've suffered a great loss too. I can feel it. I feel you have so much to offer each other."

"You flatter me. As far as I'm concerned, Robi's the best new painter since the war." Remembering the excitement he had shared with Scot when they had discovered his work at a show a few months ago, his heart contracted and he felt the sting behind his eyes. He blurted out the first thing that came to mind: "I'll be damned. You're really expecting him here?"

"You know of him? What did I tell you? You'll have a lovely time together. I understand he's a spectacular lover. Of course, I've known him since he was a child. So beautiful."

54

Lance forced laughter. "You're getting things a bit mixed up, aren't you, Flip? I'm living with Luisa."

"Good heavens, a man of imagination and cultivated tastes—surely you don't make such trivial distinctions."

Genuine laughter swelled in his throat. Her absurdity was rather endearing.

She introduced him to everybody with a proud and proprietary air. It was a largely middle-aged gathering although Flip had a quartet of good-looking men about his age staying with her. From the way she introduced them, Lance gathered that they were two established couples. This was new to him. He didn't know that homosexuals attempted permanent unions, or if they did, that they expected to be accepted socially. Another mark in Flip's favor, as well as Puerto Veragua's. Maybe in a place like this he could be accepted on his own terms. Maybe he should have insisted on Luisa's staying. He talked with a plump Frenchwoman named Madame Fournier who cheerfully volunteered bits of gossip about the other guests.

"That is Monica Freeman," she explained as a frail, haggard blond woman drifted past down the long sweep of the terrace. "They say she murdered her husband. I do not know. I remember when I came here, the first party I went to, I was introduced to her and I spilled my drink all over her dress. I said, 'Oh, I am so sorry. You will want to kill me.' It caused the most awful *scandale*. Of course, I didn't know about her husband."

She pointed out a German couple who had been there since before the war and a middle-aged man in a wheelchair propelled by a good-looking native boy ("They say it is only his legs that are paralyzed," Mme Fournier said) and a pretty young woman called Mrs. Stroud who smoked, according to his informant, "more opium than is really good for her."

"And that is my husband," she went on, indicating a short, sharp-featured man whose black hair looked as if it were painted on his skull. "He couldn't make up his mind who he was for during the war, poor dear, so now we rest here. It's not France but it's not a bad life. And what about you? Have you murdered someone? Do you take dope? I believe Flip told me that you are very celebrated but I'm not good at names. You look to me like a most attractive and most healthy young man. You're surely not here alone?"

"Not exactly," Lance said with a smile. "I'm not even exactly sure I'm here."

"You came and talked to Flip and found yourself taking a house? Yes, that is the way it usually happens. She is wonderful—so enthusiastic and so generous. Puerto Veragua would not exist without her. She has a curious gift. She makes things happen when people are determined that they shouldn't. I've seen her do it and yet I do not understand. She is—what do you say?— the fly in the ointment. Perhaps we need her. She gives us something to come up against." She spoke detachedly between sips of her dry martini, making them all seem very remote, the place itself remote in the soft luxurious night.

Flip Rawls's arrangement of terraces and gardens was ideally suited to the evening's purpose. There was plenty of room to move around in; there were quantities of inviting chaises longues in which to loll. The food and drink were excellent. Somewhere in the garden a group of native musicians twanged out haunting Latin refrains. The lights flashed on and off intermittently due to some failure of the current but there were candles in mirrored brackets hung all along the terrace, the flames rising stiff and straight in the motionless air, so it didn't matter.

It was late enough for Lance to be thinking about leaving when he noticed a crowd gathering along the edge of the parapet and wandered over to see what was going on. Far below, a light flickered among the rocks. As Lance joined the others, he saw M. Fournier lift a glass and hurl it into the night. There was a moment's silence and then the faint tinkle of shattered glass. The flame darted up, caught by some breath off the shifting sea. There was general laughter, some disparaging comments on M. Fournier's marksmanship, and another glass was hurled. Flip Rawls appeared from somewhere at Lance's side.

"Have you tried your hand at our local sport?" she asked, tilting her head up at him beguilingly.

"What's the point? You going to let them break all your glasses?"

"They always do. The light down there is the target.

56

They try to knock it out and then the party's over. Of course, they always miss but the point is throwing something. It's a reaction against the peace and tranquility. I must say I rather enjoy it myself. Try it. You'll see. It's very soothing." Lance looked at his glass and smiled, thinking of her as the fly in the ointment.

"Let me finish my drink," he said.

There was another burst of laughter from the glass-throwing group. He stepped forward to the parapet, took careless aim and let fly with his glass. There was the instant of silence and then almost simultaneously glass tinkled and the light winked out. There were cries of approval as Lance turned away, smiling to himself. Whether he wanted it or not, he had made a place for himself in the community.

When he got home he found Luisa waiting for him, still wearing her little housewife's dress and sitting primly in the pool of hissing light. She rose as he approached. He looked at her and shook his head ruefully and touched the top of her dress. "Not here," he said with a fond smile. "Never this dress here."

She loved the dress. It was her wedding dress. By presenting her in public to Señora Rawls, he had made her his wife in the foreigners' eyes and offered her a foreigner's liberty. Her father and brothers would disown her if she lived sinfully with one of their own people but to live with a rich foreigner would be a lesser sin that they could overlook. "Did you have a good time?" She had learned from films that foreign girls asked questions that the men she had grown up with would consider impudent.

"Pleasant. I wished you there. I meet the people here. Slowly, you will think it is natural to meet them, too."

Slowly? There is going to be time, she thought. He had said it. He would stay, especially if she gave him babies. Her heart was beating lightly and rapidly with anticipation of his being inside her and starting a baby. It would be more thrilling than anything she had guessed could happen to her.

They drifted along the terrace toward the bedroom while Lance tried to tell her about the people he'd met, discarding his clothes as he went. Naked, he lighted the candle at the washbasin and sponged himself down. It had been a sweaty walk home. When he turned to the bed, she was in it with a sheet over her. He lay down beside her and threw it back.

She had nothing on. He looked at her with astonishment and slowly ran a hand down from her breasts over her belly. He felt her body being shaken by little convulsions as he moved it between her legs. She had only a sparse fringe of pubic hair. He caressed it. Suddenly all the hurt and shock and bitter loss of the last weeks seemed to gather into a great knot that threatened to burst his chest. He felt as if he would drown in tears.

Tensions mounted in him that he felt would tear him apart. Something seemed to snap in his mind. It was an almost physical sensation, a crumbling, a disintegration opening fissures in his soul through which a ray of joy penetrated. He uttered a strange sound, part sob, part groan, and all his muscles went slack. His body accepted the commitment that her young body at last invited. She had waited long enough for him to feel that she must have weighed the consequences of offering herself to him.

"You wear nothing, little one," he said gently, to give her time to reconsider.

"There's no need now."

"I take you truly?"

"Yes. I went to the party as your wife. You said so. You have the right."

"But not real wife. My real wife is in New York."

"That's very far. I'm your wife here."

"This way we make babies. You understand?"

"It's my wish." Her hand slid to his erection and pressed it. "This will put many babies into me."

"We not know how long I stay."

"I will do everything I can to keep you here."

"Fair warning," he muttered in English, smiling as he lifted himself over her. Joy spread, his body's simple joy, robbing doubts and questions of their urgency. It had been a long time since a girl had given herself to him. Her desire for him to enter her made him forget her virginity. The question of whether he wanted her to give him a child was answered as he felt the generous opening of her body to him and saw her eyes light up with rapture and her lips part ecstatically. He had made no promises but once she was pregnant, he would want to stay. Other questions would be answered as he went along. She was little more than a child herself but now that she had gone beyond their childlike games and was learning for the first time the adult joys of their bodies, she became within moments a woman whom he could love as a potential mother, if not with all the passion that he knew was in him.

She lay back and felt him filling her and her breath stopped. He felt so beautiful entering her, wanting to put all the great hard length of him inside her and make her his woman. She would never belong to any other man. He was inside her, mastering her. He was planting his image in her. She would give him a son. She was sure she was in love.

He was moving in her in a way that filled her head with rainbows of bright colors and turned her body to liquid gold. Strange waves of indescribable bliss kept surging up from her depths and breaking over her, washing her in celestial balm. She was sure that nobody had ever felt anything like it; only he could make her feel it. She swore a great oath with her blood that only death would take him from her.

The next day, Lance found that everything about his being here had changed. The way he looked at the place had changed; he saw all the improvements he could make for greater comfort. When he looked at Luisa, he saw in her a mother, a gently compliant mate, and was almost reconciled for the loss of the intensity of passion that had blazed in him for a year. The prospect of paternity made him feel more like a father than all the expensive mumbo jumbo surrounding Angela's birth had permitted him to feel. He wanted to defy his heritage by bringing Vanderholdens into the world who wouldn't be burdened by his name. Children of the sun.

The sense of growing into his own skin was sharply heightened and he finally understood it. He was faced with a total break, not just from his very special background but from the urban civilization that had always been his natural habitat. Perhaps whatever there was in him that was essentially his would be freed if life were stripped to its essentials.

He still hadn't learned to worry seriously about money. The money he had set aside for his summer's travels would last for a year or more at the rate he was spending. He had plenty of time to find out if he could do anything to make a living here. He wondered if he could be a gardener. Several of the foreigners last night had marveled at Flip's garden and complained of not being able to find anybody who could make something of theirs. He'd like being a gardener.

He went into town before lunch and paid another three months' rent and came back with a hand pump and some lengths of pipe. A tank was following. If Luisa became pregnant she couldn't go on drawing water from the well indefinitely. He also ordered some utilitarian furniture—a couple of tables, a few chairs, some lamps that shed a softer light than the hisser, a cot that would serve as a sofa on the terrace. Several vague invitations had been extended to him last night. If he started going out, he would have to have people here. Luisa would get used to foreigners on home territory.

That evening she asked if she could wear the dress to go see her family. "I want them to see that I'm being well taken care of," she explained.

He supposed it was natural for her to want to reestablish contact with her family after what had happened but was surprised when it turned out that she intended to stay the night. Nights could still be bad. All in all, he supposed it was good for her to feel free to go. He didn't want her to cling to him. He had to start thinking in terms of the future.

Luisa thought of the visit as a sort of official confirmation of her new position. Without the blessing of the Church, she had only the men in her family to protect her from the misfortunes a woman could suffer from a man—his betrayal of her with another woman or his neglecting his duties as a father. Her family would tell her what was acceptable and how to defend herself if he went too far. She didn't expect her father to make trouble when he understood that she had become the foreigner's woman so long as the house agent continued to pay her wages to him. Later, if she became pregnant, she hoped that her man would understand that her family would expect a present of money to compensate for its shame. If it was a big present, they might not make her marry another man.

She was proudly wearing her little dress after supper when Lance kissed her good-night and saw her off into the dark. The lamp hissed. It stitched the silence in close around him. A pang of loneliness threatened second thoughts about the months to come, thoughts that he struggled to suppress. Flip Rawls's expatriates might turn out to be fun. He thought of Robi the painter. He should prove a momentary diversion. If people like him came down here, there must be something to be said for the place. For the rest, he was going to have to find work to keep him busy. Boredom was as great a danger as loneliness.

The next day, the letter that he had been waiting for arrived. He tore it open in high excitement, only to learn that Andy wasn't coming. There was no arguing with his explanation—complications had arisen in his legal business that required him to return to Washington immediately—but it was a bitter blow. He wrote that he had sent Lance's luggage on in care of the hotel and wanted to know as soon as possible what his plans were.

Lance's first plan was for flight. Start running and catch up with Andy. He had made love to a virgin. It was unlikely that Luisa was already pregnant. He could get out before he had done any real harm. He could catch a midday bus to the capital and maybe find an evening flight for Washington. His luggage? He didn't remember what was in it. Andy had taken care of all that. It couldn't be anything he needed.

He caught a glimpse of Luisa as she crossed the terrace to the kitchen, back from her night with her family, naked to the waist, trusting him and content. He read through Andy's letter again, unreasonably hurt by its legal precision. It confirmed what he had known instinctively—in losing Scot he would also lose Andy. Life would separate them. He was, after all, Scot's brother-in-law, part of her family, married to her younger sister, Carol. He was also the only intimate friend Lance had ever had, the only person he could say everything to.

They had loved each other from the evening they'd first met a year ago, a few months after Lance had dedicated his life to Scot. Andy was just starting his legal career as a clerk in a Washington law firm. Scot mentioned one day that he was coming to stay with her for a few days on his firm's business. Seeing that this involved Scot's moving her child in with her so that Andy could have the boy's room, Lance suggested that the visitor could stay with him. He was living in a little furnished apartment within a few minutes' walk of Scot's place. He had a spare bed and was delighted to be able to offer it; it was the first occasion that made him feel as if he and Scot were part of a family.

When they met at Scot's for dinner with several other people, Lance was astonished by Andy's youth. This boy couldn't be a trained lawyer with a responsible job, let alone a husband and father. He looked as if he were barely out of school. After a few minutes' talk, Lance realized that the youthful impression was due to the boyishness of his features and that his unobtrusive good looks were the mature image of what might have been great beauty a few years ago. He forgot his looks as he fell under the spell of his sweetness and warmth. He had never known anybody so at ease with himself and completely lacking in self-consciousness. He joined in the general conversation quietly and intelligently but Lance felt that he directed his winning smile and his clear humorous eyes at him with special affection. He said he was glad his being here wouldn't upset Scot's household and thanked Lance for the bed. Lance couldn't remember being drawn to anybody so powerfully and yet so comfortably; he felt as if neither of them had to make any effort to become fast friends.

The small gathering was composed of people who had jobs to do in the morning and broke up early. Kisses were exchanged. Andy and Scot. Scot and Lance. Andy picked up a small suitcase in the entry and Lance led him around the corner. Lance's "apartment" was in fact one room with a token division, consisting mostly of molding, to suggest a sleeping alcove. There was room for two beds, a closet, a chest of drawers. The rest of the room contained a table and chairs for eating, a desk, a sofa. It was slowly filling with books as Lance tried to define his future. There was a bath and a closet—kitchenette. Lance kept it spotlessly clean; he was proud of having learned to do housework. It suddenly became very small with Andy in it.

They joked about it as they moved around trying not to bump into each other. Having spent the evening establishing close ties of easy friendship, they became shyly aware of their bodies. Lance wished they had reached the point of being able to touch each other easily. He didn't see how there could be any sort of sexual problem between them.

He noted attractions that he must have already registered subconsciously. His blondish brown hair was thick and looked as if it would be softly furry to the touch. There was a gloss on his skin, a velvety sheen that Lance couldn't explain but that delighted his eye. When he removed his jacket, his slim, well-proportioned body was visible beneath his shirt. Lance wondered if all his skin had the sheen of velvet.

He helped him hang up a few things and then moved off to the other end of the room to let him finish undressing. He glanced at him when he pulled off his shirt and saw a hairless chest that looked like any young man's chest that hadn't been subjected to rigorous athletic training. Nice smooth shoulders surmounting the masculine V of torso that ended in narrow hips. Nothing seductive, but strongly appealing.

They exchanged a few words about the bathroom and Andy went to it, wearing shorts and carrying belongings. Lance undressed and put on a dressing gown. Andy returned wearing immaculately white pajamas, shining with cleanliness, the velvet sheen of his skin having somehow acquired dusky undertones. Was Andy a Negro? It was a subject he avoided in Scot's world except when important issues were involved; he had learned that a tone of voice or a careless word could cause appalling misunderstandings. Scot's ex-husband was white. He had assumed that Carol's husband might be white, too.

He looked at his mouth for the first time. He had been so moved by the sweetness of his smile that he hadn't been able to see the lips that formed it. They were full but not particularly negroid, all tender curves, sensitive and expressive, from which sensuality hadn't been excluded. He saw the ambiguous beauty he must have possessed a few years earlier. It was almost gone but glimpses could still be caught by a watchful eye.

They smiled at each other as Lance went in his turn to the bathroom. Getting ready for bed, he felt the powerful tug of attraction drawing him back to the main room. For some reason, he was sure that Andy felt it too. Their response to each other was deeper and more unguarded than was usual between two guys.

To Lance, the feeling was as simple and steadying as the person who inspired it. He had loved him all evening. He needed him. Scot kept him strung up to a high pitch of endeavor, striving to prove himself to her, constantly searching for something in himself that he could feel was good enough for her. But until Scot was truly his physically as well as emotionally, he needed somebody he could relax with, to whom he could acknowledge his failures and weaknesses. He shoved his hands into his dressing gown pockets and returned to his guest.

He was in bed under the covers, propped on a pillow. Lance perched on the edge of the bed. "Are you going to be comfortable enough?" he asked.

"It's perfect. I'm not going to be in the way?"

"You know you're not. I love having you here."

"I'm glad. I think I'm going to be in the city quite a lot in the next few months. We should work out how I can pay my share. It would be like having a place of my own. I'd even let you stay."

"That's decent of you. I don't know. Scot says I don't know how to be poor. Maybe taking money from you would be good for my soul. Do friends usually pay when they stay with each other?"

"Sure. They share. It makes them closer friends."

"I'm all in favor of that."

Lance moved a hand to his shoulder to seal the agreement. Andy curled a hand around his wrist. The small physical contact was as satisfying to Lance as putting their arms around each other. They looked into each other's eyes and had no need for words. Andy edged over and pushed back the covers and Lance slid in beside him, discarding his dressing gown as he did so. His hands were lover's hands as he helped Andy out of his pajamas. They lay with their bodies pressed to each other and their mouths joined. Their lips declared their peaceful need of each other while their bodies flowed gently into each other. Holding Andy was like a plunge into cool spring water, fresh and pure and exhilarating. It seemed to Lance the ultimate lovemaking, requiring no further expression of desire.

They moved against each other slowly, their tongues

leading them to consummation. They locked together briefly and had orgasms against each other's bellies. They laughed softly as their lips parted.

"Well, well, well," Andy said.

"That's what I was thinking." They laughed again. "Stay still. I'll try to get up without making a mess." Lance disengaged himself carefully, sprang up, and hurried to the bathroom. He washed quickly, feeling no strain or self-consciousness about what had happened, only amazement that Andy had wanted it so much, and returned with washcloth and towel, as happy and relaxed as if he'd known Andy all his life. He crouched beside the bed while his new friend mopped himself up and dried himself.

Andy looked at Lance with his melting smile. "We're very juicy guys," he said. "I love you, man."

"Oh, man, I love you, too." Lance pulled the covers over him and leaned down and kissed him lightly on the lips. "Get a good sleep," he said.

"Thanks. You too, you hear? We'll get a chance to talk tomorrow."

They got up together, got ready for the day and had coffee together without exchanging a glance, a word, a gesture that acknowledged the physical bond that had sprung up between them. They laughed together and looked into each other's eyes with unguarded loving appreciation and acceptance of each other without its encroaching on their lives outside the room.

Proceeding with his self-imposed reading program during the day, Lance's thoughts wandered occasionally to Andy. Perhaps what they had done was extraordinary but it seemed wonderfully natural to him. He was glad of last year's experiences for having prepared him for it. Experience must have made it possible for Andy to take it for granted too. He couldn't imagine any problems with Andy, so it was hardly worth worrying about. It didn't make any sense to think of him in connection with the other two. Andy hadn't made even a tentative move to do any of the things Lance might have expected.

Andy came back unexpectedly in the middle of the afternoon. They greeted each other as old friends, not lovers. No physical contact was made. Andy joined him at the table, where his books and notes were spread out. Andy handled the books, glancing at them, and they talked about them and about Andy's day. He looked tired, like a lawyer and a husband, not beautiful but good-looking in a not particularly striking way, like thousands who passed unnoticed in the streets, with regular features and a mouth that was seductive only when it smiled. Lance knew the feel of the furry blondish hair and the velvety skin and the body under the subdued businessman's suit and he loved him. A silence fell between them while they looked deep into each other's eyes.

"Shall we talk about last night?" Andy asked.

"I've been thinking about it."

"Good. Do you want to start or shall I? Let me. I'm a reformed homosexual. When I was a teenager, I thought I might go that way. I wasn't very active but it happened often enough for it to begin to look like a pattern. There were girls but they didn't cure me of my fantasies about boys. It scared me. I don't have anything against it but most people do. It doesn't make life any easier. When I fell in love with Carol, the problem just went away. I didn't make a secret of my lurid past. I told her about my fantasy dream-boy—a beautiful blond with a perfect body and big cock. I met him for the first time last night but it didn't scare me. I wanted you in bed with me, of course, but I wasn't going wild for it the way I would've once upon a time. Why did it happen so easily? I'm nobody's dream-boy."

Lance looked into unguarded, humorously loving eyes. "I love you. I did all evening. When we got back here, I felt something happening between us and it seemed natural to get into bed with you. I knew we both felt the same way."

"Did we? That's what I'd like to know." He reached across the table and held Lance's hand. "The homosexual in me didn't go away. It's just not a problem anymore, not even with you. Last night was a big test. Was it for you?"

"Not that I know of. You mean, do I have a lurid past? It's happened twice."

"At school?"

"Nothing at school. Nothing in the navy, but I was never really *in* the navy, shut up with guys for long stretches at a time. It happened about a year ago. I

66

wanted to find out what it was like more than I wanted the guys, if that makes any sense. They weren't much more than names and bodies. I'm not even sure I like the sex. There was something sort of compulsive about it. What does that make me?"

Andy's enchanting smile wreathed his face. "A crazy mixed-up kid like the rest of us. I must say, I used to think the sex was sensational. That's what's changed about me but I wasn't absolutely sure until last night. I'm glad we didn't want to do much of anything. I don't want to relapse. The guys I fell for mostly took me. You know, fucked me. I didn't get a chance to become a dedicated cocksucker. It doesn't show anymore but I was a very pretty kid."

"It shows. I'll bet you were much more than pretty. You're damned good-looking now."

"We better not start telling each other what we think of our looks. I might embarrass you." Their hands stroked each other and Andy's smile faded as his eyes grew intently searching. "Let's just say that we love each other."

"That'll do. It's an extension of what I feel for Scot. You make me feel much more part of the family than she'll let me be yet. Being in bed with you made all the difference. Someday, she'll let me make love to her and we'll be all set. I don't know how homosexual I am, but holding your hand could easily give me a hard-on."

The smile returned like a light being turned on. "Same here, if I can mention mine in the same breath. Yours is a major event. Let's hold hands a lot and play with each other like kids. That can't do anybody any harm."

"It's a deal. Are you a Negro? That sounds as idiotic as this whole business about race. You're you. You're Andy. I love you more than any guy I've ever known. That's all that counts. Are you?"

Andy laughed. "Of course. I thought you knew. My father is as black as the ace of spades. My mother and I look alike. I can pass when there's some reason to— like at school, for instance. I work for a Negro legal firm, one of the few in the country. I'm useful when there's business with whites. My boy's a throwback." His smile filled his face with pride. "He's a beautiful little pickaninny. I guess you and Scot have talked about that possibility."

"Sure. She thinks she can frighten me with the idea. There might be problems—there always are for anybody—but I think I'd love it. Can I tell her about us? It might be important. She won't be able to go on talking about the color bar. If I can't have a black girl I'll have a black boy." They laughed, totally at ease with each other.

"You can tell her anything you like. You don't have to tell her we love each other. I told her last night. I spoke for both of us. How's that for an uppity nigger? I've talked with her a lot about you even though I didn't know you. I told her she shouldn't keep you dangling. I said she should let you go or really live with you and see what you could make of it. She's a wonderful lady and you're a wonderful guy. If anybody can make it together, you should be able to."

Lance's throat tightened with the affection he heard in his voice. "Thanks. Most people warn her against me."

"I know. I've read a lot of silly stuff about you but I knew you weren't like that. Everything Scot said about you made that obvious. You've got to beat some sense into her."

"I'm trying but she has a lot of sense on her side. Maybe I'm not enough of a caveman. I sometimes want to stamp and holler but I can't force myself on her."

"Her husband did but that didn't work very well. You need me. We know all the things she's frightened of but you can't make a life being frightened. Do you expect to be late tonight?"

"I shouldn't think so. I'm taking Scot to one of those meeting things of hers. We're never much later than eleven."

"I should be free by ten-thirty. We'll talk all night. But right now, I need a shower. This city has a way of coming off on you. You can come with me. I've always had a weakness for groping guys in showers."

Lance had an ally. Andy's strength was becoming a part of him; he would have the strength of two. Any doubts he might have had about the course he had chosen vanished. With Andy at his side, he was going to get Scot.

They hitched their chairs out from the table and sat side by side while they removed their shoes and socks. When they were naked to the waist, Andy leaned forward and put his hands on Lance's shoulders and kissed him, testing him, while Lance's hands strayed caressingly over his chest. He drew back, intent eyes searching Lance's. "You really don't care about race, do you?" he said.

"No. I just don't think about it, I don't know why. I love her. I love you the way you are, whatever you are. She can't believe it."

"I'll tell her. I believe it. She does too, but she's a woman. She thinks too much."

They stood and finished stripping themselves and turned to each other. Andy laughed and gave his head an incredulous little shake as he slowly looked him over. "Here you are in broad daylight. They say seeing is believing but I'm not so sure. Lordy, Lance baby. I used to think my fantasies were pretty hot stuff but I never dreamed up anything like you. If this had happened five or six years ago, Carol wouldn't've stood a chance."

Lance conducted his own survey, smiling with pleasure. As long-legged as Scot. Slim torso. A dusky hairless sheen on a light ripple of muscle. A sudden friendly erection, compact, vigorous, manly, with no extra for show. It was ridiculous that men weren't supposed to feel anything about each other's bodies and he was glad that he could let himself enjoy this physical intimacy. He moved closer. Andy held up a warning hand.

"Don't come too close until I've washed. All niggers smell funny. You know that."

"A good scrub should help." Lance reached for him and held him in front of him.

Andy ran a hand along his cock. "Man, that feels *good*," Andy exclaimed appreciatively. "Such a big fat baby. It's been needing some attention. I'm going to take care of it from now on."

Lance looked down at Andy's trim instrument, finding its lively thrust very nearly irresistible. Did Andy want his in him as much as he wanted Andy's? They were playing with dynamite but Andy had defused it with playfulness. They would keep it that way. He ran

69

a hand over Andy's furry head and headed them toward the bathroom.

Lance spent the next few evenings with Scot as usual, but afterwards he and Andy talked late into the night, going around and around the familiar problems that stood in the way of a happy and reasonable life for him and Scot. Could they have children, possibly black, when Scot already had a white child? Where could they live? Did Lance have any hope of getting a divorce? Andy was pretty sure he couldn't so long as Pam remained under his mother's control.

"Why did you two have to fall in love with each other?" Andy said with a sigh late one night. "It would've been much easier if it happened to us. Think of it. No children. No need for divorces. It would've ruined my career but I suppose that would've been a small price to pay. We both could've become Western Union messenger boys and lived happily ever after."

Lance laughed. "That's the sort of job I'd be good at."

"Everybody's so alike these days, all of us in our little cubbyholes. You forget how difficult it is to be an exception. You and Scot are exceptions. You're going to have to break all the rules."

For those few days and later, all through the odd winter of frustration and hope and an indispensable sense of slow progress, affection flourished between them like a sturdy growth that bound them to each other and nourished Lance. He had never had a friend and knew that a few years ago the assortment of predigested opinions and attitudes concealed by his cultivated, handsome facade could never have attracted one. He was continually amazed and delighted that he could hold Andy's interest.

Sex had as little to do with it as they both had expected. After the first few times, they knew without saying anything that it wasn't going to become an addiction, but Andy loved seeing Lance with an erection and he was happy to oblige. They frequently showered together and always pushed the beds together on Andy's brief but fairly frequent visits to the city. At moments they felt such satisfaction in each other that Scot seemed almost irrelevant, although all their thoughts and plans were directed at overcoming her resistance

70

to the good life Lance was preparing himself to offer her.

Unexpectedly, as the winter wore on, Lance began to concentrate on art history. He had always liked to sketch and had a deft hand but had never taken it seriously. The discovery that interested him was that he had an eye that cut through the cant of much art literature. A new world opened to him. He began to frequent museums and galleries. He was particularly interested in the contemporary work being shown in the city. It was an interest that he could share with Scot. When something caught her eye at an exhibition, he was able to explain its strengths and weaknesses in a way that enlarged her appreciation.

Andy followed this development with practical encouragement. He investigated the working future Lance might have in curatorial positions with museums or in art criticism. Lance was uncomfortable with the dilettantism implicit in such work. It was getting too close to the family tradition of patronage, too far removed from the gritty reality of Scot's civil rights work. He wanted to be *doing* something, not following what other people did.

"You'll never completely escape your background, baby," Andy said. "You shouldn't try. It takes a black boy to understand the Negro's problems. People work hard to pick up the culture and education that was handed to you. You're already free of all the phoniness that came with it. You can relax, Lance baby. Scot's really excited about what you're getting into."

New York could never be good for them, they agreed at last. It was Andy's idea that Lance should know his own country better. He wanted him to go away for a couple of months during the summer, look for a place he thought they'd like, find out how the majority of his compatriots lived. When he came back, his savings would be almost gone and he would have to start doing some of the things they had talked so much about.

Once she was won over, Scot was enthusiastic about the plan. His absence would give her the time she needed to assess how impossible life would be without him. She had known him a year and everything she had learned about him had strengthened the love that had been declared between them at the start.

71

Spring was a time for euphoria. Lance was gripped by it. He could see an end at last to the waiting. Andy heard that he might be sent to some Central American country on business. If so, he might be able to travel for a couple of days with Lance and get him started on his way. He wanted him to make the trip by bus and train so that he would see what went on between airports.

Lance knew that as the time for his departure approached, Scot was on the verge of giving herself to him; any small incident or word might bring her to him. When it happened, it would be for life and the long wait would be forgotten. Euphoria kept him at a joyful pitch right up to the instant when his dream was shattered forever.

Replying to Andy's letter, Lance found it difficult to put into words exactly what he thought he was up to in Puerto Veragua. He couldn't say he had fallen madly in love. He couldn't say that he'd found work that satisfied him more than art criticism. He ended rather lamely by telling him that he was living with a pretty local girl whom he might have made pregnant and had decided to await developments.

He went ahead with the improvements he had planned before hearing from Andy, finding confidence in manual labor. He installed the tank on the roof, with one pipe running up from the well and another pipe running down the corner of the house with a shower head partway down and a faucet. He pumped: the tank filled with water. He turned the tap: water flowed. He felt as if he deserved a degree in hydraulic engineering.

For diversion after his successful labors, he walked along the sea for twenty minutes to the beach where he'd met Flip Rawls. He found her there with her two male couples. The latter were pleasant and friendly and, unlike Flip, didn't seem unduly impressed by him. He waved at some of the other foreigners he'd met at Flip's party and felt himself blending into the local scene. They all compared tans—Lance was turning as dark as the natives and his hair was the color of white gold. He asked about Robi and was told that he was still due in a week or so.

"I'm so pleased you're interested," Flip said. "Of

course he'll fall in love with you. How could he help it? You're meant for each other."

Lance laughed while the young men cast amused and speculative glances at him and expressed regret at missing the momentous meeting. They were leaving in a few days. Lance declined an invitation to lunch and they all helped Flip gather herself together and the party left.

Lance wanted to see if he could swim home but had a book with him. He was wondering what to do with it when a boy approached and straightened the chairs Flip's friends had been sitting in and demanded money. Lance pointed out that he'd been sitting on the sand. The boy insisted. He was a man, really, about as old as Lance, so it didn't occur to him to treat him like one of his children. He told him that he must speak to the *señora* or her friends. He was sure that as a regular, Flip must have some sort of permanent arrangement about chairs. The young man wanted to be paid now. It was his right. Lance had brought a little money folded into the book. He pulled it out, tempted to end the squabble, but the young man's sullen insistence made him balk. He had spent a year learning not to react like the rich; you didn't pay people to avoid annoyance. He had a new obligation to use his money carefully. He shook his head.

"No use chair. No pay." He started to return the money to the book. The man leaped forward and snatched it from him and turned and ran. Lance sprang up and overtook him, flinging himself on his back. They fell together in a tangle of arms and legs. Lance seized his hand and pried the money from it and, freeing himself, kneeled over his adversary. "You take money," he protested indignantly. "You steal." He looked into eyes that blazed with hostility and caught a sexual taunt that sent a shiver down his spine. He scrambled to his feet, retrieved his book, and started for home, prepared to fend off an attack.

The look he had intercepted stayed with him, leaving him vaguely uneasy, but he made a joke of the incident when he told Luisa about it, acting out his physical prowess for comic effect. She looked at him with unexpected gravity, speaking obscurely of blood and using other words he didn't understand. "You must be careful," she said more plainly. "You touched him. If he feels insulted he must have revenge."

"The insult was to me."

"I will ask my brothers," she said with decision. "They will know."

Lance shrugged. He knew so little about the place he proposed to settle in. Flip Rawls would have to sort it out. He'd read about primitive societies with complex codes of honor. He was becoming part of the native life whether he liked it or not. He wondered about the sexual gleam in the young man's eyes. They had been equally naked, wearing only swimming trunks. Had they touched in some way that might have been considered an invitation? He had been too busy recovering his money to notice. He was ready to forget the unpleasant episode but Luisa seemed genuinely upset.

He built a palisade around his shower installation and noticed that the water drained off into a patch of land that didn't look like ordinary mud. It hardened and held its shape when it dried, like clay. He experimented by fashioning a grotesque little devil-doll and put it in the sun to dry. It dried into a firm texture that didn't crumble when he handled it and shattered into fragments like pottery when he dropped it. He wondered if the stuff would hold paint and made a note to pick up a few tubes of primary colors for further experiments when he was next in the village.

Still nagged by a little undercurrent of apprehension because of his scuffle, he decided to pay another visit to Flip's beach to find out if she had heard any repercussions. He would take Luisa's advice and be careful. The last thing he wanted was any kind of publicity and he knew that an enterprising reporter needed very little to make a story.

He found Flip alone at the paper-strewn table, presumably writing her book about China. She greeted him with her usual disjointed charm and it took several minutes for him to work around to the question he had come to ask. No, she hadn't been asked to pay extra for chairs since the morning Lance had joined her group; she settled for her beach services on a monthly basis. While they chatted, he kept on the lookout for his adversary but wasn't sure he would recognize him unless he looked him in the eye. Lance remembered him as

74

good-looking in a hard-featured Indian way, like many of the young locals. Flip bemoaned the difficulty of saving her children from corruption now that tourism was increasing.

"I don't mean you, of course," she assured him. "You were quite right not to pay. You already understand the natives."

That evening, Luisa asked to wear her dress again to go to her family.

"You wish to see them again?" he asked.

"I should go every Sunday so they can expect me. The neighbors would think there was something wrong if I never went. It's the custom."

"By all means. We want your family to be pleased with you." The arrangement would have suited him very well if there were anything to do to fill an evening. He often read at night while she went about her chores. She probably supposed that he would be just as happy reading by himself. Boredom and loneliness.

"I will speak to them about your fight," she said when she appeared in her dress.

"On the beach? No fight, little one. He take money. I take it back. That's all." Flip had helped him to dismiss the incident as too trivial to worry about.

The next day, however, it was again a subject for discussion. Luisa reported that her brothers had warned her against "bad men" who frequented the beaches to prey on the foreigners. The younger ones, she said, sold themselves to the foreign men who didn't want women, but laying a finger on anyone in anger was considered a mortal insult. Lance gathered that the equivalent of an American sock on the nose could give rise to a blood feud that might encompass whole villages and end in killings.

"Does your family understand about you and me, little one?" he asked.

"They understand that I'm your woman. When I'm pregnant, they'll say I'm married. Because you're a foreigner, it will be believed."

"They won't want to kill me?"

"They will have to kill you if I disgrace them. They will expect you to pay for me."

"In what way?"

75

"A bride-price." Her eyes widened with trepidation as she named the equivalent of fifty dollars.

He chuckled and touched her breasts. "You must tell me these things, little one. You must tell me how to behave."

Social conventions were emerging to which he would be expected to conform. As they were unlike anything he had known, he was prepared to. He would be granted the privileges extended to any foreigner, but other than that, it was up to him to find his own place in an unknown world. He realized that he was unexpectedly carrying out at least part of the program he and Andy had outlined together.

He devoted his time to experiments with the clay. He made a series of devil-dolls, heads with vestigial limbs, perfecting his technique. He found that by hollowing them out in varying thicknesses they made different sounds when he broke them—pops and thuds and sometimes nearly a tinkle. He thought of Flip Rawls's party game with the light and decided to make a set for her. She could economize on glasses. He painted them bright outlandish colors and was so pleased with them that he rather hated to think of their being broken.

Watching him concentrating on his little clay figures, Luisa marveled that he could work so hard on something so useless. "Did you learn how to make such things in North America?" she asked.

He laughed and shook his head as he applied paint to the fifteenth of the set of twenty-four he was doing for Flip. "No. Here. Right now."

"You learn very quickly. Can you learn to make useful things that you could sell?"

"I think of selling," he said. "I have much to learn. These things will sell maybe."

It was possible. He had been struck by the poverty of the local market. Tourists would buy anything if they thought it was authentic native handicraft. He enjoyed working with the clay more than anything he'd ever done. He had learned something about pottery in his art studies, glazes and so forth, and was eager to make something he could use, but it seemed premature to start looking for a wheel and a kiln. He didn't even know how much clay cost or whether he could get it in sufficient quantities to turn out sets of plates. He intended to find out. First, he wanted to give the set of devil-dolls to Flip and see if anybody was amused by them.

A note arrived from Flip full of exclamation marks. Robbie Cosling was coming!! At last!!! And so forth. He and his "delicious child" were to save the evening of the 28th to welcome him.

Lance had to ask around town to find out when the 28th was and learned that he still had a few days to complete his set. Luisa said she would rather not go. Having learned something about local customs, he didn't insist. He would let her get used to foreign ways slowly.

His devil-dolls got off to a flying start under false pretenses. Flip gasped when she opened the box that Lance presented on arrival. "For me? But, Lance dear, you mustn't. They're priceless. I found some in Burma rather like them. Fascinating."

"You like them?"

"They're bewitching. Cambodian, of course. You see them in the temples. Absolutely priceless. I don't see how I can accept them."

Lance was tempted to let her put her foot in deeper but took pity on her. "No, Flip. You're not looking at them carefully. I made them to throw at the rocks. You can save your glasses."

She snatched one up and studied it. "Of course. I see now. The light's so dim. How clever of you. Such good copies. In this light I'd've sworn they're the real thing."

He found the light almost blinding and he didn't know what he was supposed to have copied but he was pleased with her reception of his gift. "Where's your star attraction?" he asked.

"I can't wait for you to meet. I'll bring him to you the minute he appears."

Lance picked up a glass of wine and wandered along the sweep of terrace, greeting familiar faces. He was talking to Mme Fournier when his eyes wandered to a nearby group and his attention was riveted by a stranger. Glossy dark hair crowned a poetically handsome head. Aside from the rare good looks, what struck him most forcefully was an air of sensitive intelligence and quiet authority. There was no doubt who it was; it couldn't be anybody else. All the others were quite ordinary and he'd seen most of them around for weeks.

When he'd absorbed the impact of the guy's looks, he began to lose interest in him. Robbie looked so exactly like what he was—a successful and important young man, well launched on his own life with his own preoccupations. He looked older than Lance had expected and everything about him marked him as one of the world's elect, the sort he had been thrown with all his life.

Their glances crossed. Lance found himself looking into enormous eyes, smoky and purple but curiously luminous. He saw the click of recognition in them and the painter turned toward him, moving effortlessly away from his group and approaching with a dazzlingly welcoming smile. He stopped in front of Lance.

"You must be my betrothed," he said. They shook hands.

"Has she been carrying on about me to you, too?"

"The minute I arrived. We're made for each other. I can't think of anything more likely to make us hate each other on sight."

"Exactly. I find you quite loathsome."

They looked into each other's eyes and burst out laughing, immediately enveloped in a warmth of mutual attraction. Flip wouldn't have had to make a point about the painter's sex life for him to have picked up the signals. Without being effeminate, he struck Lance as even more confidently homosexual than Bryan.

"What're you drinking?" Robbie asked.

"I've found some rather marvelous white wine."

"Good. Let's commandeer a bottle and go over there and tell each other everything that's important about ourselves."

Robbie put a hand on his shoulder as they turned to the table where the drinks were set out. He was a shade taller than Lance, with a handsome athlete's body. They were dressed alike in open shirts and slacks. Robbie's were beautifully tailored and he wore them with great style. A heavy gold chain hung around his neck. His voice was charming, the accent mixed Anglo-American with a flavor of French in the vowels.

"Lance Vanderholden," he said. "This makes coming all the way down here worthwhile. I saw you in your

78

show two years ago. It was the silliest play I've ever seen, but you—you were stunning. I went with Maurice, my dear friend of many years, and we both fell in love with you. I'm sure Flip has told you about my sexual preferences, so we don't have to mince words."

He picked up the bottle of wine that Lance had sampled, allowing a moment for his point to sink in. He gave Lance a chance to beat a hasty retreat. He remained.

"Pouilly Fuissé?" Robbie commented. "I think we can manage to choke down a bit of that. Better make it two," he said in Spanish to the boy who was acting as bartender and pointed to the two chaises longues he had already indicated to Lance.

They crossed the terrace, followed by the boy with two bottles of wine in an ice bucket. "Supplies secured," Robbie said with a ripple of mirth. "Will it be terribly rude if we don't speak to anybody else for the rest of the evening?"

"Not if we have to say important things to each other. It would be rude for anybody to interrupt."

Robbie gave the small of his back a little pat. The boy put the wine on the floor as instructed and they pushed the chairs closer together. By the time they were luxuriously settled, Lance had studied his companion's striking features. The V of his open shirt revealed a sculpturally hairless chest, deeply tanned. His upper lip had a slight fullness that gave his mouth a bee-stung and seductive look. His hands were remarkably big and powerful, almost brutal-looking, at odds with his general air of refinement. His great eyes were hypnotizing, direct and penetrating, seeming to see through everything. Lance had tried to teach himself to be wary of appearances, but there was so much about Robbie that pleased the eye that he couldn't help being disposed in his favor.

"I know quite a lot about you, naturally," Robbie said. "You're the darling of the press. I must be rather a blank to you. Do you know I'm a painter?"

"Of course. You had a show in New York a couple of months ago. Everybody was raving about it. I was too impressed to rave. Struck dumb was more like it."

"You're interested in painting? That's the most important thing about me. My work is everything. I try

79

not to let sex interfere. Do you know we're practically twins? We were both born in '21—I have the impression you were born *at* 21—March for me, August for you. We're both tottering toward thirty but I'm older."

"You'd better tell me how long you're staying. If we're made for each other, I hope you're not leaving day after tomorrow."

"I'll be here maybe as long as a month. It all depends on the work. If I can get a little work done here, there's nothing very urgent to take me away. If I did portraits, I'd stay and paint you for the rest of my life."

His painter's eyes had dismantled Lance, examined the parts and put them together again, deciding that nobody could make any improvements. The slight upward sweep of his brows and his wide-set, heavy-lidded eyes were enough to keep him absorbed all evening. The marvelously quirky curves of his generous mouth required separate study. The golden hair and the odd masklike quality of his face in repose reminded him of his first love. Lance was presumably as disinclined to take a male lover as Toni had been. He was resigned to a platonic passion but Lance was still the sexiest man he'd ever laid eyes on. He'd known it since he'd seen his show. Then his body had been superbly revealed but he hadn't been able to reach out and touch him. He was going to have to keep himself firmly in check.

"Do you think I can stand Flip for a month?" he asked.

"It would be marvelous if you could stay with me but you'd be miserable. The house isn't made for guests."

"I doubt if the house would have much to do with it. I've lived in all sorts of peculiar places. You're a family man, aren't you?"

"Was. I left all that in New York some time ago. I have a girl with me here. She speaks only Spanish so she's self-conscious about coming to Flip's parties. She begged off tonight."

"Bless her for letting me have you all to myself. Shall I tell you about some of the peculiar places I've lived? Your marble halls probably lack variety."

Within a quarter of an hour, Lance had fallen completely under his spell. It was the quick immediate closeness he had felt with Andy, although he couldn't

80

think of two people who were less alike. He had led a wonderfully full life. At seventeen, he had been praised by Picasso. At the same age, he was having lovers, male lovers at that, and was leading the cosmopolitan life of prewar France, surrounded by famous writers and painters and theatrical luminaries, while Lance was imprisoned first in a suffocatingly exclusive Catholic school in Connecticut, then in an equally exclusive Catholic college in Virginia, cultivating a worldly manner to conceal his total ignorance of the things that made up life for most people. Robbie offered him the untrammeled youth he had dreamed of having, and illuminated what he wanted to be. His quiet authority made him seem much older, a little bit the father he had never had.

"My father always made a big point about bringing me up in the sun," Robbie continued. "For a long time, there weren't any servants and when there finally were, they were just part of the family. Old class-conscious Europe is a lot more democratic in many ways than the brave new world."

Despite his American passport, he had always thought of himself as French more than anything else, but he had lived the first ten years of his life in New York and assumed when he returned for the first time as an adult a few years ago that he would feel at home there. Instead, he felt like a foreigner, welcome for the wrong reasons. He was taken for an aristocrat, an exotic, although he had been brought up on a run-down vineyard by shabby, hardworking parents whose good looks were their only passport to social acceptance.

His father's flukish real-estate fortune, acquired just before the war, had made possible the instant status of a legendary house on the Côte d'Azur, completed in time to be destroyed by the war. He had witnessed his father's murder of his mother's lover, who had been his lover too. There had been a war on and the victim had been a German, so his father had got away with it. He had lived openly as an older man's lover for ten years. It was of such strands that the fabric of his life had been woven, beyond the ken of plain-thinking, wholesome, self-righteous Americans.

"You know, incredibly enough, I think Flip might've

n right," Lance said. "I think maybe we *were* made each other, if not entirely in the way she means."

If we were, I'm sure we'll find out about it sooner or later. Meanwhile, don't encourage me. I have enough to cope with as it is." He leaned forward suddenly and for a moment, their eyes—Lance's blue and guileless, Robbie's unfathomably purple—met and delved into each other. "I get so damn lonely sometimes. It's apt to distort everything. You don't know what it's like to live with someone you love for almost ten years and then—" He made a helpless little gesture with his big hands. "Nothing. Maurice was killed in a plane crash, you know. I was supposed to be on it with him. A last minute change of plan. I often wish that I had been, except—" He took a deep breath and a smile strayed across his lips. "If I had, you would never have met me." Their hands moved to each other and almost touched.

"I know about being lonely," Lance said. "I may even tell you about it someday." Their hands gripped each other briefly and Robbie sat back and held up an empty bottle. "Well, that's where one bottle has got us. Let's see what's in the second one. I hear you're Cambodia's greatest gift to art."

Lance laughed. "She can be pretty silly sometimes."

"I don't know much about Cambodia but those things didn't look Cambodian to me. They looked like very sophisticated Western work by somebody with a witty feel for primitive art. Were you copying anything?"

"Not that I know of."

"I didn't think so. They're very original. I feel a highly personal imagination at work. I love them. I know somebody in New York who could sell them like hot cakes."

"I'm not sure I could make them like hot cakes. I don't have enough technique. Do you know anything about pottery?"

"Quite a lot, actually. I worked a bit with Picasso in Vallauris a few years ago. Right after the war."

"You see? We *are* made for each other. Will you teach me?"

"I'll teach you anything you're willing to learn."

His smile and tone of his voice didn't hint. He was talking about sex. Lance was thinking about sex. He was wishing that he'd carried his experiments further so that he wouldn't be torn by doubt or uncertainty. He didn't have to be told that Robbie was a spectacular lover. He had never felt such sexual self-assurance in anybody.

"Don't make fun of me," he said. "I can't help it if I like girls. You make me wish I didn't. Flip says it's a trivial distinction." He was grateful to Robbie for being outspoken about himself so that they could talk about it easily.

"I assure you there wouldn't be anything trivial about it. It might even be the love affair of the century." He smiled composedly as if he were prepared to bide his time. "You're very sweet. Nobody else would sound apologetic for being straight. Naturally I'm going to try to take advantage of you. You're the most exciting man I've met in years—maybe ever. Whether or not I fall in love with you is another matter but I'll want you every second I'm with you. I won't stop trying to get you. It doesn't matter if you encourage me or not."

"I probably will without meaning to. I want you to like me as much as I like you. You're the most fascinating guy I've ever met so we're almost even. We're going to spend the next month together, aren't we?"

"It'll take me at least a month to teach you all I know about potting. I hope getting you into bed will be quicker."

Lance put a hand on Robbie's knee. "I have to touch you to convince myself that you're here. Is it all right if I touch you?"

"At your own risk," Robbie warned.

Food and more wine were brought to them. Flip had assumed her duties as their guardian angel. Their conversation didn't flag. Everything they mentioned led to something else. Lance was surprised that he had so much to say about himself without touching on the major experience of his life. Obviously, Robbie's life had been a series of major experiences. He was passion and creative fire seamlessly wedded to the high refinement of his mind and tastes. He was a man of the world who hadn't lost touch with the primitive forces of nature.

As they talked, Lance wondered how long he could resist him. He felt increasingly that he must. He couldn't imagine Robbie being satisfied with the games he'd played with Andy. He would expect a complete homosexual response from a lover. He didn't quite know what that meant but he was sure he hadn't had it even with Bryan. Inadequate sex only risked spoiling the happy connections they were making with each other. Worse, it might end all Robbie's interest in him.

Time flew by without their being aware of it. They were feeling agreeably boozy on the wine. They made each other laugh a lot and their eyes sparkled with their delight in each other's company. They sat forward with their heads together while Robbie sketched with a long, big-knuckled finger on the arm of the chair the layout of the old *manoir* where he had lived with Maurice. It was his now. Talking about it made him want to get back to it. It was time to go home.

"I'll have to come see it someday," Lance said. He turned Robbie's hand over and laid his own on it. "I love to hold your hand. Do you mind? It makes me feel safe."

"Is it possible for the rich and glamorous Lance Vanderholden not to feel safe?"

"Oh, God. A month ago I didn't think I'd ever feel safe again. I hope you'll stay a long time. I'd like to know that we'll always be near each other."

This was getting serious. Lance said things that even somebody offering himself as a lover wouldn't say. If they followed the book, they would spend the night together and possibly find that they wanted to have a serious affair. That would occupy him for a month. When it came time for parting, there was the unlikely possibility that by then they would have discovered that they wanted to be near each other always. Lance seemed to expect him to make a commitment without the incentive of satisfied passion. What about the girl?

"Now that we've absorbed the shock of finding each other," Robbie said, "do you want me to go ahead and fall in love with you?" His smile playfully mocked them both.

"It's not up to me, is it?" Although Lance had never gotten used to the idea of men falling in love with each other, he knew that Robbie was speaking of a serious possibility. His heart skipped a beat and he felt obliged to remind him of their different natures. "When I've fallen in love with girls, nothing anybody said made much difference. If they wouldn't go to bed with me, I went on pining."

"I see. You recommend pining. I hope I won't look too woebegone." Their eyes played with each other and they burst out laughing.

Robbie remained puzzled but entranced. So far, he had accepted Lance as straight. But straight men didn't open themselves so quickly and sweetly and ingenuously to other men. Maybe he wasn't as straight as he pretended. Whatever he was, he wasn't a coquette. His artlessness was the most striking thing about him. To his alarmed surprise, Robbie realized that deeper feelings had somehow become engaged. He cared about this paragon of male beauty. He wanted to know what went on inside him.

For over a year he had lived with the conviction that he had lost the capacity for any deep emotional attachments. Maurice's death had left him feeling physically diminished, as if he had been severed from a Siamese twin on whose organs he had partially subsisted and now needed time to grow new ones of his own. Because it offered him greater freedom for his work, he had reconciled himself slowly to the loss. Lance threatened his freedom. For better or worse, suddenly, within the span of an hour, he had become once more emotionally intact and appallingly vulnerable.

"You don't look remotely woebegone," Lance said. "You look as if you've got a secret I should know. I don't want to miss anything with you."

"Fall in love with me and I'll be an open book."

"Wouldn't it be marvelous? Flip would be so pleased. How do you get to be homosexual? Is that a silly question?"

"No—discouraging. Your asking is the most convincing way you could find to tell me you're not." The wistful note in Lance's voice had pierced Robbie's heart. In his heightened state of awareness induced by reawakening emotions, he felt quite clearly the melancholy in his new, disconcerting friend that had seemed only a few minutes before a lack of character, an emptiness. Despite his vivid beauty and his air of intense physical well-being, Lance was sad. Robbie gripped his hand and wished the contact could grow until their bodies were swallowed up together into it.

"Unfortunately, the answer's simple," he said. "Being a homosexual is like being hungry. You just are. Of course, there *are* cases of retarded development."

"Stick around."

They looked into each other's eyes again and laughed but now Robbie's heart was wrung by the longing that echoed in the rich mirthful sounds that issued from Lance's throat.

Flip intervened. She stood in front of them and clapped her hands together and tilted her head at them when they looked up slowly, as if they'd been awakened from a dream. "It's too thrilling to see you together. Wasn't everything I said true? Haven't you discovered that you're made for each other?"

Lance intertwined their fingers and sat back and held up their joined hands. "We're at the hand-holding stage. We've decided on a long engagement."

"You're a devil," Flip exclaimed delightedly. "Make fun of an old lady if you like, but you'll thank me for bringing you together."

Robbie looked at Lance with a playful smile. "Shall we thank her?"

"I wouldn't know where to begin. You thank her if you can think of any words worthy of the occasion."

They let go of each other and Robbie pulled himself to his feet. "We're speechless with gratitude, Flip. You'll have to be satisfied with that. I think it's time to anoint the good earth with some of that excellent wine we've been drinking."

Lance rose and took Robbie's arm. Robbie hugged his hand against his side. The erection that had been more or less with him all evening had a moment of intense energy and then slowly subsided as they wandered along the terrace to the garden at the end. They stepped out into the night. A full moon was riding the enormous sky. They laughed at the seemingly endless streams issuing from them. When they went back, the guests were lined up along the parapet hurling glasses.

Lance was quite pleased to see that his devil-dolls hadn't been contributed to the sport. "Can it be that late?" he wondered. "Is the party over?"

"What an evening," Robbie said. "Let me drive you home. I hired a car to get down here." He hoped Lance would refuse. A grope in the car would be almost too great a temptation to resist. But if he was falling in love, there wouldn't be much point in it unless Lance fell in love, too. He looked at him as if he might. All the more reason to let him come to it in his own time. Robbie knew that as soon as he was gone he would regret not having made a more determined effort to have him. He was beginning to remember what it was like to fall in love.

"It's only a step. I'm used to walking."

"It's just as well for your peace of mind. I understand I'm irresistible at the wheel of my runabout."

They laughed and moved in closer to each other, face to face, holding each other's hands.

"Tomorrow?" Lance asked.

Robbie almost burst into tears. The trust and sweetness and need in the one word touched him to the depths. If they weren't lovers yet, they were loving friends. It was a start. "Of course tomorrow," he said.

"You'll be going for a swim with Flip. It's one of the immutable laws of Puerto Veragua. I'll meet you at the beach. We'll start making plans." Lance withdrew his hands and put them on Robbie's shoulders and looked at his seductive mouth. "I want to kiss you good night. Would that count as encouragement? Blame it on the wine." He gave his shoulders a little shake and smiled into the purple eyes and tore himself away. He said good night to Flip and others without really seeing them.

He was aware of a flurry of movement near him as he stepped out of the blue door and in a moment saw a figure racing away under the trees ahead of him. The moon was high in the sky, so bright that everything was bathed in silver light or obliterated in inky shadow. He wanted to sing. He was filled with elation at the evening's developments. He had found a friend. He had skirted the sexual pitfalls and could count on Robbie to treat it as a private joke. If he didn't completely kill his hopes, maybe he'd stay longer. He no longer feared boredom. A month. Why only a month? He had said there was nothing urgent to take him away. Time to find out if Luisa was pregnant. Time to find out if he could do something with pottery. Life was mending itself.

He drew a great breath of air into his lungs and burst into a full-throated rendition of "Ol' Man River." He

87

laughed to himself as the deep notes reverberated in the night.

His song caught in his throat as he rounded a bend in the road. Three men moved out from the shadow of the trees and barred his way. His first reaction was astonishment at finding anybody out at this hour. He continued walking slowly. The menace he sensed all around him was a trick of the weird light. They were black-and-white figures in a black-and-white landscape. When the light caught their faces, they were featureless chalk marks. From the hang of their clothes, the loose cotton shirts and pants like pajamas, he could see that they were young and lean. His eyes dropped to their sides and he stopped dead.

All three of them were carrying lengths of rough wood like clubs. His heart leaped into his throat. His mind was blocked with Luisa's warning of blood feuds and revenge. He couldn't think of anything to do to save himself. They were moving now, advancing on him slowly and soundlessly. They were less than fifteen feet away. In a moment, he would be within reach of the clubs. He remained motionless for an instant, poised for flight, and then whirled and pitched into two others who seized him from behind. He swung at them but all five of them were on him, pinning his arms to his sides. He cringed, trying to pull his head between his shoulders, waiting for blows to start raining on him. They dragged him off the road among trees. Four of them clung to him, grappling with him to subdue him. The fifth stepped up to him and seized his shirt and ripped it off. He looked into eyes that were hard with triumphant lust and he instantly recognized the boy on the beach. Shock made him forget to struggle.

His hands were bound with a strip of the shirt. Another strip was passed through the crook of his arms from behind, pulled tight, and tied in back so that his hands were bound securely against his chest. It made the lower part of his body feel terrifyingly defenseless. It wasn't going to be a simple beating.

Anger pounded up in him and turned sick with fear. They must know he'd go to the police if they didn't kill him. If he pretended docile acceptance of anything they did, would they let him go? His heart settled into a steady pounding against his ribs as they pushed him forward and jostled him along over rough ground under trees. If he didn't free himself before they reached their destination, he was doomed. His feet were his only weapons but the men stayed in close against him, leaving him no room to maneuver, and kept their hands on him.

They moved out from the trees into a clearing of hard-packed earth with a well in it. They stopped in a circle around him and the ringleader stepped up to him again and gripped the top of his slacks and ripped them open. They all yanked at his clothes, stripping him. His naked body was violated by lewdly groping hands, squeezing his buttocks, pinching his nipples, pulling at his cock. His outraged senses registered that it was hardening. He sank instinctively to his knees and bowed over it to conceal it. He saw clothes dropping around him.

His scalp crawled with terror. His hair was seized and he was jerked up straight on his knees. They came at him naked, their erections swinging, teeth bared in the moonlight, uttering a savage chorus of jeers and laughter. Their erections beat against him as they wrestled for position around him. Dread hollowed out the pit of his stomach. He began to shake violently. A wild perverse exhilaration jangled through his body like an electric shock.

An erection prodded his mouth. He jerked his head away. He was struck hard across the face. His head rocked and tears sprang to his eyes and his mouth dropped open. The erection was thrust into it. A man gripped him painfully by the ears and thrust himself back and forth in his mouth. Lance gagged. He wanted to bite it but thought of what they might do to him. He opened his mouth wider and worked his lips and tongue to placate the aggressor.

Moist hands were groping between his buttocks and fingers plunged into him. He bucked and twisted his hips and strained against his bonds. His legs were seized and his knees pulled apart on the hard ground. His body was torn open by the violence of the assault. He was being entered and possessed. The rape was complete.

Pain lowered a dark film over his eyes. He groaned in his throat. He heard a grunt and his mouth was

89

flooded with thick fluid. It trickled down his throat and he was forced to swallow. His stomach turned over. Another erection lifted toward his face, a hand moving on it. An ejaculation leaped from it and spattered into his eyes, blinding him, and onto his cheek and nose and lips. His labored breathing drew it up his nostrils. He choked and retched and began to sob as a hard cock stretched his jaws again. He was going to suffocate.

The flesh that had filled him was torn from him and all his insides seemed to spill out of him. Pain seared him again as he was once more ripped open and possessed. His mind reeled and he sank toward unconsciousness. He could no longer identify any part of his body. He was a broken mass of agony and filth. He remained swaying on his knees as his assailants backed away from him. The silence was broken only by his sobs.

Lance's vision was blurred. He saw a bare foot lifted threateningly in front of him but he was beyond fearing its impact. It came to rest on his shoulder and toppled him over onto his back. If they were going to kill him, he hoped they'd do it quickly. He could see no reason why they shouldn't. They wouldn't be caught. They must see him as a threat. He would never report them to the police but they had no way of knowing this.

A voice spoke briefly with a note of command. There was movement around him and sounds he couldn't identify. His heart accelerated, reminding him that he wanted to live. Two men stood at his sides and emptied buckets of water over him. He shook his head and his eyes cleared. The ringleader stood over him, naked now, his erection lifted victoriously above him. He looked into his eyes and saw a glitter of dangerous triumph in them. A foot was planted on his chest, flattening him to the ground, its toes fondling his nipples. The foot moved on over his body caressingly, smearing it with mud as it restored identity to its parts and reawakened sensation. Everything still capable of response in Lance surrendered to an intimation of compassion. His only hope lay in convincing his captor that he had won, that he could take his revenge without fear of retribution.

Their eyes met again and Lance's heart pounded up in his chest so that he could hardly breathe. The drumming in his veins made his head swim. His cock stirred, lengthened, inched out from between his legs. It swung up and lay rigid on his belly.

A murmur arose around him that was stilled by another word of command. They all edged in closer. They could no longer harm him. His cock was hard for their leader. His body craved violation. He felt as if layer after layer of the insulation that held him together as an individual were being stripped from him. Will was gone, pride, dignity, all sense of right and wrong, leaving only a small naked twitching shred of ego, the will to survive. It was all that he was.

The voice of command spoke again. Two naked figures darted forward and crouched over him. They gripped his arms and lifted him to a sitting position. They pulled him to his knees once more, handling his erection roughly in a way that indicated their contempt for it. Lance looked up at the man who had won him and it lifted into greater tense rigidity. Hands worked on his bonds and a sob of gratitude escaped him as they were loosened. His hands dropped lifelessly to his thighs.

The night was suddenly silent. His reason had ceased to function. He knew only that he was free to perform a ritual of voluntary debasement. He lifted his hands slowly as circulation was restored to them and slid them up amorously over hard thighs and abdomen. His eyes were on the erection in front of him, ghostly in the moonlight. He tilted his head back and his mouth dropped open slackly to receive it. It forced his lips open wider and displaced his tongue as it made its victorious entry.

A collective sigh arose around him as he wooed his conqueror with his lips and tongue. A hand gripped his wet hair and held his head motionless while the shaft of flesh slowly probed his mouth, demonstrating his slavish subjugation. For a moment he felt that pleasure had placated his enemy, but then he heard an angry snarl. His head was wrenched back and a foot landed on his chest, knocking the wind out of him. His head hit the hard ground, stunning him, and he lay sprawled out on his back again, gasping for breath.

Merciless hands were on him, flinging him over, spreading his legs, and lifting his hips, making an obscene display of his defilement.

He was entered brutally in one long searing thrust.

91

He shouted as pain returned and tore at his entrails. He prayed for unconsciousness while all his body opened to the assault. A clamor of grunts and snorts and jagged laughter sprang up around him, becoming a rhythmic accompaniment to the thrusts that began to rock his body. He rolled his hips with them and found a sudden harmony in their fierce copulation. Nothing else remained of him: he existed to be raped.

Together they prolonged the harsh harmony they had found. He realized that his crazed body was being led to orgasm. He struggled upright on his knees and reached back to straining haunches and incited the aggressor to a further murderous penetration of him. He cried out as his ejaculation shot up into the circle of witnesses. A muffled collective animal growl was followed by the appeased silence of consummation.

He slumped forward into the dirt, spent and insensate, scarcely aware of lust's climax being discharged into him or of withdrawal. He heard the sound of quick movement, the rustle of clothing, the brief thud of footsteps, and then silence. He rolled over onto his back under the bright moon and was seized by a paroxysm of dry, racking sobs. They ended abruptly, leaving him calm and purged. He had been ravaged and defiled beyond any possibility of his hiding from himself the enormity of his participation. He couldn't remember what had led him from resistance to acceptance, or when acceptance had become a nightmare of welcome. Nothing he had ever known had any further relevance. He had to recreate himself out of what was left to him — his shame.

A small glow of exhilaration flickered through his shattered body, recalling him to life. He was no more than the lowest common denominator of humanity. All the doors had been smashed and he had embraced the horror that raged behind them. He recognized the source of his exhilaration. There were no more secrets. He was what he was. Whatever was to come would be his own.

He sat up painfully. He ached everywhere. He felt as if there was an open wound deep inside him. He pulled himself unsteadily to his feet. He had to wash without Luisa seeing him. Nobody must know what had happened to him. He had to guard his humiliation for himself or it would be too great to bear. He gathered up scraps of his clothes and found enough to serve as a loincloth. He made his way back to the road and dragged himself the short distance home.

He circled the house and took the steps to the sea one at a time, cautious with pain. He would tell Luisa that he'd fallen. His knees were scraped and his ears were swelling. He dived in and felt the cool sea healing him. He repeatedly filled his mouth and drew it up his nose, washing away all traces of his defilement. He washed between his buttocks and held his head under water to wash his hair.

He climbed out tingling with cleanliness. He was amazed that his body felt relatively undamaged. The internal wound was painful but already felt as if it were mending. Feeling clean, after feeling that he would never be clean again, lightened his spirit and brought him a measure of peace. He had atoned for the haughty, self-advertised superiority of generations, for greed and acquisitiveness disguised as public service, for the hypocrisy on which his noble line had flourished. Money had been its firm foundation; it was fitting that he should have suffered so loathsomely for wanting to hold on to a few pennies that were his. He had won the absolution he had longed for.

He climbed back naked to the house and crept to the bedroom door. He heard Luisa's even breathing and saw her dark shape against the white sheets. He nodded absently and went to bed in the other room, repelled by the thought of physical contact with anybody.

He woke up late and his mind recoiled with incredulity as he went over the events of the night before. Had it really happened? His body told him that it had.

Luisa seemed to accept the story of his fall. He explained that both sides of his head had hit rocks as he lost his footing and blamed it on the wine he'd drunk at the party. She agreed that it might have been worse and brewed something medicinal to bathe his ears. A bruise on his cheek and his scraped knees were the only other visible signs of the horror.

He spent the rest of the day recuperating in the shade. Even if he'd felt better, he wouldn't have been able to face Robbie. The thought of Robbie engaging in acts even faintly resembling the things that he had done last night made his skin crawl.

He was increasingly convinced that he had invited the assault by the look he had exchanged with the boy on the beach. Although he had closed his mind to it at the time, he remembered a shock of excitement at the contact of their bodies. He had felt as if demons had been stirred in him that were getting out of control. Something had happened between them that left Lance at his mercy. If he commanded, Lance would follow.

As the day wore on, he knew that he had to see Robbie, if only to find out if he was still capable of a decent friendship. Like everything before the rape, Robbie was beginning to seem like a hallucination. You didn't decide against sexual involvement with a hallucination so he must have been tempted by a flesh-and-blood man. Whatever was in him that responded to male lust was vile. He didn't want to soil Robbie with it.

By evening, he felt and looked much better. The swelling of his ears had subsided. He didn't want to make love with Luisa but he supposed that would pass. He was beginning to worry that his failure to appear today would cool Robbie's interest in him. He wanted to hear him say again that he would stay a month. With Robbie, maybe he could cure himself of the sickness he'd fallen victim to last night.

Associating him sexually with the rapists had been a morbid reaction to shock. Robbie was a race apart. If everything he remembered about him was true, they would become devoted friends. He would be a protection against demons.

He was uneasy venturing ou⁴ into the world when he set off at noon the next day for the foreigners' beach. He knew that he wouldn't be able to identify with any certainty four of his five assailants, so that any young native male was a potential enemy. He looked out along the smooth curving sweep of beach bordered by peaceful sea, and told himself that it was ridiculous to sense danger here. The account had been settled. What remained was within himself.

In the distance he could see Flip's cabana, surrounded by people. The intervening stretch of beach was dotted with the usual scattering of dark figures, disporting themselves in groups or singly in and out of the sea. He averted his eyes as he passed them, not wanting to encounter the flicker of a glance or a shift of expression that might betray a witness to his degradation. He wondered if the leader was observing his arrival and his heart began to beat heavily.

As he approached Flip's entourage, he saw that she was holding court for a handful of familiar foreigners. He covered the last short distance slowly, his eyes on Robbie, who was sitting in one of the beach chairs talking to Flip. His eyes didn't stray from his handsome face, humorously intelligent, sensitive, dashingly romantic. He felt immediately comforted and his heart resumed a normal pace. He was safe with Robbie. He wasn't quite ready to allow his eyes to dwell on his body.

He had almost reached the circle when Robbie looked up and their eyes met. Lance stopped and Robbie jumped up and joined him, slightly removed from the others. He put a hand on Lance's arm, his deep purple eyes looking down intently at his face.

"Did you hurt yourself?" he demanded with no preliminary greeting as he lifted lightly exploring fingers to his cheek.

Lance pulled back sharply. He had thought the bruises were no longer noticeable. "I fell down after I left you the other night. Does it show? It wasn't serious."

"Not serious enough to keep you from meeting me yesterday?" Robbie continued to hold his arm.

"I'm sorry about that. I felt awful. I'm not used to wine."

"I was feeling a bit fragile myself but I was here." Robbie made his displeasure felt. "Couldn't you've sent a message or were you too drunk to remember everything we said? I worried. I was afraid I'd gone too far." He dropped his hand to his side.

Lance immediately restored contact by putting a hand on his shoulder. "No. Please. I'm sorry. I guess I didn't think you'd be counting on me. It wasn't just a hangover. I had sort of a problem. It's okay now."

Robbie tried to identify the change he felt in him. The odd melancholy had been replaced by a suggestion

95

of anger and fear held in taut control. He lifted his hands to Lance's hips, completing the casual embrace. Their bodies were brought tantalizingly close to contact in crucial areas. Robbie was getting an erection. He smiled his forgiveness. "Don't let it happen again. You're not supposed to have problems I don't know about, not while I'm here."

Although the light revealing clothes Robbie had been wearing the night before last had prepared him for it, Lance was stunned by his physical splendor. He looked as if he had been polished and ripened by long exposure to the sun, beautifully smooth-limbed and smoothly muscular, lithe and graceful and powerful. What made him a spectacular lover was spectacularly revealed by his brief trunks. He looked as if he had a hard-on. Lance shrank from it and hastily lifted his eyes.

"What can we do to make up for missing a whole day?" Lance asked, allowing his hand to slide down Robbie's arm before letting go of him. He realized that it might seem like a sexual provocation and reminded himself to avoid physical intimacies.

"Spend every day together for the rest of our lives maybe? Isn't that what you were suggesting the other night?" Robbie laughed. "Being Flip's houseguest is a heavy responsibility. She sleeps in the afternoon. Shall I sneak out and come see you?"

"Wonderful. I want you to meet Luisa and I'll show you that clay I've been playing around with. The house is easy to find. How about dinner?"

"No such luck. Flip's an organizer. Every day is an event. It's like being on a cruise ship. She's got some expedition laid on for tonight."

Robbie continued to look into Lance's eyes, reestablishing the rapport they had found together the first evening. He hadn't deceived himself, despite yesterday's torments of uncertainty, wondering if he'd frightened him off, resisting the almost unimaginable fact that Lance had become a necessity to him. He was an even greater threat to his freedom than he'd feared. He wanted much more than a night or a month with him. All day, he had thought longingly of home and had known that he could never go back to it without Lance. He wanted what Lance had so recklessly demanded. He wanted to be near him always.

Now that his eyes had possessed his body, breaking it down into its components of line and form and texture and concluding once more that there was no room for improvement, his glance returned fleetingly to the heavy, tautly stretched pouch of his trunks, and he was more helpless than ever. Lance's eyes remained thrillingly ambiguous, offering love, not quite excluding passion, with a new hint of desperation in them today as if he were pleading with him to force the issue and bring it to a head. What was he to make of a man who seemed to permit everything but accepted nothing?

He had no experience to guide him. Maurice had been his art teacher at school when Robbie'd seduced him, and they had lived happily together thereafter except for a wartime separation. There had been the usual strains and stresses of outside attractions but he had never allowed himself to make a prolonged effort to win a reluctant lover. Temptations had to be well-nigh irresistible and mutually urgent; a day or two's delay disposed of them. When he and Maurice had seen Lance on the stage, they had both admitted that they might fall for him in a big way if given the chance. Everybody in New York had assured them that Lance Vanderholden was straight so they had been able to joke about their infatuation. The joke was on him. He felt as if his heart had been pierced by a thousand arrows as Lance's face lighted up in the way that had so bewitched him at their first meeting.

"You know, you'd be much better off if you took a house of your own," Lance exclaimed. He settled his hands on his hips and dug his feet into the sand as if he were planting himself permanently in front of Robbie, barring his departure. "Flip would probably be delighted. She could claim the first distinguished recruit to her private paradise."

"Anything you suggest sounds like a good idea to me." Robbie's smile mocked himself. He shook his head. "I'm ridiculous. Two people who look like us? Look at us. Light and dark. Black and white. We're two sides of the same coin. We even think alike. I can see into your mind. You have a secret that you didn't have the other night. Don't worry. I'll winkle it out of you."

A shadow extinguished the light in Lance's face. "Don't," he said.

97

There was a haunted resonance in his voice that made Robbie's throat ache with the desire to hold him and make him smile again. His sunny innocence had dimmed. His appeal had acquired the poignancy of shame. Love burrowed deeper into him. He wanted to groan with it. He wondered if the capacity to love grew greater with age. After seeing Lance only twice, he had begun to fear for his future if he didn't manage to join them to each other permanently. He took a step closer to him and put his hands on his shoulders.

"Don't worry," he said. "I don't want your secrets. Not yet. We'll soon know all we need to know about each other."

"I know. I told you. I feel safe with you. I want you to make me feel safe with myself."

Their eyes held each other. Lance's were clear and candid but deep within them Robbie detected the plea. He gave up wondering. He was in love. "Let's pretend that we met night before last and are going to spend a few carefree holiday weeks together," he suggested.

Rich laughter burst from Lance, seeming to clog in his throat and sending a tremor of delight through Robbie that almost lifted him off the ground. "I'll pretend but I know we've known each other always," Lance said.

Robbie threw an arm around him and turned him to join the others. They performed their social duties. They swam. Lance told Robbie how to find the house and left. Walking home along the beach, he wanted to sing again but decided not to push his luck.

Lance told Luisa that a friend was coming to see them and when she said she would put on a blouse, he told her not to. "No need, little one." He wanted Robbie to see her at her best—his Balinese drawing. "He is not like other foreigners. What is good with me is good with him. He will see only the beauty."

He wondered if Robbie were ever attracted to women. He supposed not. All the more reason to call attention to the difference between them. He would see a couple leading an ordinary normal life and would know that his desire made no sense. The demons would be dispelled. Already, after the short time with him this morning, the rape had begun to seem a hallucination, Robbie the reality.

Robbie turned up in midafternoon and at the start

98

charmingly directed his attention to Luisa. He talked easily and fluently with her. He made her laugh her high fluting laughter.

Pleased and grateful, Lance pointed back and forth from Robbie to himself. "We are much friends. We are brothers," he told her. He laughed and turned to Robbie. "For heaven's sake, tell her we're going to see a lot of each other. Tell her we've known each other for years so she'll understand why I'm so pleased for you to be here."

Later, he showed Robbie his patch of clay and they discussed Lance's interest at greater length. "You're very clever to've made those things without any tools. But it's hot, dirty work if you want to do it right," Robbie commented.

"That's probably why I think I'd like it. I like feeling I'm really working and I love making things—you know, things I can shape and make into something I like."

"Like me and painting."

"Me and Picasso."

Robbie laughed. "Maybe. He has a feel for it. You obviously do, too. I do a bit."

"Then stay and pot with me."

"A proposition at last." They laughed. "Can we spend the day together tomorrow?" Robbie asked. "If I give her fair warning, Flip can do without me. I'd like to drive around and look at the country. We can ask questions. You can't go on digging here or you won't have any place left. There's bound to be somebody who knows about pottery. We can pick up something to eat along the way."

"You see how much I need you? I couldn't get anywhere with my Spanish."

"I learned it to prove to Picasso that I could. He was impressed."

They were launched again on a flood of talk. As he deployed all his charm in his campaign to make Robbie a permanent resident, Lance found himself flirting and he didn't like it. He was intruding a false note into their easy affectionate companionship. If it was spoiled, he would be to blame.

"Listen," he said abruptly, interrupting himself in midsentence. They were sitting under the eucalyptus tree at the top of the steps leading down to the sea,

Lance wearing a sarong, Robbie in shirt and shorts. Lance had been describing how he had fallen. He dismissed the story. "I just fell. It's unimportant. I've got to talk about the things we said the other night. You said you'd want me whenever you're with me. Is that still true?"

Robbie took a deep breath. Lance had changed again since this morning. He was no longer keyed up with an effort at control. He seemed more sure of himself. The strange beauty of his face was more openly expressive. His mouth was a marvel of sensuality, yet tender; his great, heavy-lidded eyes were capable of subtle provocation, yet could light up, as now, with innocence and candor. It was a passionate face in which male and female weren't firmly differentiated. Robbie thought he might go quite literally mad with joy if he were his.

"I told you the truth as far as I knew it then," he said. "The whole truth is that I want you even more when I'm *not* with you. At least at the moment, my eyes are satisfied. I can even touch you." He put his hand lightly on his bare shoulder. "If we're talking about sex and not love, I can put it simply. I get hard for you all the time."

"That's because I flirt with you. After I left the other night, I thought of sort of playing along with you, letting you think you might get me in order to keep you here. I'm ashamed of myself. I want desperately for you to stay, but not under false pretenses. I've got to stop flirting with you."

Robbie chuckled, abandoning hope of a confession. "Why stop? It's exciting even if you don't mean it. Maybe you will if you keep it up. Is it impossible for you to imagine our making love together?" He watched Lance's brief struggle to reply.

"Yes," he said, his conviction shaded by regret.

"You don't think you have any homosexual urges?"

"No." The word was almost inaudible. Even if it wasn't true, he owed it to Robbie to say it. His voice rose defensively on a note of defiance. "What are you talking about? What do you mean? Is there anything about me that makes you think I'm like that?"

"Like what? Queer? Homosexual? Like me? *Appelles ça comme tu veux.*"

He hadn't expected Lance to be conventionally sen-

100

sitive about his masculinity. If that was all it was, it shouldn't be difficult to get him over it. "I don't think you can always tell about people. There's so many reasons to hide it, not only from others but from yourself. If it hadn't been for me, Maurice would probably have got married sooner or later and been quite happy. I'm not suggesting that you're a screaming queen, just a bit ambivalent like lots of people, maybe most. You said you liked to touch me. You said you wanted to kiss me. Men don't usually say things like that unless they're thinking about sex."

"I know. I shouldn't have. I got carried away meeting you. Flip had turned it into sort of a joke. I don't want to be a cock teaser with you. Seeing me with Luisa, don't you understand?"

"Seeing you with Luisa puzzles me more than anything. She's sweet but you're not in love with her. When you talk about having children with her, I understand, but are you ready to live without love?"

"I'd have to tell you so much to explain it. Now that you're here, I don't want to live without *you*. Does that satisfy you?"

He spoke with passionate innocence. Robbie sensed danger in the contradictory mixture, a lack of balance and maturity. He knew that Lance had rejected the identity provided him by birth and suspected that he was prepared to adopt any role in his search for a new one that suited him. His topless girl was part of some sort of role-playing. Taking a male lover should appeal to the iconoclast in him. Thinking of it, he could hardly keep his hands off his beautiful naked body. He was an irresistible mystery waiting to be unraveled.

"I don't want to live without you," Robbie said, "but when *I* say it, I mean I want us to be lovers. Good Lord, the things we say to each other. We better give it a week to see if we mean them. Meanwhile, you can be a heartless flirt. Go ahead. Lead me on. Who can it hurt but me?"

"Please, darling. I don't want to hurt you. I love you to put your arms around me but I'd hate more than that. I wish you could seduce me. I want you to, but believe me: it wouldn't be right for us. I can't explain it. I just know."

101

"Did you call me darling?" Robbie asked, trying to take it in his stride.

Lance laughed. "I guess I did but that wasn't flirting. Everybody in the theater calls everybody darling. I guess it just slipped out. I sort of like it."

"So do I, darling. Goodness, yes. It relieves the pressure marvelously. It's almost as good as a kiss."

Robbie couldn't believe that this conversation would be possible with a straight man. He couldn't get over the feeling that something had happened since their meeting that had stiffened his resistance to his own ambiguity, something that had kept him away yesterday. The story of his fall was unconvincing. He told it as if he didn't believe it himself and it was almost impossible for the bruise on his cheek to have been caused by tripping on steps. He wanted to know who had hit him and why.

He lifted a gentle hand to the bruise and, suddenly sure that men had made love to Lance before, leaned forward and kissed his eyes closed and brushed his lips with his mouth. His breath caught and his soul trembled with the promise of bliss. He drew back and took a deep breath. Lance's lids lifted heavily, with the sleepy satiated contentment of a lover.

Robbie's fingers strayed over his cheek. "There. Was that chaste enough? I told you I might fall in love with you. It's obvious that I have. We don't have to say any more about it. I want you. I'm in love with you. Those are the basic facts as matters now stand. You've very honorably discouraged me. Everything is clear between us. Well, as clear as a good rich mixture of mud. I'll now resume pining." He leaned forward again and ran his tongue along Lance's lips, testing progress. Lance drew back.

"No," he said softly.

A ripple of laughter burst from Robbie. "No. You know, if you practice your wiles to keep me here, sooner or later you'll have to kiss me to keep me from getting too discouraged. I've kissed men I didn't want to, just to create a friendly atmosphere. It's something that raving beauties like us have to learn to do in the interests of peace and harmony. If you're not going to practice any wiles, you'll eliminate all the suspense. I'll get bored."

Laughter swelled in Lance's throat. "You're mad. I love you." He took Robbie's hand and put it on his knee. *"There's* some suspense for you. My voluptuous knee. What'll I let you have next?" He felt as sexually invulnerable as if he were impotent. He had known he would be safe from demons with Robbie. They looked at each other with sly merriment and, recognizing that the exchange had run its course, pulled themselves up from the rocky ground.

They rejoined Luisa. She made them fruit drinks and Lance laced them with rum. They drank and chatted tranquilly, both of them glad of Luisa's presence forestalling any additional advances or retreats for today.

Robbie came for him the next morning, full of news. He had learned that there was a clay pit not far away that turned out a commercial product. He had heard of a Señor Diaz who had actually run a pottery works just outside of town. He had arranged for them to see Señor Diaz the next day.

"You're fantastic," Lance exclaimed. He put his arm around his shoulder and hugged him as Robbie started the car. "All that's the sort of thing I've never known how to do. I'd've sat here messing around with the muck in the garden and trying to invent the plate but you get out and do things."

They drove up into desolate hills and found a shack and some derelict machinery and a few holes in the ground. A somnolent man under a straw hat assured them that they could buy all the clay they wanted. They drove east and west on roads that quickly petered out into dirt tracks, although road-building equipment was abandoned here and there as if improvements might be getting under way. They passed a building site near the sea that Robbie had heard was to be a luxury hotel. Flip deplored it. It didn't look as if it would be ready for the dreaded tourists in the immediate future. They encountered a few men who appeared to be asleep on donkeys.

They found a deserted, palm-fringed beach and quickly stripped and leaped naked together into the sea without permitting each other to see much more of their bodies than they'd seen already. For Robbie, it was an opportunity to demonstrate to Lance that he needn't fear him. His quick connoisseur's eye noted that he was well hung but he had expected nothing less. He was resigned to perfection when he thought of actually winning Lance.

Lance couldn't remember having been so simple-mindedly contented. He'd been a bit nervous about being naked with a guy who said he was in love with him, but Robbie seemed to have accepted his terms of friendship. After playing around in the sea for half an hour, he felt peacefully relaxed. He wouldn't object if Robbie took advantage of his nakedness to fondle him a bit as he had yesterday. Inject a shot of suspense. It would be quite safe. His cock's detachment made him feel as if he didn't have one. Not a quiver disturbed its sexless repose. He climbed out of the water and lingered at the edge, waiting for him.

Robbie came splashing out, raising a curtain of spray around him. He had almost reached him when Lance caught an unnerving glimpse of his cock and turned quickly from him. A hero's body, every part of it on a heroic scale. His heart began to pound, his stomach churned, chaos scattered his thoughts. As vividly as if it were actually happening, he felt himself being crushed in Robbie's arms. Robbie's great cock lifted to assert its will, overturning resistance, commanding his surrender. He dragged his feet a few yards through shallow water, putting space between them, head down, pretending to scan the beach. His breathing was labored. He mustn't allow Robbie to touch him. He would be powerless against his potent sexuality, reduced to a cowed and sex-crazed animal. He shuddered as the tumult within him subsided. He would remain his loving eunuch.

Robbie's eyes doted on his love, wondering what he was searching for so intently in the sand. Their experiment in nakedness was a success. It had created no strain between them. He was capable of control; he hadn't been tempted to make any move that might embarrass his reluctant prey. After a few more days like today, Lance would have forgotten whatever it was that had made him raise his guard, and the time would be ripe for drastic action. He had never before felt that his life depended on getting a man, and he found it stimulating.

After quickly dressing, they drove to a refreshment

104

shack on another beach and sat under palm trees and ate dozens of delectable little clams that squirmed when they squeezed lemon on them, and drank icy beer. Remembering that Sunday was only a couple of days away, Lance explained about Luisa's weekly visits to her family.

"I'll be on my own if you want to come see me," he said.

"The rules. The rules. They're very stringent. I know this Sunday's no good because people are coming down from the capital. Flip talks about inviting you but I've discouraged it. I hope you don't mind, darling. I know what she's up to and it's a bore. She thinks if you bring Luisa a few times you'll see how unworthy she is of you and then you'll be free for me. It almost makes me want to pretend that I'm not remotely interested in you. I've told her to manage somebody else's life."

"I wondered why the invitations weren't coming thick and fast. Do you think Luisa's unworthy of me?"

"Of course not. I think you're damn lucky to've found her, up to the point where she gets in my way. She's adorable without a top. If it weren't for you, I'd probably be looking for a local boy to fill in the empty hours. I doubt if I'd find one as sweet as Luisa."

"I love you, darling. I really do. Thank you. Don't let Flip's ideas prevent us from seeing each other." He hesitated, his skin beginning to crawl with the memory of a few nights ago. "What about the local boys?" he asked as casually as he could.

"In what way?" Robbie's attention was immediately alert. He had caught a shift in tone.

"I don't know. Is there much of that sort of thing here? Homosexuality?"

"They're around, I imagine, mostly on a commercial basis. Flip has a selection. Always the perfect hostess. I haven't investigated."

"Maybe you'd better. A house of your own and a boy. I'd have you where I wanted you."

Robbie laughed. "We shall see." He suspected an ulterior motive in Lance's questions. There had been something stiff and forced about it that wasn't like Lance. Had he had some trouble with a local boy? Flip had a very knowing houseboy who might have an idea. He put it aside for future reference and led the conversation in another direction. "Talk to me some more about you, darling. Tell me about being disinherited. I'm fascinated by your squalid past."

"Oh yes, I want to tell you about that. I'm rather proud of it because it was the first time I ever stood up to my mother. And the last. She doesn't give you a second chance. She loves me, of course. I was always her favorite. That's what makes it sort of sad. Love doesn't come easy to her. She thinks it's unladylike. I think she was always particularly severe with me to prove that she hadn't given in to it."

He tried to get quickly to the point but Robbie plied him with questions, trying to fill in all the details. He wanted to know about Pam. His interest cast a new light on the past. Lance found himself speaking of her with unexpected gratitude as the first person who had allowed him to pretend to be something other than what he was expected to be. When he told her of his dreams of being an actor, a fantasy he had never shared with anyone, she assumed that he meant that that was what he was going to be. Being English and an aristocrat, she was less in awe of convention than he. She courted him, frankly and determinedly, and when she maneuvered him into kissing her for the first time, she made him a man.

Feeling like a man made him think that he'd fallen in love. Falling in love meant that he was going to get married. He didn't remember which of them had suggested it; it was an understanding that had hardly been put into words before Pam was acting as if it were all settled. He pledged her to secrecy until he was out of uniform, thus permitting him to postpone the dread moment when he'd have to tell his mother that he'd reached some fairly momentous decisions without consulting her.

As it turned out, even his mother couldn't find any fault with Pam as a prospective daughter-in-law. She brought the family close to another title. If fifteen of her nearest and dearest dropped dead and a good many others died without issue, Lance's son might be a lord. The splendor of his marriage made it easy for his mother to ignore his hints about the theater although Pam talked about it as a *fait accompli,* predicting a dazzling success for him as soon as it was known that he was available.

His mother had more important things to think about. An army of Vanderholden minions was drafted to prepare another family bastion in the city. A big apartment in a suitably nearby neighborhood had to be found. Servants were carefully screened and selected. Wedding presents were coordinated so that the newlyweds would be surrounded by luxury without too many duplications. Money was shifted about to provide Lance an annual income of one hundred thousand dollars, after taxes. None of it had anything to do with him.

"But what a lovely lot of lolly," Robbie commented.

Robbie's questions even led him to tell about the ghastly moment of failure on his wedding night, which Pam somehow managed to help him through without its becoming a major trauma. He had a lot to thank her for. Without Pam's jolly enthusiasm, his mother would never have accepted his giving up a honeymoon in favor of working at a summer theater.

Through a man he had known in the navy, he was put in touch with a manager who was sufficiently aware of the value of his name to take him on as an unsalaried bit player. He minimized its importance to his mother, pointing out that it was simply an opportunity to observe how a theater operated at close range. Pam insisted that it would be much more fun than traveling so soon after the end of the war.

"It seems an odd way to spend a honeymoon, my dear," Mrs. Vanderholden said dismissively. It was passed over so smoothly that it didn't occur to him that she might be taking precautions. Minimize it as much as he could, he was as proud of the job as if he had been offered a starring role on Broadway. It was proof that he could get along on his own. Not being paid was a detail. Everybody had to start somewhere.

Summer was well advanced when he began to receive incomprehensible letters from the family lawyers suggesting that there was some question about how his income was to be handled. There were some papers to sign. They had lived lavishly all summer on wedding checks and Lance paid little attention. When the theater season ended, they drove back to town in their Cadillac, a wedding present, and went directly to the new

107

apartment they'd never lived in. Servants were due but there was no sign of them. Lance left Pam in their handsome living room to pay his respects to his mother.

Telling Robbie about his last meeting with the formidable old lady played tricks with time. Every detail remained so vividly in his mind that it could have happened last week rather than almost three years ago. He felt the special city quality of the hot late-summer evening as he waited to be admitted to his mother's fortress. He felt again its airless oppressive silence as he entered it, doubly suffocating after having been away from it for almost three months.

"How are you, Morris? Is my mother at home?" he asked the footman who opened the door.

"Ah, Mr. Marcus. Yes, sir. She's in her study. I hope you've had a pleasant summer."

"Fine, thanks," Lance called over his shoulder. He crossed the funereal marble foyer, deciding not to bother with the elevator, and leaped up the stairs two at a time. He found his mother at her accustomed post in front of her littered desk, attended by her secretary.

"You may go, Miss Conner," she said when she saw him at the door, and the young woman rose without a word and nodded to Lance as she slipped by him. Mrs. Vanderholden pulled herself heavily to her feet and held out her arms to him.

"Marcus, my dear. How nice to see you," she cried in warm greeting. He went to her and kissed her, smelling the familiar lavender with which her skin had always been impregnated. It was incredibly soft skin and he could feel its wrinkles against his mouth. Her hands patted his shoulders lightly.

Although she was dressed severely in black and her only makeup was a bit of powder, she had rather the air of a ruined actress. Her style and manner suggested a gracious acceptance of adulation. Her movements were full and emphatic as if they had been rehearsed. In her youth, family lore had it, her looks had depended on coloring and expression rather than fineness of feature and her face was now only an astonishing compendium of age. Her eyes were small but so ringed about with flounces of withered skin that they had usurped a large area of her face. Her nose was stumpy and all that was left of her mouth were two puckered, slightly obscene ridges of pink flesh. Her abundant white hair was piled on top of her head in an elaborate and old-fashioned arrangement that could have been a wig. She was content to let the years have their way with her and was indifferent to the fact that her body had grown wide and ungainly. She often said that she couldn't bear the rich common women who haunted beauty parlors in an effort to turn themselves into ghastly caricatures of their own granddaughters.

"It's good to see you, Mother," he said, stiffening himself against the effect she had of canceling him out, canceling out his marriage, canceling out his job and all that he had done and learned, turning him into a little boy again. "Did you have a nice summer?"

"Quite pleasant." She turned from him and seated herself heavily on the sofa, patting the cushion beside her. "It was a little difficult getting used to not having you with me. However, one expects to be more and more alone as one grows older. You look splendid. You must've enjoyed yourself, although all the family was frightfully shocked."

"It was interesting," he said temperately. She laughed lightly and flipped his hand in hers playfully.

"Well, it does no harm to do something a little unconventional every now and then, and I told them so. Where's your adorable Pamela?"

"I dropped her off at the apartment. I came right over. I wanted to find out about the servants for one thing." Lance relaxed into the sofa, feeling a man once more as he talked about his wife and his own household.

"Yes, of course. I thought Pamela would prefer to be there when they start. I'm not going to be a meddling mother-in-law, you know. They're to come tomorrow."

"Fine. Do you have some cash in the house? I'm broke."

"I might have known it," she said with another indulgent flip of his hand.

"Well, it's only because of some confusion about my allowance," he said defensively, determined to keep his own identity in focus. "Do you understand what it's all about?"

Mrs. Vanderholden lifted her free hand heavenward and shook her head in mock dismay. "What a time I had with them, my dear. They came to me and said that the arrangements had to be altered. Taxes. Heaven knows what. They carried on in the most absurd fashion so I told them to do as they wished. It appears that your major expenses will be handled by the office. You'll have an account for your daily needs, of course. I believe several thousand dollars has already been deposited. Nothing has really changed. It's a question of method."

It took Lance a moment to grasp the fact that he wasn't to have any control over his money. He didn't like it; it put a severe limit on his actions. "That isn't the way it was done with my brother," he protested. "I'm going to look into this."

"Other times, other customs," Mrs. Vanderholden said comfortably. "You have no idea how difficult the tax collector is making it for us to keep any money at all. Roosevelt. The war. Life isn't going to be the same as it once was. I think you will find, as I have, that the less time you spend with lawyers, the pleasanter life will be."

Before Lance could reply she released his hand and clapped her own together decisively in front of her with a flash of precious stones. It was her way of issuing official proclamations. "One thing, Marcus, rather more important than money. I'm told that several items appeared about you during the summer concerning your theatrical ambitions. Those disgusting scandal sheets, I daresay. I've told you repeatedly that you must be very careful in your dealings with the press. I must warn you that I do not wish to hear of such things appearing about you again."

Lance straightened slowly and the oppression that had been growing in him since he entered the house came to a head. It was all so damn dull. That damn marble hall and the obsequious footman and Miss Connor slinking about. He wanted to shout with the dullness of it. The fun and excitement of the summer was still fresh in him. He had had a house of his own. He had invited the people he chose, which included just about everybody. People had liked him. He had been a success professionally, too. He had been given two quite important parts toward the end of the season and everybody had agreed that he had been very good, consid-

110

ering that his only experience had been in school and college theatricals.

If all the pleasant people he had worked with this summer could be actors, he'd be damned if he wouldn't be an actor, too. What was the point of having money if you couldn't do what you wanted? All this was vividly present in his mind as he rose deliberately and crossed the room to the fireplace. He was momentarily conscious of his movement, imagining how he would play this scene on the stage, so that there was something a little theatrical in the way he turned to face his mother.

"I'm sorry about the papers, Mother, but it can't be helped." His heart began to beat faster at his own audacity. He expected a scene but he didn't see how it could change anything. "You see—I might as well tell you—I've decided to go on with the theater. I've decided to be an actor."

"Must you talk such nonsense, Marcus?" Mrs. Vanderholden asked placidly. She was apparently confident of her control over him. She glanced at a small diamond watch on her wrist and when she spoke again it was as if Lance had never opened his mouth. "When are you to pick up Pamela?"

"We didn't set a time. That doesn't matter. Listen, Mother, I'm serious about this. Everybody thinks I have a lot of talent. I want to use it. I played a couple of good parts this summer and people said I was the best young actor to come along for years." He paused and dropped his eyes with embarrassment. One could boast about oneself with theater people but in front of his mother it seemed in very bad taste.

He looked up and saw her haggard eyes gazing past him, her mouth pursed, her expression of passive submission as if she were waiting for an unpleasant odor to pass.

"Don't you understand? I've got to try to make a success of it on my own. Being a Vanderholden won't help. Even if I have talent for it, I've got a lot to learn just like anybody else. It's something I've got to do."

"I don't wish to discuss it, Marcus," Mrs. Vanderholden said at last. They were words that had served her well on many occasions and she spoke them in a voice accustomed to command. "It's absolutely out of the question. You mention talent. I'm happy to say that you're too well born to be talented. I know your interests are intellectual and artistic, my dear, and I'm glad. I daresay your brother can take care of the business for the family. With your taste, you could become in time a real force in the cultural life of the city. You'll soon find that the theater could never be more than a secondary interest. When you've found your place in the city, I daresay we'll be able to straighten out any little financial difficulties. An actor? You're too absurd. If it makes it any easier for you to put it out of your mind, I forbid it. Is that quite clear?"

"I don't see how you can forbid it, Mother," he said reasonably. "It's what I want to do. You said yourself you don't want to run my life."

"I've said I don't wish to discuss it, Marcus. However—if you force me—" She made a slight gesture with her hands and sat forward. "You're quite right. I have no wish to run your life. But you forget that you are dependent on me in many ways. I think that gives me the right to advise you. If necessary, to *direct* you. Does that answer your question?"

Lance flushed angrily. "I'm shocked by you, Mother." He turned back to the fireplace and again his heart began to beat faster. "If you're trying to say that you won't give me any money if I go into the theater, then I don't want your money. I don't want to be dependent on you in that way. I'll just have to get along as best I can."

"Be careful, Marcus." There was an awful majesty in the warning; silence eddied about them after she had pronounced it. She allowed the silence to have its effect and then went on. "If you should pursue this insane scheme, you would not be welcome in my house. I would not feel justified in aiding you in any way. You would no longer exist for me. It is a dreadful thing for a mother to have to say, but you force me to it."

Lance turned slowly to face her. It was incredible. She was threatening to throw him out on the street. Such things didn't happen. He looked at her dumbly with his hands hanging helplessly at his sides. "You certainly don't mean—" His incredulity rendered him incoherent.

"I never meant anything more in my life." Mrs. Vanderholden looked at him implacably, doubtless seeing

112

in his limp look and his downcast eyes the signal of his surrender.

"Well, then, Mother, I suppose I might as well go," he said as if in a dream. Her glance sharpened and she clasped her hands convulsively in her lap.

"I warn you, Marcus." There was a new note in her voice, a note of urgency and perhaps of fear. "If your own good instincts fail you under the circumstances, I think you should consider your wife."

Lance wondered briefly if there were any room for compromise but experienced an unfamiliar sensation that was far more powerful than prudence. He was feeling for the first time in his life what it was like to be free. It felt wonderful. A fierce exhilaration seized him. He threw back his shoulders, lifted his head, and took a quick glance at the mirror. The odd, hooded look went out of his eyes. He looked proud and self-confident.

"Pam thinks it's a fine idea," he said, "so I guess you'd better tell the servants they're fired. We'll move out of the apartment right away. Of course, I can't be responsible for what the papers make of it. Shall I tell them I've been disinherited?"

"This is an odd time to be making jokes, Marcus. Have you no thought of what you're doing to me?"

The plea in a voice so keyed to command was shocking. He could feel the struggle taking place in her, the struggle between love and self-discipline. "I don't see that I'm doing anything to you, Mother," he muttered with embarrassment. "I'll come by in a couple of days when you've thought it over." He knew suddenly that he had to go and go quickly if he was to preserve his newfound freedom. Without looking at her again, he hunched his shoulders slightly and quickly left the room.

"Marcus!"

The cry rang out after him. Lance ran lightly down the stairs with it ringing in his ears. He hurried to the door and was out of the house before the footmen had time to assist him. He crossed the sidewalk to his car, half expecting to hear voices raised in pursuit, to be seized by servants and dragged back into the presence of their outraged, perhaps heartbroken, employer.

The great house gave onto Fifth Avenue but the front door, if the imposing array of grill and glass and attendant lions could be thought of in such modest terms, was in the side street. The sun was setting across the park, an inconsequential little blob of color against the vast unnatural majesty of the city. People strolled or hurried by but Lance didn't see them. This street, so like a hundred others to a casual observer, held for him scores of intimate and unique reminders and he was saying good-bye to it. Good-bye to the iron fence in front of No. 7 which rang with a particularly satisfying tone when struck by a stick and to the tall stoops of Nos. 10, 12, and 14, that for some reason he had once thought served as a protection against flood so that for a time his own house seemed very insecure. Good-bye to the poor little tree in its tiny fence which had always been there but which had never grown any bigger, and to the drug store on the corner where, in indulgent moods, his governess had sometimes bought him an ice cream soda.

This street was his hometown; it held him and he didn't want to be held. He wanted to be free. Vast areas of the city were as strange to him as a foreign land. He and Pam would explore them. They would start tonight. They would go to a hotel, not one of the nearby hotels patronized by people the Vanderholdens knew but one of the midtown theatrical hotels frequented by some of the kids from summer theater. That would be fitting to start this strange and exciting new life. It was going to be fun.

"It began to get rather dramatic when Pam discovered she was pregnant," Lance explained to his attentive listener. "It turned out that she didn't know how you could tell. She was four months along when she found out what was the matter with her. If I'd known when I should have—when I went to see my mother— I might've backed down, but I doubt it. For one thing, I thought everybody would be offering me plays the next day. Don't forget, I was used to seeing my name in the paper. I thought I was somebody, without ever having done anything. For another, I hadn't a clue about money. Literally. I didn't even know how to buy a postage stamp. I was pleased as punch when I sold the Caddy for five hundred dollars. I found out afterward it was worth thousands. It was always like that. If it had gone on a little longer I might've begun to discover

114

what real life was all about but along came the dream of a young actor's life and I was right back where I started: the rich and glamorous Lance Vanderholden. When I saw what success amounted to, I lost interest. With you, I feel as if I might finally be finding something."

He looked at Robbie. With his dark hair tumbled over his forehead, still damp from their swim, the exquisite arch of his brows accenting the enormous searching eyes, the long, straight nose, the sculptured hollows of his cheeks, and the lean, hard line of his jaw, Robbie was the most triumphant product of human evolution he had ever seen, male or female. No matter what happened to Lance, he always ended up with the elite. He wondered what he would have to do before he was fit to associate only with the dregs.

"Too well born to be talented," Robbie said with a dismissive laugh. "What a line. You of all people. You're bursting with talent. That stunning performance in a silly play. The things you've done with little blobs of clay. I'm going to make you a potter if it's the last thing I do."

Robbie ached with tenderness for him. He longed to lead him out of the maze in which the conflicting pressures of his life seemed to trap him still. Lance was attempting to assemble a personality out of ingredients totally divorced from anything he had been or known before he had chosen freedom. But Robbie didn't believe in self-created men. His own rebellion had erupted over the relatively straightforward problems of sex and once he had battled his way through that he had been able to revert gratefully to the values and virtues he had absorbed as a child. Once he had won him, he could offer Lance peace. They needed each other. He reached across the table and gave one of his fingers a tug. "This is the best day I've had since I've been alone."

"And the best I've had since the thing I haven't told you about. Flip goes on being right. Shall we go home and have a drink and watch the sunset before I have to give you back to her?"

Luisa was waiting for them with drinks that had been cooled in the well. Robbie sat with her and talked about her family, as far as Lance could follow the con-

115

versation. He loved Robbie for making his interest seem genuine and giving her all his attention.

Robbie's attention was fixed on Lance but his interest in Luisa was genuine enough. He was trying to fit her into a picture where she didn't belong. Sweet, passive, devoted, undemanding, and, of course, very pretty—she was all that but what had happened to make Lance think that it was enough? She would never be able to arouse and absorb the passion in him. She was obviously one aspect of his struggle to re-create himself. He wondered if Lance had brought on himself the personal disaster that had been the cause of the recent headlines in all the tabloids that Flip had referred to. Something about a car accident.

"Too terrible," she had said in her habitual rambling style. "He was arrested, you know. I remember something of the sort happened to one of the Roosevelt boys. Which one was it? You must remember. Dreadful. A hit-and-run killing and—"

Robbie had cut her off by pretending that he knew all about it. He didn't regard Flip as a reliable reporter and he wanted Lance to tell him of his own accord anything he wanted him to know. The suppressions would be interesting. So far, he had made no reference to the year that had passed since his show had closed. What had he been doing? Why was he here? "The thing I haven't told you about." Robbie felt sure that he would be told everything before very long. If Lance wanted to enlist him in his struggle, he wouldn't have any trouble recruiting him; Robbie had already taken charge of it.

"Luisa and I are going to give a party," he said, turning to Lance, happy to have won the girl's confidence.

"Really? Am I invited?"

Robbie repeated the question to her and she uttered her fluting laughter. "We're going to invite you and Flip and the new lot of houseguests that're coming in a week or two and a few of our more intimate friends. We think Flip should get to know the native life."

They laughed and Luisa joined in, looking questioningly from one to the other. Lance was proud of her for having taken such a big step in overcoming the taboos of local custom. Robbie, by kindness and speaking easily to her in Spanish, had obviously done more to break

116

down her resistance to foreign ways than he. "You're a sweetheart, darling," he said. "I'm touched by your thinking of it."

"I didn't. It wasn't exactly her suggestion but she asked if you didn't want to have other friends come here. She says that if I'll teach her, she'd like to learn how to behave with foreigners. I'm a demon cook. We're going to do a meal together and I'll dream up some sort of rum punch that'll get them all pissed and we'll be in business. She didn't realize it was so easy. She's in speechless awe of you, darling. I don't blame her."

"Tell her that anything you say goes, as far as I'm concerned."

"I might ask you to sign a paper to that effect, darling."

She heard them using the word constantly. *Dar-leeng*. She had a friend who knew a little English. She might know what it meant. It was apparently useful. It would be her first word of English.

Robbie picked up Lance the next morning to take him to their appointment with Señor Diaz. The moribund pottery works was a shed in a dusty field on the outskirts of town. It had slat walls to shoulder height and the rest of it was open. Señor Diaz, an old man in a faded blue cotton suit, was waiting to show them around. Lance didn't know how Robbie had arranged it, or why. The old man let them into the unpartitioned shed. There were ovens at one end, a few foot-operated wheels, a sort of trough with running water, some wooden racks against one wall suitable for stacking crockery. Robbie talked to Señor Diaz at some length and then they all shook hands and Lance and Robbie returned to the car.

"What do you think?" Robbie asked without starting the car.

"What about?"

"About this place. Do you think you could work here?"

"For God's sake. Is that what you were talking about? You mean working for Señor Diaz?"

"Don't be silly. Working for yourself. You'd need a couple of locals to keep the kilns going and help with some of the dirty work. Diaz has recommended a man who's had some experience keeping the fires at the right

117

level. That's the only tricky part. The rest would be up to you."

"Are you talking about my starting a business?" Lance asked incredulously.

"Isn't that the idea?"

Lance grabbed him and kissed the side of his face and burst out laughing. "Let's go to the beach and get out of these heavy clothes and *talk*."

Robbie laughed with him, touched and delighted by his excitement. "Maybe being naked together will give us all sorts of bright ideas about pottery but I doubt it."

They threw off shirts and shorts as they ran down the sloping sand and were naked when they plunged into the sea. They swam vigorously, racing each other to a draw. Panting, Lance swam in behind Robbie and put his hands on his shoulders as they headed in toward shore. "I've got a thousand questions to ask you," he said.

He couldn't resist letting his hands move with the flow of the water and the play of Robbie's muscles, getting the feel of the powerful body he was clinging to. Robbie felt the caress in his hands, although he supposed Lance thought they would seem only affectionate. Their touch gave him away. As he had already guessed, Lance had known physical intimacy with a man, if not men. Robbie wondered if he had suppressed it so successfully that he could caress him without its visibly affecting him. He knew what his thrilling cock looked like in repose. He would recognize the first sign of its being aroused. His own erection might do the trick.

When they could stand, Lance let go of him and marveled at the sculptured symmetry of his back and buttocks as he emerged from the sea. There was no denying that he had the sexiest ass he'd ever seen. He moved up beside him, resisting the temptation to touch it. Robbie reached for his hand and pulled him around to face him. Lance glanced down and choked on a gasp. Robbie's cock had become a mighty bludgeon, jutting out with an upward lift, terrifyingly compelling. Lance felt his own shrinking as he cringed from raw desire. The sickness suddenly raged in him. He heard animal grunts and obscene laughter. Men came at him, defiling him with the discharge of their loins. The exquisite veneer

118

of Robbie's cultivation was gone. He belonged to the dark forces that menaced him.

He lifted his eyes to Robbie's strong, gentle face and the seizure passed as suddenly as it had gripped him. Robbie looked relaxed and unselfconscious, a beautiful guy making no attempt to hide his hard cock. Lance's remained quiescent; he was safely impotent with Robbie. Lance smiled into his eyes. "My God, you're magnificent," he said.

Robbie met his eye while he stretched luxuriously with his arms over his head. There was no reason to let himself be inhibited by Lance's inhibitions. It wasn't the first time he'd been offered an erection. Robbie was sure of it. He let his arms drop to his sides with a grunt of satisfaction. "God, it feels good. Think of the fun we could have."

"I suppose I ought to be shocked. Bring all that up where we can talk." Lance slapped his shoulder, forcing the playful gesture, and ran off up the beach, gathering their scattered clothes as he went. He mustn't be lulled into thinking of simple pleasure. It couldn't be that with Robbie. Remembering that would keep him impotent.

Robbie followed, wondering. A straight man faced with a friend's erection didn't have a wide range of reactions to choose from. He might be indignant or disgusted or bawdily amused. Lance didn't even seem interested. A mystery.

As his erection dwindled, Robbie laughed at himself for not accepting the evidence that Lance simply didn't want him. He preferred the evidence of his caressing hands and of his eyes when they sometimes seemed to swim with love. If he hadn't reached the point of wanting Lance wholly or not at all, he would go to him now where he was spreading out towels and take him in his arms and make love to him in whatever limited way he would be allowed. Lance might not get a hard-on but wouldn't object to somebody trying to give him one. The thought restored his erection's vigor.

Lance didn't look at him as he approached and he dropped down onto a waiting towel so as not to go on making an insistent display of himself, sitting with his cock more or less out of sight between his thighs. Lance lay on his stomach beside him. Palm trees shaded them. Lance asked the question he felt had to be answered before the pottery works could be considered seriously. "How much does it cost to start a business?"

"I found out how much it would cost to start this one. Señor Diaz wants five hundred dollars down for letting you have the use of the place, lock, stock, and barrel, and five hundred dollars a year rent, paid in advance."

"You mean a thousand dollars down? You may find it hard to believe, but I don't think I can manage it. That's a big hunk of my total fortune."

"We won't worry about that. We're going to be partners. I'll be the money man. You'll provide the talent. Backing a Vanderholden surpasses my wildest dreams of material success."

"Wait a minute. I haven't learned much but I know I don't want things handed to me ever again. Isn't there some other way we can work it?"

"I know what you mean, darling, but you don't have to think like that with me. You're naked and I love you. That puts a different slant on business." He put a hand on Lance's shoulder and kneaded it, making a more possessive point of it than anything he had yet permitted himself. Lance turned his head and rubbed his cheek against his hand. Robbie was transfixed by a sweetness that paralyzed him with delight. He managed to pull his knees up so that his cock could lift freely without standing up under Lance's nose. It was odd having an erection with somebody who presumably didn't but he felt no embarrassment on either side. He wondered what was going on in Lance's mind. "I'll show you what a smart businessman I am," he continued, picking up the thread of his plan. "I know those little idols of yours will sell. There're people who specialize in that sort of art gimmick. I don't know much about prices but a shop would charge at least five dollars. They can't cost more than a few cents to produce. Let's say I find somebody who'd pay two dollars apiece for five hundred of them. Are you good at arithmetic? If so, you've doubtless deduced that we've already got back our original investment and are sitting pretty. Do you follow me?"

"I'm fascinated by you, as always."

"It might be a bore to turn out five hundred of them but you need a month or two to experiment with the ovens and find out about glazes and so forth. You could make your dollies while you're learning to do other things."

"I'm amazed at how practical you are. I'm sure I can do something but I need you to tell me what sort of things will sell. God knows that's important. You're going to be teaching me glazes and firing, aren't you?"

"I seem to've blurted it out in my impetuous way." He paused, giving himself a moment to think. What if he'd got everything wrong? Impossible. He couldn't imagine leaving here now except with Lance. "So be it. I told you I don't have anything very urgent coming up at the moment."

"You said it all depended on your work."

"You've so thoroughly swept me off my feet that I haven't had a chance to find out about that but I'm not worried. I'm getting the feel of the place. I'll be able to work once I get you off my mind and into my bed where you belong."

"But, darling—"

Robbie smiled and shook his head. "Don't interrupt your elders. Let me dream." He withdrew his hand and hugged his knees. Lance giggled and looked up at him. Robbie disengaged his eyes from the limpid blue gaze and let them wander slowly from the wide hunched shoulders down to the narrow, tautly masculine but-tocks. Every particle of him was precious to him, the golden hair swirling around his ears, the shoulder blades, the exquisite concavity at the base of the spine. He could feel their bodies fitting sublimely into each other. The dream caused a hollow agitation in the pit of his stomach. He was almost sick with desire. He looked again into unguarded blue eyes and his smile broadened. "Let's stick to business. We'll take it one step at a time and see how things stand when we're finished."

"What's the next step?"

"Señor Diaz will have to have papers drawn up for us. We'll go see him again tomorrow. No. Tomorrow's Saturday, isn't it? We'll have to wait till Monday. I think we have to pay some sort of tax to register as business partners. It sounds rather sweet, like getting married at last. We'll have to ask Flip to be a witness— our maid of honor. The paperwork will probably take a little time, a week or two. Then we order a load of

121

clay and hire a couple of peons and get on with it. All in all, it'll probably be more like three months before you see what you want to do. We can comb a few more beaches in your spare time."

"Three months. You've agreed to three months. Don't forget that."

"Three months. A mere drop of time compared to what I want to think about." He put a hand out and stroked Lance's hair, amazed by his restraint. He would give Lance a few days to get used to being fondled and then perhaps a demonstration would be more effective than words. He caressed the faint traces of the bruise with his fingertips. Lance's chest heaved with a deep contented sigh and he moved his head to acknowledge the caress. Robbie was once more transfixed by an ineffable sweetness.

"I don't want to think about time at all," Lance said. "This is the beginning of a whole new life. It's what I've been praying for since God knows when. I can do anything with you here."

"I'm planning a new life myself. If you've got only about a thousand dollars, it's time we turn you to some profit. I'm going to take twenty-five percent, you know. I expect you to provide for my old age. Is it a deal?"

They looked at each other and laughter swelled in Lance's throat. "It's fantastic but it seems more real to me than anything I've ever done. Tell me how you managed to be so perfect. You seem so completely yourself, the way I've always wanted to be, as if you'd sprung full-grown from somebody's brow. I always forget that you must've had parents."

"Yes, the usual—one father, one mother. I'm an only child. My father's married to a young English girl. She was a friend of mine before he even knew she existed. He's started a new family. We've arranged for me to be disinherited so my little half brother will be Lord Barstlow. We seem to go in for lords, you and I. Heaven knows I don't want to be one. My father doesn't care any more about the title than I do but it seems only fair to Grandpa. He went to all the trouble to get himself made a peer. Oddly enough, my parents were never married. I have some sort of legal status as Dad's son but I'm a bastard. My mother's married a Frenchman and they all live next door to each other in lovely old farmhouses in the south of France, as thick as thieves. It's such a relief to have one's parents out of the nest, all settled and taken care of. It wasn't always like that. Dear me, the dramas, what with my being queer and everything. Ah well, it all came out right in the end."

"A simple little family history," Lance said. "How I envy you. It sounds so alive. A bastard. I knew you'd made yourself up. What would've become of me if you hadn't?"

"The question is, what's going to become of you now that I have you in my clutches? A life of sweat and toil, poor baby."

"If that's the way it's going to be, we'd better get all the sun we can. You might not love me with a working man's pallor." He rose, his towel trailing at his side.

Robbie looked up at the golden figure, his eyes lingering on the discouragingly inert cock. More and more mysterious. At moments, the current flowing between them was so sexually powerful that it brought him to the verge of orgasm. It was humanly impossible for Lance not to feel it. He gave his head a little shake. "We really are quite sinfully beautiful. I can't help knowing what I look like. I'm not quite a match for your mindless beauty but I'm no mud fence. As I said, two people who look like us don't end up together. It defies the law of averages. Well, that's one more law we have to defy."

"We're together. I want us to stay that way. Come on. Let's go lie with our feet in the water."

"You keep exposing me to the most shattering temptations. Our feet in the water, like two old cooks by the seaside. Do you have any idea what you look like standing there the way God, in a moment of inspiration, made you? It's not queer of me to be in love with you. It would be very queer of me not to be." He dug his feet into the sand and rose in one easy movement. His erection swung up and almost touched Lance. Robbie saw his eyes widen as they fixed on it.

"My God, darling. I wish mine were like that. I don't just mean that big. That hard."

"If you let me, I might be able to make your wish come true."

"No." Lance looked startled by his own vehemence. His tone softened. "I'm sorry. I've told you. As much as

123

I'd like to be queer with you, it just wouldn't work. I should think you have only to look at my cock to see that."

"I've been careful not to take any liberties so I'm not *too* discouraged by your cock." He laughed at his persistence. "I admit that you don't look as if you're absolutely wild with desire for me but maybe with practice it'll become an acquired taste."

"I don't see how I'll acquire it if it can't even happen the first time."

"Can you honestly and truthfully tell me that you've never had sex with a man?"

"I didn't say that," Lance admitted, unable to lie to his friend. "I said that nothing's ever happened to me to make me think I can make love with you."

"Ah ha. That *is* a difference," Robbie exclaimed. "This is getting interesting. I won't pry but you gave me the impression that you were a virgin as far as the love-that-dares-not-say-its-name is concerned. What's wrong with me except for the law of averages?"

"Maybe it's that. You know you dazzle me. You're giving me so much. I couldn't bear for anything to be less than perfect between us. Let's just say that things have happened to me that make me sure that sex for us would be far from perfect."

"Am I going to have to rape you to prove that you're wrong?"

Lance's expression underwent a dramatic transformation. He looked haunted, hunted, as if he were looking for somewhere to hide.

Robbie's erection lost its thrust and lowered till it slanted downward. He wished it would go away so that he could put his arms around him without its intruding. He took a step closer. "What's the matter, darling?" His voice seemed to pull Lance together. He lifted his head and managed a rather distracted smile.

"It's nothing. I was talking about things I'd rather forget. For you to mention rape with that enormous thing of yours waving around can frighten a guy."

"I think I meant that I wish you'd rape me." He knew as much of Lance's secret as he needed to know. He'd been on the right track. Perhaps a careless flirtation had been misunderstood, blows exchanged. Dabbling in homosexuality was apt to lead to trouble. Lance may've

felt he had learned his lesson but, Robbie thought hope-
fully, lessons often didn't stay learned for more than a
few days. He was glad he hadn't tried to keep his erection a secret. Lance knew by now that it could be that
way without his forcing himself on him. Soon he would
find himself touching it simply because it was there. It
was obvious that they were going to make love but
Robbie wanted to be sure that the first time wouldn't
be the last. He wanted Lance to ask for it.

One day melted into another while they waited to
get on with their business. They spent hours naked and
alone together in the sun and sea. They told Luisa about
their plans and she was very happy about them. With
Robbie, Lance almost forgot Scot, only feeling her loss
as an ache deep within him, something missing. At
moments, he was seized by a sort of rapture unlike
anything he had ever known. At such moments, he
wondered if he were falling in love with a man, really
in love the way a man fell in love with a woman. He
was getting closer to believing that it could happen. If
it could, making love would follow naturally and without torment.

Even though Lance didn't like to look at it, Robbie's
cock in varying degrees of erection was a constant re-
assurance that he still wanted him. Sometimes when
they were lying side by side, lightly touching here and
there, his companion would spring up, his cock a powerful spear raised for attack, and run down to the sea
to swim it off. Lance wished desperately that he could
offer him relief, imagining their playing together the
way he had with Andy, but when he looked into Robbie's unfathomable purple eyes and saw the depths of
desire and tenderness in them, he knew that there could
be nothing halfhearted in the meeting of their bodies.
Only a passion equal to his own was good enough for
Robbie.

They got back to the house one evening to find Luisa
wearing her dress. Lance had forgotten that it was Sunday already, the first evening he and Robbie could've
been alone together. He turned to him impatiently.
"When are you going to get out from under Flip Rawls?
Think what a lovely evening we could've had. Damn
this house. I wish you could live here."

"Not here. Not *à trois*. We'd get on each other's nerves."

"The only time you get on my nerves is when you leave me. You're a crashing bore when you're not here." He tried to laugh his impatience away. He had only himself to blame for Robbie's being such a conscientious guest. Their eyes met. He saw the question in Robbie's and couldn't answer it.

"I hope you're all ready for tomorrow," Robbie said. "The die will be cast."

"With Señor Diaz? I can't wait."

"Good." He put his arm around him and walked him to the parapet and sat with him, his arm still around his shoulders, in closer physical communication than they'd ever been. "I'm sorry about this evening but we have time. We'll get everything squared away this coming week and then we'll be set for life."

"For life?"

"Nothing less. We're not going into reverse."

Lance felt rapture enclose him but there was a new completeness in it tonight, a rapture of his body as well as his spirit. There was something so all-inclusive and flexible in male comradeship. Why resist expressing it physically? Maybe Robbie was finally proving to him that he was a homosexual. Hesitantly, testing himself, he let his hand brush lightly along the hard ridge of flesh confined between Robbie's thighs. He wasn't afraid of being impotent tonight. A sound behind them reminded him of Luisa and he brought his hand to rest innocently on his knee. Robbie's arm tightened around him and the sides of their faces touched. They both were breathing rapidly.

"I'd like it to be for life beginning right now," Lance murmured.

Robbie took a deep breath. "Okay. It's your turn to pine. I hope you have a miserable evening."

"The trouble is, I will, you shit." His erection wasn't subsiding. He wanted Robbie. He wanted him more than he'd ever wanted anybody.

It was dark when Lance finished supper and Luisa was ready to go. He kissed her good night and roamed the terrace restlessly after she was gone. He was still shaken by his long-delayed erection. His cock had stood up for a guy who hadn't laid a finger on it. He wished

126

Robbie had seen it. All his resistance had vanished. He wanted them to be together all the time, in bed or out. He wanted him here when he closed his eyes at night and still here when he opened them in the morning. All his thoughts of him had become powerfully erotic.

He dropped into a deck chair and let his mind go to him. He thought of the slight, seductive fullness of his upper lip. He felt it pressed to his as their mouths opened to each other, his extraordinary hands on him, brutally powerful but gentle with love, caressing him, wanting him, tuning his body to ecstasy. He wanted their mouths on each other everywhere. He wanted to feel their bodies moving against each other. He avoided thinking of specific acts they might perform, assuming that two people who were in love couldn't do anything offensive with each other. They were going to be lovers.

He gave his sarong a tug and let it fall away to his sides and looked down at his erection. It looked unimpressive after his exposure to Robbie's.

He rose, waiting for his cock to calm down. He retrieved his sarong and hung it on himself and laughed as it descended slowly like the lowering of a flag. He gathered it up and wrapped it around himself properly and wondered if he dared go to Flip's with some pretext for asking Robbie to come home with him. If falling in love with a guy was the same as falling in love with a woman, he wouldn't hesitate. He had a lot to learn. He knew now that men paired off as if they were married. He still found it difficult to imagine.

He wandered about collecting things—the bottle of rum, glasses, some suntan oil from the parapet—arranging them neatly on the table, concentrating his thoughts on Robbie, willing him to come back. His hand straying along Robbie's cock must have told him that he was ready for him at last. He surely wouldn't let his opportunity pass tonight.

As if in answer to his mind's summons, he heard a sound from the end of the house. His heart leaped up joyfully and he held himself motionless, listening. Light footsteps were approaching on the path that led down from the road. He sprang forward to welcome his hoped-for visitor, stifling a fleeting doubt about whether he was ready for whatever was coming. They would kiss at last and doubts would end.

He saw movement in the shadows and a figure emerged into the light. His blood froze. Shock rooted him to the ground. He shook his head slowly. "No. Please. Not here," he murmured almost to himself.

His assailant from the beach continued to advance toward him. He moved with stealth, alert and light on his feet. Lance felt the menace in him. "My name is José. Why not here? Your woman is out. You are alone," he said in a mixture of Spanish and broken English.

"I wait for somebody," Lance protested. His heart was pounding so violently that he was hardly able to get the words out. He took a step back away from the young man and got a close look at him for the first time. He had a jutting nose and deep hollows under prominent cheekbones, a handsome savage's face. There was a feral glitter in his eyes. His black hair was combed down low on his forehead like a cap. He was dressed as before in the local uniform of loose cotton shirt and pants. Lance had the advantage in weight and height. He had bested him on the beach. There was no need to be afraid of him. "You must go," he ordered.

"You don't want to know why I am here?"

"No. I can have you in jail."

The corners of José's cruel mouth twitched in a hint of a smile. "For giving you pleasure? The others punished you for insulting my people. You *wanted* me." He whisked his shirt off over his head and dropped it as Lance tensed to fend off an attack.

A warning flashed through his mind: others might be waiting in the dark. The hell with it. He'd beat the shit out of this one if he didn't clear out. His enemy looked at him with the hard glitter in his eyes. His hand moved suggestively along the top of his pants, then let them fall.

"I am a strong man. That is what you like. We do the things you wanted last time."

"You son of a bitch." Lance took a step forward and swung his fist. Everything happened very quickly. His fist was deflected. He was struck hard across the face. His sarong was torn off. Their naked bodies were locked together. He had placated this man before. He must placate him again.

The grip on him loosened. He slid down and made love to his torso with his open mouth. He knew they

128

risked being discovered but he couldn't help himself.
The fever raged in him. He was driven to perform the
ritual act of surrender that was expected of him. He
wooed the hard unyielding body, dry skin forming a
leathery cover to flat muscles and bone. He smelled of
dust and the sea. He crouched in front of him and framed
his erection, his hands flattened against his groin. It
looked stunningly purposeful, a dark compact weapon
made for quick conquest. His own looked overdeveloped
and cumbersome by comparison. He opened his mouth
and rolled his tongue around it hungrily. He had become its servant. He felt it hardening further, its reach
extending. He whimpered for the reward that was coming. A rush of thick musky fluid flooded his mouth. He
swallowed it and continued to draw on slackening flesh
with lips and tongue to receive it all.

They sank to their knees together and Lance pros-
trated himself before the man he was serving, unable
to free himself from his craving for total surrender. It
required that he restore the cock in his mouth to po-
tency. He felt it slowly filling out again as his hands
and mouth applied pressures to arouse it. He was proud
of performing the service so well. When it stood upright,
he released it from his mouth and drew back, his eyes
on it. It was ready for him, hard and lean and rapacious.
He felt José's approval. He was a good servant. Having
an erection so soon after orgasm made him proud of his
virility.

He straightened and moved a few feet on his knees
and stretched out to the table for the suntan oil. He
turned back and looked into José's eyes as he applied
it to himself. He put the bottle on the floor and slid
across to him. José waited for him, his eyes watchful
and unblinking. Lance leaned in against him and kissed
his throat and shoulders and chest, brushing his body
against him, trying to make himself desirable. He trailed
his hands down over his hard body and held his cock.

"You speak the truth. I want you." His voice caught
on the words. He shifted around, still holding him, and
guided it into him. José dropped his hands lightly on
his hips and entered him slowly, in full command.

Lance gasped and cried out and twisted his hips to
hasten the possession of him. He wanted a man inside
him. He wanted to be taken. The rape had taught him

how profound his need was. There was nothing left in him to be violated. He shuddered as José drove deeper into him, establishing his mastery of him, and shouted with the release of his massive orgasm.

He seemed to emerge from a daze of submission as he became aware of spasms shaking the body that was joined to his. They subsided. The flesh within him diminished. José shifted his weight.

"Shower is there," Lance said, shame making it difficult to find his voice. José withdrew from him and stood. Lance lifted himself on an elbow and pointed without looking at him, then dropped back and lay without moving. He felt profoundly transformed. His romantic dreams of Robbie seemed remote and irrelevant. He knew finally, beyond any further temptation, that he mustn't make love with Robbie. Robbie was a good, decent, normal guy, capable of love and complete loving relationships with men. The force in himself that drove him to commit homosexual acts was an aberration, servile and abject. He couldn't bear for Robbie to discover it in him.

He rolled over and sat up. Robbie might still come. It had been unreasonable to hope for him so soon. It was early by Flip Rawls's standards. There was time to get rid of this man. He pulled himself to his feet as José returned, his dark lean body leaving a trail of water behind him. He moved with tightly controlled pride, taking possession of the place as authoritatively as he had taken possession of its tenant. Lance found his presence jarringly natural. They were somehow linked by destiny.

"I'll get a towel," Lance said, still serving him.

"No. I am cool this way." He leaned a hip against the edge of the table and folded his hands protectively over his genitals.

"You must go." Lance heard the order turn into a request.

"You pay me?"

"No," Lance said bluntly although he felt a flutter of fear in his chest. He had half expected something of the sort, an attempt at extortion or blackmail. "I not ask you here. Why not you pay me?"

"You want money?" The twitch of his mouth was more a sneer than a smile. His lips looked as if they'd been chiseled out of wood, the curves sharply delineated.

"Not from you."

"We will make money together. I know big men. Rich. Important *politicos* in the capital. I find them boys. They will pay plenty for you. I give you half."

Lance thought he was having a language problem. He started to laugh but laughter died. The proposal was serious. He stared at him incredulously. "Why you think I am willing to do this?" he asked.

"You will do what I say. You know what will happen to you if you do not."

"You can do nothing to me."

"I can make you want very much to leave. I think you like to stay. We will make much money." He lifted himself from the table and put his hands on Lance's shoulders. Lance instinctively flinched from them. He moved them over his body without erotic undertones, as if he were assessing merchandise. "When I saw you on the beach, I knew. You were angry but you wanted me. Men like boys like you. Your body feels good like a woman's." He turned Lance and his hands continued their assessment.

Lance's skin prickled with excitement at this cool impersonal handling of his body. He was getting hard again. José wanted him to whore for him. He remembered his incredulity when he'd first heard that male whores existed. It was hard for him to imagine anybody sinking so low but what could he know about it when he'd never had to face rock-bottom necessity? He'd been practically whoring with Robbie, inciting him with his body while he accepted his money and his love. If he brought a clear firm halt to their flirtation, it would be none of Robbie's business what he did with his body. At least it was more his own than anything else about him. Any shock he felt at José's suggestion was absorbed into his dark craving for the unknown. He was still learning the depths to which he could descend.

José's hands circled his buttocks. "You are like a man here. Some boys have soft, plump behinds like women. Still your back is pretty. It will give men pleasure to see strong gringo boy serve them." José turned him again to face him. Lance's erection lifted. José ran a

131

hand along it. "It is big and quickly ready for love. That is good. It will please my patron and his friends."

"It please you, I think."

José slapped his face hard and spat. "I am a man," he asserted, his voice rough with warning. Lance wiped spittle from his cheek as he was thrust around against the edge of the table so that his erection lay on it. He let himself be doubled over on it, exhilarated by the violence he had provoked. His wrists were seized, his arms outspread and pinned to it. José drew his hips back and drove into him. Lance's body leaped with the sharp momentary pain. José understood him. He didn't want homosexual love. He wanted his body to be used savagely.

"You make me strong," he said, as he thrust his cock deeper. "You are a woman. Others will pay for you. That is what I came to tell you."

Lance's mind was filled with images of hairy obese middle-aged men taking him for money. His erection hardened on the table. "You not come here again."

"I know how to get you. My patron is not here now. When he comes, I will tell him I have you."

"Yes. You have me," Lance said, closing his mind to the insidious peace he might find in Robbie's arms.

Robbie was immediately aware of another change in him when he came for him the next morning. He had withdrawn again, this time more troublingly. He was unresponsive, coolly cut off, polite but indifferent. He seemed to have become his own man overnight.

They saw Señor Diaz again, going over the final details, and told him to have the papers drawn up. When they had concluded the business, they returned to the car. Robbie didn't start it immediately. "Well, it's all settled. Are you sure it's what you want?" he asked.

"My God, darling. Why ask? It's what we both want."

"I hope so." In spite of his determination to let Lance make the advances, he put a hand on his thigh, as Lance had done to him the night before. Lance pulled his knees together.

"Don't," he said. This was his chance to demonstrate to Robbie that the sexual games were over. Being so nearly in love with him made it painful.

Robbie unhurriedly removed his hand. "It's doubtless a figment of my fevered imagination but I had the

132

impression that you did something of the sort with me last night."

"I know. I've been meaning to say I'm sorry. I shouldn't have."

"Don't be sorry. It was one of the most exciting things that ever happened to me."

"You misunderstood. I was teasing you."

"You mean it wasn't an uncontrollable impulse? You were just making fun of an infatuated fag?"

"Yes. No, that's not true, not the way you put it. If you must know, I had a hard-on. I was amazed. If it hadn't been for Luisa, I might've let it go on from there. When I had time to think about it, I realized that it couldn't be what you want. I came as close as I'll ever come to thinking that it might be."

"I wonder if you know what I want. I want so very little more than what we already have." He slipped his arm around his shoulders without getting closer or exerting pressure. "I'd love to sleep with you. I mean, be in the same bed with you and go to sleep with our arms around each other. That would be heaven."

"If you'd come back, I'd've gone to bed with you and that would've been the end of us."

"Or the beginning. What happened with us last night will happen again. We belong to each other. Our bodies are part of us. It's as simple as that."

Lance looked into the calm intensity of the love in his eyes and ached to give himself to the sweet comradeship they offered. One of the men he admired most in the world loved him. Then he thought of José and the sort of madness that overcame him when a man was taking him brutally. Rapists. Rich *politicos* who paid for their corrupt pleasure. It was the logical answer to being trained to be useless. A good body always had a market value. He shifted away from the arm that wouldn't be holding him if Robbie knew what he'd done last night. "Please don't," he said gently.

"Okay." Robbie withdrew his arm. The tone of Lance's voice doomed his dreams. He felt a melancholy happiness in sensing in his beloved such unfamiliar mature control—no shadows, no secrets, no ambiguities. "Let's talk about me. I decided last night to do what you've suggested. I'm going to take a house. I admit that getting groped made me feel that we were on the verge of major developments but I don't like making decisions with strings attached. If it made sense to take a house last night, it makes sense today. I want to be with you, regardless of sex. I want a place where we can do things on the spur of the moment without thinking about Luisa." Watching Lance's face fill with radiance was as gratifying as a kiss. He could understand that an unexpected erection might be troubling to a man who thought of himself as straight.

"That's marvelous. God, I couldn't be happier," Lance exclaimed. The unequivocal delight in his voice made Robbie's spine tingle. "Shall we look for one together?"

"No. I'll be looking mostly for working space, not a place where we'd like to live together. I don't want you to throw me off."

They were both impatient to get their project under way but Robbie warned against visibly committing themselves further. If Señor Diaz saw them moving in, he might stall to get better terms. They spent the better part of the week cleaning up the shed but postponed making the few repairs that were needed. Through their prospective landlord, they talked to the man who knew about firing the kilns and learned that he was ready to work. He had a cousin who would help him. They were both called Juan.

When they had time for the beach, Robbie noticed that Lance kept a towel handy to cover himself casually when he wasn't lying on his stomach. Robbie tactfully followed suit. If this new phase had been brought on by Lance's having an erection with him, he didn't expect it to last. He was too deeply in love not to be spellbound by his many faces and knew that he would find the true one when they finally made love. The longer they waited, the more completely Lance would be his.

Lance grew uneasy at the approach of another Sunday. He'd have to ask Robbie to spend the evening with him because he'd think it odd if he didn't but he wouldn't be sorry if he couldn't get away from Flip. He didn't want his successful evasion of Robbie's embraces to be undone by a few drinks and the seductive night. He didn't trust his controls.

When Sunday came, Robbie was reassuringly non-committal about the evening. "I shouldn't even let myself think about getting away," he said. "I'll be leaving her so soon that I mustn't neglect my duties as a guest. I want to finish in beauty, as the French say. After all, I owe her you."

When Robbie had left him, followed soon by Luisa, Lance pulled the cot out into the middle of the terrace where there was more air and placed a table and lamp at one end and stacked up cushions for his head. He stretched out with a glass of watered rum beside him and a book, which he didn't open, on his chest. His mind was on Robbie. It had been like this with Scot, sexual desire sternly relegated to the background once he had resigned himself to her prohibitions, but a deep need to be near her, to look at her and hear her voice. Robbie had replaced her. He was condemning himself once more to being in love without the fulfillment of physical union.

He rose to pour himself another drink and returned to the cot. He opened his book but still couldn't concentrate on it. How long had he been lying here? Time was simply something to struggle through when they weren't together. When they were both working, it would probably be easier to do without him.

The silence was so intense that the sound of a rock rolling down the path at the end of the house fell into it with startling clarity. He lay still, listening. Anger flared in him as he thought of José. He sprang up and gave a quick twist to his sarong to secure it and ran silently along the terrace to the corner of the house where the path ended. His fists were ready. He wasn't going to let him start acting as if he owned him.

A figure moved out of the darkness, almost on him. It was Robbie. Lance flung himself forward and threw his arms around him and kissed him on the lips. "My God. It's you," he cried.

Robbie smiled and gripped his arms, holding him close. "Hey. If this is the sort of welcome I get when I'm not expected, I'll never make a date with you again."

Lance was trembling slightly with the shattering thrill of their mouths meeting. He pulled himself away hastily, stunned by the effort it required. "It's about time I kissed you," he said, trying to make light of it.

"With practice, you might get better at it." Robbie laughed gleefully. He had felt the surrender at last in Lance's body. Joy exulted in him, a giddy eruption of triumph. He was going to have him tonight. He wouldn't miss his chance again.

Lance turned back to him and saw that he was wearing a sarong with an open shirt hanging loose over it. "You've joined the South Sea Islanders," he said, still slightly breathless. "Come have some warm rum. We'll get pissed. How'd you get away?"

"Who can be a perfect guest forever? I had a diplomatic seizure at the end of dinner. Flip was sweet when I told her where I was going. She insisted on my wearing a sarong so I could get out of it easily."

Lance eased his nerves with laughter. "Take your shirt off and make yourself at home." He poured drinks, evading Robbie's hand as he gave him his glass, and hurried back to the cot. He felt suddenly shy and in need of distance between them. He remained stunned by the effect the brief kiss had had on him. If he could want Robbie as straightforwardly and uncomplicatedly as he had always wanted women, there was nothing more to worry about. He wasn't afraid of homosexuality. He was afraid only of whatever it was in him that turned it into a madness.

He stretched out, propped up on an elbow, while Robbie pulled up a chair. "I've been lying here sending you messages. Here you are. I have amazing extrasensory powers. If you ever go, I'll burn the books and embezzle your twenty-five percent."

"Not if I handle distribution. I'll collect at the source."

"Wouldn't you know. Do you really think I can make enough for you to bother? What if I'm no good at plates and cups? Oh, I might stoop to the odd bowl, but I'd like to make crazy things. Beautiful toys. I want to be the Cellini of mud."

Robbie looked at him with happy adoration. "You're changing again, darling. It's all coming out now. You're going to be you. I can't wait to see what you do. The world is full of dishes. Let's have beautiful toys. More and more galleries are beginnning to show pottery. You could show with me. Wouldn't that be exciting?"

They let themselves get sidetracked by details of shipping and marketing. Robbie told him about the outlet he was counting on in New York. He had already written about the devil-dolls. He'd heard that an airstrip had been built recently a few miles up the coast and that plans were going ahead to start an airmail service that would also handle light freight.

They discussed the advantages it would have for them at greater length than their interest justified. They were both glad to postpone the moment they felt was inevitably approaching. To Robbie, its promise was too momentous to be rushed. Lance still saw it as being fraught with danger. They were both grateful for the momentary respite.

They finished their drinks and Lance rose for refills. He paused, just out of reach of Robbie, and their eyes met, telling each other more than either of them felt capable of putting into words. Faced with the depths of love in Robbie's, Lance's courage faltered and his cock became painfully inert. He wished they could lie in each other's arms without any thought of sex. He fixed the drinks and touched Robbie's bare shoulder as he gave him his.

"Enough potter talk," Robbie said. "I have a surprise for you. I'm buying this house."

Lance sat up. "You're joking. What for?"

"Why not? I asked about it when I was house hunting. It seems sensible for you not to have to pay rent. I had a message about it tonight. I told you I'd have you in my clutches."

"You've actually *bought* it?"

"In the process. For a song. The papers will be ready sometime this week."

"But my God, darling, how marvelous. You can stop looking for something for yourself. We can enlarge this one so you can work in comfort. I could do a lot of the work myself. I want us to live together."

"There's a bit of a problem, isn't there? What about Luisa? I suppose we could build a separate house. Where would you sleep?"

"Well, with Luisa I guess. What about that boy you mentioned?" Lance's heart began to pound with inexplicable erratic violence.

"There isn't going to be a boy. We both know that." Robbie's voice was cool and playful but decisive. "There's going to be you and me. And Luisa, of course. I know you want a child. We won't do anything to upset Luisa. That's why we'll have to decide who's going to sleep where."

"But, darling, even if we were lovers, what difference would it make so long as we're together?"

"You'll see. Flip had another message for me when I got back this evening. That house I wanted is available. I can move in a couple of days."

Lance wanted to jump up and throw his arms around his amazing friend. "It's all really happening, darling. We've found each other in this ridiculous place. I'm going to do everything in my power to make you glad you stayed."

"Your power over that is considerable. I'll take the house by the month and await developments."

"It's wonderful." His cock felt invincibly rigid. If Robbie found it that way, there should be nothing traumatic about their lovemaking. "Where is it, this house?" he asked.

"Down at the other end, past Flip's. The last house on the Hill where the road turns down into town, an easy walk to our potting shed and close enough to here too. I'll get you coming and going."

Lance shifted so that his erection filled a fold in his sarong where he hoped it would be visible. He thought of giving his sarong a tug to show it, and it immediately subsided. He resumed his chatter. "You're right about deciding where we sleep. Why not use your house for work and sleep here? We shouldn't be parted at night."

Robbie's smile was triumphant. "If you say things like that, I might get the idea that you want to go to bed with me."

Lance's heart stopped. When it resumed operation its rhythm was slow and steady and peaceful. He looked into Robbie's eyes and knew that the moment could no longer be postponed. "Do you think I do?"

"Of course. We both know that now."

"I know so little about it. I've always associated homosexuality with ugliness and depravity. You're not like that. I want to be homosexual like you. I wish it could just *happen* somehow without our thinking about it. I'm terrified of doing something that'll spoil everything that's wonderful between us. I think I'm in love with you but I don't know what that means with a guy."

"You've had boys, haven't you?"

"Things have happened. I've told you. Things that you might not even consider really homosexual in the

138

way you understand it. Nothing that had anything to do with love."

"We're in love with each other. Is that the problem?" Robbie hardly dared breathe. He had reached one of the turning points of his life. They had both grown very still and spoke lightly but with hushed intensity.

Lance nodded. "Yes. Nothing would matter if we were just doing it for kicks. I've done things for kicks, things I don't want to tell you about. With you, everything matters desperately. If it weren't perfect for us, I'd be miserable. Or you would be, which would be worse. I'm not making any sense. I told you, I'd do anything to keep you with me. I want to kiss you. I want to put my arms around you and feel you holding me and then I get frightened. Have you ever been impotent? With Pam it was horrible. Stupidly enough, I hated her. I don't want to hate you."

"I won't let you. After all, nobody can blame you for not being homosexual. The joke would be on me."

"I can only pray that you know what's right for us and won't let us do anything that'll make us ashamed or unhappy."

"I think maybe we'd better let it creep up on us and catch us unaware. As you say, let it just happen somehow. It's getting late. If I—"

"Oh no. Don't go."

It was a spontaneous, heartfelt plea and Robbie smiled his gratitude. "I was going to suggest staying. You'll save me from that long drive home in my cups. It's time we got into bed together. We belong everywhere together, regardless of sex. Who knows what might happen when we're tossing and turning in our troubled sleep?"

Lance's laughter burst from him with youthful exuberance. They would go to bed together without his having to make a commitment in advance.

His laughter was infectious. Robbie's died as he looked at him with the awed knowledge that what he wanted most in life was his.

"With my usual subtlety, I've brought a few amenities. My *baise en ville*." Robbie stood and stretched and snatched for his sarong as it started to fall off. "I think I can still walk. I'll run up to the car and get it."

Lance lay back, trying to concentrate on the fulfill-

139

ment of his dream. Going to sleep with Robbie. Waking up with Robbie. No need to think about what might happen in between. His heart began to pound erratically again. He heard his footsteps approaching along the terrace and he craned his neck and looked at him upside down as he put a small toilet case on the table.

"Here's your new roommate," he said. He moved in behind him and ran his hand over his hair. "This is sex creeping up and taking you unaware." He toyed with the hair on the back of his neck and moved his fingertips lightly along his shoulders.

Lance took a quick deep breath. Robbie was touching him at last, amorously, insinuatingly, deliciously, establishing physical intimacy without hurrying him. He didn't want him to stop. He lifted his arms and reached behind him and held Robbie's ribs.

Robbie ran his hands down his arms to his armpits and stroked them. "Does that send any little thrills racing up and down your spine?" he asked.

Robbie made his hands as provocative as he knew how and let them stray over Lance's chest, feeling his nipples pucker when his fingertips circled them. Lance arched his back and made a contented little sound in his throat. Robbie laughed, hardly daring to believe the signals he was receiving, and dropped to the floor at the end of the cot. He nuzzled his neck and ears while his hands swept over him, finding places where his caresses elicited gasps and murmurs and small cries of pleasure. The time for withdrawal and equivocation had passed.

Robbie grabbed his toilet case and moved around on his knees to the side of the bed to take whatever his lover offered him, his own sarong trailing away behind him on the floor. His erection was trapped against the frame of the cot as Lance pitched in against his chest.

"It's as hard as a rock for you," Lance blurted through choked laughter before their open mouths met and their tongues lunged out to each other. He wanted to open all his body to his lover, to be taken and possessed by him, to be absorbed into him. He writhed against his chest with a wild longing to become a part of him.

Robbie struggled for control to meet the passion he had unleashed. He had known it was there but he hadn't been prepared for it to come boiling to the surface so soon. Violent passion hadn't entered his life for years, never with this raw urgency. It charged him with vitality, making him feel that he was emerging from a living death. Hands clawed at him. His mouth was being devoured. His cock felt as if it were being torn off. He bit the devouring lips that were pressed to his. Lance's grip tightened on his cock and he moaned with longing.

"Fuck me," he whispered into Robbie's mouth. "Oh God, please. Fuck me. Put it inside me. I belong to you. Take me. I didn't know it would be like this. I'm insanely in love with you."

Robbie drew back slightly, gasping for breath. His mind remained cool and cautious. Ready for almost anything, he had thought of this as the least likely possibility. He fumbled for his toilet case and extricated the lubricant. "Are you sure you don't mean the other way around?" he asked breathlessly, giving caution a final say.

"I'm ashamed of being so stupid. I didn't exist until you." He moved his hands up to his shoulders, clinging to his smooth chest, and curled himself in so that their cocks met at the edge of the cot. He threw his head back with an anguished cry. "Oh God. Please want me always. Don't ever leave me. I worship you. I've never felt anything like it. It's terrifying to feel so much for you."

"I love you with everything in me. I've never been in love before." Robbie held him closer.

Lance knew he had somehow outdistanced the furies. Robbie kissed his neck and chin and ran his tongue over his nose. Then he struggled to his feet.

Lance flung himself out flat on the cushions and threw his arms back over his head and spread his legs wide, opening his body to his lover. He wanted to be taken like a girl, on his back with his legs in the air. His heart was pounding. Robbie stood over him, his erection thick and straight.

Lance was able to look at it at last. It tapered slightly from the base to the elliptical head, designed for coupling. Looking at it gave him goose bumps. He wouldn't know who he was, he wouldn't know anything until it had possessed him.

Robbie dropped to his knees on the cot and moved in between his legs. Lance sat up and threw his arms around his waist and pressed his face to his cock. "I worship it," he said, his lips moving against its silken surface. "I want to suck it. I want to give myself to it. I want everything with you." He dropped back among the cushions, tense with anticipation but prey to no torments. There was nothing more to fear in himself. He belonged to a man.

"You're beautiful like that." Robbie's heart was wrung by the abandon with which Lance offered his radiant body. Joy and love lighted up the candid blue eyes. He prayed that he was about to join them to each other for life. He put some lubricant into the palm of his hand and Lance lifted his hips for it. Robbie was sure that this wasn't an initiation.

Lance was convulsed by a spasm of longing. The pleasure of his body was being restored to him. He hadn't realized how alienated he had been from it by José's violation. Laughter swelled in his throat. He lifted his legs and dropped them over Robbie's shoulders, watching him apply the lubricant. He was braced for the brutal shock of submission but felt Robbie enter him with slow, gentle care. No submission was demanded of him. Their two bodies were becoming one. They hovered together on the brink of sublime consummation. He lay motionless, breath held, while he was transformed. Robbie had created him. He was his father.

"What beautiful things a cock can do," Lance crooned. His laughter choked on sudden pain but he refused to let his body flinch from it, accepting whatever Robbie required of him. He rolled his hips to ease the familiar sensation of being ripped open. A shout of outrage dissolved in bliss as Robbie completed his entry. His cock was moving freely in him, asserting its right to him, offering him the bliss of belonging to it, taking all of him and thrusting its own new life into him. Strong hands gently gripped his hips and moved them to open him completely.

Something extraordinary was happening to his body, a metamorphosis, a discovery in it of needs that transcended everything in his experience, an annihilation, a birth. The body that was unlocking all his body's secrets was Robbie's. He loved Robbie and had become his body's slave.

He drowned in bliss. All the strands of his life were

142

joined to be woven into an unknown pattern. He was without a past, without a country, a sexual outlaw, free of all bonds and restraints except those imposed by the man who possessed him. He was Robbie's. Robi's. He was Lance Cosling.

"Oh my God," he cried. "I'm going to come."

Robbie bowed over him and lifted his cock to his mouth and received his ejaculation. Lance drummed on his back with his heels while his body was flung about in the grip of ecstasy. He shouted and laughed and sobbed. Tears were streaming down his face when Robbie raised his head to him.

Lance's bruised beauty was more moving than anything he'd ever seen. Lance had become so wholly his that he felt as if he were in love with himself. Nobody had ever made him so aware of the size of his cock. By receiving it so easily, he permitted him to measure and define it in him and brought him rushing to an orgasm that became a continuation of his own.

They rocked and shuddered together, then doubled over on each other. Robbie stroked Lance's shoulders and dropped onto his side so that he could cradle the body that was so astonishingly his on his chest, still joined to it. He licked his tears away and kissed his eyes and nose and mouth. He had never before owned anybody. "I didn't hurt you, did I?" he asked tenderly.

"God no. Only for a second. I wanted it. I'm crying because I didn't know it was possible to be so happy."

"I know. I want to remember every second of it forever. The way the light falls on you. The night around us. The heat and silence and the air on our skin. I won't forget this ghastly cot. It's the beginning of everything."

"I wanted it to be the best you've ever had."

"I don't see how anything could be better but I'm a novice too, you know. For the last few days, falling in love with you more and more, I never dreamed that this would happen. I assumed you'd take me the way it's always been. You've very welcome to, whenever you want."

"No, never, darling. I want a man. That's pretty obvious. I want you and your cock where it is now. It's already hard again."

"You make me feel as if my cock were made for you."

"It is. Feel mine. How's that for being impotent?"

"I don't think you've quite grasped the meaning of the word."

They laughed as they rolled up and over and settled Lance once more on his back. He goaded Robbie to a rage of possession which brought them to breathless, simultaneous orgasms.

"I don't think you'll ever find anybody who belongs to you as completely as I do, darling," Lance said when their breathing had returned to normal. Robbie was lying on top of him, slowly slipping out of him.

"It's frightening, isn't it? How could Flip have been so right? What'll we do when we have to be apart?"

"That's easy. We won't be. I'm going to change my name. From now on, I'm Lance Cosling."

Robbie lifted his head. The abrupt movement dislodged him. "What do you mean, my beloved?"

"I don't know now. You're gone. Let's go take a shower and make each other hard again and fuck some more. I can't stand your not being in me. That's when I know what I mean. I'm going to change my name to Lance Cosling. I worship you. I want your name. I want everything about you."

"Oh, darling, you're such a sweetheart." He ran his tongue over Lance's lips.

"It makes great sense. You don't use Cosling professionally, so that's all right. I'll be Lance Cosling, your cocky bride. Come on, darling. Let's see how cocky we can still make each other."

Robbie sprang up and headed for the enclosure that Lance had built around the shower. Lance supposed that he might bear traces of their copulation and let him go, following with a lamp. His eyes were fixed on his delectable buttocks, ripe globes of masterfully sculptured flesh. No wonder he'd always been fucked.

He put the lamp on a shelf he had installed for the purpose and stepped into the shower. Robbie already had the water on and his body glistened sleekly under it. He took Lance's arm and pulled him in and kissed him.

"This is the first time I've seen you without some kind of a hard-on," Lance said.

"You can certainly stop worrying about being impotent."

"Yes, but I'm getting an inferiority complex again. I wish mine was as big as yours."

"It is practically. You haven't really looked at them together yet. You can make clay models of them and sell them as bookends. People will hardly notice that they aren't a matching pair." They laughed with their heads together and their arms hanging loosely around each other's shoulders, looking down at themselves while their cocks straightened and lifted. "When I was a kid, I found out that most men are more or less the same. I called it the norm. You exceed the norm so you can't object if I do too."

Lance swayed his hips against Robbie's. "You can't imagine what it does to me to feel you inside me. No girl could want it as much as I do."

Robbie heard the insistence of his voice, the determination to force himself into any role that was offered him, the urge to adopt extremes of behavior in his effort to break with his past. Robbie owned him until circumstances changed. He intended to keep him even if it meant doing some changing himself. "We'll forget you were ever straight," he said lightly, denying his vague uneasiness. "You're as twisty as a corkscrew. Let's say you're in love with me and leave it at that."

"In love with you? Insanely. I'm already jealous of you. I can't bear to think of you with anybody else. Put it in me, darling." He turned and Robbie entered him. "There. There's just a second when it hurts and then it's like this, as if this is the way we're meant to be. I know I must seem peculiar to you. An hour ago I thought I was straight. I hoped we could get over sex somehow. When you came back and touched me, all of a sudden I wanted you more than I've ever wanted anything. I thought I really would start screaming if you didn't take me. I've got to get used to being an entirely different person. I hardly know where to begin."

Robbie pulled him in close to feel himself defined in him. "It *is* peculiar, my beloved. So peculiar that it's not very convincing. Why don't you begin by telling me everything?"

"What makes you think there's anything to tell?"

Robbie put his hands on his hips and moved himself in him. "Feel me in you, darling. You want me there. You're mine. I know an awful lot about you."

"All right. You better stop fucking me for a minute if you want to know everything." Robbie withdrew slowly while Lance crooned with pleasure. "That's marvelous—your putting it in and taking it out whenever we want. That makes me feel just the way I want to feel, as if I were a natural part of you." He turned the water off and they stood face to face, their hands moving lightly over each other, while he told about Jim and Bryan, trying to explain as fully as he understood it himself what each had meant to him. "I had orgasms with them but pleasure wasn't the point. It was more as if I was trying to punish myself. You can see why I couldn't connect you with anything that happened before."

He told Robbie about the rape and the incident that had led up to it. The sequel no longer had any significance, so he didn't mention it. Robbie's face was frozen in an expression of horror-struck repugnance.

"I felt as if there were demons in me, driving me crazy." Lance's erection had swung up between them. He put Robbie's hand on it. "You see what happens when I think about it. It was horrible but something in me wanted it. When you hold my cock, it's all right. Everything's all mixed up in my mind. Being brought up a Catholic has something to do with it. Atoning for my sins, or the sins I've inherited. That's the queer part of me. You make me feel normal."

"This happened just the other day?" Robbie asked, his mind still rocking with what he'd been told.

"Yes. That's just it. The night we met."

"That's why you didn't come see me the next day?"

"Yes. I couldn't face myself, let alone you. I was sure I'd never let a man touch me ever again, not even in a friendly way."

"I guessed something of the sort. I knew you hadn't fallen." Robbie now understood the distinction Lance had been making about their lovemaking. He wouldn't want to take him until he stopped thinking of homosexuality as punishment. He understood the importance the size of his cock would have in keeping his lover. His erection revived. "Thank God you've told me, my poor darling. If I hadn't guessed a bit of it, I might've made some awful blunder."

"I was afraid you might stop wanting me. Damaged goods. I'm pretty silly." He put both hands on Robbie's

cock, still getting used to wanting to. "God, it feels good.
I never wanted to touch the others. I had to force myself
to. It feels so heavy, darling. I don't see how you get it
up."

He dropped down to it. It gave a little leap at the
touch of his lips. He wanted it in his mouth, not as an
act of self-abasement but with love and desire, proud
of displaying his worship of it. It was so much bigger
than the others that he had to improvise a technique
for making love to it. He couldn't put much of it in his
mouth, only suck on the head of it. He rolled his tongue
around it and bit it gently all along its length. He could
feel that he was pleasing Robbie.

"Imagine waiting so long to do that. We hardly know
each other's bodies. I can't believe it. Don't let's stay in
here all night, darling. I want to take plenty of time
for this."

He picked up the lamp and they careened back along
the terrace toward the bedroom, playfully challenging
each other with their bodies and making sport with
their cocks. It was incredible. Robbie was here with
him. Robbie's cock had been in him. Robbie had chosen
him for life.

"I can't wait for everybody to know," he exclaimed,
bursting with high-spirited pride. "I want to be introduced at parties the way Flip introduced those guys
who were here before you. Everybody will know that
I'm your mate, your partner, your lover, whatever we're
going to call it. Your wife is more like it. We belong in
bed together now, don't you think, darling? Our bed.
Let's take drinks and talk all night. So much to talk
about."

"Some pretty basic things to begin with."

"Just a second, darling. I'll fix us some nice warm
drinks." He kept Robbie beside him while he poured
rum and water into their glasses. "It's such a relief to
know I'm queer and not crazy. What's it going to be
like? Being queer, I mean. Am I going to want every
guy I see?"

"We'll find out quite soon enough," Robbie said with
a chill of disapproval in his voice. He lifted his hand
and laid it against the side of Lance's face. He had
committed so much of himself to his love that he didn't
even care if he never painted again; he couldn't joke

147

about sharing any part of him with others. "It's new for me too. I've wanted men to take me all my life. Taking you is the most exciting thing that's ever happened to me. It's made me downright insatiable. Does that mean I'm going to want to fuck every guy I see?"

"No. Please. You believe in fidelity, don't you? You've got to be faithful to me."

Robbie laughed softly at having scored a point. He held Lance's head in both hands and drew his mouth to his and opened it with his tongue and kissed him deeply while their erections surged up against each other. Lance whimpered in his throat as Robbie's kiss became voracious. He cried out and his chest was heaving when Robbie pulled his head back. They stared into each other's eyes with a rage of desire.

"There," Robbie said. "That's to tell you that I'll never want anybody else. The only time I *wanted* to be unfaithful to Maurice was when I saw you on the stage. I've got you now."

"Quickly, darling. Let's get these glasses out of our hands so that we can hold on to things that matter." Lance looked down at the imperious swing of Robbie's cock as they headed for the bedroom. "Sweet little Jesus. If I'm not making love to that in ten seconds, I'm going to throw these drinks on the floor." He ran ahead and put the glasses on the bedside table and seized the lamp from Robbie as he entered. "There. Get into bed and stay there forever."

Robbie stretched out on his back, and Lance dove for him, landing between his legs. He gripped his cock with both hands and lifted it and pressed his face to it, ablaze with untested desires.

Robbie shifted them so that they lay with their feet at opposite ends of the bed and showed him the wonders they could perform with their mouths. Only Lance's longing for Robbie's orgasm prevented him from lying back and rejoicing in his lover's skill. His heart began to pound as he felt him approaching his climax. He longed for it but was terrified that he would still find it abhorrent. He heard Robbie moan with ecstasy. Robbie's cock swelled hugely. A great jet hurtled into his mouth and he swallowed avidly. His own orgasm became a part of his ecstasy. They were exchanging a distillation of themselves, their life's substance. It was the consecration of their union. They lay quiet finally, together at the core of life.

"Oh God, that's everything," Lance sighed. He sat up and gazed at the magnificent body that he was part of, amazed that he could still move independently of it. "I love sucking your cock. That's something else that's new for me. You're big, darling. Give me time to make it as wonderful for you as it is for me."

"There's no room for improvement. You've got a marvelous mouth, like everything else about you."

Lance laughed. He dropped over and stretched out beside him, propped up against him so that he could look at him. "What more do we have to talk about? Isn't that as basic as we can get?"

"It's right for you, isn't it, sweetheart? Nothing we've done makes you ashamed?"

"No. Nothing. I love it all. That's why I can't help wondering if I'm going to be tempted by other guys."

"You're bound to be. I've trained myself not to be. Maurice and I got into sort of a rut. We were creatures of habit. Where's that drink, beloved?" They hitched themselves higher against the pillows and sipped tepid rum. With the windows open, a draft played through the room. The night was finally cooling off. "I adored Maurice but he put me to sleep in a way. You've waked me up with a jolt that still has me reeling. At least I don't think I'm apt to go to sleep with you."

"Not unless you can fuck in your sleep." Lance leaned in and kissed the side of his face. He spoke urgently against his ear. "Fuck me a lot, darling. Don't want anything else. You've got to make me yours. There's something in me still that frightens me."

Robbie turned his head on the pillow and looked at him. "Your demons? I'm going to exorcise them."

"It started with Jim. After Bryan, I thought I was all right. For the last year, my life has been devoted to a girl who made me better than I ever thought I could be, full of high ideals, dedicated to all the good things she believed in, seriously concerned with serious things. I'll tell you about Scot some time. We weren't lovers so I thought I was ready for sainthood. When I was raped, it all came out again—a conflict with what I suppose you'd call my decent instincts, a need to debase myself, to cancel out my gentlemanly upbringing. I've even..."

149

He was on the verge of telling him about José but checked himself. He wanted to deny José's existence. "I've wanted to renounce the Vanderholdens even if it meant rolling in shit," he said. "I want to be yours."

Robbie took a deep calming breath. His heart ached for the torment he heard in the beautiful resonances of his voice. "You're talking about what the French call *la nostalgie de la boue,* I suppose. They're realists. They know that we've all climbed out of the mud and sometimes wish we could crawl back into it. Somebody called it the great urge downward. You were never allowed anywhere near the mud. Those closed doors. You've rather heroically tried to find the mud on your own. Aren't your feelings for me mixed up with the idea that I'm dragging you into it?"

Lance's eyes blazed with denial. "No. It's just the opposite. I was afraid of you at first. I was afraid that making love with you would bring out everything that's twisted and queer in me. The demons. I love you too much to let that happen. It hasn't. It can't because I'm in love with you. I always thought of homosexuals as the lowest of the low. I can't anymore because that's what we are. Anything you are is what I want to be. I'm not too well born to be buggered."

Robbie frowned and gave his head a little shake. "No, I just hope you want it because that's the way you are, not to prove you've escaped your bloody background. You're a Vanderholden whether you like it or not. Be a good one. They can't all be bad, especially if there're any queer ones."

"Queer Vanderholdens? What a peculiar idea. I don't suppose it'll shock anybody here."

"You might not shock anybody but you'll certainly attract attention." There was a grim note in Robbie's voice. "Once everybody knows we're lovers, if you want them to know, the guys will be swarming around you like hornets. Flip will keep us supplied. If I hadn't been so obsessed by you, I might have had quite a jolly time."

"It's hard to believe that you've been living a life of your own without me. There won't be any more of that, will there?"

"No. Which gets us back to the big question. Luisa."

"I know." Lance drained his glass and put it on the floor beside him and rolled in against Robbie, half on top of him, with his hands folded flat on his chest and his chin resting on them. "She'll have to know we're together."

Robbie touched the white-gold hair where it curled enchantingly around his ears. His beloved was suddenly looking devastatingly young, pure and untroubled and innocent again. The upper part of his face, upswept brows and wide-set eyes, was an image of candor. His mouth was a perpetual contradiction, spoiled, generous, outrageously sensual, fleshy without being weak, humorous and, as now, boyishly guileless. Looking at him, feeling his body against his, made him conscious of how profoundly altered his life was going to be. He wondered if he would ever again draw a tranquil breath. "Yes, she'll have to know," he said thoughtfully. "I've told her we've known each other a long time. I think I'll tell her we're half brothers and pretend I thought she knew. My father used to talk about my maybe having a half brother. He'd be older but you'll do. I don't think any of it will mean much to her. The people here expect the foreigners to be strange and different, like another race. You're a sort of god to her, with the divine right to lay down the law. The women are trained to take a back seat and don't have our northern ideas of romantic love. Brothers being lovers should fit in easily enough."

"You know everything about everything, darling. Thank God you agree with me about not making a secret of it. I want to be good with her but I'd kill her if I felt we had to change anything because of her."

"We have to change quite a lot because of her, don't we, sweetheart? I had no idea what was going to happen but I've never intended to take you away from her. That's why I've rented another house."

"I don't see how you can take something away from her that she doesn't have. She doesn't have any part of me. You know that, darling. I would never've got involved if you'd arrived when Flip first said you were due. Nothing mattered and she was willing and the thought of having children gave me *something* to live for. That's—"

"And you wanted a girl. I understand all that, my darling. So you've got her."

"The big shock for me is realizing that I'm not going

151

to want girls anymore. It's just beginning to hit me. Until a year ago, running after girls was my major occupation. I'm glad Scot prepared me for love. I may not want men but I want a man. A man, not girls anymore. It's unbelievable."

"And not necessarily true, sweetheart." Robbie found him touchingly absurd. He was forcing himself into homosexuality. It was all there in him, as he had suspected from the beginning, but he couldn't relax into his natural inclinations. He had to re-create himself into the image of what he thought a homosexual should be. "You don't want to take me because you're afraid it'll make you go on wanting girls. Why shouldn't you? You don't have to be all one way or the other. Plenty of men aren't. Follow your feelings. You want children."

"Yes, but it's probably too late even if I didn't. I'd love Luisa to give me a son. His name would be Cosling. I'd love that."

"You're going to go on doing what's generally done to achieve that result, aren't you?"

"I don't know if I'll be able to. I suppose so. Is that all right?"

"Of course, darling. I told you I've never thought of taking you away from her. I can share you when it's something I can't do for you."

Lance's eyes widened as if he were staring in at himself. "Wow," he exclaimed. "You can't imagine what that did to me. Your saying that. I wish you could make me pregnant. There's an awful lot of feminine in me." He shifted his hips and pressed in closer against Robbie. "There. Feel that. How many girls do you know with a cock like that?"

Robbie laughed, helplessly under his spell. "It's fairly unusual even for a boy. The father of a Cosling. We're starting out with your being unfaithful to me with a girl and not even knowing when we're going to sleep together but for some reason I'm happier than I've ever been in my life."

"You're crazy if you think we're not going to sleep together. I'm never going to be farther away from you than I am right now." He lifted himself over him and dropped down between his legs again. He drew his inert cock into his mouth and released it. "I know it's too soon but I don't want to make it hard. It's such heaven to be able to have all of it in my mouth. Talk to me, darling. Say things I don't have to answer. I was taught that it's not polite to speak with your mouth full." He chuckled as he drew the velvet softness of the flesh into his mouth again and kneaded it with his teeth and tongue. He felt it stirring and the throb of life in it.

"I've been thinking a lot in the last few days," Robbie said. "I didn't dare hope for too much, but just in case, I thought, what'll we do? We can't stay here forever. We need time for you to get started with the pottery and for Luisa to have a baby. She'd be miserable in the States because of the color thing. So would children eventually if they take after her. I'd like us all to go home to France. There're outbuildings I've been dying for an excuse to convert. You'll pot. Luisa can have as many children as you like in a place of her own. We'll be next door in our own bed where we belong. If it doesn't work for her, we could always bring her back here and spend part of the year with her and the kids."

Lance heard a life being outlined that guaranteed his future—with a man. His wanting it didn't make it any less startling. It was more than he and Scot had ever been quite able to believe in. Robbie was a miracle-worker, making the impossible seem simple and attainable. He had already turned him into a homosexual. At least he hoped so. Thinking of how long it had taken him to arrive at this acceptance of it, he hoped he would never be attracted to a girl again. He pulled himself up to the pillows beside him. "I love to hear you talk about what we're going to do. You seem about twenty years older than me, so sure of yourself. I have to keep reminding myself that you're Robi, one of the people I admire most in the world. You're rich and famous and I belong to you. Do know the date?"

"The date? It's Sunday. The 17th of July, 1949, to be exact."

"Well, don't forget it. It's my new birthday. I hope you like making love with babies. I'll be only two when you're thirty. I'll grow up in France. How extraordinary for you to've worked everything out for us, to've thought of the color business and all. I've had plenty of experience with that. Scot's a Negro."

"You're kidding. You don't do things by halves, do you? She's not dead?"

"No. I suppose you've heard some garbled story. No, she's not dead."

"You'd better tell me about her, hadn't you?"

"Yes. I can talk about her now. I thought I'd never be able to, even with you. Have we finished fucking for now? I haven't got used to being able to start again whenever we want to. Let's have another shower and I'll fix us soothing drinks and tell you about Scot. That'll take care of the past. The end of Lance Vanderholden. From now on, you'll know everything that happens to me. That's marvelous."

They acted on Lance's suggestion. When they were back in bed with tepid drinks, Lance snuggled in against his lover, hoping that Robbie would want him again soon. Being in the shower without anything happening had made him feel that the initial intensity of passion had already cooled. Would Robbie go on wanting him now that he'd had him? "You're not *very* rich, are you, darling?" he asked, laughing at himself for asking such an impolite question.

"Why're you laughing at such a serious matter?"

"Because I feel so good, I guess, but I was thinking what a joke it would be on me if I've ended up with a millionaire."

"You can stop laughing, worse luck. You said I was rich. I didn't. I'm not rich at all. Maurice left me enough to live comfortably. Plus the house, of course. It costs quite a lot to keep up. I don't have anything to worry about but I never have had really. I've known since I was eighteen that I could make my living as a painter."

"Well, that's a relief. I couldn't stand it if you started acting like a rich man. I guess I'll have to accept the fact that you're perfect and try to get used to it."

"That's a reasonable point of departure. We can afford to get you started in a businesslike way. Maurice made life easier in lots of ways but I wasn't dependent on him after the first year or so. You won't be dependent on me. Not in that way. Naturally we'll be dependent on each other in every possible way. Everything I have is yours but it works the other way around, too. I'm sure you're going to be a success. We'll decide together how we want to spend our money. That's the only way it can work for two men living together. Everything equal between us."

"You make it sound as if it's actually going to happen. Nobody else has ever acted as if they really believed in me. I've never given them any reason to, I suppose, but I'm going to do my damnedest now. For the first time I feel as if I had something I could really get my teeth into. I don't just mean your cock. Life and love and work all wrapped up in you, in your wanting me and my belonging to you and being your mate. Nobody's ever made me feel that they wanted me to be myself."

"Scot didn't?"

"Well, naturally she wouldn't've wanted me to be queer but that didn't come into it then, even though— I haven't told you about Andy, her brother-in-law." Lance did so. "Scot knew. That was no problem. She hated my being a Vanderholden more than anything. You say I've got to accept it. You accept it. You accept everything about me, even the way I want you to make love to me. You're going to make it possible at last for me to be whatever I am. You've got to go on being in love with me."

"I will, beautiful. I couldn't stop even if I tried. Everything you tell me makes me more and more sure that we're made for each other. God bless Flip. You're not as straight as you let me think. What have you been doing since you gave up the theater?"

"With Scot? I told you I was thinking of specializing in art somehow. That was for Scot, trying to fit into the real world. She's very important in the civil rights movement but art is her big interest outside of work. She was as impressed by you as I was. It's so hard to tell about her. You see, I thought it was impossible for me to be in love with a man because of her. We were in love with each other, but very sanely, the way men and women are, or the way she wanted us to be. Tonight, I've discovered that being in love is a sort of divine madness. It turns life into fireworks, the way I always thought it must if I could just open the doors. She would've hated seeing me the way you've seen me tonight, going wild with wanting somebody I love, yet funnily enough there's a lot about you that reminds me of her. Your strength. Your grip on what life's all about. Maybe the male and female in us were just enough out of balance for it to've worked. We were getting there.

The last few months I felt as if we were really going to make it." He paused and she was there, filling his mind's eye for the first time since the disaster, and he knew that even if he never wanted another girl, he had been in love with her. He had even felt with her at moments the lifting of rational restraint, the sort of lunacy that thrilled him so with Robbie. His mind made a connection. A black girl and a man. Equally forbidden. "She was funny-looking," he said abruptly. "Beautiful and funny-looking."

He saw the big mouth that could spread into the most wonderful, warm, happy grin and the big soft eyes that could contain all the misery of the world, topped by thick brown hair chopped short with deliberate eccentricity. Strangers rarely noticed the slight duskiness of her skin.

Trying to describe her, he was stunned that she was being replaced in his heart by Robbie. He knew nothing about making a permanent passionate relationship with a man. Despite the barriers Scot seemed to erect at times between them, he had had the experience of marriage and his season of promiscuity to give him a rough idea of where they were headed. Without that, he never would have felt that the difficulties they faced were worth overcoming. Robbie could demonstrate that he was a homosexual but he couldn't give him the experience Lance felt he needed. He would have to count on the moral laxity he associated with sexual deviation to fill in the gaps.

He told Robbie about Scot in fragmentary bursts, broken by silences, trying to give him an impression of what they'd been like together, while his mind reproduced scenes and episodes, the clothes they'd been wearing, the way they had looked at each other, what it had felt like to touch each other.

Robbie watched him closely. He lay very still with a distant look in his heavy-lidded eyes but he had altered again. He had become the man he had been with his girl. Robbie felt an unfamiliar purposeful masculinity in him that he seemed to have lost. He was spellbound by him as always, but also impressed.

Lance sighed and shook his head, edging in closer to Robbie. "It's all right now. Everything's all right when I feel you beside me. I hope she finds somebody as right for her as you are for me. We went to your show together. That's amazing. Oh God, I want everybody in the whole world to know I belong to you. Robi's mate. That's me."

"My dearest. I've felt a funny gap in your life. It's good to have it filled in. To feel as if I know almost everything about you. How old is she?"

"That's odd. Almost exactly the same age as you. A few months older than me. Her birthday's in February. She was the youngest graduate in the history of the University of Pennsylvania's law school. You've never been interested in girls but there's a lot to be said for them."

"Not interested sexually, sweetheart, but otherwise they seem more or less human. Yours sounds nice. Why aren't you still with her?"

"That's what I'm trying to tell you. A couple of months ago when the weather began to get nice, we started to drive out to the country. A friend of hers had asked her to take care of his car while he was away somewhere. We always took overnight cases, like your *baise en ville,* in case the car broke down. That was our joke. It was really in case Scottie's will broke down. She said she refused to have important decisions influenced by whether or not we had toothbrushes with us. She always drove because she felt responsible for the car."

Robbie heard the roughness in his throat as his words came more slowly and he stroked his hair and kissed his eyelids and lay a finger on his lips. "You don't have to go on if you don't want to, beautiful."

Lance shook his head. "It's all draining out of me. I'm getting it all out of my system. How much did you read about it in the papers?"

"Not much. I saw headlines and didn't read more. Flip tried to talk about it but I didn't let her. Something about being arrested. I knew you'd tell me anything you wanted me to know."

"What about the others here? Do they say I'm a fugitive from justice?"

"You know them. I'm sure they'd love it if you were."

"I'm not. The papers made it sound that way but they made everything different from what it was, starting with the accident. I never knew much about that. Scot was driving pretty fast but it was an open road. I

157

caught movement out of the corner of my eye and then suddenly there was the motorcycle and then nothing. Nobody ever saw the motorcyle again. I haven't seen Scot again. They found me wandering around several miles away about an hour later. I had a slight concussion and had no idea what was going on. They took me to a hospital where there were a lot of policemen. I found out that Scot was there unconscious and it all began to come back to me. I said I was driving. I don't know why. I suppose a gentleman automatically shields a lady. It just made it worse. I hadn't gone for help or reported the accident. I knew I wasn't running away because I didn't know anything had happened. Maybe in my subconscious I had an idea that if I disappeared I wouldn't be connected with it and it wouldn't get into the papers. If she'd died without recovering consciousness, I could've been had up for manslaughter or worse. It was a nightmare. It got as lurid as they could make it. The decadent playboy off for a weekend of illicit sin with a pillar of the civil rights movement. When Scot came to, it got even worse because she told the truth, naturally, and I had to retract. It made me look as suspicious as hell, although I never knew what I was suspected of. As soon as we knew she was going to be all right I started going wild wanting to see her. Andy was there and did everything he could but she wouldn't listen. I understood. Everything that happened was just the sort of thing she had been afraid of all along. People have accidents every day and nobody hears anything about it. We hadn't even hurt anybody but ourselves. Because of me, it became a nasty scandal. Fortunately, the police had enough to go on, with tire tracks and the way the car was turned over, to see that she'd almost killed both of us to avoid the fucking motorcycle. Andy convinced me that I'd only make it worse for her if I went on insisting on seeing her. Nothing I could say would stop me being Lance Vanderholden. The police were pretty decent. They saw what the papers were doing to me. As soon as she was out of danger and they had their record straight, they told me I could go. Maybe I shouldn't have let Andy bring me down here. More headlines. Vanderholden Flees Country, and so forth. The papers followed us. Not that I cared by then. I hung around the capital for a few days to show that I wasn't

158

hiding and when the excitement began to die down I cleared out and came down here. Exit Lance Vanderholden. You can understand why I'm glad to see the last of him. Don't let Lance Cosling screw everything up."

"Why say that, beautiful?" Robbie searched for his hand and was moved by the little spasm of gratitude with which it was seized. "Forgive me if it upsets you, but it seems to me *she* screwed everything up. Taking the rough with the smooth is what loving somebody is all about. Does everybody have to be so ordinary that there's no danger of getting their names in the paper?"

"I hadn't thought of it like that. There was a bit of that in her—you know—slightly straitlaced—but it was because she took her responsibilities seriously. I admired her for that."

"Oh, I don't doubt that from her point of view it was an impossible situation. Thank God we could land on the front pages in bed together and it wouldn't bother me in the least. I can't imagine anything you could do that would make me not want to see you again."

"That's what's so exciting about you. You're you. You make your own rules. You'll make them for me too. Our own. Just for us. I'll probably never see Andy again but if he turned up and we discovered we wanted to make love for real, would that count as infidelity?"

"Why wouldn't it?"

"Even though it all started before I knew about us?" he asked, thinking of José with a pang of alarm.

"There's no way of being rational about it. Maurice said way back at the beginning that the act itself, jumping into bed with somebody, might not have much importance but we should try never to do anything that could hurt the other. That just about covers it. It worked for us."

"Does that mean that you might not want to know everything about me?"

"No. I'll always want to know everything. It means that if there's anything you don't want me to know, it's up to you to take care that I don't find out."

"It doesn't sound very honest. I want you to know everything, good or bad. It frightens me."

Robbie heard the tremor of torment in his voice again. "Still worried about your demons, sweetheart?"

159

"I don't think so. Just waiting to find out what Lance Cosling is going to be like. I'm worried about Luisa but I won't let her come between us." He lifted himself and propped himself on his side and handed his empty glass to Robbie. He was purged of Scot but how could he be sure of his homosexuality? He didn't have a hard-on. Perhaps the impotence he feared was simply the lack of a strongly defined homosexual urge. Panic stirred in him. He had to be in love with Robbie. His life depended on it.

He moaned and fell away onto his back, tugging at Robbie to bring him with him. "Please, darling. On top of me. All of you. All of your body on me. Yes. Like that. Oh my God. Let your weight rest on me."

Lance's hands slid to his sides and Robbie linked his fingers loosely with his. They lay inert, chest to chest, belly to belly, hard flesh pressed to hard flesh, breathing together. Lance felt all of Robbie's strength entering him as he made himself an offering to love. He had no need of anything more for himself, only to be wanted by the brilliant and beautiful man who lay on him. He had found where he belonged at last. He let his mouth go slack as Robbie's tongue filled it and their teeth ground lightly against each other. Their saliva mingled and they swallowed it. Their mouths tasted of rum.

Robbie could feel peace replacing torment in his beloved and the profound acceptance of him in the body beneath him. Male and female had ceased to exist. Lance was no longer a victim; Robbie could take him now without his wanting to be raped. Their inertia became communion. They entered into each other's minds and spirits and senses. They were approaching orgasm together gently, without the convulsions of unappeased hunger. Neither of them had experienced anything like it before. The moment would lie at the heart of their lives, joining them forever.

They awoke in bright sunlight, without ever having been fully asleep. While one had dozed off, the other had continued to make love to him. At times, they woke up simultaneously and made love passionately but without violence, Lance giving himself sweetly and gratefully and docilely.

When they heard movement outside, they knew that

160

Luisa had come back, but they didn't let it break into their time together. Sometime during the night, Robbie had written her a note saying that he was here and they didn't want to be disturbed. They looked at each other dreamily and smiled.

"Are we awake?" Robbie asked.

"Yes. And happy. This is the happiest moment of my life. A whole night gone and we're still together."

"We better get up before things start happening again. It feels late." Robbie made a move to rise. Lance shifted against him. "Oh well, it was an idea. I guess you've got to act quickly around here."

"What do you expect? We haven't come for God knows how long. An hour or two at least." Lance laughed and rolled away from him, springing to his feet, fully awake. "Anyway, I was faking. It's only just beginning." He stood in front of Robbie with his hands on his hips, his erection sufficiently advanced to assure him that he hadn't reverted to heterosexuality overnight. "Am I still the most desirable man you've ever seen in your life?"

"Yes." Robbie lay back and looked at the sparse golden curls in his armpits and the froth of gold that surrounded his tauntingly elongated cock and up over the smooth, exquisitely modeled muscles of abdomen and chest, a body all radiance and grace. "It's almost more desirable that way than when it's hard. It looks as if it would go on growing forever."

"You love it, don't you? You love it as much as I love yours." He laughed again and turned to the window and urinated out onto the steep rocky end of the property where nobody ever went. He turned back to the washstand, washed his hands and face, and brushed his teeth as he had done repeatedly all during the night. He emptied the basin out the window and picked up the enamelware ewer. "I'll get some more water, darling." He started for the door.

"Luisa's there, isn't she?" Robbie reminded him.

"Sure. I guess so." He stopped at the open door and saw that Robbie's eyes were fixed on his midriff. "Oh. You mean I'm naked? I'm naked most of the time."

"You look as if you'd just had a hard-on, or were well on the way to one."

"She's used to that too."

"She's not used to your having been in bed with me."

161

"But she soon will be. We agreed about that. You said you'd tell her. Seeing me like this will break the ice."

His deep-throated laughter trailed banners of joy behind him, bringing a bemused smile to Robbie's lips. Robbie had just had the most memorable night of his life. He was in love and about to embark on a life with a man he wanted more than he'd ever wanted anybody, yet he was filled with foreboding. What was wrong? Was it simply too good to be true? Was it wrong for Lance to want his girl and everybody else to know about them? Was it wrong for him to want to change his name?

Yes, touching and wrong, lacking the moderation that would give it substance. Lance was a Vanderholden. That was what was wrong. That was what made everything vaguely unreal. Guiltless, he wanted to be punished. Robbie knew as much about Lance as he was ever likely to know and had yet to find a core of self in him. He had embraced poverty, or a working middle-class equivalent to it, with Scot. Now he was embracing homosexuality. What next?

Robbie was seized by an impulse to escape. It would be hideous but he might be able to save himself from what suddenly seemed to him a threat to his whole life. He had been obsessed by Lance for two weeks. He had had him more thoroughly than he had dreamed possible or dared hope for. It had been the transcendent sexual experience of his life. What more did he want? He'd had no experience of giving all of himself up to another person in the way he felt himself doing with Lance. Now Lance was off naked with his girl. Would Luisa accept the situation as casually as he had suggested? Lance had learned the ugly lengths to which the local people would go to avenge their honor. Luisa had brothers. Would they feel that her honor required that her man's friend should be eliminated? He had made commitments that he intended to honor but he could do so from a safe distance. Run if he was still able to. Or stay and fall more helplessly under his spell. There was so much sweetness and devotion in him waiting to be shaped into a coherent human being. Would he know how? He could love him, if that was enough. Or he could leave him, which might be more effective.

162

Lance came striding in jauntily with the water, lighting up the room with his morning's joy. Robbie's thoughts fused into mindless adoration. Nobody else existed for him. He was on his feet, his erection swinging up to claim him. They were in each other's arms, Lance's golden cock standing up against his, as hard as it had been the first time he'd touched it last night. This was something that couldn't be forced. Lance wanted him and he wanted Lance's body against his always.

"I've been wondering if I could live without you," Robbie said. "I can't."

"Oh no. We can't live without each other. You shouldn't even wonder. It's all settled."

"Yes, my sweet darling. It's all settled. I won't wonder again."

Their eyes looked into each other, extracting promises, confirming them, looking for more, insatiable. Their faces grew closer, their mouths opened, their whiskers scratched each other as they touched. Their hands moved urgently on each other. Lance pulled his head back with choked laughter. "Oh hey. Wow." He cried. "Why haven't we tried this before? Is this what schoolboys do together? Hold them both together. Oh God, feel that. Look at us. Oh, darling. Now." They fell onto the bed and rolled about together, spilling their seed liberally on each other. Lance heaved himself over onto his back. "Oh God, it's such fun. What a beautiful mess. It can happen, can't it? I mean, our being together for always."

"Yes, my beloved." Robbie made no attempt to qualify the simple affirmation although he knew Lance was rushing it. They needed time to find themselves in each other and learn the limits beyond which one or the other of them couldn't go.

"You've got to go on loving me and wanting me," Lance insisted rhapsodically. "You understand that, don't you? You've started something that it's going to take all your life to finish. So many firsts last night and I loved all of it. I kept waiting for you to do something I didn't like, but I just wanted it all more and more. Only you could've taught me how much I need a man." He squeezed Robbie's arm and sat up. "We better mop up." He jumped up and hurried to the washstand

163

and poured water into the basin. Robbie joined him and they sponged themselves off.

Robbie thought he'd learned his slim athlete's body by heart during their hours on the beach but apparently he had been so consumed by desire for it that his eyes hadn't functioned accurately. He saw for the first time the almost feminine delicacy with which it was put together. There were no hard lines of resistance in it, none of the knots of strength usually produced by muscular development, no suggestion of masculine toughness or coarseness. It was made to belong to a man. A man? He suspected that he'd unleashed a sexual whirlwind. He was ready to fight to keep him but he mustn't try to impose his experience with Maurice on him.

They faced each other, holding opposite ends of a towel to dry themselves. "Is it as late as I thought?" Robbie asked, stepping closer for more towel.

"Almost noon. Is coffee enough for breakfast? Luisa seems pleased that you're here. I told her the house belongs to you now."

"Good. Even better, let's tell her it belongs to her. That should please her almost as much as marrying you. Maybe more. It'll certainly please her family."

"But, darling, can you afford to give away a house?"

"Can we afford it? We won't do it if you don't want to. It's about three thousand dollars, to be exact. If you count it as a year's rent, it's not too wildly extravagant. Youthful indiscretions often cost a great deal more. We've got to pay for your past, beloved."

Lance's eyes widened and grew liquid. His mouth worked as if he were swallowing and he lifted a hand and touched Robbie's cheek lightly before he spoke. "My God. We're beginning to live together. Isn't that what's happening? Of course I want her to have the house. I should've said so myself."

Lance rolled up the towel and dropped it onto the washstand. They held each other lightly, body to body, comfortably, neither of them feeling any need of a sexual response. "I guess I'd better know exactly how much money we have."

"Now you're talking. That's the sort of thing I'd like you to want to know. OK. I have about twelve thousand dollars a year from Maurice. That's more in France than it is in New York, especially in the country, but the

French still have strict currency controls so I can't get at it easily when I'm not there. Otherwise, there's what I make from my painting. That varies but it's been building up the last couple of years. Last year, it was close to fifty thousand but I've been spending carelessly and I haven't done any of the things people do to avoid taxes. There're all sorts of tricks but it sounds so boring that I haven't bothered. Now that there's some reason to, I will. We will. At the moment, I think I can get my hands on around ten thousand dollars. That's what we have to live on until I find out if there's more coming in or our company starts making something. The house will come out of that and the few thousand we'll need to get you started. I've been thinking we should buy a car, too. What do you think, beautiful? It seems silly to waste money renting one."

"Can it belong to the company?"

"Sure. That would probably be better. We'll both want to use it. As soon as the company's registered, you should start drawing a minimum salary. Say fifty dollars a week as an advance against profits. Is that all right?"

"It's more than I'm spending now. I can't wait to get started. It's a bit nutty counting on something I know so little about but I'm positive I can do something with it. As you said, now that you have me in your bed, or vice versa, we can start to think about less important matters."

"Don't forget Luisa. She won't be paid by the rental people anymore. She's been getting eight dollars a week. I checked. I thought we might raise it magnanimously to twelve with the understanding that she gives it to her family."

"That's something I'd pay out of my salary, isn't it?"

"Of course."

"You see? I'm getting the hang of it. Oh my God, darling." He moved his hips against Robbie and laughed. "I guess neither of us finds money very sexy, but you— my God, you. I'm so in awe of you that I won't dare to want you for at least a minute or two."

He lifted his hands and ran his fingers through Robbie's dark hair and kissed him slowly on his face everywhere, his brows and eyelids and cheeks and mouth, and put his chin in his mouth again. His whiskers were getting scratchier. "You're incredible, darling. We're just beginning to live together and you've got us all organized as if it were meant to be, as if you'd expected it all along. You somehow make me feel as if I had a right to all of it—a house, a car, a salary, you. When Mother threw me out, she made it clear I had no right to anything. It was the best thing that could've happened to me. This is different, you make me feel I have the right to everything because I'm yours."

"Oh, sweetheart. You do." He was pleased to be taller than Lance. It fortified ownership. He could lay down the law from on high. Their lips touched and they broke apart hastily.

"Quickly, darling. Let's go." Lance laughed. "I knew awe wouldn't stop me wanting you for long. It's all right. The damage isn't extensive. We can still get by in public."

"A sarong will cover a multitude of sins."

"No, darling. Don't wear anything. I never do. It'll look strange if I'm naked and you're not. Come on. I want a swim with you. I want you to fuck me. You haven't for hours. I want you to fuck me down on the rocks in broad daylight. Another first. Come on, darling."

Robbie shrugged. "I'm a nudist by nature. I don't mind if she doesn't. I'll carry a towel just in case." He picked one up and followed Lance out onto the terrace.

Luisa greeted him with subdued, childlike pleasure. She was looking her sweet self again, without the ugly little dress, bare-breasted above the long full skirt. He thought of the momentous hours that had passed since he'd last seen her. All their lives had altered and she remained unaware of it. It made him want to treat her with extra consideration. He kept the towel casually in front of himself. She could see that he was naked, which was apparently the point Lance wanted to make, without being exposed to the basic facts about himself. She poured coffee for them and they sat at the table.

"He is here with me now, little one," Lance said in his steadily improving Spanish. "He has a surprise for you. He can explain better than can I." He put his hand out to Robbie and switched to English. "Tell her, darling."

"*Si*, dar-leeng." She clapped a hand over her mouth

and giggled. They looked at her and at each other and laughed. She pointed at Lance. "Dar-leeng?" she asked.

"Absolutely," Lance agreed delightedly. "Where did you learn English?"

"Dar-leeng?" she questioned Robbie.

"Most definitely." Robbie reverted to Spanish. "Do you know what it means?"

"I'm not sure. Is it a word for a man to use with his woman?"

"Yes, but not only that. It's a word to use with anybody you love. Men use it with each other when they love each other. I can use it with you. You see?"

"It's a very nice word. Dar-leeng."

"More like dar-*ling*." She made a stab at it and covered her mouth and giggled again. "You'll get it with practice. It's the only word you really need with the foreigners. We can go ahead with our party now. The big difference is that it'll be in your house."

"My house?" She looked puzzled. "Where?"

"Here. This is going to be your house. Lance told you we're buying it but we want your name to be on the paper. You will sign it. It'll be your house. That's the surprise."

She uttered her effortless fluting laughter. "You're making a joke with me. Why do you say these things?"

"It's not a joke. It's true. Tomorrow or the next day, we'll take you to the lawyer and the man you work for will sign the paper and you will sign and the house will be yours. You can tell us to leave if you want to. I hope you'll let us stay and give the party on Saturday to celebrate."

She had grown very still and her eyes were round with wonder. "I can't believe what you're saying. I don't understand such things. Only the rich buy houses. The rest of us have a little place where we are born and that's all. Only the rich have houses like this."

"We're not rich. We just want to take care of you. He wants you to have his children. You'll have his children in your own house and we'll take care of you. The man you work for is selling the house, so he won't pay you from now on but Lance will give you more money every week to give to your family. Are you pleased?"

Lance squeezed his hand. "You're being so sweet to her. Thank you, darling." He rose and, challenging the

167

world, leaned over and kissed Robbie lightly on the lips. He turned and managed to give Luisa a quick kiss before he swung hastily away to conceal his increasingly conspicuous cock. He stood with his back to her, letting Robbie see it, and laughed. "I'll be back when it's ready to behave itself. Explain about beds, darling." He headed for the shower and outhouse.

Robbie wondered if he should be jealous. Which one of them had aroused him? The answer might be simple: neither of them. Lance had probably given himself an erection, exulting in his daring at being the center of such an unorthodox situation. He was growing more aware of this side of him—he was a narcissist of rebellion, his unidentified torments swept aside by the intoxication of defiance. On the whole, he found it reassuring; he must be reaching the limits of nonconformity. He tore his eyes from his retreating back and turned with a smile for Luisa. "Are you happy, darling?" he asked.

"I think I'll believe it more if I see a paper. It will be in Spanish? I'll be so proud if I can show it to my family. He *is* very rich, isn't he? Everybody says so."

"No. His mother is very rich but families aren't the same in North America as here. She won't give him money unless he does what she tells him. She won't give him money if he stays here. She wants him to go home to his wife."

"It is very strange for a mother to tell her grown son what to do. What is this wife?"

"Just his wife. They have children but it wasn't a good marriage. You know your church allows a man to have only one wife unless the first one dies. When he said he wanted to stay with you, I came because he always wants me with him when he's settled with a woman he likes. We have good times together. He doesn't want other girls when I'm with him. When two men love each other and one of them has a woman, they both look after her, especially if they're brothers." He hoped it wasn't too farfetched; he didn't have very promising material to work with.

"But you're not brothers," she pointed out peacefully.

"Not full brothers. Half brothers. The same mother." Thinking of what Lance had told him about his mother, he expected to be turned to stone. "I told you. Remember? He sometimes uses my father's name. Lance Cosing. That's the name he wishes to call your children."

"I didn't understand. You're very alike. I see it now."

"Everybody says so." He plunged on. "We like to sleep together, to look after each other at night. I'll have a house not far away. He may stay with me sometimes. If he isn't here, he'll be with me, never with another woman. You need never worry about that. Do you understand?"

"Will you have a woman?"

"No. I don't need a woman. I have my work which is like a woman. And I have him. You don't mind his loving me, do you?"

"Brothers always love each other. Mine do. The two younger ones always sleep together. We tease them. We say they'll never get married unless they find sisters who will sleep with them. If you love him and keep him from other women and will stay with him and take care of his family, that will be very wonderful. If you want to be with him, why don't you stay here, like last night?"

"I must have a place to work. He wants a place for you and the family. Maybe we'll all live together later."

"I would kill any woman who tried to take him away from me, but that's between women." Her manner remained peaceful and matter-of-fact but Robbie thought she probably meant it. "At the beginning, I was afraid I couldn't keep him here. The rich foreigners never stay. What is there for them here? I had nothing to talk to him about. I didn't want to commit a sin with him unless he would stay and have a child. I was glad when you came and found things for him to do all day. I understand now. If you stay, he will. I'm very glad."

"We're going to be busy starting the factory so he can make a living. That's another reason why we'll be together a great deal. You won't mind being alone?"

"Women don't mind being alone. Soon, when I know I'm going to have a child, I won't be alone."

"When will you know?"

"I know now but in a few days it will be sure. It's time."

She said it with such quiet conviction that he accepted it as fact. He was moved by an irrational sense of participation. He felt his possession of Lance's body so intensely that he had to remind himself that they

169

hadn't known each other at the time of conception. As he imagined him poised over her, the delicate thrust of his golden flesh was so unforgettably part of his experience that he was ready to believe that he had somehow witnessed and blessed their union.

Life was amazing. After the placid years of his working routine, he was being drawn into the vortex of a domestic drama, the drama of birth. He was uprooted, in love, responsible not only for the man he adored but also for his family. It had been a big night. "You haven't told him," he said. "He'll be happy."

"I think so now. I wasn't sure before you came. We'll tell him before your party."

"Our party."

Lance reappeared near his tropical shower stall. "I'm going down to the rocks, darling," he called. "Get everything settled."

Robbie lifted a hand to acknowledge him and looked at the radiantly naked body as it turned from him. He wanted to leap up and follow but ordered himself to remain with the girl. It was important for her to trust them and be content with the life they were planning. She could pose problems that he didn't think Lance was ready for yet. Robbie didn't want him to reject her and his child any more than he wanted to impose restrictions on themselves for her sake.

They talked about the party and the guests they would invite. He offered to cook a big fish and make an *aioli* sauce to go with it and told her what the sauce was made of. They agreed that the rest of the meal would consist of her local specialties. She was quietly and sweetly responsive and obviously grateful to him for including her in the plans so that he enjoyed being with her as much as he could enjoy being anywhere without Lance. He was freed by her mentioning lunch.

"I'd like a swim first if there's time," he said.

"But certainly. Lunch is ready whenever he wishes it."

He rose, forgetting to cover himself with the towel. When he remembered it seemed a bit late to bother. He smiled as he turned from her and threw the towel over his shoulder and headed for the eucalyptus tree that marked the descent to the sea. He leaped lightly down the rough steps, remembering that this was where

Lance was supposed to have had his unconvincing fall. Thinking of the rape made his blood stir with protective rage. Lance was his. He'd always thought hitting people was barbaric but he was ready to fight anybody who threatened his possession of him. He was rather pleased to discover there was a bit of the caveman in him.

He rounded the last outcropping of rock and came to an abrupt halt. A flat, narrow ledge sloped to the edge of the water. Lance was sprawled out on his back, eyes closed with unguarded abandon, his burnished rose-gold body offered to any taker on a battered mattress. He took a few silent steps closer. This was the familiar body of their beachcombing days, stripped by the sun of its exquisite nighttime ambiguity, athletic, manly, unattainable, except that, instead of being nestled between his legs, his cock was stretched out rigidly on his belly.

The heavy lids lifted slowly and their eyes met. Lance's body contracted with a quick intake of breath and his hands jerked up and fell to his sides. "I got myself ready." His voice was darkly tense.

Robbie sprang forward and Lance rolled up onto his hands and knees as he reached him. They both cried out with the impact of their bodies' reunion. Lance shouted, a strange cry of triumph and disbelief, and gave himself to his lover's conquest. This was what he wanted, subjugation to the will of a man who wanted him, a celebration of lawlessness, public and defiant. They couldn't be seen from above but people sometimes passed in boats. They could watch all they liked while Robbie fucked Lance Cosling.

An hour later, surfeited with sex, invigorated by the sea, light-headed with love and physical well-being, they started back up to the house.

"Don't let me forget I have things to do this afternoon," Robbie said.

"Oh no. This is the first day of our life together. You can't go anywhere."

"I've got to, beautiful. I have business to take care of. You can come with me if you want to."

"Want to? I'm glued to your side. What's the business?"

"I have to tell the lawyer to put Luisa's name on the deed and I want to make sure my house will be ready for me day after tomorrow. I want to move in and get to work."

Lance stopped and turned to him. They faced each other on the steep rocky path. "I understand that but what'll you move in where? Will I move anything?"

"It doesn't look so, does it. Our life suddenly seems so simple. I'll get my work set up there and you'll be going to work at the shed. When we finish, it'll be nice to come back here for a swim and drinks and dinner and bed. We can't swim from my house. We'll go off together in the morning. I think Luisa would like that arrangement."

"She understands that we're going to sleep to gether?"

"I told her so, not necessarily every night but I told her that we like to. Telling her we're brothers was a stroke of genius. Once I said that, she seemed to think everything was perfectly normal. The people here must lead very peculiar family lives."

They laughed. Lance touched Robbie's smiling lips with his fingers. "As usual, you know what we're doing."

"I know about homosexual marriage. Women are *your* department. I'm just trying to put it together so it works, first of all for us, but for her too. Eating here, for example. It's convenient for us having a cook but it'll make her feel that she's doing the job that's expected of her—keeping house for her man. Have you been a very constant lover, sweetheart?"

"Well, more or less every day. Not dozens of times like us but usually once. Often in the afternoon before you came."

"Once you're working you won't have afternoons off. That'll help but do you think you can keep her happy if we sleep together? I want to know everything so we don't hurt her unnecessarily."

"It won't be a problem when she's pregnant. I know of Catholics who renounce sex while that's going on. Fucking for pleasure is a sin."

"We're in luck. She says she'll know any day now."

"I guess that's about right. It started a few weeks before you got here. Why're we standing here? We have the most fascinating conversations in the damnedest places. I could stand on the bottom of the sea with you and not notice I was drowning."

172

Robbie laughed and put an arm around his shoulders as they started up the uneven steps again. "I've got to have dinner tonight with Flip. It would be too damn rude not to. It's bad enough skipping lunch. I'll come back to bed with you but I'd like to go through the rest of the day as if everything I told Luisa were true—about having lived together this way for years and so on. I don't want her to think there was anything special about last night. Let's just act as if we don't know whether I'm coming back this evening or not. If I'm not here by the time you're ready to go to bed, don't worry. I'll knock over some furniture to let you know I'm ready and waiting. We'll be in the other room?"

"I guess so, if you don't want to change her routine. I hope you appreciate how reasonable I'm being about your leaving me for the evening. I don't feel at all reasonable. I'm devoured by ugly suspicions. Does Flip have a houseful of bewitching young men?"

Robbie chuckled. "You'll see. I'm going to ask her to invite you for dinner tomorrow. She'll want to make a big fuss about us when I tell her what's going on. I'll bring all my stuff back here afterwards and be ready to move the next day. I hope you appreciate how reasonable *I'm* being about Luisa. God. How could I have fallen in love with a man with a pregnant girl friend?"

"Love has driven you mad, darling."

"Probably. I even think we all might get used to each other. As soon as she knows the house is hers and is sure about being pregnant, I doubt if she'll bother much about what we're up to. When I told her that I'd keep you away from other women, I knew I'd won the day. She's so sweet that I'm apt to fall over backwards making everything pleasant for her. We'll be doing her a favor if we keep her busy in her house, doing whatever pregnant women are supposed to do. She might not notice how difficult it is for her man to escape the clutches of his gentleman friend." They laughed with happy complicity. "It's probably a better life than she'd've had without you."

"That may be true now that you're in charge but I ought to be shot for starting something I hadn't the slightest idea how I was going to finish. You're making everything too easy for me. I've got to prove that I'm worth your bother."

173

They hugged each other as they reached the top of the climb. Lance saw Luisa moving about in the shade of the terrace and waved without disengaging himself from Robbie's embrace. They took a quick circumspect shower and put on their sarongs for lunch.

"I always dress for meals," Lance explained. "God knows why but I feel funny being naked when I'm eating."

They sat side by side for the fiery meal with Luisa opposite them. She thought it very splendid to have two men to look after her, both of them so handsome. They made her want to laugh because they were laughing a lot.

She looked contentedly at them. They had their arms around each other, Lance's around Robbie's shoulders, Robbie's holding Lance's waist from behind. The way Lance looked at his brother reminded her of a very bold girl trying to win a man. She could understand his wanting to please him. She imagined that the great Spanish lords who had come here long ago must have been like Robbie. He had the princely air of a man accustomed to command, a powerful master, yet gentle and kind.

They let go of each other to eat the pineapple she put on the table. Perhaps Robbie could teach her enough English so that she could follow what they said and even speak a little to them. There were many things in life she had never dreamed of wanting for herself. She had hardly even dared dream of having a bed all to herself, although she had always thought it would be pleasant to sleep without being crowded by others. At home, she was used to sharing with one or another of her brothers. It was nicer with Lance but she would feel like a queen if she had her own bed in her own house. She felt that Robbie might make many changes but she trusted him. She was glad that he was here to make Lance happy, to save him from being tempted by other women and to take care of him at night.

"I'll teach you how to peel a pineapple so that it looks pretty with no skin," he said, turning his big dark eyes to her. "That's something else we'll do for the party. We'll get all kinds of fruit, oranges and bananas and pineapples and mangoes, and make a beautiful salad with sugar and rum. It will make them more drunk. That's what a party is for, to make people drunk."

"Do you think I can have another dress for the party?" she asked, feeling very daring but sensing that they were both in a mood to indulge her.

"I'm sure Lance would love to get you one but I'm going to give it to you. I'll pick one out with you."

"You're very wonderful. You'll show me what I should wear, what the foreign women wear." The party gave her the unfamiliar pleasure of having something to talk about and she continued to explore its inexhaustible possibilities with the man who had become, she realized, the head of the household, as much Lance's master as hers, the lawgiver.

Pineapple disposed of, Lance's hand stole under Robbie's sarong to his cock. He hadn't known that simply holding it would be so thrilling, a hard column of smooth warm flesh that swelled prodigiously under his touch. He wanted to goad Robbie into some overt demonstration of their love, to involve him somehow with Luisa so that his own exclusive connection with her would be broken. He pushed folds of cloth away and freed it. Towering, it threatened to emerge from under the table. Robbie continued to talk to her about the party as if he hadn't another thought in his head.

He let his hand stray slowly, tantalizingly up and down Robbie's erection, gripping it to feel it straining against confinement, releasing it to stir restlessly against his teasing fingertips. Robbie shifted in his chair. "Careful, sweetheart," he said without turning his head.

"You know what I want?" Lance addressed his handsome profile.

"I think so. More or less."

"Will you?"

"I don't know. It might make sense. Let me handle it, sweetheart. I don't want to shock her."

He could feel Lance building up to some madness. He probably wouldn't be satisfied until Luisa saw them in each other's arms. Robbie suspected that it wouldn't bother her in the least if they managed somehow not to make her feel excluded. She had been trained to obey men. She was eager to learn about the great world. She would probably accept anything if they acted with sufficient authority to make her feel that it was quite commonplace where they came from. He slid his arm around Lance and began to caress his shoulders and chest. He felt Lance's breath catch and was aware of sharply questioning eyes on him. He continued to look at Luisa.

"Do you want to go to bed with us now?" he asked, wondering if Lance understood what he was saying. "I know he would like it. So would I. Would you?"

Her eyes widened but her expression remained placid and unperturbed. "I understand. You're brothers. It's natural for me to be for you both."

He turned to Lance and dropped his hands to his elbows, urging him up. He saw the hesitation and uncertainty in his eyes and laughed with delight at turning the tables on him.

He got a firm grip on his arms and pulled him up. Lance uttered an exclamation of protest as his tangled sarong caught on something and fell off. His erection swung up close to Robbie's face. Robbie laughed and darted his head forward and touched it with a flick of his tongue. He turned to Luisa and caught an unexpected gleam of humor in her eyes. "He's a fine man, isn't he?" he said, exchanging a glance of collusion with her. "I envy you having his child."

He had an arm around Lance's waist and held him against his side and caressed his balls. His erection was no novelty for her. She had lived close enough to nature so that he imagined she wouldn't be disconcerted by a second one. He rose, leaving his sarong over the chair.

"My God, darling," Lance muttered.

Robbie chuckled, feeling wonderfully adaptable. He was pushing it but he thought it was going to work. He felt unexpectedly self-confident as he moved to take charge. It seemed natural to let Luisa see his cock in vigorous erection, establishing its authority. He circled the table and touched her bare shoulder. "Let's go, darling." Holding Luisa's hand lightly, he led the way to the bedroom they had all shared.

"What're we going to do?" Lance sounded bewildered.

Robbie gave his shoulder a reassuring hug. "Whatever you were thinking about. It's your party. I imagine I'm going to lose my virginity, or at least a bit of it. She expects it. It'll make everything seem simpler to her."

Robbie was taking over, as Lance had hoped he would. His heart was beating with anticipation when they entered the bedroom. Robbie made their being naked together natural and unselfconscious, lively with promise, rather than the furtive display of physical intimacy that Lance had originally had in mind.

Luisa slipped off her skirts as if they were an unfamiliar nuisance to her. Lance quickly applied lubricant to himself. Robbie caught his eye and smiled and winked with comprehension. Lance and Luisa lay side by side, Lance on his stomach. Robbie climbed up over them on his hands and knees. He laughed down at her and said something that Lance didn't understand. She laughed with him. She seemed more relaxed and uninhibited than she'd ever been with Lance. They played with each other and laughed softly together. Lance was amazed. The visceral flutterings of jealousy were swept away in a burst of euphoria. He and Robbie were entering into each other's existence more deeply and intensely than he had thought was possible.

Luisa lifted her knees eagerly when Robbie dropped down to her. For a moment, Lance felt cruelly mistreated but it was so amazing to see his lover's magnificent body in sexual action that he forgot jealousy again. He could tell from the little sounds Luisa was making that Robbie pleased her.

Robbie's mouth played with her breasts as if he were accustomed to a girl's body. The thrust of his hips accelerated and from the look on his face and his quickened breathing Lance knew that he was approaching orgasm. The shudder that passed over Luisa told him that hers had started. Jealousy became a knot somewhere around his heart but his vicarious excitement was bringing him close to orgasm, too.

Robbie suddenly withdrew from the girl and flung himself on Lance and drove into him. Lance uttered a cry as his body was charged with ecstasy. It was what he'd been longing for. They were publicly demonstrating the nature of their love; everything was open and acknowledged.

"Don't come yet," Robbie ordered against his ear. "I want you in her." He pulled him upright on his knees and moved him to her. He pushed him forward and they lowered themselves to her, she lifted her hips and Lance

177

entered her, Robbie managing somehow to remain in him without limiting his freedom of movement. He had achieved an incredible union. Lance felt as if he were taking her with Robbie's cock. They were having her together. Their orgasms were simultaneous.

After a moment, Robbie took him from her and they lay beside her with all of Robbie's weight on top of him, still hard in him. In the deep silence, their breathing was faintly audible. Luisa sat up. "I must go back to the kitchen," she said in a normal voice.

"Yes, little one," Lance murmured.

She slipped out of bed, not wishing to disturb them, and stepped into her skirts and left them, startled but pleased. Robbie had been kind to her while establishing himself as their master. Any woman would be proud to have him lie with her. His brother, the father of her child, was as much his dependent as she was. It made her his equal. Their letting her watch what they did together must mean that they had nothing to be ashamed of. She had a lot to learn about foreign ways, but her own position in the household was secure. Robbie wouldn't let his brother have other women. He had promised her and she understood now his power to decide. Lance was her man but in a different way than he had been before. It was puzzling but it settled everything. She could love Lance without fearing the future.

Robbie lay on his back while Lance washed and dried him as Luisa sometimes did for him after their lovemaking.

"How did you ever think of that?" Lance asked.

Robbie laughed. "I've heard of people doing it like that. You were Lucky Pierre."

"It was amazing. Something tremendous happened. I don't think I can be jealous of you anymore. Everything you do is part of me. All of a sudden, I feel human. I don't think I ever have before."

Robbie stretched a hand out quickly to grip his knee, touched but alert to his shifting moods. He wondered if he was talking about the sort of revelation he remembered from his adolescence when the amorphous, vaguely hostile forces surrounding him had dissolved into individual people. Lance was still so incredibly young. "Welcome," he said, purring with delighted laughter. "How do you like the human race?"

178

"It feels real. I'm getting perspective. Being in love with you isn't so blinding anymore. I can see who I'm in love with. That's wonderful. I'm going to get to know you more and more, not just want to go to bed with you. That must be what makes falling in love so exciting. It was like that with Scot except that sex has more to do with it than I realized. Did it seem funny to you having Luisa?"

"Not particularly. I was thinking about you all the time." He watched adoringly as Lance rose and carried the washing things back to the stand. "It was pretty peculiar but I think it turned out right," he said. "We couldn't go on hiding from her in this place, with everything open."

Lance returned and stretched out beside him. Robbie's arms were waiting for him, drawing him closer, fitting his body in against him, asserting his possession of him. There was only Robbie now. His homosexuality had become a public fact. "It was sort of like burning the bridges," he said thoughtfully.

"Yes. I know what you mean. Don't come out with me. Stay with her this afternoon. It won't take long for me to do our business. If she seems upset, jolly her along until I get back. I don't think we have anything to worry about."

"Imagine anybody being upset by your fucking them."

Robbie relinquished him and threw his legs over the edge of the bed and sprang up. "Give me some shorts, beautiful. It'll save me a trip back to Flip's. I can't wander around town in a skirt."

"Do you think I have anything you can get your beautiful ass into? Help yourself. I want to see." He waved at the flimsy curtain of the makeshift closet against one wall.

"Have you seen my knickers around?"

"What do you mean by knickers?"

"My smalls." He chuckled as Lance continued to look blank. "I forget you Americans don't speak English. My jockey shorts. Here." He found what he was looking for on a chair with his shirt and put them both on before looking behind the curtain to complete his costume.

Lance watched entranced as he wandered around the room as if he lived here. The pale blue shorts he put on were a skintight sheath for the seductive curves of

179

his buttocks. He had a friend who could wear his clothes, take his girl friend, do anything he liked with his body. He was getting ready to take care of business that concerned them both. Their shared life was beginning to acquire shape and definition. It would soon grow up around them and acquire its permanent form, excluding everything else. He was as queer as a coot and bubbling with happiness.

"My God," he exclaimed. "If *you* don't get raped, there's no justice in the world." He gathered himself together and bounced to his feet. "You better go before I take my shorts back." Going somewhere was part of being together. Life was partings and reunions. When they were apart, they would find out what living together was going to be like. Robbie offered him the smile that had become a signal of his love, touched him on his cheek, and left.

Lance wandered around the room, touching things without seeing them, waiting to find out what he was when he was alone. His happiness was Robbie's. It slowly dwindled as Robbie's absence permitted what still seemed an irreconcilable contradiction to move to the front of his mind: was it possible for the sublimation inherent in love to coexist with perversion? The revelations of the rape were too fresh to be ignored. José's threat was a menace he might not be able to escape. What of the great urge downward? If Robbie could label it, he must see it clearly as a danger.

Homosexuality sat on him like an ill-fitting suit; he wondered if he would ever grow into it. Only Robbie could make it feel right for him. He didn't want to act or think for himself until Robbie came back. He didn't want to be anybody without Robbie. He heard the familiar sounds of Luisa washing up in the kitchen, alien to him now, no longer the sounds of his own household. Robbie wanted him to spend some time with her while he was gone. Thinking of what Robbie wanted made him feel more sure of himself.

He paused, looking around him to reestablish connections with his surroundings, retrieved his sarong, and wrapped it around himself. His nakedness belonged to Robbie. Luisa looked up from the sink as he entered the kitchen. He had to make a small effort to meet her eye. He realized that all this time—how long had it been? Over a month. Not yet two—he hadn't really felt involved with her until today. She had been a peaceful, decorative presence who satisfied him in bed. Now she had witnessed him in an act of unnatural passion. She must have been affected by it in some way. He went to her and touched her breast, in the way he often did, to show her that nothing had changed between them. "Are you happy, little one?" he asked.

She looked at him, her expression clear and untroubled. "Yes. I'm happy he is here. He makes you happy. It was a sin for me to do it with him but you're brothers. It's almost the same as with you. I'm proud that he wanted it. It is usual, what you do with him?"

He blushed but she sounded curious rather than shocked. He made a little shrugging movement with his shoulders. "We love each other. That is the way it is."

"Here, it's considered shameful but I know everything is different for foreigners. He says you like to be together at night. May I have the room we've never used?"

"You not wish the same as always?"

"No. I would like a room that's my own. It's my dream."

"Why you not say it?"

"It's usual for a woman to lie with her man if he wishes it. When the baby is in me it'll be a great sin if I lie with you."

"I have the same thought. We do as you wish."

She looked at him in a way that was new to him. Her smile was playful, almost coquettish. "Then bring me all the linen from the room and anything else you want washed. I must do the laundry later." She looked at him as an equal. He had always wanted to make her feel his equal. Sensing the change in her, he knew that it was Robbie who had managed it. "You can help me make the beds before he comes back."

Amazing. She had always balked when he offered to help her. He had never seen her look so lively and awake. There was something almost comradely in the way she was treating him. He remembered Robbie's warning not to let the day seem special in any way. "He maybe not come back tonight. He stays with Mrs. Rawls until tomorrow."

181

"I think he'll be back. He would rather be with you than Señora Rawls. This is going to be his home even though he says it's mine."

Making the bed they had never used, the bed she had chosen for herself, he thought he detected a faint trace of teasing superiority in her smile and realized that she would think of this as woman's work. Blushing again, he had an impulse to tip her over onto the clean sheets to remind her that he was still her man, but his heart wasn't in it. He was all fucked out. The thought of performing his manly duty on her sweetly passive body struck him as flat and uninspiring. His erotic potential had been stirred and stretched, he had learned to give himself to a man.

He took care of his own chores, looking after the chickens, collecting a few eggs, pumping water, and began to get restless for Robbie's return. Washing and shaving wasn't much of a diversion. He wanted to hear Robbie's voice, see his smile, feel his hand on him. He hadn't understood what guys meant when they talked about being in love with each other. Now he did.

He had told himself for the dozenth time that there weren't enough cars on the road for there to be any serious risk of an accident when he heard Robbie's returning footsteps. He held himself very still, discovering what it was like to have everything he wanted in life, to have all his wishes fulfilled, before rushing to the end of the house. They met where they had exchanged their first awkward kiss. Their eyes flew to each other, halting them a few feet apart, searching, questioning, reestablishing connections. He flung himself into Robbie's arms and welcomed him with his open mouth. He sucked in his stomach and let his sarong fall off. He wasn't all fucked out with Robbie. His mind erupted with fragmentary images of orgiastic violence and he ground his hips in against him, flaunting his erection. He wanted Robbie to take him on the spot, commit some outrage with him that only men together would be capable of. Hands soothed him. His mind cleared as peace returned. He drew back with a little shudder.

Robbie looked at him wonderingly. "Do you really want me so much, my dearest?"

"Oh God," he blurted with choked laughter. He gave

182

his head a shake and lifted it. "I'm glad you went. Now I know what it's like to get you back. Heavenly choirs announce your entrance, just like Radio City Music Hall."

They laughed and Robbie held up a dripping paper bag. "I found a bar with ice."

"My goodness, what luxury." He snatched up his sarong and tied it carelessly around himself and hastily adjusted his manner to conform to the occasion. Robbie was so sane and decent, like the sanely sensitive beauty of his face; he probably hated his outbursts of unbalanced emotion. He'd been gone a couple of hours, not a week.

They strolled back along the terrace to the table where Luisa had left glasses and a pitcher of pineapple juice and a bottle of rum. "I like living with you," Lance said, as if bringing him up to date on the latest developments while he poured drinks. "Not twenty-four hours yet. Shall we try it for another day?"

"I think we're going to have to. We have a lot to do. Everything's happening at once. We can sign for our company tomorrow and the lease with Señor Diaz. We ought to order a load of clay and a few tons of wood for the kilns. The lawyer says it'd be a good idea to have a local connected with the company so I told him to make Luisa a director. We'll take care of her house the next day."

"Everything was fine with her this afternoon. You were right. Nothing to worry about."

"I'm glad, dearest. Did you mention what we did?"

"She referred to it quite casually. She's got the picture." They wandered with their drinks to the parapet and looked out at the sky's evening display of fireworks.

"I ran into the bank manager. My money came this afternoon, so that's all right. Our money."

"All I want is a salary and I'll live on it. That's what I've always wanted—a weekly wage that's gone when you've spent it and no fuss with banks and charge accounts and all the boring business with money. We can put my traveler's checks in our account so that our money is all mixed up together like we were this morning."

"I hope our money enjoys it as much as we did. You're adorable. Pascal would've loved you. Maurice was al-

ways quoting him. Pascal said that a workman dreaming of being a king would be almost as happy as a king
dreaming that he was a workman. I like the 'almost.'
You don't even have to dream. You're going to *be* a
workman."

"Make fun of me all you like but you're giving me
the life I've dreamed of without even knowing it, any
more than I knew I was dreaming of belonging to a
man. I wonder what Pascal would've said about that."

"Something sensible, I'm sure. What do you know
about cars, sweetheart? I haven't had a chance to tell
you. I talked to the car-rental people the other day.
They want to sell us a three-year-old Dodge for a couple
of hundred dollars. I told them that if it survives the
trip down here, we might consider it. It's supposed to
be coming in the next couple of days. Will you be able
to tell if it's worth buying?"

"Oh, darling, you know I don't know anything practical. You're absolutely amazing. You talked to them
how?"

"The telephone, sweetheart. That's the thing with
wires. Flip has one. It takes half an hour to get through
to the capital but it works. We'll probably have to have
one, either here or at the shed. Mail is pretty quick,
about the same as Europe, but when orders start pouring in, we might have to be in direct touch."

"Amazing. I've had one letter since I've been here. I
was in such a state coming down that I haven't had a
very clear idea where I am. Telephones, telegrams—I
just assumed they didn't exist."

"I could do without them but they have their uses.
I still have a lot to do. I've got to write to Paris and
change my will. Don't push me over a cliff till I let you
know it's arranged. My little half brothers and half
sisters, if any, will be destitute. Fancy leaving things
to a Vanderholden. The world is full of surprises."

Lance was silent. His throat and the muscles of his
cheeks were working in a struggle for control as his
face was contorted with anguish. "Oh, well. What's the
use," he said thickly. A sob broke from him and he
laughed as tears began to stream down his cheeks. All
the strains of the last few years seemed to gather in
him, blocking his chest as he choked on a sob. His tears
flowed with gratitude. "How is it possible?" he said

through labored breathing. "Even if you've been in love with me for a week, how can I mean so much to you? Are all queers like this?"

"I don't know, my beloved. I learned a lot from Maurice. If our lives are going to be joined, they might as well be joined in every possible way. No loose ends. Nothing held back." He moved in closer and leaned forward and tasted his tears. "So sweet. My sweet beloved darling. Your eyelashes all starry with tears. So precious. Each eyelash more precious to me than the whole world." He ran his lips over them and licked them dry.

Lance let his body go against him and made an odd little wailing sound in his throat. He put a foot up on the parapet. "I've got a hard-on again. You said you'd give it an hour to recover. It's been closer to two. I hope you're not going to think up some sensible reason why we shouldn't go to bed." He sounded indignant through his subsiding tears.

Robbie chuckled. "I've got a hard-on, too, but if we go to bed every time that happens we might as well stay there. Where's Luisa? She usually joins us when we're having drinks. I don't want to change the routine today."

"As it happens, she's doing the laundry but I thought we agreed we wouldn't let her come between us."

"We won't—just give her time to get used to a new routine, even if it turns out to be our spending all our time in bed."

"That's more like it." Lance flipped his sarong and his erection swung free of it and pointed at the sky. "I don't see how you can resist doing something about that. I couldn't if you showed me yours."

"Who says I can?" He ran a hand under it and lifted it higher. "Such a scandalous big thing. Let's go."

They held on to each other as they made their erratic progress toward the bedroom, laughing breathlessly, wrestling with each other, getting Robbie out of his shirt. They threw discarded clothing onto a chair and fell onto the bed, grappling with each other, trying to talk and laugh and kiss and make love to various parts of each other all at the same time.

They dived for each other and gathered their ejaculations into their mouths. They laughed and rolled over each other and ended up on their backs with their heads together, breathing heavily. After a brief silence, Robbie found Lance's hand and squeezed it. "That might have lacked artistry but it was certainly fun," he said.

"Mmmm. It was, wasn't it? Everything is fun with you. How can anybody help being queer when you are? It's the only way to be."

"I've always thought so." Robbie sat up and dropped his legs over the side of the bed. "What're we doing in here? I thought we were moving to the other room."

"That's all settled. She wants it to herself. I told you she might have scruples about sex when she's pregnant. She's glad you're here to satisfy my low animal needs." He moved up against Robbie's back. "Are you still going to have dinner with Flip?"

"I must, beautiful. It's the last time I'll do anything like that without you. Today is our engagement. A short one, thank God. Tomorrow night she can introduce us as a couple and then we'll be married."

"Don't forget to tell her about my name."

"Did you mean that, darling?"

"Of course. I never want to hear of the Vanderholdens again." He leaned forward over Robbie's shoulder and rubbed his cheek against his. "Such a whiskery guy. It's sexy. I may make you grow a beard."

"If we're still together when I'm forty, I might oblige. That'll give you something to aim for."

"We're really talking about a lifetime, aren't we? It's so hard for me to imagine. After ten years, did you want Maurice as much as you did in the beginning?"

"Yes. More, actually. As time passes, sex with someone you love becomes so complete that it doesn't make any sense with anybody else. That's the way it was with Maurice until I saw you. I said I might've left him for you but it's probably not true. There was so much of us that existed only for each other. He took that part of me with him. Everything we have will be just for us."

"That's what I want. That's the way it's bound to be anyway because there's so little of me so far. It's wonderful in a way. We've found each other just at the right moment, just when I'm ready to start being somebody. I realize that sex for me from now on is giving myself to you. In ten years there should be a lot more of me to give you."

Robbie swiveled around to him and hugged him. "Shall we have another drink before the ice melts?"

They drifted back along the terrace in their sarongs. Luisa emerged from the kitchen. Robbie went to her and took her hand and looked her in the eye. Lance was right. They could all be together without strain. Lance poured her a glass of pineapple juice and put some ice in it. She looked at it suspiciously before taking a cautious taste. She wrinkled her nose.

"It's so cold. It has no taste."

"You're a born Englishman," Robbie told her. "I think we should buy an icebox for your house. There's an icehouse in town. You'll be able to keep food longer."

She liked being compared to foreigners, although she didn't understand what made her like an Englishman. At the party, she would try to find out whether the foreigners' houses were more like North American houses than this one. She sat with her cold tasteless drink and watched them with enjoyment. They had sprawled out at either end of the cot. Lance had his feet up on Robbie's knees and they were playing games with them and making each other laugh. She found them very endearing, like children. She finished her drink and, as night fell, lighted the lamps and returned to the kitchen without distracting their attention from each other. They were beginning to ignore her presence, the way she expected men to treat a woman in her house.

Lance refilled their glasses and dropped the last of the ice into them and took Robbie his. He settled down on the cot again but close to Robbie with his legs tucked under him and his arm along the back of Robbie's shoulders. He leaned in against him and ran the tip of his tongue around his ear. Robbie murmured with pleasure. Lance laughed and snuggled in closer and dropped his head on his shoulder with a contented sigh. "My goodness. This is something new. I think maybe this is the best of all—just feeling as if I belong to you without making love. Not that I'm not thinking about that too."

"We just have, remember?"

He swallowed his drink and put down the glass, taking Lance's hands in both of his. He looked into the candid clarity of his blue eyes. Not even their mysterious hooded look could rob them of innocence. There was so much simple goodness in him.

"I've got to go, sweetheart."

"Go on, darling, and hurry back to me. I'll be fairly ready for you if I stay hard for the next few hours." He kissed him with a brief play of his tongue on his lips and then gave him a little push. "Hurry up and get it over with. I want to hang on to you until you tear yourself away from me, but we're living together now. We can't have a big farewell scene every time you go to the bathroom. Have a nice dinner."

"You weren't expecting to include Luisa in tomorrow night's events, were you?"

"Oh no. That's for us to make our debut. That's when the hornets start buzzing around me. We don't want Luisa to throw them off the scent."

"Okay. Here I go. Never again. I won't be late." He gave Lance's cock a caressing pat and rose, looking down at him. He looked peaceful and contented and totally angelic, as delicate as the odd exquisite delicacy of his strong body.

Lance pulled himself to his feet. Their erections swung out under their sarongs. He giggled. "It seems to be contagious." They returned mirthfully to the bedroom to collect Robbie's shirt and toilet case. Lance took the lubricant and put it beside the bed. "I'm not going to let you take *that* with you to Flip's," he said.

They joked together until they reached the path at the end of the house. They stopped and looked into each other's eyes and their laughter died. Lance spoke with awed constraint. "It's almost impossible, isn't it? I'll cease to exist again until you come back. I'm yours, darling."

"You're all I'll ever want. I adore you, my beloved darling." Their bodies swayed to each other but Robbie got a grip on himself and turned quickly with a wave of his hand and was gone.

Reverting to his established routine, he sat opposite Luisa for their supper and Lance began to wonder if he'd invented the last twenty-four hours. Watching Luisa eating placidly, he found it hard to believe that a week ago he'd been ready to accept an evening like this as the best he could hope for from life. No silly fun, no electrifying excitement, no danger from his body's violent ecstasy.

When they'd eaten, he gathered up plates and followed her to the kitchen, staying to help her wash up. She already seemed to take it for granted and clearly enjoyed the new sense of companionship it created between them.

When the time came, he couldn't help feeling uncomfortable about letting her go off alone to her new room. He eased his conscience by following her to the door and telling her that he would join her later if Robbie didn't get back.

"Oh no. He'll be back." She stood near the end of the bed and looked around the room wonderingly before adding, "It's very wonderful to have a room of my own."

Robbie found him naked and asleep on the cot, covered only by the open book on his chest. His eyes took in the tube of lubricant on the table beside the cot as he removed the book cautiously and stood in rapt contemplation of his golden beauty. Talk of Lance had dominated the evening. Flip's house party was agog at the prospect of meeting him. They had all, except Flip herself, seen his show. One of them had tried to sign him for Hollywood. They all agreed that he was one of the most glamorous figures of the age. They knew that Robbie had been seeing a lot of him and when it emerged that they were going to start a business and settle down here, innuendo had become rife.

He smiled to himself, looking down at him, and silently stripped. He wanted to learn every subtle line and contour of him before his eyes grew careless. The time would come when he would no longer see him but only feel him, his physical and spiritual presence, while his eyes were eternally held by the light in his face and the play of his mouth. He lifted Lance's hand away for an unobstructed view of the rigid flesh it had been guarding. The intricate network of veins under the golden skin held his absorbed attention. Forms unfolded in his mind. He was suddenly filled with a consuming need to work. Life was beginning again. Ghosts had been laid to rest.

Until now, all his life had been shaped by his origins—parents, France, work, Maurice, one had led

189

to another to form a homogeneous block of experience. As much as Lance, he had been born anew last night. He and his life's companion were starting from scratch together. He wanted to find out how it would affect his work. He was alive and whole and bursting with energy, ready to take Lance as fiercely as Lance wanted to be taken.

He closed his own hand slowly around Lance's cock and a shiver of delight ran down his spine as its hard bulk filled his fist. Once a size queen, always a size queen. He had heard the expression for the first time in New York not long ago and had recognized himself in it with amusement. He leaned over and lifted it to his mouth and indulged his passion for it while he imagined being taken by it. That would come. Meanwhile, his cock was positively afire to reestablish his possession of his sleeping beauty. He had never felt it so full of inflexible male determination.

He reached across to the table for the lubricant. He eased himself over beside his sleeping love and gathered him into his arms. Feeling their bodies against each other was almost fulfillment enough and he lay still for a moment, letting the glory of it seep into him before he began to cover his face with light playful kisses. Lance awoke adorably with little grunts and murmurs and a burst of soft laughter. He stretched, snaking himself in closer with his eyes still closed, and lifted caressing hands to Robbie's face.

"Oh, God, you're here," he murmured. "I left the stuff there. I don't want to wake up until I'm part of you again." He rolled away onto his side.

Robbie was almost paralyzed with tenderness. He had to learn to balance it with the cool high-handed authority Lance expected of him. He prepared them and entered him slowly. Lance's body was inert and motionless with surrender. He seemed to make himself a receptacle for all the love that Robbie could offer him. There was no fierceness in him tonight, only a tranquil passive giving of himself. Robbie's throat ached with tenderness as he felt his cock growing into him, making a spine-tingling advance, joining them. He pulled him gently in against him, feeling his cock deep inside him, long, imperious, taking what was his.

"There," Lance murmured. "You're huge in me, darling. Have you ever felt anything so complete? Let's stay like this all night. I don't want to come for hours. Have you been back long?"

"I managed to keep my hands off you for a minute or two. You'll never know how devastating you are when you're asleep with a hard-on."

Lance gurgled with laughter. "You've got me." He worked obscure muscles. "My God, have you got me. Does everybody know now?"

"Flip drew some fairly obvious conclusions from my absence. I told her it was for life. She wanted to know about Luisa, of course. I said we were setting up a very civilized *ménage à trois*. Everybody's wild to meet you."

"Did you tell her about my name?"

"Yes. She got into quite a tangle about Vanderholdens and Lord This and Lord That. She seemed to think it was a suitable match."

"Can you imagine our having different names now?" Lance pressed himself closer, rotating his hips slowly to feel him moving in him, making his possession of him deep and absolute. He made a crooning sound of contentment.

Robbie lowered his head so that their lips almost touched. Lance closed his eyes and opened his mouth wide like a bird in the nest waiting to be fed. Robbie filled it with his tongue. His lips were soft and slack with the inertia of his body's surrender. Their saliva flowed to each other and they swallowed it gratefully as if it were a precious elixir.

Laughter cut through Lance's voice again. "You shaved. God, you're handsome."

"Oh, I almost forgot," Robbie said. "I got some mail. My friend Larry has come through with an order for five hundred of your dollies."

"You're kidding. Somebody's paying money for those silly things, sight unseen?"

"They're not silly, sweetheart. They're fascinating. I told you so. I did some sketches and described them. I knew they'd go. He says he can't pay more than a dollar apiece but that's all right for a start. We'll screw him when he wants more."

"My God, we're really in business." His face was alight with what he turned into a shared success. "Oh darling, how exciting. We're in business together. Don't

191

worry about Larry. Screw *me*. Hard, darling. Screw me till I holler for help."

Lance freed his hands and seized Robbie's hair, writhing against him and biting his neck, his chest beginning to heave. Robbie rolled up on top of him. Lance's body thrashed about under him, arms and legs flailing. Robbie's ownership was being challenged. Understanding the nature of the challenge, he met it, using his cock ruthlessly, reveling in its punishing size as it ignited lust. He locked them in against each other and drove them to orgasm while Lance shouted and bucked with his body's powerless rage.

By morning their union had become so much a part of them that they didn't feel Luisa's presence as an invasion of their privacy. They came up from a morning swim with towels wrapped around themselves sarong-fashion and joined her for one of her peculiar breakfasts of cornmeal and beans and eggs. They both gave her a brief good-morning kiss and she sat with them while they planned the day's program. The language barrier permitted them to speak freely in front of her. When Lance referred teasingly to something they'd done during the night, Robbie hoped she wouldn't get beyond "darling" in her English studies. They switched to Spanish to tell her about meals.

"We'll be very busy all day," Robbie explained. "We'll have lunch out as usual. Tonight we'll have dinner with Mrs. Rawls. Not a party, just a few people because I'm leaving her. She thinks she speaks Spanish but she doesn't. I thought it would be tiresome for you to have to pretend to understand what she's saying."

Luisa lifted her head and uttered a few high clear notes of laughter. "All my people say she speaks to them very loud in English."

"That's when she thinks she's speaking Spanish." He laughed with her, finding her very endearing. Their girl. He supposed what they were doing to her was appalling by all known standards but he didn't see what they could do about it. Lovers were bound to be callous about others' feelings. When she'd had her baby, there would be plenty of time to decide what they should do for her. "Lance and I will invite people tonight to our party. We'll make sure that one or two of them speak

Spanish so you'll enjoy yourself. We'll have twelve or fourteen, including us. Tomorrow, we'll take you with us to sign for the house."

"You're both very good to me." Her eyes widened and she continued slowly as if she were trying to grasp the meaning of unfamiliar words. "What you say about the house, it will really belong to me, like my dress? I can do anything I want with it, even sell it to somebody if I want to? My father won't believe me."

"Yes, it'll be yours." Robbie put his arm around Lance's shoulders to bring him into the conversation. Lance dropped a hand onto his lap and held his cock. "Selling is different. I think you're too young to sell without your father's permission. Lance thinks you're seventeen. Is that right?"

"I think so. I'm older than the brother who is sixteen and younger than the others. It's all written down at the church but for girls they sometimes don't bother with dates."

"Well, even if you were older, you'd have to have a man's permission—your father's or your husband's if you had one. Women don't have the same rights as men in your country. The house will be yours according to the laws here."

"I'll tell my father so."

Lance leaned forward against the table. "Were you happy in your new room, little one?"

"Oh yes." She looked surprised that he should ask. "Only the rich sleep in beds alone. I felt like a queen."

Lance and Robbie exchanged a glance and laughed. "What did I tell you?" Robbie said.

"You see how much I count around here." Lance rubbed his shoulder against his and gave his thigh a squeeze. "I'm glad *somebody* wants me."

"We're about to make it legal. Our appointment's at nine. We've got to go."

Within an hour, they were partners in the Puerto Veragua Pottery Works, with Luisa's name on the paper as a "director." They signed the lease, complete with official seals, and money changed hands. Señor Diaz accompanied them to the dusty shed where Lance's work force, the two Juans, were waiting. The Juan who had worked with pottery and knew how to fire the kilns was

193

the older one. They were both dark and dour in the local way and neither was young.

"A comedy team," Lance commented. Exuberant laughter broke from him. He looked at his partner. His lover. A lover was nothing compared to what he and Robbie were to each other. He felt it intensely, standing in the hot dingy shed, thinking of the papers they had signed, aware of the helpers' eyes on him while they awaited instructions. Everything stemmed from whatever it was that he and Robbie had created together, not individually but in concert, something dense and immutable without the panic and striving of love.

"This is going to be a fun factory," he announced. "What's happened to the doors of the ovens?"

"Kilns never have doors," Robbie said, his eyes dazzled by the radiance of his beloved's happiness. Was it possible that his simple little plan had led to this? They were going to be happy together. He would devote his life to it. "You have to brick them up for each firing," he said, collecting his thoughts. "There's a reason but I've forgotten what it is. Something to do with drafts, I think. You have to maintain an even heat. That sounds reasonable."

"Of course it does. Everything you say is reasonable." His euphoria carried him to Señor Diaz who was lingering by the wide sagging door. "All very fine. Thank you. Now we work."

Señor Diaz seemed unaccountably cheered by the few words. He handed over the big key to the door, making a little speech of welcome, and left. Lance returned to Robbie's side, waving the big key.

"Look who's boss. What shall we do with these jokers?" The two Juans waited, as stolid as oxen, patient and leaden-eyed.

"Why don't you tell them what you're going to pay them? It can't make them any gloomier than they are already."

Lance told them they would be paid the equivalent of fifteen dollars a week, the amount Señor Diaz had mentioned as reasonable. The two Juans looked at each other and grunted in acknowledgment. Lance began to move around the premises, asking the names of things, the kilns, the water troughs, the foot-powered wheels, both of which he had tested and found to be in working order.

Robbie watched his sweet infectious gaiety produce an effect. The helpers didn't grow notably animated but interest enlivened their bodies and eyes and they followed Lance about, pointing at things and saying words.

Lance circled around and ended up in front of Robbie again. "Things are really beginning to hum around here. They keep saying some word I don't understand. Do you know what they're talking about?"

Robbie allowed himself a moment of pure pleasure, feasting his eyes on his radiant friend. Once again, he was totally transformed but this time there seemed to be some stability in it, a solid base. Perhaps this was what he really was, the truth of him that he'd been waiting to discover. His unique physical splendor had acquired clarity; he was bursting with vitality, superbly self-confident, his infectious *joie de vivre* lighting the world around him.

With an effort, he shifted his attention from Lance to the docile helpers and asked questions. He nodded and turned quickly back to their boss as if the special glory that had entered him might vanish while his back was turned. "He wants to know about preparing the clay. He's talking about what we call coils. I learned the word from Picasso."

"Are you going to share your esoteric knowledge? What's a coil?"

"It's a way of building up a pot. You form the clay into sort of ropes and put one length on top of another up to any size you want. You smoothe the sides and you've got a pot, more or less. I shouldn't think you'd bother with that for your dollies. I ordered you a couple of 'How To' books. They arrived yesterday. Pottery hasn't changed much since man began to walk so I think you'll be able to figure it out."

"Thanks." They looked at each other and laughed at nothing but the sheer pleasure of being together, the urge to put their arms around each other nearly irresistible. Lance took a step closer. "We better stop talking about it before my ignorance overwhelms me. Let's go get some clay."

"Clay. Firewood. I know where you can get ceramic glazes. They don't have much in stock but they say they can order anything you want from the capital. Immediate delivery, which probably means more like a week. What about these men?"

"They might as well wait in case we can get anything delivered today. I'll check up on them later." Lance spoke to them with unaccustomed fluency as if a grasp of the language went hand in hand with his grasp on himself and on the world.

Robbie felt staid and colorless beside him as they returned to the car. He'd been waiting to see what sort of figures they would cut in public, having noticed that among homosexual couples, more so than among straight ones, one partner always seemed to dominate socially. Lance was obviously going to be the star of their act. He happily adopted the secondary role and set out to cultivate it, reminding himself that they were fixing the pattern for a long future.

They drove a few hundred yards to the drab central square and parked in front of the hotel where Lance had stayed for a couple nights. It seemed like a long time ago. He remembered very little about its interior but the square had become familiar in subsequent shopping expeditions: the tattered fronds of the palm trees lifted to the hot cloudless sky, the half dozen unshaven men who seemed to remain permanently crumpled against the war memorial, the stray mongrels scavenging in abandoned flower beds, the dust. Attempts had been made to cheer things up for the tourists with a few tables under faded umbrellas in front of a few bars and a restaurant. There was one shop with a modern show window displaying electric light fixtures and another whose front wall was hung with junk, blankets and cheap embroidered shirts and wide-brimmed straw hats, masquerading as native handicraft.

"My God," Lance exclaimed as they got out of the car. "I think I've got some bags here. Andy wrote that he was sending them just before you arrived. I forgot all about them. Let's see if they're here."

They entered the vast, dun-colored hotel lobby, empty except for a few scattered islands of shabby chunky department-store—modern furniture. Lance remembered the cement counter at one end where he had first heard Flip Rawls's name. A head was just visible over the edge of the counter. It was the only sign of life. The head was attached to a body that rose lethargically as the clerk became aware of a foreign invasion.

Robbie watched as the man's somnolence was dispersed by the sunny charm of Lance's greeting. He brightened and turned almost flirtatious. Of course. Señor Lance. Of course his things were here. He'd been just about to send word to Señora Rawls. He had kept them at his side for safekeeping. Two bags eventually emerged, Lance deftly planted a small bill under the edge of a travel folder on the counter, and the transaction was completed amid smiles and bows and expressions of mutual admiration. Robbie lugged one of the bags out to the car. Lance staggered along in his wake.

"What in the world do you have in here?" Robbie inquired as they hoisted the bags into the back of the car.

"I haven't a clue. I don't remember packing." A shadow dimmed the luster of his eyes.

Indifferent to what people thought, Robbie leaned forward and kissed him quickly on the mouth. The shadow passed.

Lance moved in against him behind the cover of the open car door, murmuring with laughter. His groin thrilled with response. "How funny," he said, holding Robbie's arm and staying close to him. "I remember. Andy said he'd packed books. That shows I'm all right now. I've been locking out everything to do with leaving New York. That must have a lot to do with being happy."

Robbie slipped an arm around his shoulders and gave him a hug. "Come on. We have plenty to do." He directed them along one side of the square and around a corner into a wide unpaved street flanked by one- and two-story shacks, most of them frame, but a few of cracked and discolored cement. Tin roofs projected over raised porches. Shops were crowded in among the shanties, nothing more than dark open-fronted rooms with shutters stacked at the sides to close them. Bananas appeared to be a popular commodity.

The street was strangely quiet. Business seemed to be conducted in low murmurs and slight movements of the head. They passed one stall conducting a silent sale of tortillas and other stalls dealing in less easily identifiable edibles. Pedestrians, mostly male, moved listlessly. There was sparse traffic of decrepit American

197

cars and trucks, ambling donkeys, occasional cumbersome carts drawn by mules or misshapen horses. They came to a substantial brick building with a plaque over the door and a pole slanting out from it bearing the national flag—red and green with a yellow symbol in the middle of it, like a stylized fried egg. Robbie identified it as the police station as they continued past it.

Lance was struck by Robbie's familiarity with the place. He made himself at home wherever he was, supremely and confidently himself, untouched by any pressure to be somebody he wasn't. Lance had felt so little reason or reality in his being here that he'd done his errands without seeing where he was. With Robbie, it became the place where they were going to live and work and love. Seeing it for the first time, he was stimulated by the foreignness of it and by a sense of isolation that made Robbie his only point of contact with life.

A few hundred feet beyond the police station, Robbie took his arm and they mounted four or five wooden steps and entered one of the open-fronted shops. Beyond some waist-high rolls of paper and a big table littered with paper scraps, an ungainly old printing press and other paraphernalia were crowded in. A wizened little man wearing a leather apron emerged from among the machinery to greet them. It was immediately apparent that Robbie had already had dealings with him. He introduced Lance as his friend who was taking Señor Diaz's pottery shed and the printer spread out boxes of stationery on the table along with samples of typeface.

"What do you think, darling? White, beige or blue?" Robbie asked, indicating the paper displayed before them.

"Beige is more like pottery."

"Right." Robbie picked up a pencil from the table and with a few quick strokes sketched a striking PVPW logo. "Puerto Veragua Pottery Works—what else?"

"Our names in huge neon lights. Robert and Lance Cosling."

Robbie laughed and went on with his design of a letterhead, listening as Lance struck up a conversation with the printer. He heard the latter's voice grow lively with interest in response to Lance's fanciful and ungrammatical account of his plans for the pottery works. He quickly completed the letterhead and added a few flourishes to delay stemming the flow of Lance's charm. His image of him was changing by the minute. Lance had a dynamism and a magic all his own. His charm was compounded of shining sweetness and animal magnetism. There was a commom denominator of sexuality in it that embraced everybody without his willing it.

They eventually discussed the stationery, chose type, were told a price and promised delivery in a day or two. Again they left in a flurry of smiles and good wishes.

"The people here are nicer than I thought," Lance said.

"You're extraordinary. Everybody's crazy about you."

"Really? No wonder I like them. How did you ever find out so much about this place?"

"Just wait. I told you you were going to be a potter."

They went on, thoroughly pleased with themselves and each other, feeling the snug fit of their interlocking personalities. At an intersection, they turned from one unpaved street into another and after a few minutes came to another open-fronted shop, this one unpromisingly filled with battered metal drums and empty bottles.

"The wood merchant," Robbie explained as they entered. "I'm counting on your powers of persuasion. They grumbled about delivering."

Lance winked at Robbie as he overcame initial resistance and negotiated a delivery of firewood for later in the day. Robbie was able to provide specifications for cutting it. Another mission accomplished. The partners returned to the dusty, sun-dazed street and headed for the port from which the town derived its name. It was asleep. Men lay about on their backs with hats over their faces, on the quayside, on the decks of small fishing boats. They looked as if they had dropped in their tracks in the middle of whatever they'd been doing.

From around the bow of a coastal tramp tied up at the opposite quay, a figure appeared, moving toward them. Lance came to an abrupt, involuntary halt, his heart pounding. He saw the light-footed, dangerous glide of his approach and then panic sharpened his vision and he realized that he was mistaken. The lean figure and the way it moved was similar but it wasn't José's wolfish face.

"What's the matter?" Robbie asked, pausing at his side.

"Nothing." Lance gave his head a little shake. His heart had resumed its normal rhythm. "For a second, I thought it was one of them—there, that guy crossing the street. I thought it was one of the guys who raped me. The guy I fought on the beach."

"Are you sure you'd recognize him if you saw him again?"

Lance hesitated. He should tell Robbie about José's visit. He didn't have to tell all of it, only about the proposition and the threats. It might suit José's purpose to approach him when he was with Robbie and say almost anything. Robbie wouldn't pay any attention if he knew about his visit. They could face him together and give him a good scare. He hesitated a few seconds, shrugged, and moved on.

"I can't be absolutely sure. The first day I went to the beach after it happened—the day I came to find you—I had a nasty feeling that every local guy I saw might be one of them. If they have any sense, they'll stay out of my sight." Of course he would tell Robbie, he told himself, but not until the right moment came along and they had nothing better to think about. He could cloak the story in innocence by updating it and describing their meeting as a chance encounter in the street.

They picked their way past supine bodies in front of additional shops, marked by coils of rope, loops of fishing net and chain, and invitingly stacked tins of paint. "You're on your own here," Robbie said, waving him ahead. "I don't know anything about glazes. I never liked working with them. They change color with firing. I like color to stay the way I want it. Of course—"

"Hey, watch it," Lance interrupted. A tiny brown toddler came hurtling out of the shop, headed drunkenly at Lance, and fell flat on her face in front of him. He bent over and scooped her up as she was about to roll down the steps to the street. Piercing shrieks were instantly stilled as she clamped herself to her savior, eyes swiveling with wonder. She was wearing only a short torn undershirt. Robbie couldn't help noticing that she wasn't very clean and knew that he would've thought twice before rescuing her but Lance seemed serenely unconcerned with questions of hygiene. He crooned Spanish endearments to the infant while she gurgled with delight. Two older little girls stationed themselves warily in front of him, looking up at his captive as if they were afraid he would make off with her. He included them in his nonsense talk and, after glancing at each other for mutual support, they began to giggle at the extraordinary foreigner.

Robbie was astonishingly touched. Lance was so endearing. He imagined him with children of his own. They would be formidable rivals for his affections. Was he mad to suppose that he could build a life with a man who was so obviously ordained to be a father? He melted with tenderness as he watched him gently detach the little creature from himself and restore her to the custody of her waiting caretakers. She looked as if she was considering a howl of outrage but he crouched down to her and made funny faces and she decided on mirthful gurglings instead. Love made a lump in Robbie's throat. He must never do anything to divert or dam up the extraordinary flow of his warmth and humanity. Robbie envied him the gift. He sometimes felt a coldness in himself, especially when his work locked his mind in private visions that isolated him from others. Lance would help him open up.

"She's adorable," Lance exclaimed as they went on into the shop. "Did you notice how she hung on to me? She liked me."

"What gave you that peculiar idea?" He laughed and touched his hand. "She wanted you to take her home with you. So do I."

Lance stopped and looked into the deep gentle beauty of his eyes. He felt the twitch in his hands of wanting to touch him and the stirring in his groin. "Don't ever change your mind," he said. "Let's get a move on. When we've ordered the clay, can we have an hour on our bare-ass beach? I have a strange urge to suck your cock."

"Don't *you* change your mind."

They took time to indulge Lance's urge but by the end of the day, his work was organized. The wood and clay had been delivered and he'd found enough ceramic paint to start experimenting while waiting for additional supplies to arrive. Robbie helped him show his helpers how he wanted the clay prepared. They kneaded and folded and sliced a small batch until they had achieved an even, workable consistency.

"We're in luck," Robbie commented. "They obviously know how to clean it up there at the pit. This is pretty good stuff."

Lance scooped up a blob of the prepared clay, dropped it onto one of the wheels, and set it in motion. With guidance from his hands, the blob became a sphere and began to assume unexpected shapes as he exerted varying pressures. "Hey, this is going to be fun. I'll be able to turn out my dollies in no time."

The Juans watched stolidly, Robbie with infatuated fascination while he fashioned the clay into something resembling a plate and then a rather odd cup. He crowed with pleasure and gathered it up and tossed it back where it had come from. "My God, you've done it, darling. Did you see that? I'm a potter."

Lance supervised the stacking of the wood in a dilapidated shanty leaning against the back of the main shed, where he found a pile of old burlap bags. He dampened a couple and covered the lump of clay with them while Robbie perched on the edge of a trough, proudly watching him take charge and familiarize himself with his new responsibilities.

"That's about it for the day," Lance said, dropping down beside him. "Thanks for standing by, darling. You won't have to waste any more time here. In fact, I'd rather you stay away. I have to learn everything on my own and it'd be a bore for you. I can't wait for tomorrow to see you getting your work set up. Then we'll know where we both are and will be able to get to each other if we need each other. What more could we want?"

"A bath," Robbie said, brushing clay off his hands. Their shorts and shirts and even their faces were streaked with it. They laughed and touched each other's knees and rose. Speaking to his helpers about closing up, Lance discovered that they were planning to live in the shed. There was running water. They found the accommodations excellent and when he was firing they would have to tend the kilns at night in any case. Lance was delighted. His helpers were prepared for work he hadn't even thought of.

The sun's glare was fading from the sky when they

returned to the car. The streets were filling with lethargic pedestrians, women now as well as men. Dim lights were coming on in the cavernous depths of the open-fronted shops. Music drifted through the leaden air, plaintive Latin love-dirges. *Adios. Mi vida. Adios.*

They picked up ice at the bar Robbie had found on the port before taking the road that circled the inner harbor and led out around the promontory to the foreigners' beach and the open sea. At the fork where the Hill Road branched off, the small house Robbie had taken was visible behind a wall.

"It's no walk at all to your studio," Lance said as they passed. Neither of them thought of it any longer as a place where he would live.

"It was pretty clever of me to know what I wanted even when you were being so uncooperative," Robbie said. They touched hands as they passed Flip's blue door.

"Have you still got a lot of packing?"

"No. I've been getting organized the last day or two— dividing the stuff I want for work from what I'll take home. I'll throw it all together after dinner and from then on we'll pool our luggage if we go anywhere."

"I'm sort of nervous about tonight."

"I understand, sweetheart. Just remember, we can play it any way we like. Flip will be discreet if we tell her to be."

"And let people guess without having the satisfaction of enjoying being in love with each other in public? No, I want it to be a momentous occasion."

Today had been momentous simply because it was the first time they'd dealt with people together. How much more momentous to be with people who understood what they meant to each other. He hoped nobody would make him feel ashamed. He was queer. It wasn't something to be proud *or* ashamed of. He still needed a little time to get used to it. Being with people who knew and didn't think anything of it would be a big help.

Robbie stopped the car at the path leading down to home. "Come on, let's hurry. We're just in time for the sunset."

They careened down the rocky path together, holding on to each other. The stark little house wedged into the hillside above the sea looked different to Lance tonight, more companionable and homely, with the familiarity of a place he no longer looked at. Luisa came padding out to greet them and they both kissed her lightly on the lips.

She brought a pitcher for the dripping ice and they made themselves drinks and carried them to the parapet while she drifted off about her business. The piled-up, layered castles of color were beginning to crowd the sky. They stood close against each other and took long swallows of their drinks, watching as sea and sky blazed, a molten glow enveloping the earth.

"Another day," Lance sighed. Simultaneously, they drained their glasses, put them on the parapet, and pulled off their shirts. "God, I haven't worn clothes for this long since I've been here."

They continued to shed their clothes until they were naked while the night closed quickly in around them. They turned to each other and their erections crossed and sparred and slid up against each other as their mouths and bodies joined. They teased each other with their tongues and hands until their need to complete their union drove them hurrying along the terrace to their bed.

When they drove back the short distance to Flip's gate, Lance was keyed up with the novelty of the situation and determined to make all the adjustments the evening required. Above all, he told himself, he mustn't be embarrassed if men flirted with him. If he relaxed, he might even enjoy it. He was assuming a new identity; anything might happen. He hoped, for his own peace of mind, that men wouldn't flirt too blatantly with Robbie. He didn't want to have to knock anybody down.

After they had submitted to the extravagant enthusiasm of Flip's welcome, her "I told you so"s, and her predictions of eternal bliss, they were offered drinks and moved along the luxurious terrace among people who greeted Robbie as a familiar. He had said that they could wear shorts. He had been right. With a few exceptions, shorts were standard wear.

Robbie handled introductions. Starting with the American male couple staying with Flip, Lance was aware of something new in the way the men looked at him and talked with him, not flirtatious so much as

204

slyly amused. It made him want to do something shocking, like groping the first crotch he could get his hands on, but there were ladies present.

They talked to a woman of overpowering chic, in a machine-tooled American manner, who had been a fellow houseguest with Robbie for long enough to have developed an astonishing intimacy with him. She claimed prior acquaintance with Lance. He remembered her vaguely from New York parties. Her name was Val Carstairs and she was one of the top editors of *Women's Wear Daily*.

"So you've finally put this fascinating man out of his misery," she said, with a hand on Robbie's arm. "I'm a terrible romantic. I do like to see lovers united. You men. You're all giving us up for each other these days. I spoke to your wife not long ago. At the Comptons."

"Good Lord. How is she?" Lance asked, finding it hard to believe that Pam actually existed. He couldn't remember the last time anybody had said they'd seen her.

"Lovely. That classic English beauty never fades, does it? You haven't divorced? Ah well, there's no need to, is there? You must promise to make Robbie happy. He adores you. I always thought you were the most delicious young man in New York. Don't let Flip keep you here forever."

Lance couldn't have asked for a more public recognition of their union although his disguise as a Cosling wasn't a great success. They spoke to the permanent foreigners Lance had already met. Mme Fournier was there and Dr. Greuber in his wheelchair pushed by his companion Pablito.

"So good to see you together. So fine. So beautiful," Dr. Greuber exclaimed in Germanic gutturals. Lance hadn't paid any attention to Pablito before but felt his heavy gaze on him. Lance glanced at him and their eyes met. Pablito's were dark and bold and insistent, with a feral glitter reminiscent of José's. His haughty good looks were Latin rather than Indian and he had a lightweight boxer's build, lithely muscular with broad shoulders. Lance realized that they were undressing each other with their eyes. He smiled slightly and turned away, promising himself to avoid Pablito for the rest

205

of the evening. Robbie was talking to a gray-haired stranger.

"Here he is, Frank," Robbie said, drawing him in with an arm over his shoulder. "Frank wanted to be a surprise for you."

"Frank Schindler," the handsome gray-haired stranger said, shaking hands with Lance. "Does the name mean anything to you?"

"Wait a minute." Lance grinned suddenly. "Sure— I know. You're the guy who tried to get me to Hollywood."

"Correct. I've found you a year too late. I had big plans for you. I wanted to come East to nail you myself but I couldn't get away. I raised hell with the New York office when I heard we'd lost you. If I'd come myself, do you think I'd've got you?"

"I'm sure you'd've made it very hard to resist." He smiled amiably. Frank was one of the most important producers in the business but he didn't look like a movie mogul. He looked more like a movie star, with touches of Cary Grant. He was trimly stylish in expensively tailored shirt and slacks. Lance would have been doubtless flattered by his taking a personal interest in his film career but he couldn't imagine why he'd ever considered one.

"I knew the money wouldn't mean anything to you but I thought you might like being a star. Your first picture would be out by now. You'd've been one of the biggest. If you change your mind in the next year or two, let me know." Frank had eased them away from the others. They took a few wandering steps toward the parapet. "Why did you give up show business?"

"I was with a girl who hated actors. She made me feel they were beneath contempt."

"We've heard all about your women. My press boys thought it would be a nice rest to promote a Broadway actor who wouldn't have to be extricated from the clutches of the parking attendants at the Beverly Hills Hotel every few minutes. You've pulled a fast one on us, not that Robbie can be compared to a parking attendant."

Lance was blushing. He thought that it was Frank's way of telling him that he wasn't straight. He was sleekly attractive. His crisp, beautifully coiffed gray hair had an incongruously youthful effect. He was heavily tanned. The deep cleft of his chin was sexy. He was as tall as Robbie and his body looked fit and vigorous and meticulously groomed. "If I were in the clutches of a parking attendant, I doubt if I'd want to be extricated," Lance said cheerfully, trying out his new identity.

Frank chuckled. "They never do. That's our problem."

He put a hand on the small of Lance's back as he turned to face the party again. Lance turned with him and the hand moved down, fingers lightly caressing buttocks, coming to rest with a gentle squeeze. A spasm tightened Lance's scalp. His erection was uncomfortably confined in his jockey shorts. He stood motionless, wondering how to react. A week ago, he would have been indignant but everything had been different then. He was entering the homosexual world. He had expected it to be fairly outrageous and uninhibited. Lance was just learning. If this was the game, he wanted to play it right. Having guys after him seemed like friendly fun, especially when it couldn't lead to awkward conclusions. He flexed the muscles of his buttocks and the fingers stirred enticingly again.

"Am I making it hard to resist?" Frank asked with a lilt of amusement in his voice. "Am I making it hard, period?"

"I can't very well show you here." Lance felt that he was hitting the right playful note.

"Maybe we can do something about that later."

"I wouldn't count on it." The hand dropped away as they reached the fringes of the party.

As guests of honor, Robbie and Lance were seated for dinner on either side of Flip. The shortage of women eliminated conventional seating. Robbie had Mme Fournier beside him so that they could speak French, and Lance's partner was one of the American male couple. Lance had been cool with all of Flip's young men, perhaps even slightly contemptuous of them for being so obviously what they were, and he set out to make amends.

After a few minutes' conversation, he found that Albert was agreeable and even quite attractive in a bland, unexciting way. He and his friend Brewster, sit-

207

ting across the table and trying to keep an unobtrusive eye on them, had been together for almost two years. Their jobs, their house on Long Island, and Brewster's cooking—only a baby was lacking in the picture of exemplary domestic harmony. Thinking of himself and Robbie in such terms struck Lance as slightly comic but he didn't really see why it should. There were those who fitted comfortably into the American dream and those who didn't. It didn't much matter whom you were fucking. The evening still had much to teach him.

The meal was admirable, starting with poached fish with hollandaise, accompanied by Flip's good French wines. She kept the conversation lively and her manner toward her guests of honor had softened, as if she were genuinely moved by the passionate friendship that glowed in their faces, smoldered fiercely, threatened to burst into a conflagration when their eyes held for an extra beat. She lifted her glass and toasted them in her harsh, rambling voice.

"Happiness? Of course, but happiness is written in our stars. You've both suffered in order to find each other. I may have played some small part in it but it was meant to be. I'll never forget the day dear Lance arrived. I felt something immediately. I told him he must take a house and stay. Remember? Old ladies sometimes have these insights. Yes, you'll have a huge success with your pottery. We'll put Puerto Veragua on the map as a center of creativity. That's what we must aim for, now that you two brilliant creatures are here. Together. That's so important." She tilted her head winsomely at both of them and drank.

"This is our first night out together, Flip," Robbie said as if they were having a coherent conversation. "That's why we had to be with you."

"This is just the beginning. We're going to be such dear friends."

Robbie and Lance looked at each other with eyes full of laughter. "I guess that'll do," Robbie said. "She was supposed to say something about death parting us but there's no need to be morbid. 'This is just the beginning' is very good." He put his hand out on the table. Lance held it. "You must talk to Madame Fournier after dinner. She knows the house in France."

"Your house?"

208

"Our house." Their grip tightened. It almost brought them to their feet and into each other's arms. They let go with lingering reluctance and resumed their social duties.

Lance was aware of Pablito's intent eyes on him from time to time from across the table but he was true to his promise and didn't let himself respond to them. He invited Albert and Brewster to the party on Saturday. All Flip's house party was to be included. He knew that Robbie was planning to invite Dr. Greuber and his inevitable companion and decided to leave that to him.

After dinner, they all regrouped for coffee. Robbie and Lance stayed together, continuing to drink wine and answer questions about their plans for the pottery works. Val Carstairs knew people who would be interested and might be helpful. Robbie made a point of its being Lance's project, and Lance began to talk about it as if he were really running a business. He exchanged casual words with Frank when they happened to be standing together. Frank looked at him with an enigmatic smile that made him feel that he was missing a joke.

As before, Robbie commandeered a bottle of wine when they eventually settled down with Mme Fournier to talk about France. She had grown up outside of Orléans near Robbie's property and had known Maurice's family. She made the *manoir* sound more impressive than Lance had realized. Enough time had elapsed since dinner for them to consider leaving without being rude.

Robbie put a hand on Lance's knee. "I'll go finish up. It won't take more than ten or fifteen minutes."

"I'll come help." Lance finished his wine and started to rise. Robbie was ahead of him. He moved around behind him and put his hands on his shoulders.

"Don't. I know exactly where everything goes. One false move and we'll have to start all over again. *Excusez-moi, madame.*"

Lance refilled his glass and resumed the conversation with Mme Fournier. In a moment, he saw Frank approaching and prepared for him to join them. He slowed only enough to give Lance a smile that was no longer enigmatic but unambiguously inviting and went on. Lance finished the story he was telling about bi-

209

cycling in the Loire valley while he watched Frank's retreating back. When he reached the point where the land rose to meet the terrace, he paused and looked back. His eyes met Lance's briefly and then he stepped off into the garden. Lance recognized it as the place he and Robbie had found to take a pee in the dark the first night.

He continued to chat with the Frenchwoman while his heart accelerated. There was no question what Frank's look had meant but he wondered what would be expected of him if he followed. There wasn't the time or place for sex unless Frank was in a guest house he didn't know about. If so, he certainly didn't intend to get caught in it. He was intensely curious to find out what could possibly happen under the circumstances. Robbie had said he'd be gone for ten or fifteen minutes. There was time to slip away without Robbie's knowing. He smiled at Mme Fournier.

"I'm afraid you'll have to excuse me for a minute, too. I've had a lot of wine."

"How convenient. Now I won't have to explain that I also must be excused."

Lance waited until she had gone into the house. He glanced at the animatedly chatting guests, all of them with glasses in their hands, none of them paying any attention to him, and strolled off along the terrace, casual and unhurried.

When he reached the place where Frank had disappeared, he glanced about again and then stepped off the terrace and was swallowed up by the night. It was very dark. A segment of moon was low in the sky. He advanced across a flat planted area and could make out steps descending. He felt his way down them cautiously. At the bottom he seemed to be hemmed in by tall shrubbery. A spiky branch jutted against the sky. He moved slowly with his hands out to protect himself from invisible obstacles. His eyes were adjusting to the dark. The path wound through overgrown tropical vegetation. Its slope suggested that it led down to the sea.

He came to a bend and the path opened out into another small flat grassy area. He could make out dim shapes of furniture and then a figure moved out of the shadows. He uttered a small startled cry that ended in a murmur of flustered laughter. Frank was naked, except for a towel over his shoulder. His erection was a shadowy horizontal form. As he approached, his tanned, well-built body picked up highlights from somewhere in the night. He looked relaxed and self-confident. Lance envied him his nakedness. Frank reached for the top of his shorts.

"No," Lance blurted, holding his wrist in token resistance, but his fly was open and his erection was in Frank's hands.

There was no way of pretending to be outraged or unwilling. He pulled his shirt over his head and stretched, giving his body to the night and to the man who wanted it. Frank's hands moved on him eagerly and continued to strip him. He stooped to disengage his feet carefully from his shorts. Lance appreciated his not getting them dirty. He ran his tongue along his cock.

"A big boy," he murmured approvingly as he stood. "A *very* big boy."

Lance was thrilled by his daring and by the fact that a man knew he could be had so casually. He hadn't been allowed a moment for second thoughts. He was being handled by a man who knew what he wanted of him. He supposed this was the way homosexuals behaved together. Why stand on ceremony? The dark added an edge of suspense; he didn't know what the disembodied hands were going to do next. They were on his buttocks again, moving excitingly over them, fingers darting between them with something on them that permitted them to slip easily into him. Frank's intention seemed obvious but it was impossible for him to do it here. Lance's awareness of time passing strengthened his determination to refuse. His breath was rapid and he was making small involuntary purring sounds of encouragement.

Frank turned him and pushed him forward. Lance's shins encountered some obstruction and he fell forward on his hands and knees onto a chaise longue. Frank moved in behind him and entered him smoothly and expertly. Lance was incredulous. He was being fucked at a public party. He heard a murmur of voices and an occasional burst of laughter as Frank found his rhythm and demonstrated his easy possession of him.

Lance felt all of himself opening and surrendering to him. He exulted in being fucked as unceremoniously as if he had been picked up in the street by a stranger. He was being introduced to his sexual nature in a way Robbie couldn't do for him, baldly and impersonally, without the shield of love. His body glowed with the satisfaction of offering itself for a man's pleasure. He moaned with delight and his excitement became more highly charged as the intensity of Frank's desire mounted. He found Frank's hands as he dropped the towel under him and closed them around his cock. Their bodies pitched about with their orgasms and Frank slammed into him in a final paroxysm of lust before he collapsed onto Lance's back.

In a moment, Frank extricated himself and sat up. "You better get back and show yourself," he said in an undertone. "Leave the towel when you're finished. I'll collect it later and have it framed. Lance Vanderholden's fuck towel. You're sensational." He stood up and vanished like an apparition. It had ended as quickly as if it had never happened.

He struggled up into a sitting position and remained motionless, telling himself that he shouldn't be naked in Flip's garden. He didn't know why he had let it happen but it illuminated his feeling about fidelity between male lovers. What did his being fucked by Frank have to do with Robbie? He was simply acknowledging and accepting his homosexuality, learning to enjoy it. It was the first time he had had sex as a homosexual. Acknowledging his desire to be fucked was surely the beginning of healthy acceptance.

Robbie would despise him for what he'd just done. Fidelity—Robbie's fidelity that simply didn't allow for the possibility of being attracted to anybody else—was an ideal he was determined to pursue, but not before he had discovered everything in himself that might contribute to Robbie's happiness. Robbie said that they must never knowingly do anything that might hurt each other. Robbie couldn't be hurt by things he didn't know about.

He carefully wiped away all traces of the encounter. There was no hurry. He hadn't been gone ten minutes yet. He could see his clothes in a nearby chair. He rose and slipped them on, checking as well as he could in the dark that they were still presentable, and climbed back to the house. The timing was right. He was sure

212

he could count on Frank to act as if nothing had happened. He hitched up his shorts, assumed an innocent look and strolled back onto the terrace.

The group was seated in a circle where the light was most brightly concentrated. He noticed that several people were missing, in addition to Robbie and Frank. He went to the table where bottles had been set out and gave himself another glass of wine. Pablito joined him. Lance edged away to make sure they wouldn't touch while the young man reached for a bottle.

"José told me about you," Pablito said quietly without looking at him.

Lance's face froze. He glanced hastily around. There was nobody within earshot. "What did he tell you?" he asked.

"Just that he's had you and that you liked it. He laughed about a man with such a big prick who wants to be taken by men."

"Did he tell you what happened?"

"I understood you picked each other up on the beach."

He watched Pablito's hands as he fixed himself a drink. They were long-fingered and graceful. He was learning that he preferred the firm positive grasp of a man's strong hands on him to the soft hesitancy of a woman's. He would like to feel the steel in Pablito's. He spoke fluent English with a lilting accent. "Is he a friend of yours?" Lance asked.

Pablito shrugged. "He brings me boys sometimes when he finds ones he thinks I'll like. I pay him. He wanted me to pay him for telling me about you."

"Did you?"

The way Pablito smiled made José seem only a nuisance. He had a strong and haughty profile. Lance decided that he was more like a bullfighter than a boxer as he eyed the brown, hairless chest revealed by the deep V of his open shirt. He was slightly shocked by a good-looking guy paying for sex but he saw no viciousness in his face, only the sultry weight of desire in his expressive eyes when he looked up from his bartending with another shrug.

"I gave him something to keep him happy, not that he told me anything important about you that I didn't know already."

"What was that?"

213

"That I want you. I've made a down payment for you. Isn't that what you call it? When will I get you?"

Lance was getting a hard-on again. He was amazed at himself. A dam had burst in him. He could take it for granted from now on that he was attracted to guys and was attractive to them. It would be much easier to resist temptation if he could count on them turning up regularly. If he missed one, he would get another. Even with a hard-on, he didn't feel like taking any risks for Pablito. He put a hand on his shoulder instead and felt him easing in closer to him. The arsenal of seductive wiles acquired in his pursuit of girls could apparently be put in cold storage. Guys didn't fool around.

"You'll be coming to our party on Saturday," he said, experimenting with evading a suitor. "I guess we'll be seeing a lot of each other now."

"I hope so. You and Robbie are the first to settle here who love men. The doctor is very happy. I too of course. We'll have parties. Sex parties around the pool. Just for men. You will like it." Pablito held the glass up to the light, nodded toward the heavy man in the wheelchair and carried the drink to him.

He'd hardly had time to think when Robbie appeared around the curve of the terrace. Lance stood beside the table, smiling into his eyes as he approached. He made all the other guests look dull and ordinary.

He stopped in front of Lance, gripped his elbows and gave his lips a quick kiss. "There. Fifteen minutes on the nose. I got everything up to the car with the help of about fifteen of Flip's stalwart staff. I'm no longer a houseguest. Let me have a glass of wine while we're being polite to everybody and then I think we can ooze out."

They circulated. All the guests reappeared except Frank.

"Frank had an errand in town," Flip explained. "He said to say good night if he didn't get back before you left. He's looking forward to Saturday."

"I'm going to miss wallowing in your luxury, Flip." Robbie was charming about his stay while Lance mentally thanked Frank for his tact. By Saturday, they would be able to treat each other like casual acquaintances.

He and Robbie were able to slip away before the

214

glass-smashing ceremony began. They took each other's hands as they started up the path to the road. "How was it, beautiful?" Robbie asked. "Did you want every guy in sight?"

"Yes." Lance laughed. "Well, not really, but I enjoyed it. I was afraid I'd hate being with a bunch of guys all sort of eyeing each other but when you know you're like that yourself, it begins to seem normal. You tell me. Did you want anybody?"

"Enough to imagine doing anything about it? No. When I first met Pablito, I thought he was attractive but you finished that off. I may never want anybody else again. Wouldn't that be a bore?" They laughed and hugged each other briefly.

"You understand, darling. I can't be really yours unless I know that's the way I am. Until tonight, I haven't had much to go on. I let myself wonder about doing it with the others."

"What was the score?"

"You know I'm just talking theory—about finding out what being queer means to me."

"Sure, sweetheart. I certainly don't want you to discover you're straight after all. Frank was ready to bet me a fortune that you were. He was amazed when he found out I was moving in with you."

"How long has he been here?"

"Only a couple of days."

"It was funny seeing you so friendly with people I didn't even know. I wasn't sure he was like that."

"Frank? Good Lord. We all know about his errands to town. He's been mad about you as long as I have. I'm sure he'd've tried to get you out of your pants if he'd had the chance. What about Pablito? Didn't he make a pass at you?"

"He said he wanted me but didn't act as if he was absolutely swept off his feet by the idea." He paused, brief incredulous laughter breaking from him. "This is amazing. I sound like a woman. You don't mind my talking about it?"

"Didn't you talk about women with your friends?"

"Sure, but that's natural. All guys do it."

"Men or women, it all amounts to the same thing. Some people think homosexuals are obsessed with sex but I think it's because a man wanting a man attracts

215

more attention. A man wanting a woman isn't much of a conversation piece."

"Do you ever go to parties where there're nothing but men?"

"Sure. They're quite usual."

They reached the car and entered it from opposite sides and met in the middle in each other's arms. Robbie had been longing to hold the body that everybody had coveted all evening. His hands reclaimed him while their devouring mouths made a gift of themselves with the flow of their saliva and their plunging exuberant tongues. Robbie almost groaned with relief at feeling all Lance's ardor once more restored to him. He had seen everything, all the looks directed at his mate, every move in the little minuet of lechery while one or the other of them moved in and vied for his favor. He had seen Frank's hand on his behind and Pablito's smoldering eyes fixed on him. He had seen the American couple almost come to blows after dinner while they hissed his name at each other.

He had never been through anything like it but he had never before been paired with a raving beauty whose sex appeal encompassed everybody who came within twenty paces of him. He was going to have to learn to cope with it.

The major business scheduled for the morning was the purchase of the house; the three of them set out promptly for the lawyer. They all listened in a polite stupor as the lawyer read the deed. Including Lance's name in the document as an adult male guarantor of Luisa's rights apparently made it unnecessary for her father to be involved. The seller signed, Luisa signed slowly but with a final flourish, Lance signed, and soon they were all back in the street. Luisa clutched the deed, looking bewildered but pleased.

"Why don't you go to the shed," Robbie suggested to Lance. "Luisa and I have some errands. When we're finished, I'll take her home and come back for you. I want you with me when I take possession of the studio."

"I should hope so. Don't you dare go without me." He touched Luisa's cheek and gave her an encouraging smile. "Everything is good, little one. We will celebrate at lunch." He gave Robbie's arm a pat and left them.

He found his workmen stretched out in the shed, asleep. He woke them by moving about and making noises until they slowly pulled themselves together and shuffled to their feet. He wished them good morning and told them he had to go get a table and chair. They offered to find the things for him. The mission seemed to put them in a good humor and they went off discussing various members of their families who might have extra furniture.

He settled down on the floor with the pottery manuals Robbie had given him. He quickly learned that clay was such a versatile material that correct technique included just about anything that worked. He found technical terms for things he had learned by experiment. Everything he read suggested that anybody of moderate intelligence with a degree of common sense was highly qualified as a potter. He might just get the hang of it.

He sat at a wheel with a lump of clay and went to work. Within half an hour, he was working with intense concentration and was enjoying himself more than he had since he was eight and had spent a summer month constructing elaborate sand castles. His primary interest was in getting hollow globes the right thickness so that they would make noises that pleased him when they broke and for this the wheel permitted much more variety than working only with his hands. There was no way of knowing what success he was having until they were dry enough to break, so after quickly turning out twenty-five of them he stopped.

He was just returning some excess clay to the main supply when the Juans appeared carrying a plain kitchen table and chair. The men were more animated than he would have believed possible. They told a story whose details Lance didn't attempt to follow about a man and somebody's mother-in-law and a house that was shut up. Nobody was using the table and chair. As far as Lance understood, no permission had been given to take them. The Juans assured him there was nothing to pay. The acquisition seemed to have given the men a proprietary interest in the place. They inspected Lance's handiwork and nodded approval and rigged up racks outside for them to dry.

Lance worked with them while they prepared more

clay, which the older Juan handled expertly. Lance took to calling him Big Juan and then dropped *Juan* entirely in favor of *Big*. He detected the glimmer of a smile on the sullen face when he did so. They were going to be a team. He felt an extraordinary sense of satisfaction in sharing the simple dirty work with the men at his side. He was finding his place with ordinary men who had worked all their lives and took it for granted that that was what they were for. For the first time in his life, he had an inkling of what real life was like.

Robbie was struck by the calm, sober concentration he felt in Lance when he came to pick him up. He didn't greet him effusively, but offered him a fond, abstracted smile.

"Just a minute. I'm just finishing," Lance said.

Robbie watched, impressed by the assurance he had acquired and by the alertness of his helpers as they worked together. He had obviously stirred an active response from them. They folded away a considerable pile of prepared clay under damp sacks and Lance washed his hands, exchanging a few words with the men before turning to Robbie and giving him his full attention. "There. I've really gotten started. The books were a help. They've encouraged me to hold my breath and plunge in."

"I see you got your table."

Lance laughed. "I think they stole it. We're going to work well together."

They wandered out to the car. The back seat was still full of Robbie's things. They headed out around the port to the Hill.

"Luisa's adorable with the deed," Robbie said. "She won't let it out of her sight. She was still holding on to it when I left her. I bought an icebox. We decided that was a permissible luxury, didn't we?"

"Everything's permissible now, darling. I've discovered this place is real. I think I'm real, too, and I really hate warm drinks."

"That's the way. Spoken like a true Vanderholden. I'll apply for electricity this afternoon. As soon as we get it, I'll trade in your pump for an electric one. Luisa can have her baby in style."

Robbie's house was as lacking in charm as he had warned it would be. It's major asset for him was a long, sparsely furnished room with a row of French windows that let in a lot of light. The rest of it was built around a deeply shaded inner courtyard—kitchen, dining room, a couple of bedrooms, and a quite up-to-date bathroom. It was set in rocky ground and surrounded by an attempt at a citrus grove but with no view of anything worth viewing. There was a dark homely boy waiting to let them in.

"Thank God they didn't show me this when I was looking. In the state I was in, I'd've probably taken it. No Luisa; no sea—I'd've killed myself." They returned to the long, bare, bright room. "Is it going to be all right for work?"

"Practically perfect. Even if there's the famous rainy season everybody talks about, it should be light enough." Robbie's things were strewn about on the floor. "If you give me a hand, I'll be at work in no time." He pushed three tables into a row along one wall. He picked up a pile of newspapers from the floor and spread them over the tabletops. With Lance's help, he placed a stout wooden case on one table, another smaller one next to it and began to spread things out—paint pots, brushes, calipers and other engineering instruments, bottles, rags, knives, spatulas, and charcoal sticks, all of which seemed to fall into their appointed places on what had become one long work surface. He unfolded an easel and set it up. He untied the cord of a cumbersome, heavily wrapped package that turned out to be four large stretched canvases.

"Can you imagine anything more idiotic than traveling with those? I always do when I go someplace new and it always turns out that I have no trouble finding what I want, but I like to be on the safe side." He clamped one to the easel and stacked the others against a wall, calling Filipe. The homely boy appeared. "Have you got a jar or a pitcher in the house? A vase? Anything glass that holds liquid. Bring what you've got."

Lance looked around him at the display, marveling at the organization it represented. The place looked as if it had always been a painter's studio. "Trust you even to think of newspapers so as not to mess up the tables."

Robbie laughed. "It's my traveling circus. The show's about ready to go on."

219

"It's incredible. It looks as if you'd been here for six months."

"I hope the canvas isn't quite so blank in six months."

"I wonder if anybody watched Rembrandt set up his studio. This is something I can tell my grandchildren about. Just think, darling. We've got Luisa installed in a house, I've started my factory, here you are in your studio. How's that for fast operators? In the midst of all this hectic activity, don't let's lose sight of what it's all about. We're together for life."

"I hope you never forget it." He picked up the remaining small suitcase from the floor. "I brought a few clothes in case I ever want to change here. Also some conveniences in case you need reminding. Let's put everything where it belongs in the bedroom. That'll be that."

"I'm good at putting things where they belong." They looked at each other with teasing eyes. The boy returned with the jar. Robbie waved it to a table and dropped a fistful of brushes into it.

"Okay, Filipe," he said. "We'll be going out soon. You can relax till later. Never come in here when I'm not here. Do you understand? Never touch anything. I'll let you sweep when necessary but only when I'm here. Is that clear? This is where I work. This gentleman will come whenever he likes. He and I have the house together but we probably won't sleep here often. You're going to have a nice easy job."

Lance moved in close to his friend while Robbie gave his instructions, feeling the enormous authority of his working personality—his professional assurance and self-sufficiency. Lance had nothing to offer him but his body. He took a final step in against him as the boy withdrew. "Oh, God, want me, darling," he begged. "I'm nobody still if you don't. That's what I am—a guy who doesn't exist unless you want me."

"I want you, my beloved. I always will. I need it as much as you do." He ran his tongue over his voluptuous lips. "Come on. Let's put things where they belong."

They followed Filipe into the inner court and stepped off the covered colonnade into the first bedroom they came to. It had a wide curtained doorway. As Robbie paused to draw the curtain, he saw Filipe lingering at the kitchen door across the way before ducking out of

220

sight. Robbie gave the curtain another tug and shrugged. He opened his suitcase and emptied it onto a chair.

Lance was already naked, stretched out on the bed, his cock stiffening in its climb up his belly as he watched Robbie sorting out his things. Being naked with him in a new setting seemed to add continuity to their lovemaking, extending it from Puerto Veragua into the unknown future. There was nothing about Robbie's well-established career that could exclude or threaten him, no public opinion to be courted or appeased. They were making sense.

Robbie threw off his shirt. His hands moved to his shorts. Lance's heart skipped a beat and began to pound tumultuously. He tore his eyes away with a jerk of his hand. He was still appalled at moments by his slavish addiction to his cock. It risked driving him to wild excesses. He wanted his body to be torn apart by its savage demands.

A shudder passed through him and his heart subsided and he opened his eyes to look at Robbie as he approached, a big handsome man with a big erection who was capable of taking him with tenderness and love. He felt an odd alienation from himself, a momentary, startled disbelief. He thought of Jim's first brutal violation of his body and of the stages he had passed through since then that had brought him to Robbie. He was reaching the stage where whatever ambivalence remained in him would be completely eroded by a daily acceptance of his sexual deviation. When that happened, his dedication to Robbie would be unshakable.

He sat up and dropped his legs over the side of the bed and edged forward, reaching for his lover. He pulled him to his knees in front of him and ran his fingers through his hair and held his head while he moved his cock over his face.

"Do amazing things with it," he urged. "Make it feel as big as yours. I want you to be amazed by it."

When Lance returned to the shed after lunch, he found it occupied by a big shapeless man in a khaki uniform. He sat with one hip perched on the edge of the table with an extraordinary appearance of weightlessness. He didn't get up when Lance entered. The two Juans stood side by side against one wall, arms folded over their chests, eyes downcast, looking more sullen than ever. In reply to Lance's inquiring look, the visitor identified himself as Captain Ramiriz, chief of police.

"I know you of course, *señor*," Ramiriz said noncommittally. His uniform consisted of a shirt with an open collar and rumpled trousers held up by a pistol belt, complete with holster and gun. He wore insignia on shoulder flaps and a visored military cap pushed back on his head, exposing a shock of thick dark hair that fell over his forehead. His nondescript features were buried in folds of flesh. His eyes were alert.

"You know me?" Lance said to get the conversation under way.

"Naturally. You came two months ago. You had had an unhappy experience in North America." He spoke good English in a deep, slow voice. There was an unexpected note of sympathy in it when he mentioned the car crash.

Lance wondered if he'd come to reclaim the table he was sitting on. He had been brought up to think of the police as family servants. They were there to help his mother's enormous Packard through traffic, find illegal parking places for it, keep pedestrians moving in front of the house when she was giving a particularly conspicuous party, make kindly jokes with him when he was playing in the park with his governess, and perform other small services. He pulled the chair out in front of the police chief in case he was looking for it too. "Maybe you'd be more comfortable in that," he suggested.

"This will do unless you're afraid I'll damage it." There was a small twinkle in his eye. "This is quite an occasion. A rich and famous young foreigner starting a business in Puerto Veragua. I don't think anything like it has ever happened."

"I'm not rich," Lance corrected him hastily. "My family is rich but I get no money from them. This place is in the name of my partner, Mr. Cosling. He's a famous painter but he uses a different name for his work."

"You both wish to remain incognito. Is that the correct way of putting it?"

"More or less, except that we have nothing to hide. Everybody knows that Mr. Cosling is known professionally as Robi and I can't help having been born who I am."

Ramiriz nodded slowly and sighed. "Yet you say that nobody will know that you have anything to do with your pottery here. That means that you wish to remain incognito, no?" He said it with a policeman's patient insistence on scoring a point in an interrogation.

Lance shrugged and made a dismissive little gesture with his hands, smiling. "You may have a point. I don't like being a celebrity. I don't want publicity. If you can help me avoid it, I'd very much appreciate it."

Ramiriz nodded slowly and stared at the floor, trying to fit his words into a picture that wouldn't come clear, while he thought how much this young man had changed since he'd come here. He was much darker from the sun. He had lost the milk-fed look of the North Americans. He no longer looked shy. He looked rich and reckless.

"You don't think publicity would help you sell what you make?" he asked after a brief silence, without looking up.

"Not in the least. Pottery doesn't interest people all that much. They buy it to use or because it's cheap and decorative. Nobody would buy it because I made it."

"And you plan to export it?"

"It's a bit soon to talk about plans. I hope to. I have an order from New York. When that's finished, I'll see."

"The government's in favor of exports. You won't be selling locally? To the capital, for instance?"

"I suppose I would if anybody wanted it. Nobody's talked about any restrictions. I certainly won't do anything I'm not allowed to do."

"No, no, there'll be no difficulty." Ramiriz removed his cap and looked into it. He had more or less covered his instructions. He hitched up his gun where it was digging into his hip. "I think you'll find it easy to deal with officials here. In North America, you have hard-and-fast laws for everything. Here things are dealt with in a more personal way. Once you've started, you might find you want to employ more people. You might want advice. I could, of course, warn you against trouble-makers."

Lance was picking up the hints as they were dropped. The policeman was telling him that he wouldn't have any trouble if he cooperated with the right people. A gift would be regarded as an expression of personal esteem if he had to ask for any favors. He didn't expect his business to be the sort that would involve asking favors. "I doubt if I'll hire any more help but if I do I'll certainly check with you," he assured Ramiriz. "These men came from Señor Diaz."

"Yes. Serious, hardworking men. Unfortunately, there's no shortage of labor. You can come to me for any help I can give you." He didn't think it could do any harm to say it even if he wasn't sure that it was true.

It still wasn't clear whether young Vanderholden was to be helped or hindered. His instructions had come from high levels in the capital. Why should anybody care if he was living with a girl? Men usually did, unless there were boys. The questions about the money he was spending weren't usually asked except when illegal activities were suspected from which a *politico* might wish a share. The fact that the painter had brought the money into the country to buy both the business and the house where his friend was living with the little Fernandez girl didn't seem very interesting, but he had reported it. There was nothing more for him to do unless he received more specific orders.

Among other things, Ramiriz had developed a sixth sense about money. He could smell it and since an important function of the police was to channel as much money as possible into the right hands, it was a useful gift. This modest enterprise would never be a big moneymaker. He looked around gloomily, searching for something that might be useful to his superiors. They wanted something from this extraordinary-looking foreigner. Until he knew more, cautious courtesy could do no harm.

He sighed and settled his cap squarely on his head, lifting himself lightly to his feet. He gave his gun another hitch. "Very well. I don't wish to keep you from your work. It's been a pleasure to talk to you, *señor*."

Lance rose. The policeman was tall by local standards. He suddenly looked familiar. He had seen him somewhere before but not in uniform. For some reason, the memory of him in civilian clothes brought with it a hint of danger. "If you come back in about a week, I'll be able to show you what I'm doing," he said.

"Very interesting. Perhaps I'll drop in. You can always find me at headquarters if you want me." He managed to make his departure more social than official.

Lance rather liked him and was glad to have started out on a friendly footing with him. In a place like this, the police might come in handy in unexpected ways. His helpers looked pleased to be rid of him.

He went out to check his morning's work and decided it wouldn't do. The clay was still damp and malleable. He gathered the spheres together into a lump and carried it to Big inside the shed. "No good. Work in with the rest," he said.

He scooped up some fresh clay and went to work. Learning to vary the speed of the wheel and teaching his hands a quick light dexterity, he was able to introduce character and variety into the devil-figures. He made them droop and sag and assume comic characteristics. By evening, he'd finished fifty that satisfied him. He noticed Big and Juan commenting on them as they carried them out to dry, pointing at one or another and coming close to grinning. They probably thought he was still trying to make perfect spheres but he took their reaction as a compliment.

It was almost dark when he made the ten-minute walk to Robbie's house from the shed. The lights were on in his studio. He went through the meager citrus grove and entered by a French door. Robbie turned from the easel and his face lighted up with welcome.

"There you are, beloved. You're in luck. I'm not in a creative trance yet. I know who you are." He put down the charcoal pencil he'd been working with and put his hands on Lance's shoulders. "Isn't this amazing? We've got a routine going already. We're an old married couple. How time flies."

Lance lifted his hands to Robbie's bare chest. He was wearing a sarong. "We feel so right together. I'm not amazed anymore."

Robbie brushed the hair back from his forehead. "You look as if you've been working hard. It's getting late. I almost drove down to get you." He had kept the car for his afternoon errands with Luisa.

"The walk's nothing. I love being able to get to you whenever I want to."

"I don't like the idea of your walking on that road at night."

225

"Because of what happened? Nobody would try that twice."

"No, not in the same way, but some other sort of unpleasantness. I keep wondering why he disappeared—the one you call the ringleader. He got away with it. You'd think he'd hang around to show you who's boss."

"I may've passed him somewhere without noticing. I haven't paid much attention." Now that they would be spending some of the day apart, Lance was planning to tell him that he'd seen him, perhaps even spoken to him, but he hadn't prepared his story and wanted to be sure to get it right. He'd let it go for another day. He didn't want to think about José. "I really got going this afternoon. You've started, too." He glanced at the canvas on the easel. It was covered with intricate tracery of interlocking forms—a Robi in the making. He was thrilled to see it at this stage but wasn't sure that he should look at it closely. "Your first picture that's going to have some of me in it."

"Yes, my beautiful. It felt strange getting started again, feeling so much of you in me."

"Strange good?"

"Strange marvelous. Seeing things in a new way. Wanting to be better than I've ever been. For you."

"Oh Jesus." Lance broke from him and backed away. His breath caught at the magnitude of the declaration. "A few months ago, I walked into a gallery and saw your pictures for the first time. They knocked me sideways. Here I am with you—*with* you, seeing you start a new one. For me."

Robbie smiled into his eyes, touched by his generous admiration. "I'm so happy, darling. Let's go home now. Luisa has a surprise."

Luisa had ice ready from the new icebox when they got home. She was still excited about the house and wanted to know if Lance knew about their having been to apply for electricity that afternoon. The company hadn't been able to give them a date; they might have to wait for weeks.

"But we know we will get it," Luisa said with placid pride.

"Oh yes. We'll get it," Robbie promised.

"And running water," she prompted.

"Yes. We don't have to wait for that. They're putting pipes in next week but it won't run for long until we have the electric pump."

"You two have had a busy afternoon," Lance commented, handing Robbie a drink.

Lance went to change into a sarong. When he returned, Robbie was alone. He joined him at the parapet and put an arm around him. "Was the ice the surprise?" he asked.

"No. She'll be right back."

Lance took Robbie's glass. "If we have to wait, we better get drunk." He was headed for the bottle and ice when Luisa reappeared on the terrace from her room, wearing a new dress. He came to an abrupt halt with an exclamation. "My God. How beautiful."

Robbie moved in beside him. They stood together, looking at her. "What do you think? Weren't we clever to find it?"

The dress was of crisp white cotton with discreet ruffles and a long full skirt. It had a vaguely Spanish-peasant look but was sophisticated enough for a summer evening at a country club. It added grace to her body in a way that the little American-style dress didn't. Lance went to her and held her arms and kissed her. "You're beautiful, little one."

Robbie followed him. "You're pleased? We'll get a flower for her hair. I saw gardenias in the street today. She'll be stunning."

"You're a genius. I couldn't think how to dress her except in simple local stuff."

"We both think you look wonderful," Robbie told her in Spanish. "I told you he'd like it."

Her eyes were bright. She looked at Lance and giggled into her hands. She looked up and her self-consciousness receded into pride. "Shall I take it off now? I don't want to wear it in the kitchen."

When they all sat down to dinner, Lance didn't register immediately that she was wearing a blouse at table. When he did, he accepted it as appropriate. The owner of a house with electricity and running water didn't go about half-naked. She should be allowed to adapt to changes in any way that suited her.

For the first time, they had things to discuss about the place where they were living. They asked Luisa

227

about Ramiriz and the importance of the police. The local estimate of the police chief was a hard man but fair, she said. She didn't know anybody important enough to have any dealings with him. The police ran everything for the *politicos* in the capital. There were only a few "bad people," who had a way of disappearing. The villagers were left to settle their private grievances among themselves except for the rich, who had the police to act for them.

"Our old friend, the police state," Robbie said. "Did Ramiriz seem friendly?"

"Not particularly one way or another. Bored, mostly. He did say that it was a big event for a rich and famous foreigner to start a business here. I set the record straight but he obviously knows about my family. He tried to make some sort of point about our both being here incognito. I guess the police can't help making everything sound slightly sinister."

"I wondered if anybody would mind our little private enterprise. The lawyer didn't seem to think so. The government's very chummy with Washington. I can't imagine the *politicos* being interested in us."

By the end of the week, Lance had two hundred of his devil-dolls glazed and ready for firing. He was terrified of ruining them all but Big had already started one of the kilns and run through a few rough plates for color tests and Lance was reassured by the results. He wasn't aiming for spectacular effects. If they survived the firing, the figures would be very similar to the ones he'd made for Flip. He'd ordered more glazes and hoped to have his first order ready to go at the end of another week.

Both he and Robbie were happy with their routine. They went off to work together, one or the other keeping the car. They rejoined each other at midday and took a couple of hours off for sunning and swimming and lunch. They had their evenings and nights together. Luisa seemed placidly content; she treated them both with affection and decreasing deference. Their dish-washing sessions after dinner were conducted under her directions. Life moved smoothly and without strife.

Being with either of them gave Luisa equal pleasure. She loved them both, differently from the way she loved her brothers but with equal tranquility. Her life was in their hands and they made her feel that they were more concerned for her comfort and her wishes than she had ever expected anybody to be. She owned a house. It was still hard to believe but it was a fact. Now that she knew she was going to have a baby, she thought sometimes of how frightened she might have been if she were still alone with Lance in a rented house that he could have left overnight.

Robbie declared Saturday a holiday to be sure that they would be ready for their party without any last-minute hitches. Lance spent the morning getting his figures into the kiln, and once they were bricked in, he was free too. He picked up ice and a gardenia for Luisa's hair and went home to find the kitchen a beehive of activity.

The guests arrived more or less in a group and the evening immediately became a trial of Lance's ingenuity and self-control. Flip's couple, Albert and Brewster, were pointedly attentive. Lance found them growing more attractive with familiarity and his curiosity about their bodies increasingly insistent. Frank looked at him with knowing amusement, making it clear that he would like another chance at him. Once Pablito had planted the doctor's wheelchair in a central location on the terrace, he launched his campaign for the conquest of his blond host. Lance didn't know why they all chose him but guessed that they'd tried and failed with Robbie. He wished circumstances would permit them to succeed with him. He'd had a week to convince himself that the only thing he regretted about his homosexuality was that he hadn't allowed himself to enjoy it sooner.

"You will show me where you swim?" Pablito asked as soon as they had a moment alone together. He was holding Lance's arm and his grip tightened as he spoke. Something about his hand made Lance feel that they both knew Pablito could have him whenever he wanted him.

"Sure. Later. Probably everybody will want to go. We can't be alone here."

"You'll manage it. You're very clever. Frank says you're out of this world."

"I see." Lance blushed. It was exciting to know that

229

word was spreading that he was available. It should keep people interested.

"Robbie doesn't know?"

"No. I've got to be careful."

"Of course. We'll wait for the right moment. Later, they'll all be drunk."

It was a reasonably accurate prediction. Robbie's punch was dry and smooth and very potent. Everybody drank it like fruit juice until laughter became raucous and the din of voices made conversation more animated than coherent. Being so much smaller than Flip's, the terrace created a more informal and intimate atmosphere. It looked romantic in the lamplight, suspended over the sea. Robbie had found some gaily colored cushions that made it look more furnished.

Luisa, of course, was the center of interest for the permanent residents, who had heard a lot about her as Lance's consort and now saw her as the odd-man-out in the new alignment. With the flower in her hair she looked as exotically lovely as Lance and Robbie had known she would and there were whispered surmises as to whether they indeed formed a *ménage à trois*. She remained subdued but not ill-at-ease and everybody pronounced her charming. Robbie kept an eye on her and went to her rescue whenever she looked left out.

After an hour or more of serving punch, Robbie and Lance signaled each other with their eyes that food was advisable. Luisa supervised them while they brought it out. They laughed together and congratulated each other for the successful party.

"You're now a great international hostess," Robbie assured her.

"Your punch is a triumph," Lance told Robbie. "Everybody's going to pass out before they know they've had a drink."

"Señora Rawls is being very kind to me. She has spoken to me three times, very loud in English," Luisa said, laughing.

They made Luisa sit with the guests while they served the food. Success followed success. Luisa had filled tortillas with a variety of succulent meat and vegetable concoctions. Robbie's fish and sauce were impeccably professional. Unable to compete with Flip's French wines, they served iced beer. Everybody asked for second helpings. Lance had his first opportunity to talk privately with Frank.

"I gather nothing's sacred. You're a cad," he said amiably.

Frank chuckled. "You didn't think I'd have Lance Vanderholden without boasting about it, did you? I can't wait to tell the brethren on the Coast. They'll be fascinated to hear that you're hung like a stallion."

"Make it a good story. Tell them it's two feet long."

"Approximately two feet long. That makes it sound more convincing." They laughed and Frank ran his hand deftly over Lance's bottom. "Real star quality. I wouldn't mind it again when I could see more, just to make sure I have my facts straight. Is Pablito going to get it?"

"I wouldn't tell you. You're not to be trusted." Lance noted that everybody took promiscuity for granted; fidelity wouldn't count seriously as grounds for turning somebody down. He and Robbie might consider their union as sacrosanct as marriage, but nobody else did. "For God's sake, don't tell Robbie," he added hastily.

"Don't worry. Robbie's special. He's one of the sexiest guys I've ever known but I'd never dare make a pass at him any more than I'd say anything personal about you to him. He's got all that charm but underneath it, he's a very private guy. He makes the rest of us seem like tramps."

Lance resolved not to act like a tramp and continued to share the duties of host with Robbie. They cleared away plates and dishes, served Robbie's sumptuous fruit creation, cleared away plates and glasses, served brandy. Pablito continued his single-minded pursuit. Lance couldn't turn his head without meeting his eyes. When he paused to talk to one of the guests, Pablito moved in beside him, touching him, putting his hands on him. Lance found it nerve-racking. There was no point getting all worked up to wanting a guy if there wasn't any way of doing something about it. He wished Pablito could handle it as quickly and efficiently as Frank had.

Robbie watched impatiently. He didn't blame Pablito for trying to get Lance but there was no excuse for being so obvious about it. He was sure Lance wasn't encouraging him—accepting and rather enjoying his attentions, perhaps. He'd been attracted to Pablito himself.

To make sure he could still hold his own, he cast a

few suggestive glances at him and soon brought him to
his side. His white teeth flashed. His hands moved on
Robbie with an arrogant assumption that he was giving
his host a thrill. Robbie had watched the hands on Lance.
Lance's lack of experience might make him susceptible
to Pablito's huge self-confidence. Robbie realized that
he was competing with his lover and laughed at himself.
Why didn't he let Lance find out how to take care of
little flirtations for himself?

Relieved of his Latin admirer's insistent presence,
Lance was welcomed by Albert and Brewster with
slightly alcoholic exuberance. They clearly belonged together and just as clearly were ready to be detached
from each other for a bit of extracurricular activity.
They were clean-cut, Ivy league types and Lance wanted
to see them naked. Their empty glasses reminded him
of his duties as a host and he made the rounds offering
more brandy. He collected empties and took them to
the drink table, where Robbie was also busy with glasses.

"How're we doing, darling?" Lance asked. "Nobody
seems to be in a hurry to go. The food was beautiful.
You and Luisa are a team."

"She's good. She just needed encouragement. A couple of people have asked if they can swim. Do you want
to?"

"Sure. Let's go. We'll be famous for our midnight
swims."

"One of us should stay here with the halt and the
blind. You take them, sweetheart. There's no moon.
You know the way better than I do."

"Pablito said he wanted to see where we swim but
that was before he decided to spend the rest of his life
with you."

Robbie laughed. "You or me, I don't think he cares.
We're both supposed to fall for his irresistible body. It's
very pretty, as a matter of fact." Robbie congratulated
himself for having recovered his senses. Lance had to
have a chance to find out where his new sexual direction
might lead him.

Lance put his arm around him and leaned in against
him briefly. "I'd like a swim with you when they go.
Let's wait and see."

When they'd distributed the refills, Robbie made a
point of pulling up a chair beside the lady editor, cutting

himself off from suitors. Pablito returned to Lance's side. "Isn't it time for our swim?" He put a hand on Lance's elbow.

The touch of his long, strong fingers made Lance want to feel his hands on him everywhere. The slightly contemptuous glitter of anticipation in his eyes excited him. To Pablito, he was just another infatuated faggot. He had to get used to his new identity. He looked at the smooth brown muscular chest exposed by the open shirt and the arrogant aristocratic face and felt himself adapting to Pablito's picture of him as an easy fuck. He wanted to be taken with arrogant indifference.

"We can't swim alone together," he said. "People might wonder."

"I don't think Robbie would wonder. We'll collect some others. Are you allowed to show me the toilet without a chaperone?"

"I guess that's safe," Lance said with a smile. "It's out here." They moved along the terrace. As they passed the kitchen door, Pablito stopped and looked in.

"This is the kitchen? I want to see where you make such wonderful food." He stepped in. Lance followed and stopped in the doorway, his hands spread out on the jambs, staying in sight of the gathering. Pablito turned back to him and unhurriedly began to unbutton his fly. Lance's heart skipped a beat but he couldn't think of anything to say to stop him that wouldn't sound silly. The moment of indecision gave him time to realize that he wanted to show himself off.

Lance stood without moving as Pablito's quick, assured hand brought his cock jutting up from cover, startlingly naked and erect. Pablito ran both his hands over it with firm, appreciative appraisal, his eyes fixed on it. The danger of discovery gave Lance a familiar thrill. He braced himself with his hands against the doorframe as the first twinges of orgasm stirred in him. "Be careful. I could come awfully easily," he warned quietly.

He glanced over his shoulder along the terrace and saw that nobody was paying any attention to them. There was a burst of laughter as he turned back to the guy who was about to jerk him off in the kitchen.

"I see why everybody's talking about it," Pablito said, unmistakably impressed. "It's out of this world. You want me. That's obvious. I'll fuck you and make you

233

come." Slowly and with considerable difficulty, he set about rearranging Lance's cock in his shorts, handling it in a way that was obviously intended to keep it hard.

Lance remained innocently visible and motionless in the doorway, breathing deeply to keep orgasm at bay. He was beginning to understand that sex could crop up at any moment and without ceremony. He supposed that letting Pablito familiarize himself with his cock was as much an infidelity as anything else he might do with him but he couldn't see much logic in it. He had to allow himself a little leeway before he would feel at home in this excitingly lawless world and hoped that Robbie would soon realize that he couldn't be unfaithful in any way that mattered. That was the important truth.

"The toilet's there," Lance said to Pablito with a large gesture toward it to show everybody that they had nothing to hide. He put his hands in his pockets and stepped aside to let Pablito pass.

"I'll be back to find our chaperones," he said, heading for the outhouse.

Pablito reappeared within minutes and joined the other guests. Glasses looked reasonably full. The party was drawing to an end in a final burst of animation. Mrs. Stroud rose and approached Lance with her friend in tow.

"We all envy you so having a house right on the sea," she said. "Pablito thinks you wouldn't mind if we have a quick plunge. Sarah's quite addicted to sea baths and my house is miles away on top of a hill."

"We were wondering if anybody would like to cool off," Lance agreed. "I'll show you."

Brewster and Albert moved in beside him and claimed him with hands that slid down over his back and settled on his hips. "You can swim from this place?" Albert asked.

He put his arms around their shoulders, thinking unequivocally that it would be very pleasant to have some fun with either or both of them, and his cock began to stir again. "Sure, come on. We can play hide-and-seek for each other in the dark."

"Finders keepers?" Brewster said, hooking his fingers over the top of Lance's shorts. Lance met his eyes as they all laughed, and his cock gave a little surge of response.

Seeing that Pablito had joined the small group, he picked up a flashlight and a couple of towels before leading the way over the rough ground to the eucalyptus tree. His heart was beating rapidly and he was filled with a sense of adventure. He wished it were lighter and that the women weren't with them. Would he let Pablito fuck him while the other two watched?

"Look out, everybody," he said, pausing at the top of the steps. He shone the flashlight down them. "The going's a bit rough. I'll lead the way. Take it easy." They tripped and slipped down the rough incline, laughing and grabbing for each other. He stopped at the bottom and swept the beam of light over the rocks. "Everybody okay? We're safe now. There's nothing to worry about down here." He pulled off his shirt and threw it back toward the rocks that climbed the hillside, wondering who would pick up the signal. He led the way to the edge of the sea.

It was very dark. The rock formations that enclosed the small cove were silhouetted against the sky and there was a sheen of light on the sea. Between was a well of darkness. The group that gathered around him were dark forms against darkness. He wasn't sure who was who.

"We obviously don't have to worry about being naked. I can't see who anybody is. If you stay more or less between those rocks you can't get lost. Stay on this side if you want to dive. It's easy to get out over there. There're plenty of submerged rocks to climb up on."

He slipped away from them and headed back to where he'd thrown his shirt. When he found it, he carried it to the crumbling cliff that cut off the view of the house and sheltered his battered mattress. The bottle of suntan oil was in its usual crevice. He stripped, feeling wonderfully liberated as his cock swung out, and stiffened slightly. He hoped *somebody* found him. After the flirtatious evening, he was ready to share his body with anybody who was interested in it.

The others sounded very close; he heard them clearly laughing and chatting, and a splash as one of them went in. His eye was caught by a faint shadow. Approaching it, he felt along the cliff face and collected

235

his bottle of oil. Another few steps brought him unexpectedly within touching distance and he made out the set of Pablito's naked shoulders. He was perched on a small ledge with his feet on the ground.

"I wait here." Pablito spoke as if they had a date at a prearranged location.

Hands reached out of the night and brought Lance down between spread legs, at the same time taking the bottle of oil as if it too were part of a prearranged plan. Pablito's erection felt as rapacious as José's, taut and lean and purposeful. Lance stroked his chest, finding pleasure in the smooth swell of muscle that his eyes had lingered on so covetously.

He kissed his nipples and slid down and filled his mouth with his cock, imagining the little curl of contempt on Pablito's lips as he did so. He didn't care if Pablito thought sucking cock was degradingly effeminate. Except for Robbie's, cocks didn't particularly thrill him but he wanted to be good at it. He could tell from the excitement his mouth was generating that he was learning fast.

Oiled fingers slipped urgently between his buttocks, preparing him. He could feel Pablito's forces gathering for attack. Hands gripped him and forced him to abandon what he was doing. He was moved into position and Pablito dropped from his perch and entered him with skill and dispatch. Lance uttered a cry of satisfaction.

He was amazed by how much he wanted it. He didn't even like Pablito very much but he wanted his cock in him; Pablito's taking possession of him coldly and passionlessly heightened the excitement of it. It reduced him to a convenience, a silly faggot snatching at a chance for a real man.

Pablito shifted his hands from his shoulders to his hips to adjust his position to suit his own pleasure and drove into him masterfully to achieve his climax.

"You're out of this world," he murmured, breathing heavily, and slipped out of Lance and vanished into the night.

Lance seethed with frustration. He was so close to coming that he needed only another touch to complete the process and was tempted to provide it for himself. So much for infidelity if it only led to masturbation.

He gathered himself together and retrieved the flashlight. He heard people splashing in the water and the sound of voices. He could go have a chat with Mrs. Stroud without her noticing his troublesome cock. Smiling to himself, he turned to face the sea, poised to make a dash for it. He took a few running steps forward and collided with a naked body. The impact made them both grunt and their hands were automatically on each other to steady themselves.

"Who is it?" Lance whispered. He liked the feel of what he'd found.

"Lance? I've been looking for you everywhere. It's Brewster."

Lance tucked the flashlight under his arm and their hands swept over each other and settled on their cocks. Brewster's sprang into erection at his touch. His own needed no encouragement. Hands moved back and forth along it.

"Oh wow," Brewster exclaimed in an undertone. "My God, Frank was right."

"What about?"

"He said it was one of the wonders of the world."

Lance chuckled. "Thanks. The old Hollywood build-up."

"You don't need it. I wish I could see it."

Lance made sure his back was to the sea and snapped the flashlight on. "Here we are."

"Jesus, Lance. What I wouldn't give to be in bed with that for a night."

That was more like it. He'd found a faggot who appreciated him. He snapped the light off hastily and guided his new partner across the rocks to his mattress. Their mouths met. Lance brought them down to their knees, in happy possession of a slim inviting body. Their hands served as eyes, darting over each other and lingering on places they liked. They began to writhe against each other with an ecstatic interplay of muscle and sinew. Their mouths parted. "If you want to suck me off, you'd better hurry. I'm about to come," Lance whispered.

Brewster bowed over him with an ardent mouth. He made Lance feel as if he'd never known anything so desirable as his cock. In a moment Lance's orgasm intervened but it didn't cool Brewster's ardor. His mouth remained active and inventive. Lance wondered if he'd ever learn to be so accomplished.

He stroked Brewster's hair and ran his hands over his nice shoulders, grateful to him for making him forget Pablito. "I'm sorry I was so quick. I was with somebody who left me sort of up in the air."

Brewster relinquished him and straightened. "Pablito? He's famous for it. Hit and run."

He drew Brewster to him and began to make love to his body with his mouth, hoping that he wouldn't seem like too much of a novice. Brewster fell back, propped himself on his arms, and lifted his hips to him as he moved down to his cock.

"My God, Lance," he whispered. "How can you be so beautiful and make love so sweetly? Most beauties don't. I'm wild about you."

"We mustn't forget Albert," Lance said with his lips on his cock.

"No, but what would life be without a bit of cheating? My God, where did you learn to do that? I'm going to come, honey." He dropped down flat on his back on the mattress while Lance happily received his ejaculation as evidence of his growing skill. He was going to learn to be the best lover Robbie had ever had. He remained on his knees beside his partner, caressing his body while his tremors subsided.

"That was lovely. I'll have a dunk in the sea and then I'd better round everybody up."

The return of the swimmers brought the party to its closing phase. Everybody made a point of having just one more drink for the road. The swimmers exclaimed enviously of having the sea as a private pool. Lance had lost his brief underpants in the dark and was wearing only his shorts. It was a daring exhibition of genitalia, with every detail clearly outlined, and everybody's eyes dropped to it as he served drinks.

Robbie frowned with displeasure, but when their eyes met, Lance's were so disarmingly radiant with love and high spirits that he decided he didn't mind. He saw that Pablito's eyes still followed him with a hungry glitter, which perhaps suggested that nothing had happened to calm his passion. Brewster's eyes were fixed on him with comparable infatuation, which perhaps suggested that something *had* happened to arouse his. Robbie hoped that he'd soon learn to live with everybody's sex fantasy.

"Was it a good party?" Luisa asked when the guests were gone.

"Very good," Robbie assured her.

"It was much work for you both. I'm sorry I couldn't do it all for you."

"No, little one. It's fun to do together," Lance said. "Was it a big boredom for you?"

"No. Very interesting. Did I do everything right?" She looked increasingly pleased with herself as they praised her for her social ease as well as for her cooking. She hadn't been as frightened as she had expected to be and once she'd seen them eating her food so hungrily she'd stopped being frightened entirely. The foreigners weren't so unlike her own people as she had thought, except that they laughed much more.

Robbie told her not to wash the dishes. "We'd be be up all night," he said. "If we give any more parties, maybe you should get a friend to help. You and I can get started on it in the morning. Lance has to be up at the crack of dawn."

"I'll do it now if you wish," she said. She was still unused to being treated with such consideration and didn't dare take it for granted.

"No. We've had a big day. It'll seem like nothing in the morning."

She left them. She wanted to hang up her dress carefully before it got dirty and get into her own bed alone, like a great lady.

Robbie approached Lance and looked down at him and laughed. "You ought to be spanked for not wearing anything under those shorts."

Lance looked delighted with himself. "My knickers got lost. Does it look like a big one?"

"What do you expect? It is a big one."

"Wonderful. I didn't have much luck swimming. It was so dark nobody could tell a girl from a boy."

Robbie ran a finger along the enticing flesh and watched it grow. "Not even Pablito?"

"Well, it wasn't *that* dark," Lance said hastily. "He couldn't jump on me with the others all around. Actually, he swam off by himself. Still, I've wondered, now

239

that we're seeing guys who are that way, how indignant are we supposed to be if somebody tries to get a bit too chummy?"

"Oh Lord, sweetheart, don't let me make more of it than it's worth. Guys are inclined to have wandering hands. If they're not feeling a tit, a cock makes a nice easy target. We can sort of ease out of it without making a big scene."

"I was thinking the same thing this evening. As a matter of fact, I practically fell over Brewster when I was still naked. He put his hand on it. I got a hard-on in two seconds. I guess I get a kick of of guys being interested in it but I was afraid you'd think I should raise hell with him."

A chill of outrage passed through Robbie, immobilizing the muscles of his face. He smoothed the fabric over the firm ridge of Lance's cock; it looked as it were about to burst out of his shorts. He forced a smile and was able to speak lightly. "There. I defy anybody *not* to touch it when it's like that."

Lance leaned forward and gave him a quick kiss on the mouth. "I love you darling. Shall we finish that bottle and then go to bed?" He went to the littered table and divided what was left of the rum into two glasses and added water that was still quite cool. They took the glasses to the parapet and sat side by side.

"I've been feeling so good about being a homosexual the last few days. Flip's party and then tonight—knowing that guys are attracted to me and being sort of attracted to them—it's beginning to seem perfectly normal. At the beginning, I thought guilt would spoil anything that happened between us. I don't know if this makes any sense, but being attracted to other guys frees something in me to fall more and more in love with you."

"The more that's homosexual in you, the more there is for me."

"That sounds right. Yes. I like to tell you everything. You can probably see that I'm attracted to Pablito but it's nothing that could ever cause any trouble between us. If I happened to be alone with him somewhere, would you think it very bad if I had sex with him?"

Robbie stiffened and the chill seeped through him

again. He had to get a rational grip on himself. Lance was trying to talk honestly with him. He took a deep breath. "Of course not. Not *very* bad. Not bad at all if I didn't know about it. I've told you. I can't be rational about fidelity. I didn't know until this week that I could be eaten alive by jealousy. It's nuts but I can't help wanting to be everything to you."

"It's wonderful, darling. It's what I want to be for you. It's the way it's going to be. To tell the truth, I wasn't crazy about the way you were looking at Pablito yourself."

"Persistence pays. I'm sure we'd neither of us give him a second's thought if he didn't go on looking at us as if he's consumed with passion."

Lance giggled. "Well, that's part of it, darling."

Lance felt as if he were getting a great load off his chest. He didn't think he'd done anything very bad, but his conscience had been bothering him. He didn't want to have secrets from Robbie. He'd practically told him everything, enough for him to imagine the rest. He need no longer feel that he was deceiving him, only protecting him from little things that he'd rather not know about.

He leaned in against Robbie and sighed happily as he dropped an arm around his shoulders. "I've discovered what I like best about parties—being alone with you after."

Robbie laughed softly and hugged him. "It's always a relief to know I've still got you. Anyway, we've done our social duty. As Luisa says, it's a lot of work and I don't suppose we'll find many people here who'll turn out to be lifelong friends but I wanted to do it once for her. It'll make her feel more a part of whatever she thinks our life is. Finish your drink, sweetheart," Robbie said. "I know how anxious you are to get going in the morning."

"Yes. I've got to be there for the opening of the oven. Keep your fingers crossed."

"I'll get up when you do. That'll give me an hour to help with the dishes before I get back to my own dirty work. You take the car, beautiful."

"Okay. If you never see me again you'll know there was nothing but dust in the kiln and I've jumped off the highest cliff I could find."

Breaking open the bricked-up kiln was one of the moments of high suspense of Lance's life. As Big worked the bricks free, Lance tried to peer over his shoulder to look in. It seemed to take an eternity before the hole was big enough for him to see a row of the devil figures lined up on their bed of sand. They looked intact. Big grunted and turned to him. He somehow managed to look as pleased as Lance felt. He nodded and went on removing the bricks. Little by little, the trays were uncovered. Three figures in a row formed a little scene of ruin. There were other shattered shards scattered about, but when all the trays had been removed, Lance counted a loss of only eleven.

"Very good," Big commented as if he were proud of his employer.

Lance went to work immediately, applying glazes for the second firing, determined to have the whole batch ready for the kiln by evening. He had so little idea of what to expect that he allowed his fancy free rein. Taking care with the unknown was a waste of time so he hoped that daring would keep luck running in his favor.

He took a short break for lunch at home with Robbie but was back at work with the whole afternoon ahead of him. He made his helpers smile and nod as his assemblage of bizarre figures multipled. He stayed late while the kiln was being bricked up again and watched the fire being started. He knew now that he could count on Big and his helper to take care of the rest.

When he picked up Robbie for dinner, he was as tired as he'd ever been in his life. Luisa had already left for her Sunday visit with her family when they got home. They had been together for a week. It was their first evening meal alone together and they welcomed the chance to celebrate Lance's triumph in intimate privacy. Lance couldn't stop talking about the details of the successful firing and his plans for the completion of his order. Robbie listened rapturously, gloating with loving pride over his dedication to making a success of his project and his shining satisfaction in his accomplishment so far. Lance confirmed all the faith Robbie had in him.

"I'll get going first thing in the morning on the other lot. We'll open the kiln Tuesday morning and if that's not too much of a mess, I'll be all set." He began to count days to himself, muttering things about "leather hard" and "slip." Robbie was touched by his pleasure in the professional jargon. "By golly, the shipment should be ready to go by Monday, a week from tomorrow. That's not bad," he concluded.

Robbie cooked them a deceptively simple, delicately French meal and they ate opposite each other so that their eyes didn't have to leave each other for an instant. At moments, the depth of their lingering glances spoke to each other in ways that almost made them shout with joy. Lance shivered and hugged himself and lifted his head incredulously. "I know you love me just as much but do you love to be with me as much as you did a week ago?" he asked.

Robbie looked startled and then slowly smiled. "That's an important question. More, actually, but we're together less now than we were at the beginning. Except for sleeping together we've hardly seen each other at all for the last three or four days."

"That's what I was thinking. It won't make us get used to being without each other, will it?"

"When I'm working, nobody exists for me, not even you. I think your work's going to be more and more like that for you, too. When I get finished, I'm so lonely for you I could cry."

"You're adorable. I suppose it's an awful thing to say but I wish this is the way it could be always, just the two of us. You probably feel it even more so."

"Not really, beautiful. Sometimes, but then I think of little Lance and that's so exciting that I wouldn't want anything changed."

"No, we certainly wouldn't want to lose little Lance." His mouth opened wide and locked into an enormous yawn. He laughed and slumped over the table. "I'm absolutely *whacked*. Remember when you first said you wanted me to go to bed with you? You said we'd just lie there and go to sleep. I think for once in our lives that might actually happen. You might have to pick me up and carry me in."

Lance wasn't entirely satisfied with the results of the second firing but there was nothing wrong enough to make him start all over again. He noted some glazes that had come through almost exactly as he'd hoped and eliminated a couple that had altered unrecognizably. There were some pleasant surprises—one glaze in particular that had acquired a coppery metallic sheen that he decided to experiment with later on other pieces. He tried to remember exactly how he had used it and made a note of it in a copybook he'd bought for the purpose.

He worked without stopping for the rest of the week, throwing the figures, adding appendages as they dried and hardened, starting to pack the first batch for shipment while the second batch was bricked up for the first firing. By Saturday, everything was ready for the final firing and after watching Big start the fire Lance left him in charge to take Sunday off.

He hadn't let Robbie see any of his work yet. Since each figure was different, he didn't want to show him only one or two and hoped that he had made enough improvements in the glazing of the second batch for it to make a more impressive display. They settled on Monday morning for an official show and because Robbie didn't allow himself a regular day off, Lance spent most of Sunday at his studio dozing on the decrepit sofa at the end of it and watching him work.

To Lance, sharing in the creation of a Robi canvas was the ultimate consecration of their belonging to each other. It was uniquely theirs, something that nobody else could have any part of. The intricate forms were still being filled in with flat undercoats and he still couldn't see what Robbie was trying to achieve, but when it was finished only he and Robbie would know the structure on which it had been built.

Alone again that evening, over another dinner cooked by Robbie, they celebrated having been together for two weeks. "Another week seemed like almost too much to hope for on our last anniversary," Lance said.

"Soon we'll be counting the years, darling," Robbie replied lovingly.

They were up and off to the shed early in the morning, eager for Lance's exhibition. When they arrived, they found that Big had already unbricked the kiln and had the trays lined up on shelves. They made a splash of riotous color in the drab surroundings. Lance moved quickly along them, picking up and examining individual pieces to which he'd given special attention. All his tricks had worked pretty well. There was room for improvement but he could turn them out by the hundreds now, without even trying.

Robbie moved slowly along at his side, his eyes absorbing shock after shock as he studied the strange little figures. They were technically much more professional and accomplished than the things he had slapped together for Flip. They had extraordinary character and individuality. Some were merely comic until one felt a hidden leer. He had done things with clay that Robbie had never seen done before, finding shapes in it that seemed contrary to its nature, turning it into a medium of intense eccentricity. They had great tactile appeal; one wanted to handle them. His eye was caught by one of such malevolence that he wanted to smash it. He told Lance how it affected him.

"That's wonderful. Go on. Smash it."

Robbie did so. It gave him great satisfaction.

"I hope you're ready to get to work on a big re-order," he said.

Lance turned to him quickly. His face lighted up. "You mean it? You think they're good?"

"Frankly, I'm stunned. They give me goose bumps. We've got two artists in the family, sweetheart."

Lance looked charmingly flustered. "Don't be silly. They're crazy little toys."

"If that's what you feel when you're making them, I wouldn't want to convince you otherwise. Allow your elders to know better. What're you going to call them?"

"Call them? I don't know. Gollies, for 'golliwog' or 'oh, my golly.' What happened to my gollies? You've got my gollies. Sure. That'll do."

"We'd better start trying to make Cosling stick as your name or you're going to hit the papers again. You'll definitely be my half brother. I'll write Dad and ask him to help us with a brief biography. He'll love it. We'll make you a year or so older. You'll have to be a bastard and part French. My real half brother, if any, is presumably in Brittany somewhere."

Lance looked bewildered. He shook his head. "Have you gone nuts?"

"Far from it. If it gets out that your gollies are by Lance Vanderholden, this place would be crawling with photographers in no time. My name is worth a bit of press attention but not enough to make a circus out of it. One of the big weeklies like *Time* might query their Paris correspondent. If they don't find me, they may check with Dad. If he's all ready to tell them about his recluse son Lance who's never allowed his picture to be taken, they'll forget all about it."

"Are you serious? You mean these silly little things might get big press coverage?"

"Not if they're by Lance Cosling, dummy. But they'll attract attention in some small circles. New York is populated by specialty journalists who have nothing to write about but the latest fad that somebody's trying to promote. Ask that Carstairs lady. My half brother might make a little splash."

Lance was busy for the next two days packing and taking care of the formalities for the shipment through a trucking agent Robbie had found for him. It was estimated that delivery would be made in New York in about ten days if he paid a premium for express service. Since the alternative was a month or two and the cases were neither heavy nor bulky, he accepted the extra expense philosophically. It wasn't much but he added it to his accounts and noted that he should go over expenses as carefully as possible in the next day or two to see if there was any chance of making the profit Robbie had predicted.

With his work on its way to New York, he found it difficult to settle down to something new. He'd been intimidated by Robbie's taking what he'd done so seriously. Could he really be an original artist as Robbie insisted? He had ideas he wanted to play around with but he was terrified that he'd shot his bolt with the gollies. He welcomed interruptions, even another visit from Captain Ramiriz.

The police chief came wandering in one morning and perched lightly on the edge of the table with as little apparent purpose as the first time. He looked around him, peered intently into the kilns, pushed his cap onto the back of his head, and sighed. Lance tried to be as cordial as he could be with a man who seemed scarcely aware of his presence.

246

"We've been very busy here," he said conversationally. "You should've come a few days ago. There'd've been something for you to see."

"Yes, yes. I understand you've started to export. Now you'll make more important shipments?"

"I don't know. That was the only order I had. I'm about to start some things I might be able to sell."

"For those of us who aren't rich, that must always be considered," Ramiriz said with a glint of humor. He had been told nothing to cast doubt on Señor Lance's relative poverty. He gave the local people small sums of money to bring him information about the foreigners. The youth who worked for the painter had told him that his employer and Señor Lance engaged in sexual activities together. It was a bit to add to the puzzle that this young man represented for him but he doubted if it would be of any interest in the capital. It wasn't surprising that two such handsome young men should find each other pleasing, especially if they were brothers.

"You had no trouble with your licenses? I gave orders that everybody was to cooperate fully."

"Thanks. Everything seemed to go smoothly. I heard that there was going to be plane service soon. Is that true?"

"For mail and light freight, very soon, I think. Perhaps a month. That will be of help to you?"

"Maybe. It depends on how much it costs and how prompt the delivery is this time."

"I'll have the representative come see you. I'm sure he'll make every effort to arrange satisfactory terms for you."

"You're very helpful."

"I wish to be." He wished to have as little to do with this young man as possible until he knew which way to jump. "Will you know soon how well your things are selling in the market?"

"I don't know. Maybe in a month or two."

The policeman adjusted his cap and shifted himself onto his feet. "I'm glad to find you well settled. I wish you success."

"Thanks. I hope you come someday when I have something to show you."

When Ramiriz had made his ponderous departure,

247

Lance told himself that he had to go back to work if only to prove to the policeman that he wasn't occupying the premises under false pretenses. Ramiriz's visits and his aimless questions made him feel like a fraud. He couldn't sit here waiting to hear that the gollies had arrived safely. He'd spent a day giving the place a thorough cleaning in order to avoid work. Enough procrastination.

He scooped up some clay and shaped it into a rough phallic form. He turned it over in his hands and saw that it had acquired a vaguely shrouded look. His mind gave a little leap of imagination. He saw a sculptural composition of a grouping of such forms, their juxtaposition on a flat surface giving them expressive significance. Like fantastic visions of classic chess problems. He would set them on a fragment of a chessboard. If he achieved the effect he wanted and Robbie's friend liked them, he could go on to making real chess sets. He chuckled to himself while his mind made rapid calculations. Thirty-two pieces and the board. An order for a hundred sets would require a total of thirty-three hundred pieces. The board and the pawns would be easy but the other pieces could take at least two months.

He threw a dozen mysterious shrouded figures of various sizes, the biggest being six or seven inches tall, all of them subtly phallic, and put them out to dry before he hurried off to join Robbie for lunch. He was bursting to tell him about his plans and ask his advice. His imagination was caught by his sculptural compositions but he intended to do only two or three of them before tackling the chess sets.

Robbie was enthusiastic and promised to write New York that afternoon to find out how big an order they could hope for and at what price.

As Lance went to work on his sculpture project, his conception grew more complex. He found endless possibilities in the grouping of the figures. Moving one a finger's breadth created a whole new world of dramatic tensions. Two groupings of five with a grouping of three between produced the effect that interested him the most and he added a thirteenth figure to the ones that were already dry. He told his helpers to fire up the other kiln in the morning to see how it worked, then rejoined Robbie.

248

It took him the rest of the week to position the pieces exactly the way he wanted them, attach them to their bases, fire them and glaze them in subdued tones he hadn't tried before. By Saturday morning they were ready to be bricked in for the second firing. Before he left that evening he told Big to open the kiln in the morning and then take the day off. He was looking forward to a leisurely Sunday but when Robbie was ready to go to his studio Lance found it impossible to delay going to the shed. He had to see how his sculpture had turned out.

Big had left the three pieces together on the table. Lance circled them warily until he decided that they'd turned out nearly as well as he'd hoped they would. He thought the subdued glazing, shifting tones of beige and cream, quite beautiful. It gave the figures the shadowy eerie quality he'd been aiming for. They looked like the victims of some calamity and yet somehow threatening to one other.

Although he was much more shy about them than he had been about the gollies, he took Robbie to see them after lunch. He'd separated them, so Robbie had to move from wheel to shelf to trough to look at them before Lance joined them to each other on the table. As usual when his eyes were absorbed, Robbie had remained silent but at this he took a quick breath and exclaimed, "Jesus." He circled them as Lance had done and came to a stop in front of his friend with his hands on his elbows, drawing him close. There were tears in his eyes.

"You bowl me over, beloved. You're good, you know. Really good. What a strange and wonderful creature you are. They're really quite gruesome but underneath it I hear a great raucous belly laugh."

Rich laughter poured from Lance's throat. "I'm glad I don't leave you speechless. I want to hear more." Their arms slipped around each other and they kissed at satisfying length. Lance's laughter became a gurgle of pleasure.

Robbie left him with an uncomfortable erection, intimidated once more by the gravity of his praise. He had to get to work quickly or he'd be stopped by another block. He discarded shirt and shorts, retaining only Robbie's flimsy black briefs that he had borrowed. An

249

ideal working outfit, although he didn't think the Juans would approve.

He began to experiment with the clay, using all the bits of tools that he had accumulated, and began to achieve results that astonished him. His concentration became more intense, developing skills as he went along, and he began to see possibilities for the chessmen that he'd thought were beyond him. He kept flattening the clay and starting over again.

He'd lost track of time when he heard voices outside and then Flip's unmistakable, flat, harsh tones saying, "I don't think there's anybody here."

"I'm here," he called. He rose before he remembered he was practically naked. It didn't matter with Flip; he was convinced that she didn't notice if anybody was wearing anything or not. He started to make a dash for his shorts in case she'd brought somebody with her. She appeared in the door followed by a young man. Straight or not, it didn't matter with him either.

"There you are, my dear," she announced, advancing to him and taking a grimy hand in both of hers. "Michael would give me no peace until I brought him. He's very much interested in pottery. Michael Denis. You know him, of course. The famous dancer."

The young man smiled diffidently. "If you know Flip, you know how she exaggerates. I hope I'm going to be famous but it takes time." He said it as a literal statement of fact while his eyes rested peacefully and undisguisedly on Lance's crotch. He had very long straight pale hair and a remarkable body. He looked young, in his early twenties, and was shorter than Lance.

"Have you done any more of those fascinating idols that fooled me so?" Flip inquired.

"Not since I finished the order. That's all I have at the moment." He waved toward the table.

She took a step toward it. "How thrilling. It makes me think of a gathering in a graveyard. So macabre. The colors are beautiful. I'd love to have a set of dinner plates in those shades. May I leave Michael with you? I have a thousand chores and a call to pay on a tiresome couple who would bore him to distraction. If you're going home soon, perhaps you wouldn't mind dropping him off so he doesn't get lost." The subject of her concern had abandoned his contemplation of Lance's crotch in favor of his sculpture and glanced up at her absent-mindedly.

"I'll be all right, Flip," he said quietly. "If I'm in his way, I'll manage to get home."

"I know you two will hit it off. My dear love to Robbie." She tilted her head at both of them, waved gaily, and departed.

Lance went to the tap and washed and dried his hands before turning back to his visitor. He had seated himself on the edge of the table with his legs stretched out in front of him. He had a wide, faintly Slavic face without distinctive features, pleasant-looking but not striking. He looked like a nice, simple young man but his eyes were once more on Lance's crotch, not furtively, but gazing openly at something he wanted to look at. Lance went to him and held out his hand.

"I couldn't shake hands before, not that it mattered to Flip. She didn't even notice that she's gone off covered with clay. Welcome." Michael took his hand slowly and held it as if he wanted to keep it. Doubly aware of being practically naked, Lance removed his crotch from his field of vision by sitting beside him.

"She's nutty as a fruitcake but she's not dumb. She sees things. I think these things are remarkable." The dancer glanced over his shoulder at the grouped figures. "I've fooled around with ceramics. Ashtrays. That sort of thing. I never got into sculpture. You're good."

"I don't have anything else to show you. There's nothing to see here."

"Except you."

Lance laughed. "Just about all there is of me. I wasn't dressed for callers."

"You're dressed beautifully. Hung beautifully too. The only way I'd like you better is stark naked with a hard-on but I don't want to rush you."

They looked at each other with quiet speculation. Lance realized that all his social experience with homosexuals since his sexual switch had been with and through Robbie. For the first time he was on his own and wasn't sure he knew how to handle it. But the attraction wasn't strong enough for him to be tempted to cheat.

"I've heard of you," he said, to steer the conversation

251

away from sex. "It seems to me I read quite a lot about you two years ago."

"That's when I was getting my first big solos. After you'd opened in your show."

"I guess that's why I never saw you. You never see anything when you're performing yourself. Did you see me?"

"God, yes. I fell in love with you at first sight. I saw you five times and had a hard-on the entire time. I couldn't make love for a year without thinking of you. I still do sometimes when I want to come quickly."

He spoke quietly and literally, without humor. His long pale hair was brushed straight back but it had a tendency to fall lankly over one eye. He had a mannerism of combing it back slowly with his fingers. It gave him a cool detached quality. He didn't look as if he were smoldering with passion or even dazzled by love at first sight.

"It's pretty silly to have to come all the way down here to meet when we were working only a few blocks away from each other," Lance said, still trying to get away from sex.

"I was afraid of meeting you. Everybody insisted you were straight. It certainly looked that way but I couldn't believe it."

"Why not? *I* did."

"Guys often do for a while. I never did, not after I was fucked the first time. There're certain things a straight guy can't do with his body. That's how I knew about you. Shall I show you?"

He pushed himself off the table and, with a dazzling ripple of muscles in his shoulders and chest and abdomen, whipped his shirt over his head. His long hair fell over his forehead in disarray. He had no hair on his chest or in his armpits. Lance had never seen a guy who shaved there. He tossed the shirt onto the table and crossed the room while Lance's eyes were held by the bunched power of his buttocks. He turned back.

"The beginning of your big sort of dance number," he explained. "I knew you weren't a dancer but it didn't matter. You could do it because you moved right. The spot picked you up like this." He balanced himself on one leg and lifted the other knee in against his chest and folded himself over it with his arms at his sides,

252

stretching back. "The music built and slowly all of your body opened up." Michael unfolded like a flower, until his arms embraced the sky and his leg lifted out straight in front of him.

Lance watched, hypnotized, as the dancer effortlessly reproduced what he had worked so hard to achieve.

He lifted himself to his toes, hung poised in space for a moment, and then lunged forward onto his outstretched leg and made a running rush for Lance. His heart stopped. Michael had come to blazing life in movement. His physical appeal was electrifying. Lance's hands lifted to the sides of his chest to steady him as he drew up in front of him with his hands on his shoulders and one leg arching up behind him in an arabesque.

"Remember?" he said, his lips brushing Lance's cheek so lightly that he wasn't sure it was intended as a kiss.

"You do it a helluva lot better than I did."

"I came the first time I saw you do it. Literally. It's the first and only time I've ever had an orgasm with nobody touching me, not even myself." He slowly lowered his foot to the floor while he moved his lips lightly over Lance's face, unmistakably kissing his forehead and eyelids and cheeks. Lance was transfixed by a stab of desire and his grip tightened on his chest. When their lips met, Michael's tongue darted in and out of his mouth, challenging him to catch it. Lance's erection burst from its inadequate confinement and lifted against his belly.

They were in each other's arms, tugging at elastic, stripping each other. A startlingly bulky cock sprang up into his hands but the urgency of their bodies prevented him from giving it his full attention. All of Michael was waiting for his touch. His hands lingered on the taut muscular spheres of his buttocks while the dancer hung on him, swaying against him so that their erections teased each other deliciously.

"Oh my God, Lance. It's really you," Michael crooned. "I'm with you at last. I knew your cock would be sublime." His head was thrown back, his face transformed. Its color was heightened and a look of rapture brought out the planes and angles of its bone structure. His eyes were soft and lustrous with desire, his mouth expectantly loose and sensual. He had become the romantically handsome youth of the photograph. The current of desire ran vividly between them. Michael's inviting mouth surrendered to Lance's tongue. Lance moved his hands with delight over the powerful buttocks and let his fingers stray between them. Michael wrenched his mouth away with a cry.

"Oh God. Oh damn. I'm going to come."

Lance dropped and stretched his mouth wide to take the imposing cock, catching a quick glimpse of both of them for comparison. Not quite matching bookends but close enough. Michael's swelled prodigiously as it slid into Lance's mouth and immediately filled it with his ejaculation. Lance swallowed it. He was beginning to relax and take it for granted.

As he stood, the dancer ducked down in his turn and Lance backed up to the edge of the table and ran his fingers through his hair while his mouth took his cock with touchingly ardent adoration. Lance was exhilarated again by the danger of discovery. Naked sex-play in such an exposed place was an outrage, as exciting as producing his erection in a men's room, spitting in the collective Vanderholden eye. His orgasm was an explosion of euphoric defiance.

The dancer rose, looking dazed with grateful satisfaction. "That was worth waiting two years for," he said.

Lance laughed, seeing that he had a hard-on again. His own erection had only partially subsided and felt as if it could be quickly revived. "Come on. We've got to put these things away somehow." He let go of him and took a turn around to see that he was leaving everything in order. Aware once more of his surroundings, he expected to find eyes peering at him everywhere he looked. It had been a foolhardy risk but he couldn't remember a moment when either of them could have called a halt. It had been inevitable. Something so simple and immediate couldn't be considered an infidelity. Michael was going to be their friend. He couldn't wait to take him to Robbie. The thought of all three of them together brought his cock jutting out in front of him again.

He stepped into his shorts without attempting to close the fly. He returned to Michael, who was sitting on the edge of the table with the trunks covering himself, watching him with peaceful, absorbed eyes. Lance pushed the trunks away onto the table, uncovering his impressive erection. Their hands moved caressingly on each other.

"We're supposed to be going," Lance said. "Where to? Do you know about Robbie?"

"Flip said you live with your lover."

"Lover. Friend. My life. Everything."

"That sort of covers it all. She says you're the two most beautiful men she's ever seen. I agree with her about you." He leaned forward and brushed Lance's cock with his lips. "What about fidelity?"

"That too."

Michael looked up at him. "Then—"

"It's just that I can't see some things as infidelity. I don't want to keep you a secret from Robbie. I want us all to be friends, making love together if we want to. I don't see how this can be wrong." He lifted Michael to him and the dancer folded himself in against him as if taking shelter. "I never expected to live with a guy, so I have a lot to learn. I know there have to be rules but rules won't make you invisible. God, what a body. You're so damn sexy. Wait till Robbie sees you."

Michael laughed softly and their mouths met in a kiss that send desire racing through their bodies again. Lance ran his hands over his back and buttocks and felt muscles quivering with anticipation. He'd already guessed what Michael wanted.

"You want me to fuck you, don't you?"

"God, yes." Michael made it as heartfelt as a prayer.

"We've got to get out of here. Let's go to bed and see what happens. Don't put anything on. Cover yourself and we'll make a dash for it." Having pushed his luck to the limit, he felt suddenly that every second they remained invited disaster. They snatched up their things, Lance stuffed the little black briefs into a pocket, and they clutched bits of clothing over themselves as they ran the few yards to the car. They fell into it laughing, their hands reaching for each other.

"You're such a beautiful nut," Michael exclaimed, his face glowing with animation. "I've never been for a drive naked before. Where're we going?"

"We can go to Flip's, can't we? It's too early to disturb Robbie."

"Perfect. She's given me the guest house all to myself."

They held each other's cocks as Lance started off. He felt that his life as a homosexual had really begun. He had found a queer friend on his own. He liked him. He hadn't waited for him to make the first move but had joined in immediately. This was the sort of thing he had thought was bound to happen—the sudden rush of desire, the easy, almost irresistible opportunity to satisfy it—something that could be a constant source of irritation and frustration unless he and Robbie absorbed it into their life together. Robbie was as susceptible to a well-built, personable kid as he was, even though he didn't want to admit it; they couldn't be unfaithful if they were together. Lance thought of the last two weeks living exclusively for their work and each other. He'd loved it but he didn't want Robbie to feel that they were already getting into a rut. Michael was just the guy he'd been waiting for to prove that there could be some freedom in the close confinement of their love.

"Do you have a lover?" he asked, dropping an arm around Michael's wide sloping shoulders.

"Yes. Ever since I was a kid. Almost six years."

"Vows of fidelity?"

"Back at the beginning but Phil doesn't think it's very important."

Another couple who stretched the rules. "Robbie does," he said.

"Thank God you don't." He leaned down to Lance's cock, his head almost against the wheel, and began to do exciting things with his mouth.

"I do up to a point." Lance chuckled. "Less so when you're doing that. I'd like the three of us to be together. You know—in bed. Will you?"

"You can do anything you like with me. From what I've heard about him, it doesn't sound as if it would be a hardship."

Lance laughed. "No. Wait till you see him. I won't stand a chance. His cock's bigger than mine, for one thing. I hope you find out all about it. He's so good. I mean it. A paragon of virtue. I'd love to corrupt him enough for him to enjoy having fun with guys who attract him, like what's happened with us. It would make me feel less guilty for wishing you'd take me."

"You mean, fuck you? We both want to get fucked?

I'm stunned. You're my big sister." He giggled and worked his way down in the seat so that he could lay his head in Lance's lap. "Just looking at your cock is better than being fucked by any ten guys I can think of. God, it feels good. Not just your cock. Being like this with you." He renewed the attentions of his mouth. They erupted in brief bursts of laughter until Lance came to a halt in front of Robbie's studio. Michael sat up and looked around. "This isn't Flip's," he said.

"No. This is where Robbie works. Flip's is just a few minutes' walk. I'll leave the car here." He was glad to be so close to home, almost within shouting distance of Robbie. He had nothing to hide. "Much as I hate to, I better let you put your pants on for a minute." Michael pulled his trunks up over his legs and Lance's hands lingered on the unwieldy thrust of his cock before letting it be hidden. He put the keys of the car in a pocket beside the back seat, as usual. If by some unlikely chance Robbie came out early, he'd think Lance had left it for him and drive it home. He wasn't going to lie about where he'd been.

He pushed his cock haphazardly into his open shorts and held his shirt over his front as they set off on the short walk to Flip's gate. Michael hurried him down through the garden to a guest house that he was pretty sure was the one Flip had given him the day they'd met. He and Michael threw their arms around each other as they reached it and crowded through the door together. Their minimal clothing was gone by the time they were inside. Michael was flushed and looked younger than ever, as vibrantly alive as when he'd done the little dance movement. His flat-footed dancer's stride carried him to the bed and he stretched out on his stomach.

Lance quickly dropped over him, aware of the invitation implicit in his position, and bit his shoulders and ran his tongue around his ear and kissed the side of his face. Michael's lips parted ecstatically. He moaned and laughed and, with a thrilling fluid movement of muscles, rolled over onto his back. He flung his arms over his head and all his body seemed to lift and undulate into Lance's embrace. He lay back on the support of his arms, still and inert. He made his sturdy athlete's body an opulent offering. Lance passed his hand over a hairless armpit. It was very smooth.

Lance stretched luxuriously against him. He had time at last for a complete physical experience with a guy, free of the tyranny of love, time to examine and savor what it meant for him. He was filled with a rare sense of well-being that seemed to flow from a liberation of all his senses, a peaceful realization of his deepest erotic urges. After his meaningless little encounters with Frank and the others, he was finding something he could share with Robbie—a glowing acceptance of himself and his readiness to tune himself to male desire.

Their bodies coiled voluptuously around each other. They posed for each other, laughing like children at their shameless inventions. They discovered a strong streak of exhibitionism in each other. Michael opened closet doors to reveal full-length mirrors and they performed phallic rituals in front of them. Michael had three orgasms in astonishingly rapid succession and they laughed triumphantly when Lance restored his erection without difficulty.

Michael was an adorable playmate. The pleasure they found in each other was inexhaustible. Lance realized that only Robbie could satisfy him totally, but total satisfaction somehow blocked self-knowledge. He was learning a lot that he had to know about himself with Michael, including the knowledge that he couldn't exclude Robbie from anything good that happened to him.

When the time came to interrupt Robbie's work, they played together under the shower and dressed, Lance wearing the briefs under his shorts, Michael in a black and green sarong, presumably from Flip's inexhaustible collection, and a loose, open, vestlike shirt.

"How're we supposed to act?" Michael asked. "As if nothing's happened between us?"

"I guess so. No. I don't know. Let's just relax and let him think whatever he wants. He can't think we've fallen in love with each other and I want him to feel that everything's wide open as far as sex is concerned. If you want him, I hope you'll make him feel it. He'll probably try to resist you unless we're absolutely outrageous."

"You make me feel as if we were a couple of tarts about to make our rounds."

They laughed and kissed and hugged each other before starting back to Robbie's house. Lance felt light-hearted and guiltless. Their lovemaking had been only a prelude to what he hoped would be an adventure in sharing everything with his lover. If it worked the way he wanted it to, they would have found a safety valve in case they ever felt they were devouring each other or, worse, letting their life become a rigid routine of self-denial.

The car was still parked where Lance had left it. Robbie glanced up when they appeared in his door and, seeing the stranger, gave his easel a quick push so that the canvas faced the wall. Lance noticed it with a surge of pride; he was the only one who was privileged to look. Robbie came out from behind it and Lance hugged him and kissed him lightly on the mouth. Robbie was astonished but pleased; as far as he could remember, it was the first time Lance had greeted him publicly in this way other than with Luisa. The young stranger was evidently one of the fraternity and knew that they were a couple. Lance held Robbie's arm and turned to him.

"This is Michael Denis. He's with Flip, naturally. She brought him to the shed. He's one of the stars of the Ballet Theatre."

"I will be one of the stars next season," Michael said, shaking hands.

Robbie liked the way he established his exact position, his lack of what the English called "side." There was nothing studied in his manner or personality, as might be expected in a star of either last season or next. Even his hair, which could have been turned into an eccentric attraction, was too carelessly natural to look contrived. And he did have a highly desirable dancer's body. Robbie caught himself trying to make out what the folds of the sarong concealed. "Are you staying long?" he asked pleasantly.

"A week or so. Flip's been asking me to come for years. I haven't told Lance this but when she said he was here, I was packed and off like a shot."

Robbie laughed and glanced fondly at Puerto Veragua's latest tourist attraction. "That sounds familiar. I'd've done the same."

"You got to him ahead of me, worse luck. Not that

I hoped to carry him off with me but I've always heard about romance under a tropical moon. What did I find? The glamorous Lance Vanderholden covered with mud and sweat."

"We've got very down-to-earth tropics here." Robbie noticed that Lance looked considerably fresher than he usually did when he came from the shed. His hair was damp around the edges. Sweat or a shower? He took a closer look at Michael. His face was without striking features but there was a niceness in his expression and he had a youthful appeal. He turned to Lance. "Have you come straight from work?"

"Not very straight. More zigzag. I was a mess but it was too early to barge in on you. Michael let me take a shower at Flip's."

Lance exchanged a look with Michael that made no attempt at innocence. Robbie had been told that they'd been to bed together. A flash of rage seemed to split his brain, followed by an icy calm as he looked at Lance. He looked so sweetly pleased with himself, bringing him his conquest like a precious gift. He was boldly eager to enter perilous territory where Robbie had known he would eventually want to lead them. Robbie could teach him a lesson by trying to cut him off from his lover of an afternoon or he could give him a chance to show him a new dimension in relationships that all his experience told him was beyond human reach. He glanced at Michael and had to admit that Lance's gift was pleasing.

"I could use a shower myself," he said to give himself time to find out what was expected of him. "I'll wait till we get home." He moved to his work surface and began to clean brushes, remaining half-turned to his visitors.

"Michael's coming for a drink with us," Lance said.

"Good. Tonight's our bachelor night. Have you told him about our girl?"

"No. I was mostly clueing him in about us."

"He says you brought him out," Michael said. "If *you* couldn't, nobody could. You two are extraordinary. You don't exactly look alike but you look as if you belonged together."

"We're a matching pair," Robbie said. Lance let out a burst of laughter. Robbie looked into Michael's eyes and found a tranquil, disarming welcome in them. He was used to associating with his own kind and knew all the little signs and signals with which they communicated secret matters. He saw that Michael had made no commitment to Lance and was ready for him to take him. "Were you surprised to discover he wasn't straight?" he asked.

"I always knew it, no matter what people said. You saw his show? Didn't you think so?"

"I try not to assume everybody is homosexual, no matter how much I might want them to be. Not knowing didn't stop me from falling in love with him."

"Same here. I told him so."

Robbie looked at Lance and chuckled. "Do you like being talked about, sweetheart?"

"You're not talking about me," Lance said contentedly. "You're flirting with each other."

"We're doing nothing of the sort, are we, Michael?"

"I'm flirting with you," Michael said simply.

"I see," Robbie said, reluctantly accepting the situation that Lance had created. "Well, if that's the way it is, I'd better try to catch up with you two." He put down his brushes and went to Michael and drew him close. Michael melted in against him and their mouths met. Michael's lips were soft and thrillingly inviting. Their cocks hardened against each other. Lance had proved that, despite all Robbie had said, he was capable of being strongly attracted to others. Lance had brought him back to life with a vengeance; he was seventeen again, having his first unbridled sexual adventures. If Lance didn't like what was happening, he had only himself to blame.

Robbie broke off the kiss and looked at him over Michael's shoulder. "Is this what you had in mind?"

Lance erupted with laughter. "Oh, darling. You're sublime."

"Okay. That's enough for here. Let's go home and flirt over drinks." He returned to the table and dropped his brushes into the jar of turpentine, wiping his hands carefully on a rag. "Didn't I have a shirt? Yes. Here it is." He picked it up while Michael waited at the door. He fell into step beside him as they all went out through the citrus grove to the car.

Lance got into the driver's seat. Robbie let Michael

get into the middle and climbed in beside him with an arm across his shoulders. As soon as Lance started the motor and provided the privacy of motion, Michael eased his weight over to Robbie and began to stir against him. Robbie's arm tightened around his shoulders and their hands became active on each other. Michael's hand slipped under Robbie's sarong and found his erection with a little exclamation of startled delight. Robbie unfastened the sarong and let it slip open. If he was going to play games with Lance, he might as well go all the way. He wanted to jolt him into calling a halt.

"That's more like it," Lance said approvingly. "I want to see what's going on."

"You keep your eyes on the road," Robbie ordered with playful severity.

Lance chuckled and dropped a hand to Michael's sarong, and flipped it open. The cock that lifted from its folds was an exhilarating shock. It was almost a matching bookend. Robbie's hand met Lance's on it and they moved over it together. "Isn't it a honey?" Lance commented with the pride of discovery.

Incredulously, as their hands played together on hard flesh, Robbie began to feel that Lance might have found a new intimacy in their enjoying the same boy. An undercurrent of resentment and disapproval remained from his knowing that this had started before he'd been brought into it, but maybe that would pass. He knew that basically Lance was trying to show him that they had nothing to fear from infidelities, but the fact remained that their desire for each other was being momentarily diverted to a third person. He wanted to finish with it and get back to Lance.

"I'm in luck," Michael exclaimed as their amorous hands caressed him and each other. "The two most beautiful guys in the world coming to blows over me."

"Armed combat comes later," Lance promised and they all laughed.

Slowing as they neared home, he prepared himself for the next move. Robbie had succumbed to ordinary mortal weakness; he didn't want to give him a chance for second thoughts. He swerved over to the side of the road, braked at the top of their path, and switched off the motor, getting out of the car in seconds. "Take your

262

time. I'll run get the ice out." He went clattering off down the path.

Robbie barely had time to turn to Michael before he'd slid out of his top and into Robbie's arms. Their open mouths met and their bodies locked together while they tugged at the tangle of sarongs until their nakedness was completely exposed to their urgent hands. Lance was playing fair. He was allowing them a moment alone together in return for the time he'd spent with Michael earlier, a moment to make their own connections without being guided or dominated by Lance's prior claim. Robbie was being adaptable. For the moment, adapting was giving him great pleasure. Michael's body was a joy to explore. The dancer suddenly wrenched his mouth free with a little cry. "My God. I'm going to come," he gasped.

Robbie quickly bent over him and took him in his mouth. In another few moments, Michael's mouth led Robbie to a climax with equal ease. They sat side by side with their arms around each other, breathing deeply.

"That should help us to behave ourselves for a little while," Robbie said.

"I hope not for long. I don't think Lance expects us to. He adores you."

"That didn't stop him from wanting you."

"That was my fault. I forced myself on him. He talked right away about wanting me to meet you. He's afraid you'll get bored with him."

"I know. Variety is the spice of life. He's mad, of course. You don't mind providing variety?"

"With you two? Good Lord! The minute we joined you, I felt him bringing us all together. He's making me fall in love with both of you because you're together. You two don't have anything to worry about."

Robbie ruffled his pale silken hair. "You're sweet, baby. I should stop worrying so much about fidelity. It must seem pretty silly to you after what's happened with both of us. Let's go in. He's waiting for us."

Lance coaxed himself over the wrench of leaving them together by reminding himself that he'd spent a happy hour with Michael without its having done anybody any harm. The future would undoubtedly offer greater threats than the amenable undemanding dancer; they would be prepared to take them in their stride. He took off his work clothes and put on a sarong and went to the kitchen to get things ready for drinks. Waiting wasn't easy. He couldn't help imagining Robbie discovering pleasures with Michael that he didn't know anything about. He wanted him to enjoy himself, but not too much.

He had glasses and ice out when he heard them coming down the path and his heart gave a little leap of relief. They hadn't been as long as he'd expected. As soon as his eyes met Robbie's, Lance knew that his experiment had been a success. They were full of humor and devotion, his secret smile a guarantee that nobody could come between them. Their hands lifted to each other as he approached and they exchanged an uninhibited kiss while their cocks stirred against each other.

Robbie knew that the extra little edge of excitement he could feel building between them was due to having Michael as a witness. Since Lance was the only person in the world he really wanted, it seemed a bit pointless to have introduced an outsider into their intimacy, and yet something new seemed to have been added. He didn't quite understand what it was but supposed that it might be the open acknowledgment of their susceptibility to attractive young men. They didn't have to pretend to be saints. It made for a new ease between them. Misgivings remained but he was ready to give Lance the benefit of the doubt.

They let each other go and Lance gave them drinks. They lighted lamps as night fell and basked in the pleasure of feeling that Michael was equally attracted to them both. They didn't have to vie for his attention. His eyes moved from one to the other as they talked about things that interested them all. Lance had defused what might have been an explosive situation. With luck there would be no more Pablitos. Everything open and aboveboard.

Could a three-way sexual involvement ever be as simple as that? Robbie doubted it. His instincts continued to warn him that they were taking insane risks with their feelings.

He made a test of leaving them to take a shower and found that he wasn't wondering morbidly about what they were doing without him. There might be something to be said for sharing their pleasure if they could count on everybody always wanting them both equally.

When he returned, they were discussing the evening. "I've got to go soon to have dinner with Flip," Michael said. "I'm the only guest. She wouldn't like eating alone."

"Good Lord, you don't skip meals casually with Flip," Robbie agreed, standing beside Michael's chair. "I stayed with her, too. It's still pretty early by her standards."

"I know. She usually makes nine o'clock sound like teatime. She's already apologized. Early meals and no parties. She's let some of her help have time off during this lull. I've met the only two people I want to see here so that's all right with me." He smiled tranquilly at them.

"Another quick drink and then we'll take you home. We'll expect you back for a swim after dinner. It'll be a full moon," Lance said as he stood.

Michael reached for Robbie's hand and looked up at him. "Is that all right?"

"Sure." He gave Michael's hand a squeeze. He hadn't expected Lance to let him go until he'd made the most of the situation and he supposed he couldn't honestly say that he wanted him to. He'd given him tacit encouragement. He lifted an arm as Lance approached to collect glasses, and encircled his waist. Lance moved in against him and for a moment they were blissfully together. Robbie wished Michael would disappear. He checked himself and turned to their guest.

"Come sit with us and tell me about being a dancer," he said. Lance took their glasses to the table.

"I'd better stay where I am." Michael smiled disarmingly. "Remember what you said about behaving. Seeing you two together does make it difficult."

"We don't have to behave. We're a threesome. At least, I think that's Lance's theory."

It seemed to Robbie that they'd better put theory to the test. They couldn't be at ease with each other until they found out if they could all enjoy being together in the sense that Lance intended. He leaned over and brought Michael to his feet. He followed Robbie's guidance with touching alacrity, making him feel in masterly control of his body. The effect his hosts had on him was very evident under his sarong. Robbie let him hide himself against him, feeling his youthfully submissive appeal. He wanted the dancer, but couldn't imagine taking him in front of Lance.

His hands moved over Michael's chest under the odd vest and stroked his intriguingly hairless armpits before pushing the superfluous bit of clothing back over his shoulders and letting it slide off. His erection prodded Robbie into vigorous action. Their sarongs became superfluous as their hands rediscovered each other and their mouths met. Robbie felt a growing expectancy in Michael's soft inviting lips as if he took for granted the course their lovemaking would take.

He broke from the deepening kiss and turned toward the table where Lance was replenishing their drinks. Their eyes met. Lance's danced with fun and sly encouragement as his sarong joined the others on the floor. His display of his superbly priapic body was suitably casual. They made a rush for each other in a passion of welcome as if they were returning to each other after a long separation. Briefly, they forgot Michael's presence until they became aware of the sharpened excitement of being observed. They were committed to a threesome and they couldn't exclude Michael now.

Once again Robbie broke free from an embrace and held out a hand to the dancer, who accepted its invitation unquestioningly, advancing to them with his eyes lowered to their groins. Robbie assumed the leadership in stretching Michael out on the cot, his dancer's body automatically assuming a languorously compliant pose on his back. Robbie dropped to the edge of the cot and brought Lance down on the other side of the recumbent figure. With a final stiffening of his will, he relinquished his exclusive possession of his lover by throwing an arm across his shoulders and urging him down over Michael's belly.

Lance lifted Michael's cock to his mouth and Robbie's heart began to pound with outrage. He watched Lance's lips and tongue move with obscene familiarity on swelling flesh and tried to choke down his pain. Knowing that Lance wanted it wasn't very different from seeing him do it. He had taught him to enjoy it; he should be pleased that he took to it with such skillful enthusiasm. Michael moaned ecstatically.

To drive the image of the sucking mouth from his mind, Robbie applied his own mouth's skill to the object of his single-minded adoration. He felt Lance's body leap with passionate life under his touch. Michael's legs kicked out under him and his ecstatic moans were terminated by a succession of short whimpering cries. Lance flung himself out on the cot and pulled Robbie up to him. Michael's mouth fluttered tantalizingly along Robbie's cock and Robbie shifted his hips to make himself more readily available. He could feel Lance's body tensing with his approaching climax. He was incapable of offering Michael the grateful attention that he would have felt ordinarily was due a generous partner. All his thoughts and feelings were engaged in giving Lance pleasure. They shared simultaneous orgasms and lay still while Robbie thought how much he'd prefer their being alone.

He sat up. Michael's mouth didn't relinquish his subsiding erection, but he'd monopolized his attentions long enough. He still didn't see how sex could be a satisfactory group activity. There were too many conflicting interests and instincts involved. If you were interested in somebody, you were bound to try to monopolize his attention. If you weren't, there was no point starting anything. In any case, it concerned two people, not more.

He put a hand under his chin and lifted his head. Michael hunched himself up higher against him and put an arm around him. His other hand trailed along Robbie's cock.

Robbie held the hand motionless on himself. "We'd better have those drinks before you have to go."

"You'll have to throw me out. I want to make love to you both all night."

Lance laughed behind them. "He's incredible. He has a hard-on all the time no matter how often he comes. I bet he has one now."

Robbie wondered again what they'd been doing this afternoon. He wouldn't quite know how to act with them until Lance told him everything. He could be reasonably sure that their lovemaking hadn't gone beyond what the three of them had now had together.

Robbie disengaged himself and stood. He gathered up the discarded sarongs. By the time he had done so, his nearly restored erection was once more subsiding. He heard the other two giggling on the cot. Fair enough.

He didn't want Michael to attach himself to either one of them more than the other.

He wrapped his sarong around himself before turning back to them. They were sprawled out with glorious abandon on the cot, Michael propped up on the cushions. Shapely limbs were intertwined. He was moved by their beauty and more thrilled than shocked to see Lance so physically at ease in new unfamiliar sexual circumstances. He could actually look at his nakedness with a naked boy without wanting to kill them or himself. He was adapting. Had some subconscious defense mechanism been set in motion that would eventually arm him with indifference?

Their eyes met and Lance laughed as his hands wandered caressingly over Michael's body and lingered on the handsome erection that stood up against his belly. "What did I tell you?" he demanded with infectious glee.

Robbie looked at Michael and chuckled. "You look as if we'd neglected you shamefully. What can we do about it?"

"Don't *you* laugh at me. I can't help it." He pushed Lance's hand away affectionately and pulled himself forward to the edge of the cot and dropped his feet to the floor. He looked up at Robbie with his disarming smile. "You're the most exciting guys I've ever known. You're the way I've always thought two guys should be together—loving each other and having fun together and knowing that nothing can ever come between you. You make me feel as if you'd always been together."

Robbie found it reassuring that somebody thought they were making sense. Michael's calmly passionate eyes drew him. He approached him as Lance slid in against his back and kissed the side of his face. "You're nice," he said, "even if your cock won't lie down."

Michael laughed and put an arm around Robbie's waist and pulled him close enough to lay his head against his hip. Robbie dropped their sarongs onto the cot, feeling an unexpected loving comradeship flowing between the three of them that had somehow emerged from their haphazard sexual coupling. Having contributed little or nothing to it, Robbie was dazzled by this further evidence of Lance's instinct for finding the good in people. He stroked Michael's pale hair and hugged his head against him before handing them their drinks.

When they decided they couldn't keep Flip waiting any longer, the three of them went back to the car and Michael was delivered to her gate. The moon was already casting a silver sheen on the road; they agreed that it was bright enough for Michael to walk back as soon as he was free. Lance turned the car around and headed for home.

"He's fallen for you in a big way, darling," he said with laughter in his voice.

"Both of us," Robbie corrected him. "That's what's so sweet about him."

"You mostly. You're the one who can give him what he really wants. He knows how things are with us. He called me his big sister."

Robbie made a little face. He hated camp talk and he was less eager than he had been to find out what they'd done without him. It was a dead issue. Without Michael's presence to keep desire stirring, the little episode seemed flat and somehow shameful. "Were you just sisters when you were alone together?" he asked with a twinge of distaste.

"Sort of incestuous sisters." Lance's laughter bubbled to the surface. "He didn't make a he-man of me, if that's what you mean. He wanted me to take him but now that I know about myself I'd feel silly pretending to be a dominating male. I'm not. I don't want to be. You're the dominating male of our family. I just want to belong to my guy."

"*Your* guy, or any guy? If we're going to be a bit flexible about strict fidelity, there better not be any confusion about how far I'm willing to go. I'd never accept anybody else having you. You understand that, don't you?"

"You know nothing like that's going to happen with my little sister. I wanted him for you as much as for myself. I've been waiting to tell you how it happened. I didn't think much about him when Flip brought him. She left him with me and then he showed me that little dance bit I did in the show. It was the sexiest thing I've ever seen. There I was practically naked with a hard-on. The next thing I knew he had my cock in his mouth. I don't see how anybody could call that being unfaithful. Once I'd had a good look at Michael's body, I couldn't wait for you to meet him but it was too early to disturb

269

you, so we went to Flip's to get acquainted. He'd already made me come so there was no reason to stand on ceremony. He comes when you just look at him. It was my first chance to really relax and find out what sex with a guy was like without getting fucked or falling in love. Just plain ordinary silly sex. I'm still learning, darling."

"Yes, I keep reminding myself, but what about me? I don't have anything to learn."

"Sure you do. You have to learn that we shouldn't feel guilty about being attracted to other guys. Michael understands. He knows nothing can come between us."

"Not if we don't let it."

"*No*, darling. Nothing *can*." Lance was seized by the unique incandescent joy that lighted up the world around him, the joy that Robbie was determined would never be dimmed. "It's so exciting to know that everybody wants to be had by my guy. You can take your pick."

"What if I just happen to be monogamous?"

"You want Michael."

"Yes, but I wouldn't have if you hadn't pushed him under my nose."

"But that's ridiculous. You close your eyes because you think you have to for my sake. It cuts you off from people. Think how fed up with me you'll be after a year of it. We'll be a nice dull married couple who'll bore everybody out of their wits, including ourselves. I want us to keep each other alive and adventurous. I like competing for you, especially with real competition like Michael. I don't expect us to find guys like him every day and it doesn't really matter—because we make each other happy without anybody else—but it's good to be tested every now and then so we never take each other for granted. It's wonderful to be truthful with each other. How can it hurt us?"

Robbie made a sound of ruefully mirthful acquiescence. "The marvelous thing about you is that you really don't know," he said. "Okay, beloved. I'm convinced you know more about people than I do, so I'm ready to follow. Lead on."

He felt better about Michael after hearing Lance talk about him. Lance wasn't just making a case for sexual diversity. He was trying to achieve a total giving of themselves to each other, beyond the restraints of mod-

270

esty or a sense of privacy or shame. By making a public show of themselves, they had left themselves no choice but to belong to each other. They were together in a sense he had never known before.

All through dinner, his mind turned around the things Lance had said, trying to see himself as the lover Lance wanted him to be—licentious, male, and demanding. Perhaps he would be those things with Michael. Perhaps balance and self-control were a form of self-deception. He was finishing his chores in the kitchen when he heard Lance greeting the boy and he stood without moving, the sound of their voices acting as a powerful aphrodisiac. Thinking of Lance's familiarity with the sturdy, seductive body, he wanted Michael for himself. He didn't have to pretend anymore although it was odd, after the passive circumspect years with Maurice, to have a lover who wanted to watch him take a good-looking boy.

He found them playing together, teasing each other with their hands, whispering and giggling like girls while they teased each other out of their scanty clothing. They stopped abruptly when they saw him and then dropped the bits of clothing they'd been pretending to cover themselves with and rushed to meet him. They had a cheerfully uninhibited reunion, all trace of self-consciousness overcome in the renewed excitement of their liberated bodies. In a way, a strictly sensual way, Robbie found Michael's body almost more appealing than Lance's. It had something to do with being shorter and being able to fit himself in against him so defenselessly.

They coaxed him toward the cot and dropped to its edge and drew him closer, acting in unison as if they'd planned it in advance. Their mouths met on his erection. Their laughter was as innocent as children's. Lance made everything sunny and lighthearted. Robbie entered into their games, holding his cock, guiding it to titillate them, sliding it into their eager mouths. He got a simple-minded pleasure from the feel of it in his hand, its inflexible weight and bulk, its satisfying size. He was a pasha in a harem. He was going to take them both.

He ruffled their hair and broke from them and ran

off toward the eucalyptus tree and the sea. They followed in boisterous pursuit. They regrouped at the top of the steps, panting and laughing. The moonlight sculpted their bodies into works of art and cloaked every move they made with ethereal grace. They swam and emerged from the sea, silvered priapic gods under the moon. Robbie stretched out on the lumpy mattress near the rocks. Michael's body seemed to melt bonelessly into Robbie's. Their coupling was as natural, as effortless, almost as automatic and unpremeditated as breathing. One minute their hands were straying contentedly on each other and the next they were joined, Robbie feeling himself filling the boy gloriously, feeling the boy opening himself to him in a deep, grateful passion of submission. The communication of their bodies was too intense for Robbie not to give Michael his full attention; and yet some part of him remained acutely aware of Lance's motionless participation. He knew that somehow this was for him and that by triumphantly possessing the dancer, he was in some way taking ultimate possession of Lance's imagination.

"God, yes. You," Michael whispered against his ear.

As the sounds of ecstasy mounted, Lance clenched his fists and struggled for breath while his heart pounded. His nerves were torn, his senses ravaged, but he exulted in their daring. There could be no safety in passion. He didn't want to be sheltered by Robbie. They would learn to live with risk.

As soon as he had his body once more under control, Robbie disentangled himself and leaped back up the steps to the shower. He distrusted his romantic vulnerability. Sex was sex—except that it didn't always seem that clear-cut to him. Feelings had a way of blurring the edges. Briefly, he had felt the beginning of an emotional attachment to the dancer and he didn't want it to go any further.

When he returned to them, he felt no shift in their carefree intimacy. Michael remained equally responsive to them both in spite of the deep commitment he had made to Robbie with his body. It was natural for them to be together. When they had had another lazy swim and lingered on the rocks to admire the splendors of their bodies in the eerie light, it was natural for Michael to witness a celebration of the others' union.

Robbie took Lance on his back as they preferred. Lance laughed and shouted in an exuberant demonstration of his body's surrender. He played with himself for Robbie's pleasure and saw the glitter of lust in Michael's eyes. Michael wanted him. With luck, Michael was going to have him. When Robbie got used to their having fun with others, he wouldn't care what they did.

The next night after his dinner with Flip, Michael met Luisa and thus automatically became part of the family, their first friend. Michael knew enough Spanish to take part in a companionable conversation with her before they left her for a moonlight swim. Her being there added a feeling of permanence to the pleasure the three friends found with each other, as if they were settling down together.

They played in and out of the water together. Robbie raced off for a vigorous swim and Lance and Michael turned back. They climbed out onto a rock and sat side by side with their feet in the sea. "I want you," Michael said, his face hauntingly young in the gentle wash of moonlight.

Lance's hand slid over Michael's cock and he felt it stretch and harden in his fist. "I thought so. What happened to my little sister?" he asked.

"I wonder. I've never wanted to before. It drives me wild watching him take you. Seeing what it does to you. I can't help it."

"We can't with him. He won't allow it. I don't understand why he thinks there's something so special about it. He's certainly happy having you."

"I hope so. I adore him. Both of you. This has been—" He broke off with an odd sound of frustration or exasperation. "I thought if I just met you I'd never want more, but now I want you to be really mine for a little while."

"I want it, too. Tomorrow? I could come to Flip's again. Will you be there at five?"

"Of course. Any time. God, how marvelous."

Lance felt agreeably tense and keyed up the next afternoon when he parked the car in front of Robbie's studio and walked on to Flip's gate. Unless Robbie burst in on them, he wouldn't know what he and Michael had done together but there was always the danger of a slipup, and taking elaborate precautions with the car struck him as cheating with himself. He'd established his right to have Michael as a lover, within limits. If he got caught going too far he would have to face the consequences.

The immediate consequences were thrillingly satisfying. The other things he had done with Michael had been fun, like playing games, a harmless substitute for the real thing. Being taken by him was real.

"God, you're good," he murmured as Michael's possession of him grew more confident. "Yes, honey. Your cock. Yes. Do that. It feels good."

Michael joined them as usual after dinner that night and nothing marred the warmly affectionate friendship that had developed between them. It seemed to Lance that he and Robbie had found the formula for an indestructible future together. What could come between them now? They had embraced with impunity the greatest danger that lovers faced—a seductive intruder. Lance's confidence in the durability of their passion for each other was greater than ever. Resting his cheek against Robbie's cock, feeling Michael's erection sliding up the inside of his thigh, he reveled in their uninhibited acceptance of one another's bodies. He still had years of reticence to overcome but Michael had done wonders for him.

Despite his sweet infatuation with them both, the dancer remained refreshingly unsentimental about them. His visit was drawing to a close but he didn't indulge in lovers' laments. Their last nocturnal visit to the rocks was marked by high spirits, outbursts of erotic horseplay, and exuberant laughter. Contrary to Robbie's instincts and expectations, the odd episode had smoothed away whatever small conflicts and tensions he had felt at times in Lance. He was proud of himself and Lance for having dealt with it so successfully.

The day after they'd said good-bye to Michael, a letter came announcing the arrival of Lance's shipment to New York "in good condition." Lance was happy that the gollies had gotten there safely but was anxious to hear about how they were selling before he got too committed to the chess sets. He was also looking forward to receiving payment for the shipment. That would be an event—actually receiving a nice fat sum of money for something he'd made with his own hands. It wouldn't pay Robbie back for what he'd put into the business, but it would be a good start.

Still waiting for word, he started on his playing boards. There was nothing interesting about making the two-feet-by-two-feet inch-thick squares. He knew he wasn't going to stick to classic black and white. Any two strongly contrasting colors would do—green and yellow, red and gray, a metallic rust and blue. The same colors would predominate for the pieces, augmented by as much multicolored detail as he could crowd onto them. He wanted the sets to be a riot of color that would grab the attention in any room where they were set out.

The fires were started, the tiles were lined up in the kiln, the door was bricked up. This was the way Lance liked the place best—dirty, sweaty, working at full blast like a miniature factory. He didn't like to spend money on clay and wood without knowing that there was some demand for the chess sets, but it was even worse sitting around without making the place operate. He was bound to hear before he had time to make one full set of pieces.

He had made only a dozen pawns when the letter arrived. Robbie had it at the studio when Lance went to pick him up for lunch. He was making an obvious effort to maintain a neutral manner but Lance sensed his excitement.

"I'm sorry," he said. "I should've waited to open it till you got here. Curiosity got the better of me."

Lance pulled the letter out of the envelope. There was a check with it for the amount owed. He read:

The gollies were fascinating. The quality of the pottery excellent. Fifteen had been sold in the first hour they'd been displayed in the shop. People seemed to be hooked by them. Herewith a firm order for five hundred more. The chess sets should be a natural. A first order of twenty-five would undoubtedly lead to a hundred. It was difficult to fix a price without seeing one but somewhere between a hundred and a hundred and fifty dollars sounded right. Fifty dollars for Lance Cosling.

Lance fell into Robbie's arm with a shout. "Wow-eee! Oh, darling. How about us? We're in business. A hundred at fifty dollars. Jesus, the man must be mad! That's five thousand dollars."

Robbie hugged him, laughing with him. This development was the best thing that could have happened to him. It was the beginning of a solid sense of identity for him, of pride in his own achievement that the theater had failed to provide. "All I can say is I told you so. You're good, beautiful. What do you expect?"

"It's obvious it wouldn't've happened without you. You've done it all. Oh God, darling. I'm so pleased I haven't let you down. I never will. I swear it."

"You couldn't. You don't have to sell five hundred more gollies for me to know that." Robbie kissed his mouth but didn't prolong it. He didn't want to impose himself on his proud self-satisfaction.

"Five hundred more of those damn things," Lance repeated importantly. "I wanted to get going with the chessmen. It's all right. I'll start this afternoon. I can finish them in two weeks while Big goes on with the tiles. The chess sets may take almost two months. Jesus, I'm going to be busy. Will you write? Tell them I'll send the piece of sculpture too. You can decide how much I should charge for that. I don't believe it, darling. I'm going to be making my living. I wonder how many generations it's been since a Vanderholden did that?"

Luisa celebrated with them at lunch. She couldn't take it all in because they were too excited to speak Spanish for long but she found the bare facts extraordinary enough without all the details that they were discussing at such lengths. It was almost incredible that people in the remote dream-city of New York had seen the funny little figures that Lance made and were willing to pay large sums of money for great numbers of them. More money than her family had to live on for a year.

By the time he'd finished five hundred more gollies, Lance felt as if he were getting to be an expert with the wheel. He had finally acquired a profession. He knew how to do something. He even felt like an expert at packing them. He was in the midst of that chore the day they were scheduled to be shipped when he went to pick up Robbie for lunch. Another telegram had arrived revising the current order up from five hundred to two thousand. The text was slightly garbled and included a reference they didn't understand. Lance looked at Robbie and shook his head incredulously.

"Do you suppose they've all lost their minds? Two *thousand*. I'll be making them for the rest of my life."

"Poor baby. A slave to success. I don't know what 'gimmicks okay' means. There must be a letter on the way."

Robbie's guess was confirmed the next day. The letter explained that the gollies were apparently becoming a fad. Even Lance's name for them had caught on. People were buying them to smash them. A distributor of novelty gifts was thinking about putting them in outlets around the country—Chicago, Dallas, San Francisco, and others. *Life* had made inquiries and was considering a small feature if the fad spread.

"The trick now is to keep you out of it," Robbie said at lunch. "Thank God I thought of this ahead of time. There's going to be a great temptation in New York to drop your name into it for the sake of publicity. I think we can count on Larry and I'll write today to remind him to be careful with distributors and anybody else we do business with. I don't think anybody will bother to come see us. We're too far away and Cosling isn't a name that makes headlines. I hope to hear from Dad soon telling me what he's going to say about my brother if anybody asks. Aren't we having fun? I'm going to put the price up. We might as well be rich if we can't be famous."

Lance worked. The repetition became drudgery but he was too proud of making something that people would pay for to be bored. He attacked the job in lots of five hundred, which was a convenient number for the kilns and for shipping and gave him the feeling that the end was constantly in sight. When his hands got tired of making the same movements, he gave them a rest by throwing a few chessmen until he had a complete set.

He was delighted with it. He retained the traditional characteristics of the pieces—the mitred bishops, the crenellated rooks—so that people would know what they were, but endowed them with the characteristics they seemed to him to have in play. The pawns were anonymous gnomish creatures, backed by the athletic agility of the knights, the bishops' geometrical precision, the sweeping thrust of the rooks, the queen's fanciful omnipotence, and the ineffectual passivity of the king—all with a high glaze, glittering with color like junk jewelry.

"Everybody's going to turn into chess players when they see those," Robbie commented. "I wouldn't mind a game myself even though it's always driven me mad. Let's take it home with us, beautiful. You won't be sending it till next week."

He sold his three-piece sculpture for a hundred dollars. Robbie's father wrote saying that he'd had a call from a French news service in Paris checking on his sons' whereabouts. He had offered to send a picture of them, having available a photograph of Robbie with an unrecognizable friend taken from the side. They had said not to bother until he told them it was the only time Lance had allowed himself to be photographed.

The sample chess set drew a rave from New York and a confirmation of the order for twenty-five. The novelty company followed up with an order for a hundred but, being a middleman, would pay only twenty-five dollars apiece for them.

"Granted it'll take several months to make them but I'll still be making pretty good profit, won't I, darling?" Lance asked anxiously. He was terrified that if Robbie turned anything down they'd never get another order.

"Good Lord yes. PVPW has already paid for itself. If it goes on like this, you'll make a couple of thousand a year profit, plus your salary. I wouldn't be surprised if you're in the five-thousand-dollars-a-year bracket right now."

Lance was too busy to pay much attention to the installation of the running water and flush toilet but Robbie made a fuss about it to please Luisa. At the end of a month Lance was getting ready for the second firing of the last lot of five hundred when a renewal order arrived for another three thousand. He collapsed in a chair in Robbie's studio and covered his face with his hands.

"Oh, no. I don't believe it," he moaned. "What are they trying to do to me? Have I started making them in my sleep yet?"

"Read the rest of the letter. The piece in *Life* is due to appear in the next few weeks. Larry says that after that there'll be a spurt and then the whole thing will probably die down. He says this sort of thing usually lasts two or three months at the most. He wants this batch as fast as possible."

Lance uncovered his face and dropped his act. He was pleased as punch. "He'll get them. I've been amazingly lucky so far. I still have the horrors about something going wrong with the firing. I couldn't have done it without Big. He's good. We should probably give him a raise. Prosperity comes to Puerto Veragua."

When they got home, they found a note from Dr. Greuber waiting for them. He apologized for not having been in touch sooner but had been away on an unexpected visit to the capital to see a doctor and hear some music. He wanted them for a supper party in a week. His apologies to Luisa but it would be for men only, in the local fashion. He had added under his signature, "I found some charming young men in the city."

"Will you answer or shall I?" Lance asked.

"Whichever. What do you want to say?"

"We more or less have to go, don't we?"

"I'm not so sure."

"Oh?"

"I'll put that differently. I'm sure I don't want to. I'd rather not."

"Fine, darling. I don't particularly want to either. It's pretty silly being offered charming young men, as if we couldn't find them for ourselves if that's what we were after. I just couldn't think what we could use as an excuse without being rude."

"There's always something. Actually, I think you should go. Both of us refusing would be a bit pointed."

"Don't be silly. We're together. We do things together like any other couple. I have no intention of going anywhere without you."

"I'd really like you to, sweetheart. I heard a lot about his parties when I was with Flip. I've been through all that. I don't like it." He prayed for Lance to stick to his guns but he had to make him feel free to choose, not grudgingly but unequivocally and convincingly. He wrestled valiantly with his possessiveness and added, "I'm sure it's all good clean fun but I'm prudish enough to be uncomfortable when sex rears its head too publicly."

"I think I've got myself over being a prude."

"I hope so, sweetheart. It's a stupid thing to be. That's why you should go. It might be fun for you."

"I obviously have no way of knowing what you're talking about but that isn't the point. I just don't want to go anywhere without you. It has to do with the way we live."

Robbie gratefully sensed Lance's resistance stiffening. He could risk giving him another little push. "I couldn't agree with you more but there can be exceptions occasionally. This'll be a special sort of party. It's something you should find out about for yourself."

"Why? What do you think goes on?"

"Oh, everybody'll probably be naked around the pool. Nothing you wouldn't see at a public bath, except that it's a social occasion. That's what I find embarrassing. You don't know whether you're supposed to be discussing the weather or sucking somebody's cock. At least at a public bath you don't have to worry about committing a social gaffe if you turn somebody down. I hear the doctor takes photographs."

"And that's what you think I should find out about for myself?"

"Yes. I did long ago. If I hadn't, I'd've probably gone on thinking I was missing something. We've talked about keeping ourselves open to experience."

"Yes. Together. It wouldn't mean anything unless you're there. Experience isn't true for me if I'm alone because I don't live alone. Everything is through you."

"But if I'm there, it wouldn't be anything at all. The point of parties like that is that everybody's on his own. Couples stop everything dead. They'd just sit around and wait for us to go. It's really pretty dumb of the doctor to invite us."

Lance guessed that Pablito had told the doctor that they were an amenable couple. He felt surrounded suddenly by hidden dangers. Pablito was in touch with José. He didn't want to do anything to turn Pablito against him. He was intrigued by the party. It was the sort of thing he thought they should be able to enjoy together no matter how outrageous it turned out to be. When Robbie became deeply preoccupied with work, Lance felt unneeded. An occasional change of pace like Michael reminded them how important they were to each other. He wasn't going to let them turn into a

280

conventional humdrum couple. "Well, let's go and be killjoys," he said. "If we don't, they'll ask us again. It's easier to be on good terms with the neighbors."

"Okay, beautiful. We can accept for both of us. I'll think about it. I can always get a headache at the last minute." He was glad to let it go for a week. He had made a persuasive demonstration of adaptability. Lance had remained steadfast in his determination to act jointly. The only thing the conversation had accomplished was to convince him that he must make Lance go without him, do what he wanted to do even though he might think he didn't. He must never let him feel that belonging to him was a burden.

Lance worked at top speed for the next week, determined to finish the latest order in no more than a month. For the first time, Big had both kilns operating. Lance was developing assembly line techniques with no visible effect on the product. When Lance went to pick him up for lunch on the day of the party, Robbie announced his change of plan. He was going to spend the evening at the studio, fix himself something to eat with Filipe's assistance, and go to bed in his own house where his work would keep him company.

"Don't be silly, darling," Lance protested. "I told you I wouldn't go without you, but it'd be a bit rude to drop out now. Why didn't you decide all this a few days ago?"

"I hadn't much thought about it till this morning. I'm dying for a little time to catch up with a million things. When I'm with you, I can't think about anything else. I really need an evening off."

"Not from me, you don't. I'll sit in a corner and read a book. It'll be sort of fun being here for a change. We can send Filipe up with a note right away. I can say we both have food poisoning. That's as good as anything. Actually, it's more convincing to do it at the last minute."

"Please, beautiful. I want you to go. Your first so-called gay party. Whether you like it or hate it, I don't want to be there to make you self-conscious. You'll be the belle of the ball. If we were in New York, you'd have had lots of chances to find out how you like all-male gatherings. Now's the time. On your own, so you won't be embarrassed if things happen that you don't quite know how to handle." It was the most difficult speech he'd ever made in his life but as he spoke he knew he was right. He felt Lance's interest quicken. He was probably imagining a pool draped with beautiful naked youths. Robbie knew that they were rarely beautiful.

Lance's gaze was level and watchful as he studied him for a moment. "What is all this, darling? Why do you suddenly want to get rid of me?"

"Oh, sweetheart." He laughed fondly and leaned forward and kissed his forehead. "I just want you to go to a party I think you might enjoy more without me. You don't have to stay if you don't like it."

"No. You said you wanted an evening off. Did you mean it? Are you beginning to get bored with me?"

"What an adorable goose. It's just the opposite. I have a pile of letters I keep putting off because I never get enough of you. I think we ought to kill two birds with one stone, or one evening—my letters and your debut."

Lance studied him for another moment and then gave his head a little nod. It was Robbie's decision. He wanted to be with him but he also wanted to go to the party. "You know me, darling. I count on you to decide about these things. If you think I should go, I'll go."

Robbie sprang up, all his body immediately tense with anxiety and dismay. He was sure he was making sense. Let Lance make his own discoveries and his own mistakes. Everybody had to. He wouldn't have been ready for Maurice if he hadn't gone through a period of unrestrained sexual experimentation beforehand. For him to expect Lance to fall peacefully into the arms of his first lover and never stray again would be pure fairy-tale foolishness. He should be glad for tonight. He stretched to shake off the pall of anguish that had settled on his spirit. "Okay," he said lightly. "And we don't have to send a note about me. You can make my excuses. Pick me up this evening as usual, beautiful. I'll go home for a drink with you while you get tarted up and then you can drop me on your way."

Lance wondered from time to time during the afternoon about the unexpected evening on his own. If Pablito wanted him again with some light to see him, he didn't know how he could avoid it but he could try. He felt less vulnerable to temptation than he had a month

282

ago, better prepared to extricate himself from entanglements. By the time he had showered and put on a smart white shirt and shorts, he was feeling pleasantly keyed up, curious and slightly apprehensive. He joined Robbie at the parapet with a drink.

"Come on, darling. Change your mind and come with me. This is ridiculous. I *hate* going anywhere without you."

"You're looking too beautiful for me to attempt to compete. I hope there'll be somebody there to give Pablito some competition. He's much too sure of himself."

"Okay, darling," Lance said as he stopped the car in front of Robbie's gate. "You're a shit to do this to me. I'll probably be back as soon as we finish eating."

"You're beautiful, beloved. Don't hurry away if you're having a good time. You've been working too hard. You deserve some fun." They leaned to each other and their mouths met in a peaceful kiss.

Lance watched Robbie close the gate and turned the car back to the road that wound up the hill. He already felt such an ache of emptiness where Robbie should have been that he wanted to stop and rush back to him, but a little lift of excitement led him on.

Robbie had given him rough directions to the house. It was quite high with a dramatic view. He followed the steep winding road through scrubby trees and barren patches of rock. He passed scattered houses but they didn't fit the fragmentary descriptions he had in mind. He drove almost fifteen minutes, feeling lost and lonely. There was nothing in the world he wanted so much as to feel Robbie's arms around him, share his supper, make love with him in the house where they'd never spent the night.

The headlights picked up a drive passing through gate posts on the right and he remembered somebody saying that you could drive right up to the front door. He'd found it just when he'd stopped wanting to.

He turned in and found himself in an oasis, hidden behind the lush foliage. Half a dozen cars, not beat-up American models like theirs, but gleaming foreign jobs, were parked in front of a low, rambling house. He saw a Bentley as he got out, and a couple of Mercedes.

Open iron gates were set in a low, wide arch through which he entered a Spanish-style reception hall. Be-

yond, he could see an inner courtyard and the movement of people. He hoped he hadn't crashed the wrong
party. Pablito appeared and hurried forward to greet
him, his hands lifting to his shoulders. "You're the last.
Where is Robbie?"

"It's farther than I thought. He's been feeling rotten
all day. He finally gave up. He's sorry."

"So are we. How fortunate that it wasn't contagious."

Lance was so glad to see a friendly face that he let
Pablito prolong his welcoming kiss, hands gripping his
buttocks and pulling him in so that their cocks began
to make themselves felt against each other. Pablito drew
back, a complacent smile on his face, and slipped a hand
up the leg of his shorts and ran it along the prisoner
of his jockey shorts. It continued to swell. "My friends
are all waiting to see it. So am I. It feels very much
worth bringing out into the open."

Lance chuckled. "When is this show supposed to take
place?"

"After dinner, we'll all be at the pool."

"Maybe it won't be in the mood by then."

"We'll all help with the mood. You want me. I'll be
there. Come. I'll introduce you to my friends and give
you a drink."

Pablito led him into the inner courtyard, partially
covered, a luxurious version of Robbie's studio-house
with a decorative pool in the middle, surrounded by
riotous tropical vegetation. One side was furnished like
a dining room. Opposite was the living room, with low
opulent modern furniture. The light was brighter and
steadier than at Flip's; the doctor must have a generator
of his own way up here.

Pablito touched his arm as they turned toward the
sitting area. A dozen men rose to greet them. The doctor
swiveled his chair toward them.

"Ah, beautiful youth," he exclaimed. "Do you have
a kiss for an ugly old man?" Lance leaned over dutifully
and made brief contact with his face. "So where is the
other beauty?"

Lance repeated his excuses for Robbie, and Pablito's
hand was on his arm again, leading him forward. Faces
approached his for a kiss with each introduction. A
mustache brushed his lips. He caught a few first names.
Guillermo. Carlos. A sleek young man whom he had

met with Flip was there. Fred, a big American in his early forties, threw his arms around him. A slim American whose name he didn't hear, with lightly tinted dark glasses and a straggling blond mustache, caught his attention with a detached look in his eye. A very young, pretty, startlingly girlish Latin put his whole body into his kiss. A tough-looking muscular German stuck his tongue into his mouth. He went down the line without a quiver. He wondered if Robbie would have handled it any differently. Everybody sat down again while Pablito led him to a bar.

"Have you seen José?" he asked, pouring Lance a drink.

Lance winced within himself. "No," he said curtly.

"That is odd. I saw him in the city a few days ago. He said he was coming back particularly to see you."

"I can't imagine what for," Lance said quickly, with a pang of alarm.

"Ah. Who knows." Pablito smiled slyly and handed him a glass. "I'm sure he has reasons. Do you like my friends? Is there anyone who especially takes your fancy?"

"They all look very attractive. I haven't really had a chance to look at them yet."

"You will." Pablito's sly smile gloated over him.

"Do they all live here?"

"No, no. The foreigners are all staying with us. Guillermo and Paco have weekend houses here."

Lance glanced around at the gathering, catching a number of eyes on him. "I met one of them—I think he's sitting with an American—at Flip's."

"Ah yes, Carlos. He's staying here, too, with his friend Luis. I don't think he's for you."

"I don't think any of them are for me. I'll have to leave promptly after dinner. Robbie and I are working hard. We don't usually go out without each other."

"Then tonight you can relax. We won't have to hide in the dark."

Lance took a swallow of his drink to avoid having to answer. As Robbie said, Pablito was much too sure of himself. He saw the American with the dark glasses rise, followed by Carlos and Luis. The three of them approached the bar. The American held out his glass to Pablito.

"Is there time for another drink before we eat?" he asked. He fixed his eyes on Lance, still looking detached but amused. "You're Marcus Vanderholden," he told him in a humorous drawling voice. "What is all this Cosling shit?"

"Lance is my real name," Lance said evasively.

"Yeah, the papers started calling you that during the war. You were Marcus before. I should know. I've been in love with you all my life. I started jerking off for you when you were twelve. I considered you a grown-up. I was only ten. You were in some show or something, weren't you?"

"You didn't see it? What's the use of people being in love with me if they don't bother to see me in a show?"

"Well, I did a lot of thinking about being in love with you when *I* got to be twelve. I decided I couldn't let it rule my life. You wouldn't want me to go on jerking off forever, would you?"

Lance laughed. "I guess twelve is a good time to start branching out." The exchange had established a feeling of good humor between them but Lance didn't quite know what to make of the young man. His glasses were peculiar, sort of wrapped around his face without much visible frame so that he looked as if he were behind a window. His mustache was untrimmed and sparse, straggling wispily along his lip. His sandy hair was short and fell carelessly over his forehead, sticking out in cowlicks here and there. He was dressed in an off-white shirt and skintight pants that looked vaguely Western to Lance. He was about the same height as Lance, perhaps a shade taller, his rangy body flat as a plank with light shoulders and very slim waist and hips. His detached manner suggested that he was playing some sort of joke on the world. Lance would never have guessed that he was a homosexual. "I didn't get your name," he said.

"Tracy Cook. I'm from Texas."

"I've never been there but I hear it's quite a place."

"It's a great country. You'd better come see it. I'll show you around."

"I was planning to go before I came here. I may make it yet." Despite the offer, he felt no vibrations of physical attraction between them. He dropped his eyes. His

286

tight pants made his cock visible in minute detail, as if he were wearing nothing underneath.

The Texan's friends, Carlos and Luis, moved in beside them with glasses and handed one to Tracy.

He lifted it and nodded to Lance with a faint smile. "You know these guys? Well, I'm sure as hell glad I've met you, Marcus ole buddy." He looked at Lance's mouth for a long moment without moving and then touched him lightly on the shoulder.

Lance felt the shock in the pit of his stomach. His heart raced. Something odd happened to his knees. The trio was headed for the chairs they had vacated. Lance followed without thinking, feeling Tracy's light touch as a summons. There had been something about the way he'd touched him that announced his possession of him. Tracy knew that he could have him. Lance wanted to break through his cool detachment.

Lance saw that there was no place for him to sit. He felt himself getting a hard-on and glanced around him. The girlish boy caught his eye and pulled an empty chair closer to him, looking at him invitingly. Lance went to him and dropped into it.

"You are so very much handsome," he greeted Lance meltingly. "I love North Americans. I'm Gabriel."

He had ruby lips and soft eyes with long lashes. "Like the angel?" Lance suggested.

"The angel?"

"Don't you know the Angel Gabriel?"

"Oh, yes." The boy offered him a winsome smile, revealing small pearly teeth. "You are very much joking. I will be your angel."

"That sounds nice to me."

"I have heard very much about you. You have a factory."

Lance chatted with the flirtatious boy while his eyes kept returning to Tracy. Something about the young Texan teased and baffled him. He gave the impression that he expected people to make an effort to please him. His companions were obviously mesmerized by him. He had a quality that enthralled.

Lance forced his eyes to abandon him and looked around the room to see if there were any other attractions to distract him. He saw routine good looks and encountered eyes that conveyed obvious messages. They could all be had one way or another. Only Tracy remained aloof and impervious to the evening's temptations.

Gabriel was very agreeable to look at, almost a temptation. He had a mass of soft, dark, girlish hair and a quite delectable brown body generously displayed in a loose open shirt that looked as if it would fall off at the slightest touch. He was in his late teens probably and belonged to Guillermo, a trim handsome man who had a house here and appeared to be just about old enough to be his father. Lance found his girlishness less bothersome as he grew used to it and began to rather like him. His instant infatuation with Lance was disarming. He was studying literature at the university and wanted to write poetry.

"I will write you a love poem," he said. "We will be naked together later at the pool. I think I will cause very much scandal."

Lance smiled amiably. "Won't Guillermo mind?"

"I am young. He forgives me. We must love when we are young. I will love you very much tonight if you will let me."

"We'll see about that." Lance decided that it made much more sense to flirt with this pretty kid than to get all tied up in knots over a quite ordinary-looking American.

When somebody said something about dinner and the guests began to stir and get to their feet, he felt as if his curious quick blaze of interest in Tracy were already passing. He hadn't even glanced at him for some time but when he stood, Lance stood with him, abruptly abandoning Gabriel, and moved forward so that they drifted together naturally as they started around the courtyard to the dining room side. It felt strangely right to be beside him again.

"You're staying with the doctor?" Lance asked politely.

"Yeah. He's a friend of the family. When I finally got an idea of what went on down here, I decided to give it a look-see. I sure as hell didn't expect to find you down here."

"You didn't come specially to see me? I'm disappointed."

"That *would* be a good line, wouldn't it? I guess I

goofed on that one. He's a cute piece, that Gabriel, isn't he?"

"Very pretty."

"You got ideas?"

"No, not really."

"Just checking in case I decide to try to score. I wouldn't want to move in on you."

"Help yourself." There was nothing flirtatious about Tracy. He had told him that he wasn't included in his plans. The old brush-off. Lance realized that he'd always assumed that his problem with guys would be dodging advances, not courting them. A well-deserved lesson. He felt suddenly lost. He didn't know how to woo a guy. And why should he woo Tracy? He should consider himself lucky to be out of it. His entourage was staying close beside him. Let them have him. The only guy he cared about was waiting for him at home.

"Did you come down here alone?" he asked.

"Yeah. I guess I'm a natural-born loner. You're the only guy I ever fell in love with. These guys—Carlos and Luis—they came down from the capital with me. We've been having some laughs together."

"They're fascinated by you. I can see why."

Tracy turned his head quickly to him. "You can? That's funny. I should think you'd be so used to everybody being fascinated by you that you wouldn't have time to be fascinated by anybody."

"Are we saying that we're fascinated by each other?"

Tracy's smile was approving. "That could be," he said with his humorous drawl. "We're both pretty cagey."

As they reached the table, Pablito appeared. "The doctor would like you to sit with him," he said to Lance. "The others can sit where they like."

Lance turned to Tracy. Candlelight from the table was reflected in his glasses. He couldn't see his eyes. Carlos and Luis had moved in protectively beside him. "I guess—" Lance began.

"Okay, ole buddy. Take it easy," Tracy drawled. He lifted a hand and touched Lance's arm.

It all happened again—the wrench in his stomach, the racing heart, the weakness in the knees. Lance stood helplessly for a moment, then got a grip on himself and followed Pablito to the end of the table. The

289

doctor indicated the chair at his right and Lance started to seat himself as Gabriel slipped adroitly in beside him.

"I may sit with you?"

"What could be nicer?" He gave the boy's bare knee a squeeze as he pulled his chair in to the table. Gabriel moved in as close to him as he could get.

The insinuating pressures of the boy's body gave Lance another erection but he didn't expect it to lead to anything with his young companion. It was a reaction to the atmosphere of sexual liberty.

The food was excellent, the wine German and plentiful. By the time the exotic fruit-ice dessert was served, Lance was feeling pleasantly giddy and sexually keyed up.

When the guests began to rise, he thrust a hand into his pocket to take charge of himself as he stood. Tracy looked across the table at him. His thumbs were hooked in his pockets and one hand was curled around his very visible cock. It had grown considerably and was angled upward across his groin. Lance took his hand out of his pocket and pushed his way past the others without giving Gabriel a backward glance. He fell into step with Tracy.

"Hi, ole buddy of mine," the Texan said with a humorous glance at him. "Thanks. I like to see what I'm getting."

"Are you going to get it?" he asked, not rejecting the possibility.

"I'm thinking about it. Just circulate and leave that pretty kid alone until I get back to you."

Coffee was being served in the sitting area. Lance had his orders. He didn't know why he accepted them so unquestioningly but he seemed to be bound by some contract with Tracy. He felt a streak of cruelty in him, a capacity to inflict pain. Wooing such a masculine guy made him feel as queer as he wanted to be.

He circulated. He talked to the big American called Fred. He talked to Klaus, the German. He talked to Guillermo and Paco. They both made hospitable offers to show Lance their houses. He felt as if he were being introduced to a world to which he might belong and he didn't want to enter it without Robbie. He was friendly but noncommittal, hoping that he wouldn't seem antisocial.

Everybody remained standing, moving about, being offered after-dinner drinks by Pablito. Lance was learning that good manners prevailed even in these circumstances. He couldn't just grab Tracy in front of the others. He waited for him to break away from them and come to him, touch him, single him out. When that happened, he would consider leaving. He had to be given the choice.

There was a general drift toward the end of the courtyard where a wide archway opened onto a well-lighted garden. Lance could see grass and trees through it. He crossed slowly to the bar and refilled his glass with wine, trying to make up his mind about leaving. Tracy had said he'd be back for him. He was aware of silence growing around him as the others disappeared through the archway. He started after them reluctantly and was halted by a voice.

"Marcus," Tracy said from behind him.

Lance whirled around, almost spilling his wine. He was standing behind a chair with his hands resting on its back, a tantalizing smile playing around his lips.

"We don't want to go out there yet, do we?"

Lance felt a warm flush of pleasure at the intimacy implied by the words. "I thought you were too busy to notice what I was doing."

"I noticed. I was playing my cards carefully."

He came out from behind the chair. He paused and removed his glasses slowly and folded them and put them on the table beside Lance. He moved closer and put his arms around him and kissed him in a way that took unequivocal possession of him, deep and demanding and superbly authoritative. Lance was seized by a rage of desire unlike anything he had ever felt before, a passion to please the guy whose mouth was draining him of his will. He belonged to Tracy until he had given him everything that was demanded of him.

They dropped to the sofa, wrestling together, their legs thrashing, tugging at clothing to get to each other. They were panting and uttered little grunts in their lust for union. They slid off the sofa onto their knees on the floor.

Their shirts were gone, their chests heaving, their erections straining to each other. Tracy's was a straight cylinder with no taper or curve in it. Lance dropped

291

forward to it and took it with his mouth, worshiping it at last. "Suck, honey," Tracy urged.

After a moment, he put his hands under Lance's chin and lifted his head and pushed him out flat onto his back. He moved around on his knees, stripping him. When he was naked, he lifted Lance's cock to his mouth. He made Lance leap when he circled his balls with his tongue, laughing as he drew back.

"Pablito was right. You're a wonder." He pulled Lance up by his shoulders and cradled him against his flat, hairless chest. "We've got something going. I'm going to take you to bed and find out what it is." They unwound themselves from each other and stood.

"You better give me—" Lance began, reaching for something to cover himself.

"You won't need clothes anymore while you're here."

Tracy pushed his cock behind a flap of his fly and fastened the top button, making an obscenely enticing bulge. He put his glasses on and they went around the courtyard barefoot to a corridor. Closed doors stretched ahead of them like a hotel.

He led him into a big, brightly lighted bedroom with handsome, dark, Spanish furniture and two big beds against opposite walls. There was a suitcase at the foot of one of them, but the room looked tidily unoccupied. Tracy put a hand on his arm and guided Lance to one of the beds. He sat and reached for Tracy and unfastened the button of his pants and lifted out his cock. Tracy pushed the pants down to his feet and stepped out of them. He put his hands on Lance's face and moved it until his cock touched his lips.

"You like my cock, ole buddy?" He put a finger under it and lifted it away from Lance's mouth so that it stood up before his eyes.

"I'm wild about it."

"It has a winning personality. It's nowhere near as big as yours but I guess you're used to that. You want it inside you?"

"Yes."

"It figures. That's where it's going to be but there's no hurry. When I finish, I want us both to know that Marcus Vanderholden has been fucked for life. You're going to be mine until I let you go."

A shiver ran down Lance's spine. He was only beginning to be fully conscious of what was happening to him and he couldn't see beyond it. He realized that while it lasted, he wanted Tracy's hands on him more than Robbie's. They were straying over his face, redesigning it, lifting his eyebrows, arranging his hair, pushing his lips into a smile. There was no love or tenderness in his touch nor in the strange intensity of his eyes. He asked only his total submission and offered him the privilege of giving himself to him. Lance was exhilarated by the lack of sentiment or romance in his cool, dispassionate appraisal.

"When are you going to let me go?" Lance asked.

"I hear you have a beautiful lover."

"Yes."

"What do we do about him?"

"I don't know."

"I don't want this to get heavy. I'm going to give you back to him. You don't have to worry about that. I want you tonight. I'll give you back tomorrow."

"That's as impossible as staying away for a week."

The little smile returned to Tracy's lips. He put his hands flat on the sides of Lance's face. "We'll see. Wait till I fuck you. You can decide then."

He let his hands slide away from his face and was gone. He returned with towels and collected a tube of something. He dropped the things he was carrying and climbed up on the bed. He lowered his head to put his mouth on various parts of Lance that struck his fancy. He rolled him over and used his provocative tongue to make his buttocks dance, his cock prodding, importunate, commanding.

"God yes," Lance gasped with pleasure.

Tracy dropped over into a sitting position, his legs sprawled apart, and pulled Lance up to him. He put his hands on his face again. "Your lover's just brought you out, hasn't he? I can tell. He hasn't brought you out far enough. I'm going to turn you into a beautiful fucking machine, Marcus, ole buddy. Show me how good you are." He pulled his mouth to his and bit his lips.

Lance wanted to be devoured by him. He was gripped by a passion to break every barrier that shielded him from his body's darkest needs. The bed seemed hardly capable of containing the paroxysms of their lust. Tracy was everywhere on him, eluding him, demanding ever greater surrender, consuming him until Lance felt that there was nothing left in him that wasn't his. Only then did he enter him, plunging masterfully into him and re-creating him with his power. They were heedless of their orgasms. The intensity of Tracy's purpose carried them on. A second climax brought a lull.

"We're getting there," Tracy said. "I'll give the others a chance for now. Later we'll really have it."

"How good was I?"

"You'll do, with practice. With a body like yours, you could hardly go wrong. I wish I'd gotten to you sooner. I always wanted to be the one to turn you queer."

"You have."

"Yeah. Maybe I have. We'll see."

Tracy led the way to the shower. As Lance entered the bathroom, he caught a glimpse of himself in the mirror and stopped for a closer look. His lips were puffy. There were red welts on his neck and shoulders and below one nipple. He was struck by a pang of remorse as he realized that he couldn't let Robbie see him now. How long did it take for marks like that to go away? Maybe he'd look all right in an hour or two.

"We're going to join the others?" he asked, stepping into the shower.

"Sure. I can't hog the star attraction. You're going to get fucked. I want to see you getting fucked. I'm going to bring you out all the way. When I have, maybe I'll want to keep you."

His cool appraising hands as they soaped him under the shower made him intensely conscious of his body's responses. He was always so overwhelmed by emotion with Robbie that he hardly knew what they were doing. After Tracy had helped him explore the depths of his depravity, he might be able to contain it.

They left the shower and dried themselves and combed their hair. Lance's lips looked a little less puffy. They went out to the bedroom and Tracy put on his glasses.

He held Lance's hips and moved their cocks against each other until they were both erect. "Nice. Let's keep them this way."

They followed the corridor back to the lush court-yard. As they approached the wide archway with il-luminated lawn visible beyond, the party hum of voices became audible. They stopped at the edge of the lawn, still some thirty yards from the brightly lighted pool where the others were lying about on mattresses and deck chairs, and turned to each other for a final look.

"Everything okay, ole buddy?" Tracy asked.

"Sure. What's next?"

"Let's have a swim. The last one in is straight." He sprinted off, his slim body as swift as an arrow.

Lance followed, keeping pace with him. As they passed among the others, a cheer arose at their priapic passage. They dived in and splashed and shouted and floated into each other with their mouths meeting on the surface of the water. Others plunged in after them. Tracy swam to the side of the pool, snaked himself out and sat with his legs in the water, his cock upright in front of him. Lance followed, wallowing lazily in the water and making no effort to evade the hands that reached for him. He held on to Tracy's foot, laughing while Gabriel made a titillating underwater exploration of his body. When the pretty youth surfaced, Lance offered him a long loose-lipped kiss and then, with a quick thrust of his legs, shot up and landed beside Tracy.

Tracy leaned forward and took Lance's mouth with his own. Their arms lifted to each other and they were immediately locked together, rolling around on top of each other, wrestling on the lawn. A chorus of male voices rose around them laughing, calling out cheerful obscenities. Lance exulted in the licentious atmosphere of freedom. They could all make love openly with the open approval of their audience, naked under the sky. He had a big cock for everybody to marvel at. He felt a warm glow of comradeship linking him to the others. They were all guys together, all wanting each other. He belonged with them.

He and Tracy released each other as Pablito appeared above them. He was naked except for a towel over his shoulder, holding out glasses to them. Lance realized with a little start of astonishment that although his cock had been inside him he'd never seen it. Even in repose, it looked as purposeful and efficient as it had felt. His matador's body was a pleasure to look at. They lifted themselves to their knees to take the glasses and sat back on their heels.

"Another of your love potions?" Tracy asked.

"The doctor's," Pablito corrected pedantically.

"What is it?" Lance asked.

"He won't tell," Tracy said. "Just drink it and hang on to your hat." He made a comical little grimace and Lance drank. It was milky and rather sweet and tasted like an eggnog.

"Come with me. The doctor wishes to photograph you together," Pablito said.

They stood and Lance reached for Tracy's hand as they followed their host to the end of the pool. A sort of platform extended out from behind the diving board, raised a foot or two above the ground and strewn with cushions and mattresses. The doctor had rolled his chair to the end of it. They stepped up onto it into powerful spotlights. It was like walking onto a stage. The doctor's camera began to click. This was public exposure in the grand manner.

The others gathered around while the camera continued to click. Lance saw an array of erections. Carlos's and Gabriel's and Luis's, trim variations of Pablito's, Fred's big one, the German Klaus's also big but strangely knotted like a clenched fist, far from beautiful. Lance felt he had finally seen enough to understand why his own considerably bigger one attracted so much attention. It surged up into even more rigid erection as Tracy thrust his in beside it to offer the doctor a striking pose.

Lance's hands moved over him lightly and Tracy let himself go to him. Lance felt as if he'd reached a sort of zenith of shameless indecency. It was thrilling to give in completely to his body's bizzare appetites. They put their hands on their heels and arched their backs and ground their hips in to each other so that their cocks rolled about together against their bellies. A low keening sound began in Tracy's throat. Lance knew what Tracy expected of him.

Something suddenly gripped his scalp. He ducked to wrench his head free. Nothing restrained it. The sensation passed. He and Tracy shifted, making a maximum display of their cocks, but Lance's movements began to blur and lose clear definition. He saw hands creeping over naked bodies to infinity. Pablito was kneeling behind him, sliding into him to complete a possession of him that had no ending. Anything was possible. He had entered an ever-expanding universe. Time stopped.

Guys fell on him and took him as if he were public property. He worshiped all the cocks that were offered for the attention of his mouth. Nobody could rape him now. He wanted all of them. He reveled in excess. He wanted to be taken, ravaged, defiled, to obliterate all traces of the Vanderholden he had been.

A great block seemed to lift from his mind when Tracy crawled over the mattresses to him, wearing his glasses, and stretched out beside him. He propped himself on an elbow and smoothed back his hair. "You had come all over you. I cleaned you up."

"Have you been here all along?"

"More or less. Been having fun?"

"My God. It's wild." He held Tracy's cock. It was as hard as his own. "Mine's been like that all evening. You too?" Lance asked.

"Sure. The love potion."

"Is that what it was? I knew it must be something. You said to hold on to my hat. Did everybody have some?"

"No, just us. We're the new boys. They wanted us to keep going."

"Amazing. I wonder what it is. I guess I needed it—acting as queer as I wanted. Am I all the way out now?"

"That should do it."

"Do you want to keep me?"

"Yes, but I won't let myself for long."

"I guess it's just as well." He was in love with Robbie. He could allow himself a momentary passion without shaking the foundation of his life.

"Anybody who'd shack up with a guy like you and not expect some excitement should have his head examined. Your body is about as perfect as a body can be. You drive guys wild."

"I haven't thought much about it but I'm glad it's good if it makes guys want me. I must be a nymphomaniac. What about our big number?"

"Soon. I think people are beginning to go. I didn't want to be the first."

"Is it late?"

"I don't know. The last time I saw a watch it was two o'clock."

* * *

297

Bright sunlight streamed through openings of the heavy curtains. They stirred in a breeze, creating shifting patterns of light on the polished floor. Lance heard the whirring of a fan somewhere. It was pleasantly cool. There was no use trying to kid himself—he was awake. Tracy lay on him, moving slowly and deliciously in him.

"Hi, Marcus ole buddy," Tracy said lazily against his ear. "You returning to the land of the living?"

"I guess so but don't hurry me. Just go on doing what you're doing." He gave himself into the gentle possession of Tracy's cock while he assembled fragments of memory.

The general outline of the evening fell into place. He'd been had by quite a few guys. Four? Five? Faces appeared in his mind's eye. Five, including Tracy. He remembered kissing everybody good night and renewing contact with bodies that he'd known intimately. He remembered coming back to the room with Tracy. He'd remember it all his life. Tracy had won the right to do anything he liked with his body. He was doing just what Lance wanted now, bringing him slowly back to life, revitalizing him, filling his body with a sense of well-being to get him started on a new day.

He suddenly froze with panic. It was bright daylight. A new day had already started. His body jerked together as his nerves knotted. "What time is it?" he asked, aghast.

"It must be pretty late. Around eleven, I guess."

"Oh no! I told you I have to leave early."

"I've been trying to wake you, Marcus honey. I finally decided to see if fucking you would work. Nothing else did. Now I'm going to fuck you for real."

"I've got to go. Please. Oh Jesus. What am I going to say?"

"Relax, honey. Whatever you were planning to say at eight won't make any sense at noon. Take some time to think of something else." He rolled him over with him and held him and worked himself up until his shoulders were propped against the wall and Lance was sprawled out on his back on top of him. "There. Don't you want to stay a little longer?"

"God, yes. Help me. Tell me what I can say to him."

"I don't see what you *can* say except more or less the truth. Tell him the doctor drugged you and you passed

298

out. I really tried to wake you up. You were out cold. We can have another half hour and then you're on your way. Now do the things I taught you."

Lance lost his urgency about leaving. As long as he was with Tracy, he felt confident that there would be no trouble with Robbie. It was obvious what the experience had meant for them. If they hadn't given in to it and let it run its course, it would have plagued them both, turning into something completely out of proportion. Like this, they could part in peace.

Once he was driving recklessly down the winding road, however, his only thought was to get to Robbie as fast as he could, face whatever had to be faced, get it over with and return to Robbie's arms where he would always belong. He tried to conquer his dread. He had plenty to feel guilty about but he wished Robbie wouldn't make him feel guiltier than he thought he should be. Briefly, he had honestly feared that he might be falling in love with Tracy. If anything like it happened again, he would have sense enough to know that such things were usually fleeting. Luckily, Robbie would never *know* what had happened. It wasn't the sort of thing the others would talk about. They had all been in it together.

It was not quite twelve when he got to the shed. In reply to his questions, Big assured him that nobody had come around asking for him. He'd been sure Robbie wouldn't, even if he'd been worried about him. He had too much respect for his working independence to check up on him, and his sense of responsibility toward his own work was too great for him to break his routine. He thought of telling him that he'd been here all morning but realized that that would be worse than the modified truth he was prepared to tell him. Consideration for Robbie's feelings would oblige him to report his safe return before doing anything else.

His helpers had opened the kilns and emptied them from the last firing. He told them to load up the next lot and be ready to fire up as soon as he returned from a quick lunch. The lost morning wouldn't set him back too much if he worked an extra long afternoon.

He drove up to the studio and sat for a few minutes in the car, gathering up his courage. He had to act as if he were as upset by what had happened as Robbie might be. If he blamed the doctor for not warning him about the drink, Robbie couldn't make much of a case against him. He took a deep breath and hurried into the house.

Robbie was standing in front of his easel with his back to him. He scuffed his feet noisily as he approached and stopped at the open door.

"Here I am, darling," he exclaimed in a voice that came out easily, without sounding strained or false. "At last. You won't believe what happened. I'm so sorry. Have you been worried?"

Robbie turned. He didn't smile but he looked calm and friendly enough. "Are you all right?"

"Yes. Now." He went to him and kissed him on the lips. Robbie accepted it without response. "It was pretty stupid. Pablito gave me a drink. I thought it was some sort of speciality of the house. I didn't find out until later after I'd drunk it that it was doped. I was all right at first. Just sort of woozy. Then it hit me. I guess I passed out. They said they couldn't wake me. I just came to about half an hour ago. I was horrified."

"That does sound pretty stupid—for a doctor to give his guests dope without warning them. I'd like to tell him what I think of him."

"You can if you want to, darling. I was going to say something if I'd seen him this morning. I'd told them all I wanted to leave early."

"What time was all this?"

"You mean, what time did I have the drink? It was after midnight. I was thinking it was about time to go. I remember it was about two when I was still waiting for my head to clear enough to drive. Then I guess I just conked out."

"Where?"

"Where? I don't know exactly. I woke up in a guest room. I guess Pablito put me there."

"Alone?"

Robbie had been determined not to ask questions. He'd been wondering ever since he'd awakened at six and found his bed still empty what story he'd be expected to swallow. A drugged drink was at least ingenious. In order to save himself from going wild with worry, he'd convinced himself that if Lance had had too much to drink he might have gone home absentmindedly to sleep it off. The obvious explanation for his absence hurt too much for him to let himself think about it. He had insisted on the party. No matter what had happened, it was up to him to make covering his tracks as easy for Lance as possible.

"Well sure, alone," Lance said after an instant's hesitation. "Why do you ask, darling? Don't you believe me?"

"Of course I believe you." He wanted to close the incident as quickly as possible. He put a hand on his shoulder. He couldn't bear to think of his beauty being shared by anybody else. "I wouldn't love you if I didn't trust you."

"You wouldn't?"

"No, beautiful. Love and trust go together. I'm just trying to think if there was anything you could have done so that this sort of thing won't happen again. I *did* worry. I know it's silly here, but still. Cars are cars. That road is a bit tricky. It's the first time we've spent a night apart but as long as we don't have a telephone I don't see what you could've done about it. The main thing is, you're here. Did you have fun till you passed out?"

"It was sort of interesting. I'll tell you all about it."

He moved in closer while Robbie's words gnawed at his conscience. It was going to be all right because Robbie believed in him. He couldn't betray his trust but he needed his understanding. For him to pretend that he'd gone through the evening with a bunch of horny guys without anybody laying a finger on him was bound to raise some doubts in Robbie's mind.

If they were in bed, Lance might be able to hint at what the evening had meant for him. He could count on his naked body to disarm his lover. He put his hands on his waist and moved their crotches against each other. His hardening erection was an unequivocal demonstration of his need for Robbie.

"Let's go to your room for a little while, darling. There were some nice naked bodies around the pool, just like you said there would be. I want to feel that you've got me back safely." He thought of the bite marks.

"I'm glad you got here before I had to see Luisa. I didn't want to tell her that you'd disappeared. She sort of counts on me to keep an eye on you. We'll say you slept here. Okay?"

301

"That's probably best."

Lance pushed the sarong aside and Robbie's erection rose to his caress. He ran his hand slowly along its length, thinking of the others he had held. He had a reasonable basis for comparison now. Robbie's was in a class of its own. "There. I don't know how I got through a whole night without it."

"I missed you, beautiful. Don't let's spend many nights apart." Love and tenderness welled up in him, drowning resistance. He kissed Lance's mouth and felt love flowing between them. Whatever had happened, Lance was still his. What more did he want? He dropped his brushes on the table beside him and took what was his with his hands and mouth.

They stumbled back to the courtyard, trying to kiss and hold each other and move all at once. They made a rush for the room where they'd been before. Lance was counting on its being a rather gloomy room to be able to fling himself into Robbie's arms without his noticing the bites. Robbie pulled the curtains across the door after them and tossed his sarong onto a chair. He stood, superbly priapic, at the end of the bed. Lance stayed on the other side of the room to strip himself. The room was full of protective shadow. He pulled off his shirt, his nerves stretched to the breaking point. He wanted Robbie with all of himself. He wanted him to know how much he loved him. It was the near loss that made him so completely his now. He wished he could make Robbie understand it. He was sure he could once they were in bed together. The bite marks were a meaningless danger that had to be circumvented somehow. Once they were in bed together, Robbie would accept any careless explanation for them.

Naked, Lance draped his arms around himself with his hands on his neck to cover the red marks and started for him, trying to hold his eyes with his own. Robbie smiled his secret smile at his approach. Lance could feel his hands on him. In a moment, the danger would be past. He saw Robbie's great eyes waver and begin to stray over him. He stopped in front of him, and pulled his hands away from his neck.

"Did the drink make you come out in blotches?" he asked sharply.

A chill of dread seeped through Lance as he saw

Robbie's erection subsiding. He stood motionless in front of him, his hands hanging at his sides, his head slightly bowed.

"No, that happened," he said.

"It's fairly obvious how."

Lance lifted his head. Robbie's dark eyes were hard and cold. "You said there were things I should find out for myself," he said slowly, prepared to throw himself on his mercy and beg for understanding. "I'm finding out how to get to you, how two guys can be everything to each other. There's a lot that's strange about it. At least to me. Maybe not to you. Situations that don't make any sense unless I adapt in ways that are new to me. I don't see how you can be naked with a hard-on and not expect guys to get ideas."

"You were naked with a hard-on?"

"It was the way you said it would be. After dinner, everybody went to the pool naked. They had towels but they didn't bother with them much. They didn't wear towels when they were swimming. You can't stop guys from touching you when you're swimming. You'd drown. Maybe I get hard too easily but everybody else was the same. Maybe you shouldn't have let me go, but once I was there I couldn't act as if it were a debutante ball."

"So you didn't pass out. You were having a gang fuck." Robbie's voice was deadly calm.

"I *did* pass out. I'd've been home—maybe late but I'd've been home by four or five if I hadn't passed out. Tracy said he tried everything to wake me. I was out cold."

"Tracy?"

Lance looked into cold, probing eyes. He couldn't lie to Robbie. Everything that he was belonged to him. If he couldn't tell him about Tracy, he didn't deserve to be with him. Tracy was part of giving himself to Robbie.

"I was with a guy. I went a little crazy. It's over with."

There wasn't a flicker of expression in Robbie's face. "You let him fuck you?"

"Yes. I—"

Robbie swung his open hand with all his force into Lance's face. Lance's head snapped back. Robbie swung the other hand and delivered a blow that sent Lance reeling back onto the bed. He rolled over onto his stom-

303

ach with his swelling erection under him and put his hands over his head, waiting for it to clear. Robbie made a lunge for the bureau and pulled a belt out of a drawer and turned back to Lance's prostrate body. He lifted the belt and brought it lashing down on Lance's shoulders. His body contracted and he uttered a cry.

"I'll mark you, Goddammit," Robbie shouted. "You don't have to go looking for it. You can get it at home."

"Yes, beat me," Lance begged. "Punish me if you think I need it. I want you to. I'm yours."

"What if I don't want you? Go back to the doctor and his faggots. Go back to Tracy."

The belt whistled and cracked. He watched Lance's body leap with pain. He fought back tears of rage and sorrow. There was more pain in him than any he could inflict. He had been betrayed and was betraying himself. Everything he valued in himself was being twisted out of shape. The beloved body cringed from him as his flailing arm descended. To his horror, his erection had revived.

"Fuck me," Lance begged in a voice that was choked with sobs. "Fuck me. Don't use anything. Just spit. That's what those guys used."

"What guys?" Robbie roared. The hurt in him was deep and unappeased. He brought the belt slashing down across his shoulders. Lance shouted with pain.

"The guys who raped me. Just spit, darling. Rape me. I belong to you."

"Oh Christ," Robbie groaned, hurling the belt across the room. "Yes, Goddammit. I'm going to fuck you for the last time." He spit into his hand and wiped it on his cock and drove into him with all the brutality he could muster.

"Oh Christ. Oh Jesus," Lance shouted. "No, I can't. You're going to tear me to pieces." He struggled up and tried to twist away from him.

Robbie brought his forearm down hard above his ear. Lance crumpled under him with a whimper. Robbie ripped deeper into him. He got a grip on his hips and forced a punishing advance. Lance's body convulsed. He uttered a wail and began to beat on the bed with his fists. Robbie pulled him up and bit his neck and shoulders where they were marked until he tasted blood. Lance's legs thrashed and his body writhed while broken sobs burst from him. Robbie felt his cock reach the farthest limit of its entry. He drew back and plunged mercilessly into him again. Lance shouted with hoarse triumph.

"Yes. Oh Christ yes. Oh Jesus, darling. I worship you. Fuck me. Rape me. Take everything in me. It's all yours." He uttered a different kind of sound, a sort of shuddering moan as his orgasm spilled out over the bed.

Robbie stood under the shower trying to fight his way up out of the depths of despair. How far was he prepared to go to feed Lance's lust for depravity? Lance had been so shielded from reality that he accepted as reality any violent excess, any self-abuse that gave him the illusion of living intensely. Robbie thought he understood that much.

He reminded himself that he'd sworn to do nothing that would diminish the joy that was Lance's unique gift to the world. He thought of him as he must have been last night at the pool—naked, proudly showing off his big cock, radiant with the unselfconscious pleasure he found in people. Joy existed to be shared; he couldn't keep it all for himself without killing it.

He had rushed Lance into something that he had needed time to prepare for. Falling in love, probably for the first time, and learning the true nature of his sexuality were two profound and momentous experiences that didn't usually happen simultaneously. Robbie had had a few months to adjust to one before being caught up in the other. By tomorrow, perhaps, he might be able to look at Lance without seeing him in a stranger's arms.

It was the beating that appalled him. Feeling that Lance had wanted it, and realizing that he himself had wanted the body that he was beating made the sickness seem contagious. Could he allow Lance to arouse all the ugliness in himself without being permanently deformed by it? He was appalled by the possibility that he was adding to the tensions that at these bad moments threatened to shatter him. He had to let Lance be the guide, follow him, accept him, love him unquestioningly, even at the risk of destroying himself. He had to fight for Lance by fighting himself.

When he returned to the room, Lance was curled up in a fetal position on the bed where he had left him. At the sound of his footsteps, he scrambled down to the end of the bed and seized Robbie's hand and pressed it to his swollen cheek. "It wasn't the last time, was it?" he asked beseechingly.

A sob knotted Robbie's throat. Lance loved him. He didn't doubt it. He wished he could make his mind settle for that fact. Tears filled his eyes. He saw the long broad welts of the belt. He blinked the tears away. The bites on his neck and shoulders looked angry. He wanted to hold him and kiss him gently and weep with him. He snatched his hand away but brushed it quickly against his hair, not daring to permit himself any greater endearment, and stepped safely out of reach.

"I don't know. I'm too shocked and hurt to know anything. I've never done anything like that. It's horrible."

"No. It was beautiful." Lance lifted his face, his eyes wide with an inner vision. "You care more about me than you ever have about anybody. I didn't think you could lose your self-control. You're magnificent."

"Oh, for God's sake, there's nothing magnificent about losing control." Robbie's voice was rough with self-reproach. "It's shameful. You drive me wild as if you were doing it on purpose. Don't you want us to treat each other like civilized human beings?"

"No. I want us to be wild. Wild with love." He spoke with unexpected vigor and with no trace of either reproach or contrition. "How can anybody be a respectable, law-abiding, socially acceptable homosexual? You've showed me I'm a faggot. What's socially acceptable about that? I want you to beat me when I do things you don't like. It's thrilling. It makes me belong to you even more." He dropped back and rolled over onto his stomach. "Look at me. Have you marked me?"

Robbie averted his eyes from the ruin of the beautiful back. "Yes," he said.

"I'm glad." He threw his legs over the side of the bed and sprang up. "Look at us. Two naked guys in a crummy bedroom stinking of sex. My ass hurts from what you did to me with your cock. I'm covered with my own come. I love it. Who cares about being civilized? I should've brought Tracy back with me and let you fuck him. That sort of thing makes us closer. There's no sense pretending. Beating me gave you a hard-on. You're not all that civilized. I don't suppose last night was very civilized but at least it was honest. That's what I want. I want us to be honest with each other. I don't think you should ask me to act as if life is all tidy and pretty. I've had enough of that as long as I can remember."

"All right." Robbie passed a hand over his eyes and took a few steps away from him. He found Lance terrifying and rather splendid. He might even think he made sense if he didn't force himself to such extremes. "I know what you're saying. I know why you're saying it. You've still got a lot of the past to unload. I understand that. Do you try to understand me? I've told you that if you give yourself to other guys, I'll stop wanting you. Have you thought about that?"

"I don't believe it. Nothing could make me stop wanting you except falling in love with somebody else. There were couples there last night. They played around like everybody else but they ended up together just the way we would have if you'd been there."

"After Tracy had fucked you? I doubt it." He had difficulty getting the words out but he had to face it without taking refuge in ambiguity. "We'd better settle this once and for all. We're back to what we were talking about when Michael was here. It still sounds as if it just boils down to having sex with anybody we like."

"Not anybody. Only when it seems to really mean something. I can't explain what made Tracy special but if I hadn't let it happen it could've gone on building up into a big issue that might've really hurt us."

"God forbid you should've been hurt," Robbie said sharply.

He crossed the room, careful not to get close enough to Lance to touch him, and wrapped his sarong around himself. He tried not to look at him. The sight of him, forsaken, the unsightly marks on his body, all the light extinguished in him, made Robbie want to scream with the need to release the love he was withholding. He wanted to hold him, kiss his wounds, revive the joy in his eyes.

"Listen, you can put it any way you like," he said. "The trouble is that as long as I'm in love with you I'm not going to want anybody else. That's the way it is.

307

It's my problem. There's no reason you should be the same, but can't we go back to where we started? If you love me, you don't want to torture me. You don't know what this is doing to me. Just take my word for it. The thought of other guys having you is more than I can take. It turns me into a sadistic thug. I can't take that either. You can do things with your body that can't affect us in any way. I know it. I can say it but it doesn't do any good. Can't you take the trouble not to let me find out what you're doing?"

"So that love can be all moonlight and roses?"

"Yes. You can make it sound silly if you want to. If you'd come home this morning, seven o'clock, any time—without the bites of course—I wouldn't've let myself wonder about it. Parties can last all night. I'm not an insensitive idiot. I know what it's like to learn what you're all about sexually and I know that at the beginning you may want things that won't interest you later on. It's something we can't share. I can't discover I like to suck cock. I know it already. I'm pretty sure you've managed to do things that I haven't had to know about. That's the way it should be until you've acquired enough experience to know what's worth taking a risk for and what isn't. I found out pretty quickly that nothing's worth that kind of risk, the risk of losing something that's as precious as life itself. You're older than I was. You'll probably find out even quicker. If that's moonlight and roses, it's better than sinking into the primeval slime."

He felt Lance approaching and his muscles tensed as he steeled himself against his own weakness. This wasn't the moment for a sentimental reconciliation. He still hadn't won his point. Lance stopped a few feet behind him.

"I wanted everything to be open between us. I don't want to do things behind your back. Why can't we be honest with each other?"

"Stop being so bloody American. Honest Abe. A little deception in love never did anybody any harm. It also takes a lot of fun out of cheating, which isn't a bad idea. I think you know what I'm talking about. You're so damn spoiled. You want to have your cake and eat it. If we want each other, we'll probably have to make sacrifices. Give up your simpleminded ideas about hon-

308

esty. That's the only sacrifice I'm asking you to make now. Have your gang fucks without me. Find out about sex without hurting me."

"Oh God. I can't stand hurting you." Lance moved in against him and put his hands on his waist to turn him.

Robbie whirled around and gripped his arms. "Then don't. I've listened to everything you've said about living a full free life together but you leave out basic human feelings. There's nothing avant garde about love. It's just the same old business of two people tying each other down and then fretting against the bonds. If you fret so much that you stop wanting me, that's my tough luck. There's no other way of playing it. You saw what happened. I got a hard-on beating you. We don't want a life of hurting each other, physically or any other way. We want a life of loving each other and taking care of each other and making each other happy. I want to hear your wonderful laughter. I want your joy. I expect you to have enough ingenuity to find whatever extra you need that I don't give you. I can't change my cock every day but I can try not to be a bore in other ways. I don't want you to stop exploring until you find out all you want to know."

"I know all I need to know about parties like that. I don't need another one."

Lance knew that Robbie was shutting himself off from the side of himself that frightened both of them, the side of himself whose importance he was still unable to assess, but he was too anxious to feel the bonds tightening around him again to insist on his accepting all of him today. He had to belong to Robbie.

"You won't talk about its being the last time again, will you?"

"No. Not if you leave me my illusions."

"Oh God, darling."

Their mouths opened and healed each other. They felt horror receding. They pledged themselves to their love. They felt as if they had survived a car crash. Lance hurt all over. He treasured his pain. Robbie drew back.

"You better take a shower. I've got something to put on those sores. I'll run along to Luisa and tell her we'll be there for dinner. I'll make up some story about an accident with the kilns. The belt marks will be gone in a few hours. I can throw something together here for lunch. Are you in a hurry to get to work?"

"Yes, darling. They're waiting for me to fire up again."

They fumbled with each other tentatively like novice lovers. They were both shy of each other. The emotions that had raged in them were still too raw to be easily absorbed into the usual harmony of their daily lives.

"I think we both need a hard afternoon's work," Robbie said, moving away. "We'll both feel better this evening. I'll be right back. I'll tell her you can't take time for a real lunch."

"Thanks. I don't feel like smiling sweetly at her at the moment. We do understand each other about most things, don't we?"

"We're getting there. Is there anything else about last night you think we should talk about?"

"No. I know I don't have to say I'm sorry for hurting you."

"We don't ever have to say we're sorry any more than we have to say we forgive each other. We understand that."

"Do we understand that we'll never go out without each other again?"

"If you're sure that's what you want."

"I'm sure. It'll be good for my ingenuity."

They smiled slightly forlornly. At least they would be able to laugh again.

By evening, Robbie had convinced himself that Lance was still the same person, no matter who had enjoyed his body. His belief in fidelity remained unaltered but he knew that it was only luck that kept it from being a problem for him. The only positive adjustment he could think of making was to take special care to allow Lance his independence when they were with others. Maurice had always clung to him, and it had annoyed him. He was inclined to cling, too. He could get over it.

In the days that followed, Robbie discovered that something new seemed to have entered Lance's body, a voluptuous freedom, wanton and abandoned, that Robbie found electrifying. Whether because of the party or the beating, he had the feeling that Lance had come to terms for the first time not only with his sexuality but also with his rich sensuality.

Lance was in love with Robbie at last in the way he

had dreamed of being in love—consumingly, exclusively. He had found the violence in him and was increasingly intoxicated by the limitless passion he was learning to unleash in him. He wanted to make himself so necessary that Robbie would kill him before he would let him go. He was leading Robbie to indulge in excesses he had never before dreamed of, slowly undermining the controls that Robbie valued as a foundation of normalcy and sanity. He was preparing Robbie to accept his image of homosexuality as a divine aberration that liberated them from all social conventions and conventional morality, lawless and without constraints.

Work progressed. Robbie applied himself with the concentration of the greatly gifted. He put aside his first canvas and started on another, explaining that he always worked on two alternately. Lance found it maddening. He was just beginning to make sense of the first one, the undercoats building into a rich texture, dense forms emerging and acquiring meaning, muted color suddenly striking a dominant note. Lance was left in suspense, dying to know how it was going to turn out, as if he'd been interrupted in the middle of a thriller. Robbie laughed delightedly at his frustration.

"I may never finish it. Keep you waiting for years. I never knew I could hold somebody in my power with a picture."

Lance was jealous of his work. Robbie shut himself away in it. It was the source of the discipline and control that he was systematically attacking in bed. "Please finish it. Change your work habits. Just this once. For me. This is sort of my picture."

"You really mean it, sweetheart?"

He loved to have Lance ask him to do something for him. He was so docile, so devoted, so grateful for any small gesture of appreciation, that Robbie was afraid of getting into the habit of taking him for granted. He looked at him intently for a moment, delighting his eyes by discovering his beauty in the formation of his brow and the extraordinary mobility of his mouth.

"God, you're a miracle," he said. "Okay. Give me a few days to get this one blocked in and then I'll go back to yours. Lord knows what'll happen to it. I always put things aside for at least a month before I finish them. Maybe you'll launch me on a new period."

"I've always wanted to be an influence on contemporary painting." For Lance, it was a precious gift. Robbie was letting him get a foot in the door of his private world. He would have all of him now.

A copy of the layout in *Life* arrived, along with an order for two thousand more gollies. Larry wrote that sales were leveling off and that this would probably be the last order. Lance groaned at the thought of going through the same motions two thousand more times but was pleased with himself. He was a success. Robbie had paid himself back for his initial outlay. There was money in the bank. Lance expected to meet his self-imposed deadline of a month for the previous order. If he cancelled out another month for the final order, he could get on with the chess sets.

The *Life* piece didn't amount to much, mostly pictures of celebrities handling gollies. There was a snapshot of Robbie with a side view of a young man who might have been anybody, identified as the painter's brother. The short text contained pseudopsychiatric references to postwar aggressions to explain the craze for smashing gollies and included a brief summary of Robi's career. Puerto Veragua was identified as the site of Lance's pottery works. There was nothing that would bring a horde of reporters rushing to the scene.

One day Ramiriz dropped by for another visit. The policeman wasn't in uniform this time but in a rumpled cotton suit with a sweat-stained felt hat mashed onto the back of his head. Because he never explained what he came for, Lance was getting bored with him. He greeted him cordially enough but after a momentary pause went on working on his wheel. Ramiriz approached and stood watching while the little devil-doll took shape under Lance's practiced hands. He withdrew to the nearby plank wall and settled against it with one arm thrown over its shoulder-high top, his other hand on his hip.

"I hear you do good business," he said, gazing out over the top of the wall.

"Yes, I've been lucky. These little things have been selling very well. I expect to be finished with them in

312

another month or so. I don't know how good business will be after that."

"You managed without more help?" They both looked at Lance's work force, stretched out on the floor asleep near the bricked-up kilns, both of which were operating. Lance laughed.

"They work very hard," he explained, "but in between they have time off. Pottery is like that. I wouldn't be able to use anybody else. This place is too small."

"I believe much pottery is made with machines."

"Yes, but that's not the kind of pottery I want to make. I like making it by hand."

"It would be possible to produce a great deal in this place with machinery?"

"I suppose so. I didn't exactly mean the place is too small. I meant it's not set up for more people. Three is just right."

Ramiriz looked on while the polite young man continued his work. His interest was more personal than professional. He had been curious about this young man from the beginning. His name conjured up such vast sums of money, even though he controlled none of it himself, that it was impossible not to be curious about him.

The *politicos* weren't generally interested in modest factories, or factories of any kind. They went in for big deals on paper. But somebody was interested enough to consider taking the business away from the young *señor*. His mother's name had been mentioned mysteriously in his message from the capital. He felt something *simpatico* in the handsome young man despite having learned things about him that shocked him. Señor Lance had been drawn into the German doctor's circle. He had seen photographs of him doing things that he hadn't known a man could do. He had included a paragraph about the photographs in his last report to the capital because he didn't know what sort of case was being prepared against him.

Usually, an exorbitant tax bill was enough to close a business, but nobody had taken advantage of that useful expedient. A morals charge was also useful if he was to be deported. But mysteriously, this young man seemed to be holding a trump card.

He sighed as he stood looking around indecisively,

tugging at the rolls of flesh on his face. "You know the air-mail service is about to begin?" he asked, unable to think of any other questions.

"Soon?"

"At the end of the week. Mail and light freight. It's a great event for Puerto Veragua."

"I may use it if I have any rush orders."

Ramiriz nodded vaguely. "Take my advice. Don't put more money into this place. You won't want to stay forever."

"No, not forever. Maybe another year. Anyway, I told you. I don't have enough money to worry about."

Ramiriz noted the time limit. He'd already reported the limited funds. Maybe the interested parties in the capital would decide he wasn't worth bothering about. Ramiriz hoped so. He was getting soft. He put his hands on his hips and looked up at the exposed beams of the roof.

"You said you wished to avoid publicity yet you appeared in your big picture magazine."

"Oh, you saw that? That was all right. That wasn't my picture and they called me Cosling. I don't think the story was of much interest to anybody anyway."

"Perhaps not, although I'm sure the government was pleased to see the country mentioned without anybody being called assassins or dictators. Perhaps the ministry of tourism will ask you for a testimonial." He pushed his face into shape with his hands, nodded, and headed for the door.

"Thanks for stopping by," Lance called after him. He was coming to the conclusion that the policeman came to see him because he had nothing better to do. He couldn't find anything significant in his questions or comments. He shrugged as he resumed his work.

The next day, the rain began. Lance was driving up to the shed when he saw José dart across the street in front of him, signaling him. By the time he'd parked the car and turned the motor off, sheets of rain enveloped him, drumming on the car roof. The door was wrenched open and José fell in beside him, panting and shaking water off himself.

Lance hadn't seen him, he supposed, for about two months. He looked slightly citified, with a different, more North American haircut, wearing cheap chinos

314

with a sports shirt and shoes. He was as wiry as ever with the same predatory look but his arrival had been youthfully impetuous and not unappealing. Lance realized that he was no longer frightened of him. He even felt a little tug of gratitude toward him. If it hadn't been for José, he might not have known he was ready for Robbie.

"The rain has started," José announced unnecessarily. His shirt was plastered to his chest, outlining his nipples.

"Very sudden. I did not expect it."

"It is always like that. It will rain now every day for an hour very hard." He paused. "Did you think I had forgotten you?"

"Pablito told me he saw you in the capital."

"Did he give you my message?"

"Yes. Two weeks ago." Lance felt his attraction just as, he knew now, he had felt it the first time he'd seen him. He had a score to settle with him.

"I stayed longer. I am here now. My important friends are coming. You remember our agreement. We will make money."

"I think no."

The rain drummed on the roof. They had to raise their voices and put their heads close together to make themselves heard. It was a wall around the car. Lance could just make out the shape of the shed in front of him.

"What are you saying?" José shouted.

"I say no. No money. No agreement."

"We will see." He put a hand on Lance's crotch.

Lance made no attempt to evade it. His erection began to fill out under it. He slid an arm around his shoulders as he turned to him. He wanted to demonstrate to the beach boy that his macho preening and posturing was a fraud. If José tried hitting him again, he was ready to hit back.

He leaned forward to him, his hands tensed for violence. He encountered a mouth opening to receive his. Their tongues rolled over each other. José's hands were busy with Lance's clothes. He unbuttoned his shirt and moved over him down to his shorts. He opened them and freed his erection.

Lance pulled his mouth free and guided José's head

315

to his chest. He made love to Lance's body with his tongue and lips. Lance realized that he didn't have to exert any pressure; José's mouth was moving voluntarily toward its goal. He watched him stretch his lips wide to encompass the head of his cock. He held it and sucked on it, not with a very convincing show of desire but dutifully and efficiently. Lance's cock had brought his conqueror to his knees. His orgasm was a spasm of triumph. He held his head to make sure that he swallowed all of it. When he was satisfied, he drew José up to him.

"I learned many things in the capital to make money. The foreigners always want it that way. They pay."

"How much?"

"Twenty dollars. I think of you when I do it."

"You are not worth so much but you learn."

"You are very big. Others are easier."

"You try again more good. I must work. You wait here if you wish."

"I am not afraid of getting wet. I will come again in a week or so."

"Come back when you wish that I fuck you."

"Nobody does that to me."

"I think I will. It is something you can learn."

"What about our agreement?"

"After I fuck you, we talk."

"Maybe. You are better for sex than the ones who pay. I don't let them kiss me."

"You want everything with me. You are like a woman. Like me. We both want men." He put his arms around him and kissed him tauntingly.

José tore himself out of Lance's arms and made a lunge for the door and flung himself out into the rain. In an instant, his running figure became a blur in a liquid landscape.

Lance grinned to himself as he took off his shirt and shorts and bundled them up to keep them dry during the short dash for the shed.

He had had his revenge and the score had been settled, but he remained perversely drawn to the corrupt and squalid life that José represented. The dark side of his imagination was gripped by the thought of a Vanderholden becoming a male whore. To be a social outcast was the ultimate freedom. José would be back.

The end of the gollies was in sight. Lance celebrated his impending release from repetition by taking time off one afternoon after the daily rain to order the glazes he was going to need for the chessmen. When he had finished his business, he crossed the wide quay to the bar with metal tables in front of it that he'd noticed before. He ordered a beer and sat outside, feeling suddenly remote, adrift, cut off from the world.

Life was very strange. He had to remind himself that if he followed that road around the warehouse, he would find the place where he worked, his lover, a girl who was pregnant by him, a house where he lived, friends. He felt as alien as if he'd just stepped off the decrepit old tramp freighter tied up a hundred feet away. How had he managed to break free of the mold that had imprisoned generations of his antecedents? Lance Cosling was a fiction. His past was a dream. He felt as if he didn't exist.

He slowly became aware of a man staring at him. He hitched his chair around to stare back at him. The man's eyes didn't flinch or dart away. He lifted his glass and drank, still staring at him over the rim of the glass. They looked at each other coldly and expressionlessly. Lance felt as if they understood each other perfectly. The man appeared to be between forty and fifty, his short brown hair flecked with gray. He was lean and lanky with a hard-bitten look, dressed like a tourist in slacks and sports shirt and a cotton jacket. He was Lance's idea of a Midwestern businessman.

When he looked away, he did so with finality, severing contact. Lance knew that he wouldn't look at him again. He signaled the waiter and paid. Lance drained his glass and signaled the waiter in his turn. The man stood and left the bar without looking back. Lance dropped some coins on the table and followed.

They crossed the quay and entered a street that led to the main shopping district and the police station. A big American car was parked in it. The man went to it and let himself in, still without looking back. The door on the other side swung open and stayed open. When Lance reached it, he dropped in beside the driver and closed it. The man started the motor and set the car in motion. "You a hustler?" he asked.

317

Lance didn't know what had prompted the question but he was delighted. "Yeah," he said.

"I can usually tell. How much do you charge?"

"Twenty dollars U.S."

"You better be good. Do you take it up the ass?"

"Sure. Anything you want."

"That's a refreshing attitude. Too many hustlers are so fucking fussy. They can't do this. They won't do that. I say, if you buy a guy, you have the right to get what you want. It's like any other business—the customer is always right."

"Sounds reasonable."

"Good. We understand each other. The name's Dan."

"That's funny. Mine's Van."

"A vaudeville team." Dan uttered a brief snort of laughter.

He drove past the police station, slowed by the horse-drawn carts and the pedestrians. At the end of the street, he turned into the big central square and drove around it and parked in front of the hotel.

"You're staying here?" Lance asked.

"Yeah. Is there a better one?"

"Not that I know of. I don't want to be seen at the desk. What's your room number?"

"Eighteen."

"I'll go through to the corridor and wait for you." Lance let himself out and strolled casually into the great dusty lobby without glancing at the desk. He was fascinated by the role he had adopted. He had launched himself as a hustler without any help from José. He didn't know why he was doing it. He seemed to be acting without volition, as if he were being guided by fate. When he reached the corridor that led off to the rooms, he paused and looked back. The tall lanky man was following briskly. He caught up with Lance and led the way to his room.

"You seem to know your way around," he commented as he unlocked his door.

"Yeah. I've been here before."

Dan admitted them and locked the door behind them. "You want to take a shower?"

"I'm clean. Just my clothes are dirty."

"Okay. Let's see what I've got." He removed his jacket and hung it in the closet while Lance stripped. Exposure

318

brought his erection up to vigorous attention. He stood with his hands at his sides, offering himself for his client's inspection. Dan looked him over and nodded approvingly. "That's a sight for sore eyes—a hustler with a real hard-on. You're not bad. What're you doing in this dump? You could get fifty bucks easy in the capital." He began to undress.

Lance was amazed at how simple and direct and unselfconscious the transaction was. It wasn't even sordid, just businesslike and to the point. "I have a job here," he explained.

"You *must* be hard up. Had some trouble with the cops stateside?"

"Nothing serious."

"Just enough to make yourself scarce? Sure, that happens. Even a pretty guy like you doesn't always get all the breaks."

Dan was uncovering an ordinary male body, neither attractive nor repellent. It was carelessly put together, without grace or charm, lean, very white except for face and neck and forearms, with an ordinary scattering of hair. His erection was ordinary too. Lance was delighted. A straight might fall for a beautiful boy; it took a real queer to be excited by a guy like this.

Dan went to the bedside stand and found a tube and applied lubricant to himself. He evidently wasn't expecting any frills. He made no move to kiss or caress his purchase. Lance had been brought here to be fucked. He gestured toward the bed. "Lie down, kid," he directed.

Lance stretched out on his stomach. Dan dropped down over him and entered him easily and began a straightforward drive for orgasm. Lance was immediately gripped by the thrill of being taken by a stranger. He brought his body into action. He felt the body on him respond, its rhythm modifying, entering into communication with the messages Lance was sending. They found a rhythm that permitted Lance to offer him all the satisfactions that were contained in the intensity of his desire.

"Hey, you're good," Dan exclaimed. "You really know what a guy wants."

"You're good too, man. I like it. Take everything I've got to give. There. Smooth and easy. You're taking me now. You're really getting it. Use that cock, man. Use that nice cock."

"Jesus, kid. You're great. You're the greatest ever."

He put his arms around Lance's chest and pulled him up to his knees with him. Lance worked his hips and bore down on the cock within him. He dropped his head back and made his lips soft and inviting for his partner's mouth. Dan's hands were obviously entranced with the feel of his body. Lance moved them down to his cock.

"How's that for size?" he asked.

"I'll bet you love playing with it."

"I love somebody playing with it with me. It's big enough to play two-handed."

"You can say that again."

Lance loved to feel his body working in total harmony with another. He loved giving himself extravagantly. He knew he was surpassing Dan's expectations. He had the power to satisfy a man. If he could uncover an erotic goldmine in this man who looked as if he ran a small bank in Idaho, he could do it with anybody. He could be the best whore in the business.

Dan grunted as he came and pulled out quickly. A towel had appeared from somewhere under him. Lance sat up and wiped himself off. He heard Dan in the bathroom and went to the door. He was standing at the basin, washing himself.

"Boy. For a minute there, I didn't know what was happening to me," Lance said.

"You're something, kid. Aside from anything else, you're just about the prettiest guy I've ever seen." Dan moved away from the basin. Lance stepped forward to replace him. Dan blocked his way.

"Get in the tub," he ordered.

He did as he was told and turned back to Dan questioningly.

"Sit down. Lie back," Dan said. He moved to the tub and stood over him, his cock distended, and urinated on him.

A cry caught in Lance's throat and he started up but dropped back as the hot stream splashed over his shoulders and chest. It hit his cock. It sprang up into erection. He had an immediate orgasm. He lay back, gasping, his eyes closed while come trickled down his body in rivulets of urine. A sob rose in his chest and he choked it back, determined to accept the ugliness of his defilement.

"Maybe you should pay *me*," Dan said with a quiver of laughter in his voice. Lance opened his eyes. Dan's erection was lifted toward him once again. "Don't worry. I'll give you fifty. You're worth it. Wash yourself off. I'm going to fuck you again."

Lance gave himself more unrestrainedly than he had before. He wanted to be able to take anything that life dished out.

"How about coming back later?" Dan asked while they were still joined to each other. "There'll be another fifty bucks in it for you."

"I'm not sure I can."

"Try to make it at about ten or ten-thirty. I'll be here."

"Okay. I'll try. I could use the fifty. I want you to piss on me again."

"Yeah. You like that. Anybody so pretty is asking for it."

"You can piss on my face next time."

"That'll probably make *me* come."

Lance left the hotel with five ten-dollar bills in his hip pocket. It was the first money he'd earned on his own, without anybody's help or his name being known. It gave him a wonderful feeling of independence. He was going to earn a hundred dollars in less than two hours. The amazing thing was that he could collect the money and keep the merchandise.

When he got back to the shed, Big told him that José had come to see him. There was an odd expression on his face when he said his name that Lance couldn't interpret. Was it disapproving or simply knowing? Whatever it was, it made a more personal connection with Lance than he had ever felt with his helper before.

"He say he come back?" Lance asked.

"He will be back if you allow it," Big said, disapproval becoming more pronounced.

Lance was ready for his rapist now. Whether or not he accepted whatever proposal he might make depended on the details, but the appeal of novelty could no longer influence him. "I wish to see him if he comes," he told Big.

321

At dinner, he told Robbie that he wanted to go back to the shed for a little while. Five hundred gollies were in the kilns on which he'd used a new glaze, he explained, and he wanted to make sure the firing was a success. It wasn't yet ten when he said that the kilns were probably about ready to be opened. He didn't bother to dress. A sarong was all he need wear at this time of night. Robbie kissed him and told him to hurry back.

Lance parked the car in front of the shed so that if anything unexpected happened it would be where he had said it would be. Robbie never came here but he let himself be guided by the possibility that he might. He went in silently and turned on the bare bulb hanging over the table so that the place would look active from outside. The bulb was dim but shed enough light to prevent him from bumping into anything. He went back behind the kilns to where his helpers kept their mattresses. They were curled up on them, not quite embracing.

Lance knelt and touched Big's naked shoulder. He was instantly awake, sitting up and staring at Lance with sleep-dazed eyes.

Lance explained quietly that he was going to leave the lights on so that it would look as if he were here. He would be back soon if anybody asked for him. Lance gave his shoulder a pat and left.

When he reached the square, he found a procession in progress. The facade of the church was illuminated and a file of black-hooded figures was issuing from a side street headed toward it. Flaming torches were borne aloft, rough wooden crosses, skulls brandished on the end of poles. They looked very real in the flickering light. The thud of drums was an accompaniment to a lugubrious wailing chant. He couldn't remember any important church festival in September and assumed it must be some merry local event. There were people watching in front of the hotel. Lance slipped around them and entered the lobby. There was nobody visible at the desk. The clerk was probably asleep behind it.

Lance knocked on Dan's door, earned another fifty dollars and was home with Robbie in little more than an hour.

In the morning, he drew Luisa aside before breakfast

322

and gave her the money. He told her to put it away safely for the baby.

He was providing for his family on his own. Tracy had made him feel how insulated his life remained under Robbie's care. He was sheltered from harsh reality by his lover's financial security and his beauty. Yesterday he had come up against the grit in life. He had a premonition of losing Robbie but he wanted José to come back with a definite proposition.

Thinking about it all morning while his hands performed their familiar routine, it struck him that he had gone beyond the momentary attractions of youth and good looks. Robbie didn't have to worry about his infidelity anymore. He had given Dan good value for his money. A simple business proposition didn't touch anything that belonged to Robbie.

When he went to pick him up for lunch, he found him struggling with "his" picture. True to his promise, he had returned to it and Lance could see that it wasn't going well. He wanted to tell him to put it aside again and work in his usual way but he didn't see how he could without making it clear that he didn't like it. Robbie would see for himself that it was going wrong but he was ashamed of himself for having made such a frivolous request. Painting was Robbie's business just as whoring might be his.

"I'm learning a lot," Robbie said, putting his brushes away for the morning. "Having two pictures going at once has been a crutch. I'm going to get this bastard right if it kills me."

José turned up after the rain that afternoon. Seeing the animosity in Big's eyes, Lance took him outside to talk.

"Don Antonio will be here at the end of the week," he announced. "He wants to see you on Friday."

"Don Antonio is your famous *politico?*"

"Yes, a very important man in the capital. Much money."

"He wants me as a whore?" Putting it into words made it real and ordinary, even banal.

"Of course, he will pay for you. I told him I had a handsome North American for him. I'll give you half as I promised."

"Half of how much?"

"Fifty U.S. the first time. That is much money. If you please him and he wants you again, then we'll see."

"Twenty-five is not enough for me. If I not go, you get nothing."

"If you do not go, you may be sorry. Pablito has some pictures your friend would be interested in seeing."

Pablito had already hinted about the pictures, but there had been no opportunity to see them. As long as he didn't see them, he could tell himself that they weren't as bad as he suspected they were.

"You take half for the first time. If again, I take all."

"No. It is understood that the money will be given to me."

"Why does he come here?"

"He is from here. He has a fine house there where the great families used to live long ago." He gestured inland toward the square. "You will go there."

"On Friday at what hour?"

"At night. Eleven o'clock usually. I've been getting him boys for several years. I'll tell you beforehand."

"How long I stay?"

"An hour. Maybe two. Whatever he wants."

"No. What *I* want. For fifty dollars I stay one hour, no more."

"Very well. I will tell him that is usual with North Americans."

Lance returned to work, telling himself that he could always change his mind at the last minute, but curious. If it proved to be an ugly experience, perhaps his curiosity would be permanently satisfied. He decided to say nothing to Robbie until dinner on Friday evening. Some story would occur to him by then.

He was just finishing up his morning's work on Friday when a visitor arrived. He entered with an insolently lordly bearing and stopped near the work table. He looked as if he were dressed for prewar Palm Beach or Newport, when gentlemen wore suits and neckties for ceremonial breakfasts, except that his tailoring was too flashy to be quite gentlemanly. His lightweight cream-colored jacket was nipped in at the waist and the shoulders were padded. Something monolithic and unbending about his figure suggested to Lance that he was corseted. He wore an off-white Panama hat with a

wide sweeping brim. Under it, his features were fleshy—
prominent nose, full lips. He appeared to be in well-
preserved, vigorous middle age. He glanced at Lance.

"This is the Puerto Veragua Pottery Works?" he asked
without tripping over a syllable in almost unaccented
English.

"Yes," Lance said, still sitting at the wheel.

"It is yours?"

"With a friend. I run it."

"Señor Sanchez," the man said, presumably introducing himself. "I assume the papers are in order."

"I think so. I know the chief of police. He comes to
see me from time to time. He hasn't said anything about
papers."

"Quite so. This is all there is?"

"Yes. It is a big name for a small place."

Sanchez advanced toward Lance and picked up an
unglazed golly from a tray. "This is what has sold so
well in North America?"

Lance stood. He was slightly taller than his visitor.
"I was lucky. It was sort of a fad."

"Very amusing." His smile was humorless but not
unfriendly. ʜe put the figure back. "This is all you
make?"

"I've made so many that I haven't had time for anything else. I'll be finished with them in a few weeks."

The visitor's dark liquid eyes roamed the premises
and settled on Lance. "It looks quite harmless," he said
cryptically. "Perhaps we will meet again."

"A pleasure. Excuse me but did you come for any
particular reason?"

"Ah, yes. I should have explained. I have friends in
the capital who are interested in what you are doing.
I happened to be coming. I told them I'd take a look."

"Why are they interested?" Lance asked, wondering
why his official callers, if this was an official one, never
told him what they wanted.

"What interests people? Money and love. Both are
frequently elusive." He bowed and made a lordly but
less insolent departure.

The visit gave Lance an idea. He combined Sanchez
with José's *politico* and told Robbie at lunchtime that
a local man who was in the government had come to

325

see him and wanted to talk to him again about the pottery works.

"Maybe I'll finally find out what Ramiriz keeps snooping around about. He said that people in the capital are interested in what I'm doing here."

"Who is he?"

"God knows. Somebody called Don Antonio. He has a house here somewhere in back of the church. He asked me to come see him after dinner. It turned out he meant eleven o'clock."

"That's after dinner for people like that, sweetheart. They keep Flip's hours."

Luisa was looking at them round-eyed. "Don Antonio came to see you?" she asked.

"That's who he said he was," Lance blurted out hastily.

"He is a very great man. He has done much good for the people here. What did he say?"

"Nothing. He say he see me tonight."

"That is very wonderful. A great honor. You will see him?"

"Of course."

"He can get us electricity. Tell him we are waiting."

Robbie and Lance exchanged a look and laughed, Lance grateful for the diversion. He didn't see how he could be caught in the lie. Señor Sanchez would probably never be heard of again.

José reappeared after the afternoon rain to confirm the evening's appointment. He explained how to find the house and told him to mention his name. "I said you would not stay more than an hour. If he wants you to stay longer, he'll pay extra. Are you satisfied?"

"Yes. That is good. He's nice man? You like him?"

"You will see. He is very powerful. He expects people to do what he wishes."

Lance was increasingly curious about his meeting. If Don Antonio was a benefactor of his people, he couldn't be a bad man. He pictured an autocratic but benevolent patriarch with only a voyeur's interest in sex. He would probably know who Sanchez was and why his "friends" in the capital were asking questions about him. Don Antonio might turn out to be an important person to know. He was glad he'd agreed to go. Luisa would get her electricity.

"What was he like, beautiful?" Robbie asked as they were fixing themselves drinks before dinner.

"Who, darling?"

"The man you're going to see tonight."

"Oh, San—uh, Don Antonio. Very much like what you'd expect a *politico* to be—very smooth and over-dressed and sure of himself. He came in as if he owned the place."

"Where does he live? Is it far?"

"No, right in town. Two streets behind the church and then to the right and the first big stone house on the left." He repeated José's directions as they carried their drinks to the parapet.

"Flip says that a few of the great old houses are still kept up. It might be interesting. Did he make it sound like a social call?"

"No, strictly business. More an order than an invitation." He put a hand under Robbie's sarong and toyed with his cock while it lengthened and hardened. "He wasn't exactly rude but he wasn't spreading the charm. I guess I could've refused but I thought I'd better find out all I could. Ramiriz has made me feel that they might try a shakedown but it's hard to believe they'd be interested in the couple thousand dollars we've made."

"If they try anything like that, I should think they'd have to bring your partner into it. Try to make it sound as if I don't know anything about it." His erection thrust up between the folds of his sarong and rose against the night. Lance's joined it. Luisa came and went between the table and the kitchen. They'd forgotten the days when they'd taken care not to let her see them at play.

"My magnificent partner," Lance said, purposefully stroking Robbie's swelling cock. He ran his mouth over his chest and sucked on a nipple. They closed to each other and their mouths were joined. After a long blissful moment, Lance drew back. "We'd better go to bed for a little while before dinner. You may get sleepy waiting up for me."

"Staying up till midnight is pretty wild for us these days." They wandered off along the terrace together. Luisa made a note to take her time in preparing dinner.

It was after ten before Lance made a move to get

ready to go. "It's hot. I could use another shower. I better get dressed up for the great Don Antonio. At least as much as I do for Flip. If he's wearing a white dinner jacket, that's his tough luck." He showered. He went to the bedroom and groomed his toes and trimmed the pubic hair back from around his cock to give added emphasis to its size. He arranged his hair with care and used cologne liberally. He put on a well-cut pair of summer trousers and a sports shirt that flatteringly exposed an expanse of golden brown chest. His sandals were polished and gleaming.

When he returned to the terrace, Robbie looked at the golden head, the glowing brown skin set off by his white shirt, the ineffable grace of his body, and wondered if there was a man or a woman in the world who could resist him.

"You're beautiful, my darling," he said with an entranced smile. "It's after ten-thirty. You better go in case you have trouble finding the place. Take it easy. I know you'll handle it better than anybody else could but don't forget this isn't the States. We have to be nice to the powers-that-be. If it's money they're after, offer to show them the books."

"Of course. The books are our secret weapon."

Robbie strolled with him to the end of the house where they kissed at length. Robbie was careful not to muss his hair or disarrange his clothes except for the gratifying bulge that appeared at his crotch. Lance clung to Robbie's erection. "Keep it that way for me, darling. I shouldn't be more than an hour."

He'd spoken so convincingly about his meeting with a man he'd never seen that he'd almost forgotten that he was a whore on the way to an assignation. Robbie hadn't questioned a word he'd said. His trust in him was absolute. He drove down the hill trying to fight free of his trust, casting himself adrift from him in an effort to turn himself into a different person by the time he reached Don Antonio's door.

He found the right-hand turn behind the church and parked as soon as he saw a big house on the left in front of him set flush with the street. As he approached, he saw that the facade was ornate, with columns and corniced windows, only a few of which were lighted. He found an old-fashioned iron bell-pull beside a central door and gave it a tug. It set up a great clanging inside. Within moments, the massive door was swung open by an old man wearing black trousers and an embroidered waistcoat.

"A friend of Señor José," Lance said.

The old man stood back for him to enter and closed the door behind him. Lance followed him across a tile floor into an inner courtyard. An enormous magnolia tree was growing in the middle of it. A gallery ran around it between the lower and upper floors. He heard the trickle of a fountain. The old man led him up a stairway and along the gallery to an open door. He stopped with a bow.

Lance entered a big, high-ceilinged room with a row of tall open windows. It was as full of furniture as a secondhand shop. Lance's eyes alighted on what appeared to be a couple of fine old pieces but everything was jumbled together with no attempt at style. A man was sitting in an upholstered armchair with a lamp on a table beside him. Lance did a slight double take as he saw he hadn't lied. Señor Sanchez was looking at him.

"Good evening," his host greeted him.

"You're Don Antonio?" Lance asked, approaching.

"Antonio Sanchez, Don by courtesy. Such titles no longer exist. My grandfather was the last legitimate Don."

He was wearing a long, expensive-looking, white silk dressing gown with an indecipherable monogram on the breast pocket. A leather riding crop dangled from a loop around one wrist. He looked more distinguished without a hat. His nose was commanding. His mouth was the mouth of a voluptuary with a hint of cruelty in it. His hair was luxuriant, a flowing black mane.

"Did you know who I was?" Lance asked. "I mean, did you know I was coming tonight?"

"José said he'd found me a North American who made pottery. It seemed unlikely that there were two. I think he forgot to mention your name."

"It's—"

Don Antonio gave a flick of his riding crop. "I know what it is and what it isn't."

"Why didn't you say anything this morning?"

"I'm not used to being interrogated by whore boys."

"Oh," Lance said, flushing. "I see what you mean. I'm sorry." He pulled a straight-backed chair closer to the table and sat.

Don Antonio was on his feet with astonishing speed. The crop came whistling down across Lance's shoulders. He cried out and was almost toppled from his chair. He staggered up, his hands lifted in instinctive self-defense.

Don Antonio had already reseated himself calmly in his armchair. "You'll sit when I tell you to. You North Americans must be taught manners."

"You're quite right. That was rude of me. I'm sorry." Lance's heart was pounding with excitement.

"No harm done. Do you want a drink?" He pointed with his crop to a table against a wall with bottles and glasses. "You may help yourself."

"You're sure you don't mind?"

A faint smile crossed Don Antonio's face. "On the contrary. I'd be delighted."

Lance went to the table and found a bottle of whiskey and gave himself a slug. He wondered if the riding crop figured in his sex-play. He carried his glass back to stand in front of his host, lifting it to him politely before drinking. Don Antonio had a drink on the table beside him and he too made a small toasting gesture and drank.

"Pull up that chair. It's more comfortable," he said, indicating an armchair like his own that stood isolated in the middle of the floor. "The house is being painted. The furniture has been pushed about all helter-skelter. I hope someday to restore order."

Lance pushed the chair into position across the polished floor and stood beside it.

"Sit, Marcus," Don Antonio said.

Lance did so. "Nobody's called me that for years except my mother. Call me Lance."

"What about your mother?"

"How do you mean, 'What about her?'"

"What is her concern with your being here?"

"My mother? None in the least. I'm not even sure she knows I'm here."

"She knows." He indicated a small traveling clock on the table. "Observe the time. I'm not worried about the money but I don't wish to make you late for another appointment. Have you time to talk?"

"If it's anything to do with what you said at the shed today, definitely. I didn't know you were Don Antonio, of course, but I hoped somebody could tell me why anybody was interested in me in the capital."

"Your mother isn't pleased with the success of your little business. I think it would be to your interest to tell me why."

There was a flutter around Lance's heart. The palms of his hands began to sweat. "She must be crazy. I haven't seen her for—I think it's almost four years. She doesn't want to see me. She won't allow me in her house. She disinherited me. Why should she care what becomes of me?"

"Mothers always care, often in odd ways, but they always care. You had some success in the theater?"

"Yes. That's how it started. That's when she disinherited me."

"It must have been very galling for her if you succeeded. If it's as simple as you suggest, she doubtless doesn't want you to have your profitable little business here. She wants you where she can exercise some control over you. For some, her name is sufficient for them to do her bidding. They were prepared to close your business, but those days are over. I decide what happens in my own province."

"What importance can my mother's name have here?"

"Come, come, my young friend. You haven't heard of the United Development Corporation?"

"I think so. Vaguely. In connection with some papers I was told to sign before I was disinherited. I don't know what it is."

"It is pineapples and rubber and coffee, oil, copper— anything that can squeeze profit out of the starving peasants. All over Central and South America, it is the Vanderholden octopus whose tentacles are slowly being lopped off. Don't you know where your wealth comes from?"

"It isn't mine. Anyway, we were taught not to talk about money."

"I'm glad to hear your family has some shame. Their day is ending. Your mother will pay for favors like everybody else. I've decided to allow you to keep your business for the time being. We'll see how much the control of your life is worth to her."

"You mean you expect her to pay to have me shut down?"

"Very heavily. Enough to finance one of our many worthwhile projects, with enough left over to take care of some interests of my own."

Rich laughter burst from Lance's throat. "That's wonderful. She never will. You may be right about her wanting me back but she never lets anybody make demands on her."

"Then she will beg in vain and I will have her son, the Vanderholden whore. Take your clothes off."

Lance's heart leaped up with excitement. This was more marvelous than anything he could have dreamed of. His name was playing its part, but in reverse. He had always suspected that the mountain of gold on which the family was firmly established covered a multitude of sins. At least one man was having his revenge on the Vanderholdens through him. He was the Vanderholden whore.

He finished his drink and stood facing Don Antonio and slowy removed his sandals and unbuttoned his shirt, waiting for his erection to consolidate for the man who had struck him, who was directing his self-abasement. When it was fully functional, he stripped and waited with his hands on his hips.

Don Antonio rose, his eyes moving over him. Lance saw that his body looked softer, less compact than it had this morning, confirming his suspicion about the corset. His dressing gown covered the beginnings of a paunch that hadn't been noticeable earlier. He lifted his riding crop and ran its flexible tip under Lance's pectoral muscles and down over his abdomen and around his balls to his cock, tapping it lightly and making it strain upwards rigidly. He circled him and ran his crop over his body again, along his shoulder blades and down his spine. He slapped it experimentally across his buttocks and prodded it up between them and left it there, moving it tantalizingly.

"A superb physical specimen. A thoroughbred," he commented dispassionately. "We must give your family credit for that. If they took as much care of the starving wretches they've exploited as they have in breeding you, the world would be a happier place."

He withdrew the crop and came around in front of

Lance and moved it against his cock to make it swing back and forth.

"Interesting from an evolutionary point of view. No man needs such a penis except to excite the envy of other men. It's a tease for homosexuals. I wonder what they intended to achieve with that." He returned to his chair and sat.

"It's for conquering the world," Lance said. He was here to excite this man and arouse his desire. It was time to exercise his profession but his cock apparently wasn't a complete success. He ran his hand along the length of it. "Look at it. Every time a man takes me, he destroys a dynasty. When I jerk off, there's one less Vanderholden to lop off."

"Your idea intrigues me. Let me see you dispose of a Vanderholden."

Lance planted his feet apart and thrust his hips forward and began to masturbate, making long caressing strokes from the base of his cock to its head, slowly accelerating the action. It was excruciatingly humiliating in front of Don Antonio and brought him quickly close to a climax. Don Antonio's eyes were fixed on his moving hand. He began to tap the leg of the chair with his crop in time to Lance's stroke. The hand lying casually on his thigh moved almost imperceptibly on himself.

"Show me," Lance murmured.

Don Antonio shifted and adjusted the folds of his dressing gown and the long lethal-looking rapier of his erection whipped up against his belly.

"That must excite the envy of other men. It does me."

Don Antonio's hand began to move on himself in unison with Lance's. Lance couldn't delay his orgasm.

"Wait. Watch me come. Then we can do anything you like." He administered the last decisive pressure and his ejaculation shot from him and scattered on the polished floor.

He wiped his hand across his chest and dropped down between Don Antonio's knees and made love to his dangerous-looking erection while his hands moved up over him, pulling the robe open, baring his torso for his caresses. His body was astonishingly feminine—soft, hairless, faintly repellent. A once-powerful chest was developing breasts. His slight paunch was hairless and

333

rounded. With stretched jaws he performed the tricks at which he excelled and brought Don Antonio to a speedy climax. The emission was less copious than Lance was accustomed to. He felt the flesh softening in his mouth, released it and lifted his head.

Don Antonio looked at him with a nod as he closed the dressing gown over himself. "You know your business. You're very good."

"My business is making love, not just sex. If you let me, I can make love to you."

"I doubt if I want you to. I may want to make love to you in my fashion. It's an expression that's more appropriate for the young. I may let you meet my nephew. Can you let him take you without perverting him?"

"I don't understand."

"It's normal for boys to take each other when they're dreaming of women. It's not normal to want to be taken, although the young are forced to submit. Later, after they've loved women, they sometimes return to boys. That too is normal. I think my nephew may be a homosexual but I don't want to encourage it. An impressionable boy could easily fall in love with you. Better you than a street boy but I don't want you to introduce him to perversions that he hasn't discovered for himself. Actually he's my wife's nephew, an orphan. He's a pretty boy. I've become quite foolishly infatuated with him."

"I won't make him suck my cock if he doesn't want to, if that's what you mean. I'm a whore. I do what people want."

Don Antonio lifted his crop and pointed at an Empire desk marooned halfway across the room. He withdrew an immaculate white linen handkerchief from his pocket and handed it to Lance. "Clean up your mess, then go over to the desk." He picked up a hand bell from the table and rang it briskly.

Lance took the handkerchief and crawled across the floor in the path of his ejaculation. He was on his hands and knees when the old man entered. Don Antonio gave orders unhurriedly. Lance knew that it was his intention to humiliate him and he continued his chore while his cock swung out and began to harden. The old man left.

When Lance stood, he was near the desk. He went

334

to it and saw a pile of enlarged photographs turned facedown on its surface. He picked one up and turned it over. It took him a moment to disentangle the figures and see what they were doing. His scalp crawled. His face was burning. He turned the pile over and ran his hand across it, spreading it out. They were as bad as he had feared. He pushed them together into a neat stack and turned them on their faces again.

"Dr. Greuber is a friend of yours?" Lance asked, approaching Don Antonio.

"An acquaintance. He's tried to entice me to his parties for several years. It doesn't look suitable."

"I've done that once. I doubt if I'll ever do it again."

"I imagined my nephew in such circumstances and it shocked me. My infatuation displeases me, all the more so because I know he wouldn't resist me. It must be ended. If he falls in love with you, I would put him out of my mind. I've found you at an opportune moment."

Lance wondered if it was usual for whores to be drawn so deeply into their clients' lives. Don Antonio wanted him for his nephew. He was getting in deeper than he'd bargained for. He glanced at the clock. It was only eleven-thirty. "What are you going to do with those photographs?" he asked.

"Return them to the doctor now that I've seen the original. I think that will do for tonight. I wanted to have an idea of what to expect of you. Next time, I'll be more demanding."

"You have the right to be."

"Exactly. I have every right with you. Perhaps I'll bring my nephew with me or arrange for you to come to the capital. You may put your clothes on now. I have no more time for you."

Lance did as he was told. Don Antonio was treating him like a servant. It was fascinating. He knew finally what it felt like to be on the wrong side of the closed doors, to be consigned to the servants' stairs and the tradesmen's entrance. It freed him of all responsibility. He had only to obey orders.

"I may come back quite soon," Don Antonio said while Lance dressed. "The new airstrip is a convenience. If I'm kept in the capital, I may send a plane for you. I'm considering whether I can introduce you to my wife. I don't wish to insult her. If we do business together, it would be permissible. It remains to be seen what arrangements I make with your mother."

Dressed, Lance paused with his sandals in his hands. "None, I hope. I don't want to lose the pottery works. I'm sure she won't play along with you so I'm not really worried."

"If Manolo falls in love with you and you satisfy me, it would be a consolation. We'll discuss it next time. I can spare another ten minutes. You may replenish your drink if you wish."

"Thanks." Lance finished fastening his sandals and fixed himself another drink. He returned to the chair that he'd vacated. "May I sit?"

"Get your pe—your cock out where I can see it."

By the time Lance had unbuttoned his slacks and lifted it out of his shorts, it was partially erect. It curved out obscenely from his open fly. Don Antonio ran his riding crop teasingly along it and watched it lengthen and lift. Don Antonio was more interested in it than he wanted to admit. Perhaps it would defeat his mother.

"It's undeniably remarkable," Don Antonio said when it stood up fully erect. "I'm enough of a sensualist to enjoy seeing a Vanderholden standing in front of me like this. You may sit."

Lance did so. Don Antonio continued his play with the riding crop, keeping him hard. "Wouldn't you enjoy it more if you did that with your hands?" Lance asked.

"I'm sure Manolo would. I'll feel it before you go. Finish your drink." He indicated an envelope on the table near Lance.

"That is for you. I don't imagine you'll be so foolish as to tell José I gave it to you. He'll give you your share of what I gave him. I'll deal with him in my own way from now on. You needn't discuss our arrangements with him. You and I won't talk about money again. You'll find me generous. Very well. Come here."

Lance rose and took a step closer. Don Antonio pulled his shorts lower to free his balls and ran his hands over them and out along his cock, studying it. Lance held his shirt out of the way. Don Antonio moved the flat of his hands over his groin and rested them on his thighs. "A young man like you is a remarkable creation. At moments, I can understand the exclusive homosexual.

336

That will do. Cover yourself." He removed his hands and gave the bell a brisk swing while Lance got himself back into his clothes with some difficulty. "The old man will show you out. Good night."

Lance picked up the envelope. "Thank you. Good night." He turned. The servant was waiting at the door. He followed him down the stairs to the courtyard. The door closed behind him. Lance took a deep breath. There was something frighteningly austere and passionless about Don Antonio that made him want to shout and roll around in the mud.

As soon as he was in the car, he opened Don Antonio's envelope. Five ten-dollar bills. With the share José owed him, he would have another seventy-five dollars for Luisa and his child. It felt good to make money, no matter how he did it.

Driving up past Robbie's house, he felt so blameless that he checked back over the evening to make sure that he hadn't forgotten anything that he should be prepared to lie about. Omissions weren't lies. Any blame attached to whoring was considerably mitigated by Don Antonio's connection with his mother and his work. Except for taking money, he hadn't done anything worse than what he'd done with Geraldine Fleet to protect his job in the show.

He went clattering down the rocky incline to the house. Robbie was coming to meet him when he reached the terrace. They hugged each other. Robbie was his life. Nothing could change that.

"Well, that wasn't so bad," Robbie said, smiling into his eyes. "Only a little more than an hour. I thought you might be later."

"I can't wait to tell you. It's unbelievable. Can we have a drink?"

"I think there's some ice still. I've had a very sober evening, reading and trying to stay awake." They went to the table together and poured themselves drinks. "Did you get Luisa her electricity?"

"Damn. I forgot. There was something more important to think about. I'll be seeing him again. I'm sure he can have it connected in twenty-four hours if he wants to. He's a big shot."

"Start at the beginning and tell me everything." They

took their drinks to the cot and sat together. "Were you alone with him?"

"Yes. He mentioned introducing me to his wife and a nephew but they didn't appear. The house is impressive but it's being painted. The living room we were in was all topsy-turvy. Furniture all over the place. The point is, dear old Mum has struck again."

"How do you mean?"

"She's trying to have us shut down. It turns out that the family has big holdings here—or had. I should've known it. There's nowhere in the world where I can get away from them. Mother apparently thinks she runs the country, as usual, but Don Antonio disagrees, thank God." He elaborated on what Don Antonio had told him. "Anyway, it turns out that Mother's the one that's going to get shaken down, not us. If she'll pay enough, they'll put me out of business but for once I don't think anything bad will come of it. I know she won't pay. She expects people to do what she tells them to and not talk back."

"Poor darling. It *is* unbelievable," Robbie said.

"Can you imagine her pursuing me all the way down here? I guess she found out who Lance Cosling is. The good Don is going back to the capital but he expects to know more when he comes back. He said he'd let me know."

"When's that supposed to be?"

"He didn't say but I gather in the next few days. He mentioned the new airfield. I guess he has a private plane. Of course, if by some wild chance Mother pays the fortune he's hoping for, I'll be out on my ass."

"Did you like him, sweetheart?"

"*Like* isn't the word. He's not the flashy gangster-type I thought he was. He's impressive. He exudes power. You feel that he's used to people doing what he tells them to do. I was so busy trying to charm him that I didn't think much about liking him but I think I was wasting my time. Even if he were in love with somebody, he's not the type to let his personal feelings interfere with what he's out to get for himself. At least we know he's not interested in our few peanuts."

"Was he wearing a white dinner jacket?"

"No, a very elegant, white silk dressing gown and

338

carrying a riding crop, of all things. How's that for a combination? Very macho."

"No horse?" Robbie asked. They laughed and Robbie leaned forward and kissed his temple, which, he claimed, was one of the sexiest parts of him. Lance lay back, making himself look as wantonly desirable as possible, and began to slowly unbutton his shirt. He pulled the shirt out of his slacks and bared his chest. He moved his hands to his fly, pretending that this was their first time. He saw a light come up in Robbie's eyes. Their breathing grew rapid. Lance was amazed that familiarity still hadn't dulled Robbie's passion for him. He was doing his best to maintain the tension between them.

Robbie lifted his legs onto the cot and knelt, letting his sarong drop off. His erection swung out. He gripped his hair and pulled his head to it, holding him so that he could move his cock over his face. He felt the element of playacting in their lovemaking but it was very easy to get carried away by it. Lance was irresistible when he was playing the wanton.

The following evening Lance made his discovery about Luisa. The light fell on her as she emerged from the kitchen in a way that caught his attention. She looked different. When he saw what it was, he leaped up and led her across the terrace to Robbie.

"Look. Our little mother," he burst out excitedly. "It shows."

He turned to her and kissed her lightly on the mouth and patted her front. There was a slight thickening of the waist, a subtle change in the set of her breasts. He kissed her again. "It is wonderful. You have a baby."

She looked pleased and flustered. "I did not think you would notice yet. I did yesterday. Now it will get very big."

"Let me see," Robbie said, moving in beside them. He brushed Lance's hands away and stood back from her. "Yes, I see what you mean. You've got sharp eyes, darling. It's obvious once you look. How amazing. I've never lived with a girl who was having a baby."

They switched back and forth from English to Spanish to include Luisa as they exclaimed over it and counted on their fingers. "Is it four months now, little one?" Lance asked her.

"A little longer."

"Then he'll be— I'll bet he's born on your birthday, darling. Some time in March, anyway. He's going to be a genius like his half father." Lance uttered a peal of laughter and hugged them both. "Isn't this exciting? We'd better have a glass of sparkling rum, darling."

Robbie went to get drinks. Lance turned back to Luisa. "Do you see a doctor, little one?"

"Why? It's a baby. I'm not sick."

Lance smiled and thought of Pam, of the legion of doctors, the endless tests, her successful efforts to hide her condition with constant changes of wardrobe so that he never had the satisfaction of living with a pregnant wife until the last minute when the baby made a miraculous appearance and was immediately banished to the care of a nurse. He would be able to share in everything now. Luisa would have her baby simply and naturally, and would bring it up with him and Robbie to help.

Robbie returned with their drinks and a fruit juice concoction for Luisa. "I've had a brain wave," he said to Lance. "It's so obvious that I don't know why we haven't talked about it. I suppose I had to see what looks as if it might be a baby in order to believe it."

He turned to Luisa and continued in Spanish. "Do you want to marry me, darling? Lance can't marry you, as you know, but I can. The baby would have a legal father. That's better."

Luisa looked at him round-eyed. "I would be your wife?"

"Yes, you'd be Señora Cosling. We'll find a priest to do it. Everybody will know that you're married."

"That would be very wonderful. To be married to a foreigner and own a house—I would be the grandest lady in our neighborhood. My father will be so proud."

He turned to Lance and squeezed his shoulder and winked. "I'm sure it'll come as a great relief to *my* father too. Don't you think it makes sense, sweetheart? You don't mind my being the legal father, do you? I suddenly feel wrong about his being a bastard."

"You're an angel as always but have you thought

340

enough about it? I mean, it won't make any complication for you that we might regret later?"

"I don't see how it could. She can't even sue me for divorce. The Church doesn't allow it. I'll pass myself off as a Catholic. Maurice was. I know enough about it to be convincing. I think there's all sorts of rigamarole you're supposed to go through first but I can pay a priest to get it over with tomorrow."

He included Luisa once more. "You understand you won't be able to marry anybody else if you change your mind later?"

"Lance is the father of my child. If I'm your wife it will be the same as being his wife. I will never want another man."

"Is today Saturday? You'll see your father tomorrow? Tell him we may need his permission. I'll find out anything else we should know." He lifted his glass. "Well, here's to unborn Coslings. There won't be a single lord among them. I've thrown away their birthright."

Lance leaned to him and kissed him on the mouth. "You're all the saints and angels rolled into one. It does seem simple and obvious but still— You're taking a step that sort of involves you, even if it's only symbolic. It's almost as good as your marrying me."

"Despite what we've said, I sort of like it here," Robbie said. "Where else would I find a girl ready to marry me without expecting me to be a good husband to her? With a ready-made child thrown in. The more I think about it, the more I like it. A child of yours deserves some sort of official legal recognition."

Whenever Luisa passed near him, Lance found his eyes going to her almost imperceptibly thickened middle. The baby had become a tangible reality. No matter how queer he was, he was going to be a father. It made the future more plausible and added stability to the household. When she was ready for bed, they both kissed her lovingly and told her to take good care of herself.

The next day while Lance was working, Robbie made inquiries and found a priest who would waive formalities for a small consideration and marry them on Monday. He insisted only that Luisa's father come see him on Monday morning to sign something to make the marriage binding. Before she went to her family that evening, Robbie told her to make sure that her father

341

went to the small church of San Fernando around the corner from the police station, where the priest would be waiting for him before noon the next day.

After lunch on Monday, Robbie reminded Lance to bring his passport. They put on white slacks and shirts and Luisa her best white evening dress and the three of them went to the small church where a brief mass was said making Robbie and Luisa man and wife. Robbie had even remembered to get her a ring. The three of them kissed.

"I suppose it's silly but I found it very touching," Lance said.

"I know what you mean. It really was a bit as if you and I were getting married. I'm glad we did it."

"I must go home before anybody sees me," Luisa said. "My father doesn't want to tell anybody until the baby begins to show more. Then he'll tell them I've been married for quite a long time. If they ask the priest, he will say the same."

Lance went back to the shed and let Robbie drive the bride home. He was getting near the end of the gollies and didn't want anything to delay him. They were saving the wedding celebration for that evening, when Robbie was going to cook a special meal for her. Robbie's thoughtfulness was an endless source of wonder to him. It wasn't surprising that he made him feel unworthy of him. Nobody else would be so understanding of him, so patient of his weaknesses and failures. The least he could do was to stick to his work.

A week later, he sat exhausted and incredulous, watching Big and Juan loading the last batch into the kilns for the first firing. In another few days they would be packed and on their way to New York. He had done it. He felt so deliciously, mindlessly freed of all burdens that he scarcely looked at the man who came in and handed him an envelope.

It was a plain envelope containing a plain sheet of paper on which was scrawled: "Tomorrow evening. Supper at 9:30. A. S." It took him a moment to place the initials and then he rose and went to the door and looked out to see if there was any sign of the messenger. The street was empty. Apparently no answer was expected. He crumpled the paper and dropped it with other litter on the floor. He would think about it later. He had to make sure that all the little figures were properly settled on their bed of sand before the kilns were bricked up. Good-bye gollies.

When the bricks had been mortared and the fires started, he retrieved the crumpled paper from the floor and smoothed it out to make sure he hadn't missed anything. It was an order. Unless he refused, no reply was necessary and he had no intention of refusing. Aside from anything else, he needed Don Antonio's patronage.

When he told Robbie about it that evening, he raised a question that had begun to worry him. "It sounds more social this time. Supper. If it turns out he wants to be friendly, I don't see how I can go on seeing him without you. Do you think I could ask him here?"

"Why not? We have running water. No, seriously. Let's try to keep it businesslike. It's better for you to handle it, especially with your mother involved."

"Exactly. I'm hoping to find out tomorrow how seriously he takes her. If he's going to keep her in her place, I don't see why I should bother with him beyond being civil." That hurdle was cleared. Robbie made things very easy for him.

Don Antonio received him in a black silk dressing gown and a white scarf in the same upstairs sitting room. The furniture had been arranged in rational order during his absence and created the atmosphere of a fine country mansion, aimed at comfort rather than style. Don Antonio greeted him with more warmth than he had before, restoring him to his rank as one of his underlings.

"You may have a drink."

He indicated a cabinet. Lance noticed the riding crop lying on a table as he went to it. He poured himself a whiskey and Don Antonio led him to a grouping of comfortable upholstered chairs around a coffee table and gestured for him to sit. They both did so.

"Any more news of my mother?" Lance asked.

"She's doubtless had news of me. I informed her agents that your success has enabled you to expand."

"You still think she'll pay to have me closed down?"

"I intend to proceed as if I thought she would. It suits my purpose, one way or the other. One of the great

343

problems in this country is unemployment. Every new job helps, particularly in my province where we have no industry to speak of. Your pottery works once employed ten people. With modern methods and a small outlay for machinery, you could easily employ twenty. For Puerto Veragua, that is a great deal. I've made some investigations. I'm optimistic about growth."

"You know I have no money to expand, don't you?"

"Of course. I would provide the capital. We'll draw up new papers under which your company would be absorbed into a parent company. The financial details needn't concern us now. Within a month or two, I'll be able to import the necessary equipment to start a real factory."

Lance smiled and shook his head. "I don't want to run a factory. Even if I wanted to, I don't know how."

"I understand that. You're creative. I've discussed it with a man who has run a pottery works. He's available. He would run the factory. You would continue to do what you're doing. You understand what pleases the foreign market. You'd be in charge of design. You will produce a handmade product. The quality line, I think it's called."

"Just a minute. You're talking about setting up a business around me, without my bothering with the business or mass production side of it. I assume I'll be making at least as much as I make now. Is that what it amounts to?"

"That's a rough outline of what I have in mind. The lawyers can work out what share you should have in the new company. A small one, I imagine, since you'll be contributing no tangible assets, except for the part of you I enjoyed touching last time. You'll receive a salary as a designer in line with the prevailing scale in this country. Needless to say, the more successful you are, the higher your price will be to your mother. Shall we see now if you can persuade me to go ahead with the scheme?"

He rose, giving the bell on the coffee table a brisk swing as he did so. He crossed to the table where he'd left his whip and picked it up. The old manservant entered and he uttered a few brief words of instruction and turned back to Lance. "You may take your sandals off," he said.

344

Lance unfastened the buckles and kicked them off and stood on bare feet. "Do you want me to undress?"

"Not yet." Don Antonio approached, studying him.

Lance was his prey, paralyzed and fascinated. It had seemed exciting to sell his body but he wasn't prepared to sell his life. He had become a pawn in some game the *politicos* were playing with his mother. He wasn't going to let her exercise any control over him. He had his tangible asset to protect himself from her. He ran a hand suggestively over it, waiting for Don Antonio to make his wishes known.

"A catamite can't expect to be treated like a woman," the older man said. "The difference is what makes it interesting to me, crossing a line that can't be crossed. You think it can be. I won't make it easy for you."

Lance's attention was diverted by the appearance of a figure in the doorway. For an instant, he thought it was José because of the peon costume he wore. As the young man approached, Lance saw that they were quite unlike. This one was tall by local standards, a bit taller than Lance, good-looking in a way that was more African than Indian, with softer features and a big, wonderfully sexy mouth. His body was undefined by the loose costume but gave the impression of muscularity and strength. The nephew? He wouldn't be dressed like a peasant. Don Antonio turned to him as he entered.

"We're ready, Enrique," he said in Spanish. "Let's proceed." His riding crop twitched against his thigh as he led the way to a door at the end of the room.

Lance wondered what part Enrique was going to play in this event. Whatever it was, he felt no danger in him. From the lack of greeting or introductions, he sensed that a ritual was unfolding that was familiar to the other two. His heart was beating rapidly at the promise of something strange and unexpected.

They entered a big, comfortably furnished bedroom. A bathroom was visible beyond it through an open door. High windows were open behind swaths of filmy gauze. The sheet on the four-poster bed was turned back with mathematical precision. It was pleasantly cool in the big immaculate room.

Enrique spoke briefly. Don Antonio turned to him with a nod, the riding crop twitching at his side. They had stopped beside a chest of drawers.

At a signal from Don Antonio, Enrique moved around in front of Lance and began to unbutton his shirt. Lance instinctively lifted his hands to stop him and dropped them again to his sides. He felt the ritual evolving and wondered what was expected of him. Enrique finished with the buttons and pulled the shirttails out of his slacks.

Lance looked into his handsome impassive face, searching for some clue to guide him, and felt the bond of servitude between them, the companionship of subservience to their host. It warmed him and his erection was completed by Enrique's hands moving up over him, lingering unnecessarily on his chest while he pretended to push the shirt out of the way. Lance slipped his hands up under the blouselike top of his cotton suit. The feel of naked skin made his erection swell but Enrique gave his head a slight shake and his eyes were full of warning. Lance dropped his hands hastily while Enrique stripped him to the waist.

Enrique obviously didn't find it displeasing to uncover his body. He paused to look at it with interest before running his hands along the top of Lance's slacks. He opened his fly and gave a tug to the slacks and let them fall around his feet.

He bent over to tug his shorts down over his thighs and let the small garment drop onto his slacks. Doing it brought his face close to Lance's cock and he held it aside with the tips of his fingers and studied it for a moment before straightening. He gave it a small caressing squeeze. "José told me about you," he whispered.

Enrique turned slightly and took out a tangle of leather from the top drawer of the chest beside them. He lifted one of Lance's hands and Lance saw the tangle divide into two as he picked up a leather manacle and attached it securely with buckles around Lance's wrist. A stout thong dangled from it. He lifted Lance's other hand and repeated the procedure. The effect of them attached to his naked body was strikingly erotic.

Enrique took his arm and led him across the room to the bed. He looked at Don Antonio as they passed near him but he stood as motionless as a statue, closed in on himself, a distant observer. Lance edged in closer

346

to Enrique for human contact. He glanced at the manacles on his wrists and his heart began to pound.

When they reached the side of the bed, Enrique put a hand on his buttocks and gave him a little boost up onto it. He started to stretch out but Enrique moved in close to him and he remained on his knees, waiting. Enrique placed him where he wanted him by moving his hands over him, thoroughly caressing his body. He turned him squarely toward the head of the bed. Enrique picked up Lance's hands one at a time and, using the thong that dangled from each manacle, attached them securely to rings set into the headboard.

Only then did Lance become fully conscious of what Enrique had done to him. His arms were spread, his hands firmly shackled to the bed. He had very little freedom of movement. The rings were too high to permit him to sit back on his haunches. If he stood straight on his knees, his cock rose perilously close to the heavily carved headboard. He had only begun to arrange himself comfortably when he heard the whistle of the whip as it sliced the air, and the slap as it struck his shoulders.

His body lurched forward and he struck his head on the headboard as he shouted with pain. The next blow fell on his buttocks and brought his body snapping upright. As he feared, his cock smashed against the headboard and he shouted again with the stinging pain. He backed away as far as his bonds permitted and let his weight hang on his wrists and took the next blow without an outcry. His body was flung about and all his muscles strained in protest, rattling the rings and shaking the bed as the beating continued. He was being driven toward orgasm, charged by an ecstasy that transcended sexual satisfaction, an ecstasy that fed on abuse and degradation. His lips parted as his breath became labored and he twisted his head around to look at his tormentor.

Don Antonio was naked, his face composed but intent.

Lance fell back with a cry as the riding crop flayed his buttocks and his body was convulsed by an orgasm that shattered his senses, his ejaculation being flung out across the headboard. He seemed to swoon, then hung inert on his manacles.

He heard the riding crop clatter across the floor. In another instant, Don Antonio was on him, breathing heavily with his exertions. He wrapped his arms around Lance's thighs, spread them wide and brutally entered his splayed body more deeply than he'd ever been entered before. He remained limp, hanging from the headboard on his arms, his head lolling between his shoulders, while his body began to swing with Don Antonio's cruel violation of it.

Although he had offered no resistance, Don Antonio was giving himself the satisfaction of raping him. His stomach churned with excitement. His cock lengthened and expanded, rapidly acquiring its full dimensions, and rose up rigidly toward his belly. It began to swing like a metronome to Don Antonio's rhythm. Don Antonio gripped his hips and rocked his body back and forth unsparingly. He felt his cock expanding dangerously in him, possessing him cruelly and ruthlessly, exacting the surrender of all his instincts. He shouted with ecstasy as he felt the first spasms of Don Antonio's orgasm lunge into him and groaned as he felt the force dispersing. Don Antonio had taken him as conclusively as anybody could.

Don Antonio lowered Lance's knees onto the bed and slid out of him. He remained crouched on his knees, his head lowered, trying to recover his equilibrium.

He heard movement near him and lifted his head. Enrique dropped a towel onto the bed beside him. He was naked and looked the way Lance had expected him to look. His brown body was fleshed out with symmetry and refinement, unlike the gaunt hardworking bodies of the local boys. He reached over him and unfastened the throngs. Before Lance could thank him, he had disappeared.

Lance sat up with the towel between his legs and removed the shackles. He rubbed his wrists. Don Antonio came around the bed from behind him and stood beside him, carrying a white robe of some sort over his arm. Lance saw that it was a silk dressing gown as he tossed it onto the bed beside him.

"I brought you a small gift. I thought you might want to leave it here to save bother with clothes."

Something in Lance cringed from him but he felt drawn by his authority. It seemed imperative to please

348

him, to win from him some gesture of approval or acceptance. Perhaps the gift was it. He fingered the fine stuff of the robe. "Thank you. It's beautiful," he said.

"That was extraordinary. I sense depths of depravity in you that interest me. I should have expected it. You're rotten with generations of money and power. It excites you to be beaten. That's not unusual but I thought you might be too soft to stand up to it."

"Will it leave marks?"

"No, no. Your skin is still inflamed but that will pass in another half hour. I wish to mark you in other ways. It was a test. You suit me."

Lance turned slowly to look him full in the eye, trying to identify the gratitude he felt with something recognizable in his nature. He offered him a unique experience, an exercise in domination and submission that hypnotized him. He felt as if he were caught up in a suspense story whose ending he had to know. "I'm glad," he said into cold unrelenting eyes.

"I imagine you'll want to wash before dinner. There's a shower. You may use it if you wish."

His saying so underlined Lance's servile position.

"Thank you," he said dutifully.

"You'll find some makeup beside the washbasin. With your experience in the theater, I'm sure you know how to use it effectively."

A little tremor of complicity ran through Lance. "You want me to make myself up?"

"I'd like to see what makeup does for you. There's much that's feminine in you. You probably want me to kiss you. With makeup you might make me want to."

Lance knew how easily makeup could turn him into a beautiful girl. It was something he'd had to be very careful about in the show. Don Antonio was trying to break down the sexual boundaries. He was drawing him deeper into a fantasy from which there would be no escape.

He stood and laughed abruptly. "When I'm this tan, makeup won't show much but I'll do my best."

"I'm sure you will," Don Antonio said, turning from him as Enrique came out of the bathroom wearing his loose clothing. Don Antonio waved his hand toward the door and Enrique left quickly.

Lance showered his erection away and used lipstick

349

more freely than he had in the show to give himself a luscious mouth. With liner and shadow he made his eyes glamorous. It brought out a bizarre, secret self. Maybe he'd end up in full drag. He teased his hair softly over his forehead.

He returned to the empty bedroom, put on his new dressing gown, and went barefoot to the living room, where he found his host at the coffee table waiting for him. He rose at Lance's entrance, his eyes sharpening as he studied him.

"It's hardly noticeable as makeup but it alters you astonishingly. You look outrageously corrupt. You must wear makeup when you meet my nephew in the capital. He'll find you fascinating."

"When is that to be?"

"In a few weeks. Come. I've fixed you another drink." Lance sat with him at the coffee table. "Yes, it will take about two weeks to get our business in order. There'll be papers to sign but time for some pleasure."

"How long will you want me to stay?"

"Not long. Two or three days perhaps. It would be rude to my wife to keep you longer."

"It would be rude to my lover to stay longer. He's my partner you know. He'll have to sign whatever I sign."

"Of course. I'm sure there'll be no difficulty. Whatever arrangements we make will be advantageous to you both. When we've finished our drinks, we can have something to eat."

"Whenever you say. Can I ask you a favor?"

"I expect to be asked favors. You've exercised admirable restraint in waiting this long."

"I'm not sure you can do anything. I've been trying to get electricity at home. Can you ask somebody at the electric company to hurry it up? Two favors, actually. I'd like a telephone."

"Those hardly count as favors. I'll tell the electric company to give you current tomorrow or Monday. I've intended for you to have a telephone at your work place. It will be put in on Monday. Is that where you wanted it?"

"Either there or at home. If you want it at the shed, that's fine with me."

350

"If I call you, I won't want to talk to your family or friends. Shall we eat?"

They went downstairs where a candle-lighted table had been set in the patio under the magnolia tree. A fountain splashed coolly in the dark. They were served refined versions of local food and a good French white wine by the old manservant and a younger assistant. It was all very civilized and unpretentious. Don Antonio talked about his plans for Puerto Veragua—the roads to be built, the luxury hotel on the beach to be completed, the regular passenger flights to the capital to be inaugurated within a year. He spoke of the whole area as his private domain. He never let Lance lose sight of his position as an underling being granted the privilege of eating at the master's table.

"We'll have coffee upstairs and then you may go," Don Antonio said. "It's not yet eleven. I have work to do. I must get back in the morning. It has been a pleasure dining with you. In this light you're very beautiful, as beautiful as a woman."

When they'd finished coffee, Lance remembered the makeup. "Do you have some sort of skin cleanser? I have to take this stuff off."

"There must be something. Come. We will see." They went to the bathroom together. Don Antonio found a jar of complexion cream. "It says to use it before applying makeup. Let your hair grow. It's beautiful golden stuff."

"Thank you for the robe." He opened it and let it slide off and stood in front of him. "Do you want me again?"

"At my age, I find that once in an evening is quite satisfying. I appreciate your thought."

He stepped forward and took Lance in his arms. His mouth was fiercely possessive. Lance made his soft and yielding as he was enveloped in a gust of passion. Don Antonio's virile authority made him melt with desire. His cock lifted to him. Don Antonio bunched his pectoral muscles into breasts and squeezed and fondled them. His hands on Lance's cock were no longer indifferent. Lance felt himself establishing his own small hold on him.

"You're hard. Take me," Lance said against his mouth.

Don Antonio drew back. "Next time I'll make love to you and find out if you can be my woman. Clean your face."

Don Antonio left him while Lance removed all traces of the makeup. His erection remained. Don Antonio was exciting. He was seated at a desk when Lance entered the bedroom still flaunting his erection.

Don Antonio looked up and nodded. "You're very handsome. Next time." The episode had ended.

When Lance was dressed, Don Antonio rose and handed him an envelope as he accompanied him to the door. "You'll hear from me when you have your telephone." The old manservant was waiting on the gallery to show him out. He said good night to his host and left.

Driving home, he found it more difficult than he had the last time to reintegrate himself into his real life, his life with Robbie. Part of him remained ensnared in the fantasy of the big town house. His heart pounded when he thought of Don Antonio standing over him, the riding crop raised. It had been one of the most startlingly revealing moments of his life. He was beginning to understand Don Antonio's hold over him. He wanted to brutalize and degrade him for the best reason Lance could think of: because he was a Vanderholden. It was something that Robbie could have no part in.

He hurried down the steps at the side of the house and found Robbie already rising to welcome him. He rushed into his arms, wanting to make his return so happy and loving that all thoughts of the evening would be swept away.

Robbie held him, chuckling delightedly. "Goodness. We'll have to do this more often just for the fun of getting together again. You're earlier than I expected. Was it interesting?"

"Very. Fix me a drink while I slip into something comfortable." He kissed Robbie and hurried to the bedroom. He was married to the most beautiful guy in the world. He returned in a moment with a sarong wrapped around himself and took the drink Robbie had waiting for him. They settled down on the cot together.

"Well now. I think it looks pretty good." He told about Don Antonio's plans for the pottery works. "He still has this crazy idea that my mother will pay sort of a ransom to keep me from working here. He talks about being in touch with her 'agents.' I suppose that means the people in the family company, the United Whatever-it-is. Naturally, I haven't agreed to anything. I told him my partner has to sign any papers involved. As far as I can see, all it means is that I'll have to stay out of the way of the machines and make suggestions about design and go on doing what I've been doing. How does it sound to you?"

"Pretty good, I guess. Starting a business just to annoy an old lady strikes me as a bit peculiar but maybe he thinks a pottery factory is a good idea anyway."

"That's what he said. He wants to create employment. Everything just sort of fell into place, including my being a Vanderholden. He hates the family. I can't help liking him for that."

"Not otherwise? Is he going to be a friend?"

"I don't think he has friends—just people who do what he tells them to do and probably some enemies. I wouldn't want to be one of them. He's probably pretty ruthless. I'm impressed by him. He talks as if he owned a large hunk of the country but he wants to do things for the people. I think I can trust him to be fair in business, up to a point."

"Having you to dinner with his wife is more than just business, sweetheart."

"That's where the damn family comes into it." Lance noted with satisfaction that the wife had been included without his having to lie. "It's the same old story. I get special treatment. I don't like that part of it."

"Don't talk like that, darling. It's perfectly natural. You *are* special for him, just being a foreigner."

"Maybe. Actually, it really works against me in this case. If by some faint chance my mother gives him what he wants, I'll be out. I'm sure she won't but I want to stay on his good side. He expects me to come to the capital in a few weeks when the papers are ready."

"To stay with him?"

"I guess that's what he meant. He said his wife wouldn't want me there for more than a day or two, whatever that means. I suppose she's bored by our speaking English."

"It sounds as if you're really becoming part of the native life. We should ask Flip about him."

They laughed and their hands became playful on each other.

"I'm surprised she's never mentioned him," Lance said. "Maybe he didn't come often before he could fly down. He says there'll be a passenger service soon. I wonder what I'll do if he wins his game with dear old Mum."

"It won't be any great tragedy, will it, beautiful? If you stay friendly with him, he might let you go on using the place. You could go on with your own things and learn the new techniques with modern kilns and whatever machinery he puts in. It would be like going to your own school."

"If she wants to reduce me to begging in the streets, the deal would probably be for me to have no visible connection with the place. I've told Don Antonio he's not going to get anywhere with her. What I've got to do now is persuade him to stop trying."

By talking about Don Antonio and the evening as routine business, Lance was almost able to convince himself that that was all there was to it. He felt Don Antonio's hold on him loosening. Their sarongs had fallen away. Their hands were taking indolent undisputed possession of each other. They were together. He didn't have to think about Don Antonio again for a while.

"God, you're beautiful," Robbie exclaimed with wonder, marveling at the miracle of their having found each other. "Don't forget that you've already made as much as we thought you might make in a year. It'd be a shame to be forced to stop just when you're doing such fabulous work but it only means waiting a few months until it's all right for the baby to travel and then we'll clear out and go where you can get on with it."

"Where my mother can't find me."

"The hell with your mother."

"What a way to talk about dear old Mum. Would you like somebody to suck your cock?"

Robbie laughed. "If somebody will let me suck his."

"It's a deal."

They had the house wired for electricity while the line was brought in from farther along the road. Robbie spent an evening rigging up bottles and pottery jars as lamps. A plumber installed an electric pump. Luisa watched developments with round-eyed pride, her "condition" becoming more evident daily.

Men appeared at the shed and after an hour left a telephone attached to the wall. It looked like an instrument that Lance remembered from a country house in his childhood, with a crank on the side to call the operator. He didn't know anybody else to call.

They spent a few evenings adjusting to the novelty of electric light, adapting shades to their makeshift lamps and snapping them on and off at every opportunity. Luisa kept forgetting that they'd been hooked up to the miraculous convenience and continued to prepare the kerosene lamps every evening as she always had. They still came in handy when the power failed, which it did regularly but never for long.

Finishing the gollies took the pressure off Lance. Everything seemed to be falling into place. They both felt as if they'd reached a new level of harmony and contentment with each other. Lance sensed that the weird evening with Don Antonio might have marked a turning point in his restless search for new experience. He was in no hurry for the proposed trip to the capital. There was still the unlikely possibility that Don Antonio would succeed with his mother and that would be the end of it. It would be a relief in a way, although when he let himself think about his patron, his heart became unruly.

Robbie supposed that the period of adjustment, inevitable when two people were first reaching out to each other, had ended. The shift in Lance's sexuality had created tensions that he probably had never fully grasped. He didn't ever expect to tame him and didn't want to, but he was learning to make him happy and to anticipate the startling shifts of mood of his mercurial personality. He puzzled him at times. He had sensed some secret in the way he had talked about Don Antonio but supposed it was only the defensive self-consciousness Lance felt about anything to do with his mother. He wasn't interested in Don Antonio so long as he didn't prevent Lance from working.

Flip announced that she had to make an unexpected trip to California and gave herself a farewell party, where Pablito told them that the doctor was planning another sex party.

355

"Some beautiful boys are coming from the capital," he said, eyeing them flirtatiously. "We're counting on you both this time."

"Don't," Lance said promptly but good-humoredly. "We're both slaves to our work. We can't afford to let your beautiful boys keep us up all night."

He looked at Robbie. Robbie offered him his secret smile. He was touched and grateful. A new era. They had come a long way.

Robbie didn't want to listen when his homely houseboy introduced Don Antonio's name into a conversation a day or two later. The boy had been wandering in and out, presumably performing legitimate chores, but Robbie felt him beginning to loiter and becoming a distraction. Filipe spoke, which was definitely against the rules. Robbie paused impatiently in mid brush-stroke. "You see I'm working. What do you want?"

"I thought you would be interested. People say that your friend has become Don Antonio's favorite. Some boys I know are very envious."

Robbie's impatience grew. He didn't like the boy and wished he hadn't accepted him as part of the house deal. "I'm not interested in that," he said dismissivly.

"I thought you would be. I know you make love with your friend. Don Antonio likes young boys. José finds them for him. He pays them well. José arranged for him to meet your friend. Since then, he doesn't see the other boys. They're very envious of your friend."

A shock of apprehension hit Robbie. His hand became unsteady. He put down the brush. "I'm not interested in your gossip. You've got it all wrong. My friend doesn't know any José."

"Oh, yes. José brags that he and his gang raped your friend, but they're friends now."

Robbie was hastily assembling the facts as he knew them. Don Antonio had turned up unannounced at the shed one day. There had been no intermediary. Lance might have spoken to a local without knowing that he'd been involved in the rape. He'd said that he probably wouldn't know any of the gang if he saw them again. For a foreigner to even nod to a local made him a friend. He didn't want to hear any more of this garbled nonsense. He frowned at Filipe.

"You're wasting my time. People get everything

mixed up. My friend has business with Don Antonio. He sees him with his wife. It has nothing to do with whatever you're talking about."

"I think you're mistaken. Dona Emilia never comes here. That's why Don Antonio can have boys."

"Maybe she didn't come when they had to drive. Now he flies and she comes with him. I suppose that's why he hasn't seen the boys you know. That's enough of this. It's none of your business why my friend sees Don Antonio."

"As you wish. I'm your servant. I thought it my duty to tell you what people are saying."

Filipe was a mealymouthed sneak and a trouble-maker. Robbie was angry with himself for paying any attention to him. There was no reason why Lance would know anything about Don Antonio's taste for boys. Lance was hardly the type to appeal to a man who paid the local urchins for his pleasure. He waited while the boy started for the door, wondering if this José could have been at the doctor's party. If so, Lance might have spoken to him without even knowing his name. Filipe hesitated and turned back.

"It's not right for you to think I'm not telling the truth," he said with a whine.

Robbie supposed that he was hoping for a tip for his loyalty. He saw some coins on the table and held them out to him. The boy hurried back for them. "You may be telling the truth about what people say. Thank you for telling me if you thought it was your duty but I don't want to hear gossip."

"It is more than gossip. I know a man who was with your friend and Don Antonio last week. He's a friend of José too. I'm sure Dona Emilia wasn't there. Everybody knows that your friend likes men to take him, like a woman. Many men took him at the doctor's house. José has seen photographs. You beat him when he came here the next day. I thought that was why."

Robbie's mind had ceased to function. There was a great weight on his chest that made it difficult to breathe. He waved toward the boy without seeing him. "Please go."

"If you pay, José might be able to show you the photographs."

"Get out."

Robbie stood in silence without knowing what he was doing. Slowly, vague thoughts began to form in his mind. Moving as if his body were held in a vise, he took the canvas that had given him so much trouble off the easel and replaced it with the one Lance had asked him to stop working on. It was a small act of rebellion against the tyranny of his love. Doing it familiarized him again with the use of his limbs and he went to a chair and dropped into it with his forehead in his hands. He had to go over it one step at a time.

What had the boy told him? Very little, really. Somebody who claimed to have been there while Don Antonio had Lance, but men's boasts were often unreliable. Filipe took it for granted that there was a sexual involvement between Lance and Don Antonio, but that might be because of the *politico*'s reputation. And Lance's. It wasn't something he could know absolutely. The only fact that could be verified was whether the wife was a fiction. If Lance had invented her, it was probable that all the rest was true. Why else make a point of her?

He rubbed his forehead with his fingertips. Everything in him recoiled from the ugliness of it. The man called José. The photographs. Lance being known to the locals as a man who wanted men like a woman. Whatever was beautiful in their love became sick and corrupt. Lance could make a case for his having condoned deception when necessary to spare each other hurt, but everything seemed to point to such far-reaching deception that it made their whole life together a deception. If he had decided to make peace with the rapist, why should it be a secret? He could understand his losing control at a sex party when everything was so new to him, but there was too much here that suggested choice and volition and calculation.

His mind suddenly began to function with normal clarity and he was filled with a cold, calm fury. He lifted his head and looked around at the drab room, hating it and everything outside it. His being here was insanity. He was waking up from a romantic dream. Lance had made an utter fool of him. He didn't know what had led him from disbelief to acceptance of what Filipe had told him but believing it restored reason. He had accepted a world that was alien to him. He had lost all touch with reality.

He tried to remember what day it was. It seemed to be about time for another of Luisa's weekly visits to her family. He had to talk to Lance but not with her in the house. He couldn't risk another scene here with Filipe lurking behind the door. Somehow he had to keep up the pretense of happy harmony until they were alone together. He was appalled by the possibility of being told more than he wanted to know. Lance was prone to confession. Confession and repentance, and you were free to sin again. It was the surefire Catholic formula for geting along in life. His fury was ice in him. He wanted to cut him out of his life coldly and cleanly and forever.

He returned to the easel and began to prepare brushes while he eyed the nearly blank canvas. Work was a release, a step toward freeing himself from illusion.

When Lance came breezing in to pick him up for the evening, he immediately noticed the switch of canvases. "Is my picture finished?" he demanded excitedly.

"No," Robbie said without looking at him. "I wanted to get back to this one. I have to work in my own way."

Lance felt it like a small slap in the face. Robbie was shutting him out again. He wondered if anything was the matter and concluded that he was just fed up with the recalcitrant painting. "Naturally," he said.

Robbie cleaned his brushes while his icy fury melted. He stole sidelong glances at Lance and was shaken by the shining candor of his eyes. His deceptive eyes. Robbie was no longer able to believe in his innocence but he already hoped that there might be plausible explanations and extenuating circumstances. The case against him was not yet proven. "What day is today? Do you know?" he asked.

"Amazingly enough, I do. The day, you mean? It's Friday."

"I thought it was the end of the week."

He was going to have to act his chosen role as devoted lover till day after tomorrow. Being with Luisa would make it easier for him to carry on as if nothing was bothering him.

"Okay, let's go," he said, dropping his brushes into the pitcher. "I need a drink." He brushed past him, avoiding any of the usual loving physical contact.

"Had a tough afternoon?" Lance asked, following him.

"Actually, I don't feel my usual brilliant self. The faithful Jeeves kept hanging around and trying to talk to me. It gave me a headache out of sheer annoyance."

He knew he was obliquely apologizing for having put the picture aside. The habits of love were powerful. He was capable of deception too but he didn't see how he could keep it up until Sunday evening. If he acted as if everything were normal, Lance would win him over little by little, reconcile him to whatever he thought he knew. It was too serious for him to go on closing his eyes, letting himself be lulled by Lance's attraction. He was going to have to pretend to be really sick.

He paid more attention to Luisa than he usually did. Lance watched him closely, feeling that something was amiss. He turned over in his mind all the sources of potential danger and didn't see how anything could have gone wrong. The tiresome houseboy must be to blame.

When Luisa said good night, he moved in close to Robbie on the cot and tried to kiss him but Robbie evaded him. "What's the matter, darling?" he asked, more worried than hurt.

"I'm feeling really rotten. It's nothing, just an upset stomach. I feel sort of bloated and queasy. Go to bed when you're ready. I'll stay out here."

"Come to bed. You'll sleep better. I'll behave if you want me to."

"No. I'm better here where I can get to the toilet without disturbing you. I feel as if I might need it."

"Shouldn't you take something? I could tell you haven't been feeling well all evening."

"I'll be fine in the morning. I took those pills before dinner. Go on to bed, sweetheart. We've both been working hard."

"I'm tired. Just give me a little kiss."

Robbie allowed their lips to touch and pulled back. "My mouth tastes funny."

"I'm here if you want me."

Robbie watched him go with a wrench of anguish. It was going to be hard. Love raged in him. He had given all of himself blindly to his passion, heedless of all the warning signals—the instability of Lance's nature, his urge to defy convention, the demons—and had trusted in his foolhardy faith that love conquered all.

When he looked at Lance, his will was paralyzed. He

360

adored him. He felt an aching emptiness in the pit of his stomach when he thought of being without him and his heart fluttered so erratically that he couldn't breathe. The discipline he was imposing on himself of sleeping alone was making him sicker than any imaginary sickness he could think of. Lance would surely be able to explain everything so that they could be together again. They just needed the chance to talk it over quietly in their own time.

He woke up in the dark and instinctively reached out for Lance. Not finding him brought him fully awake and he sat up. It was all starting again, the breathlessness, the ache of hollow emptiness in his stomach. Nothing was worth this torment. Let Lance do what he wanted. He'd sworn to himself that he would adapt to his needs. If it was sex he wanted, he'd give him more sex than he could handle.

He lurched to his feet and made his way groggily along the terrace. He fell into bed and gathered him into his arms with a groan of relief. Lance rolled in to him, making incoherent little whimpering sounds in his sleep. Robbie took him as brutally as he knew how and listened to his shouts of ecstasy with agony in his heart. Deny tenderness. They could share pain. Lance would never belong to anybody else.

When he woke up in the morning, Robbie knew that there was no resistance left in him. He couldn't even try to pretend that he didn't worship him. He opened his eyes and found Lance's smiling into his from the pillow beside him.

"How about us last night?" Lance murmured. "Are you all better, darling?"

"Sure. You cured me." Hands began to move on him irresistibly. What more could he want?

As the moment of confrontation moved a day closer, Robbie couldn't get his lover out of his mind. Work was no help. Lance was lodged in his thoughts, plaguing him with questions. Was a confrontation really necessary? Couldn't he just talk to him again about their responsibilities to each other, warn him of the danger of losing each other if he was careless about them? He had forced himself to accept momentary attractions to others but if there was any truth in what he'd been told, Lance seemed set on self-destruction. The longer he closed his eyes to it, the more heartbreaking the ending would be. His heart fluttered uncontrollably at the thought of interrogating him. He knew Lance wouldn't lie.

By the time he came to pick him up for the evening, Robbie was wild with wanting him and with the determination to prove to both of them that he belonged to him. He pulled him to him and kissed him with all his troubled passion. Lance responded eagerly. Robbie released him and tugged off his sarong and backed up to the table. He sat on the edge of it, his legs spread, his feet planted on the floor, his cock pointing at Lance.

"Suck it. Show me you're the best cocksucker I've ever known."

Lance's eyes were shining with excitement. "What about that dismal boy?"

"Who cares? He says he knows we make love. Let him watch if he wants to."

Lance laughed recklessly and dropped to one knee in front of him. Robbie watched him stretch his mouth wide for him, his eyes closed in an attitude of blind worship. Robbie had taught him to want it. He had taught him to abase himself. The thought of his doing it with Don Antonio made his stomach turn over with rage. He would beat him to a pulp if he learned he had. "Take yours out," he ordered. "I want to see you do yourself."

Lance opened his pants and freed his erection.

Robbie noted with satisfaction that his cock was bigger. He was the lord and master. He felt silly to even think it but he knew that Lance saw him that way. His mouth was a provocation. Robbie gripped his hair and took what he regarded as obscenely exhibitionistic liberties to satisfy his lover's appetite for excess. He remembered the reluctant hesitation with which Lance had performed this act at the beginning. How could he begrudge him whatever experiences he had had that made him so avid now? Lance's hand moved rapidly on himself. Out of the corner of his eye, Robbie caught the flicker of a shadow at the door.

"Take your shirt off," he ordered.

Without interrupting the activities of his mouth, Lance did so and Robbie's eyes gloated on the glorious naked body crouched in submission before him. His cock

362

ruled it. He was brought to a triumphant climax and he saw Lance's ejaculation leap from him and scatter between his legs.

Robbie felt as if Luisa would never leave them alone the next day but at last she appeared in her little day dress as the light drained from the sky on Sunday evening and kissed them both good night. Watching her leave, his heart began to misbehave but he counted on a few drinks to steady his nerves. He'd had two days to prepare himself, two days to come to grips with the possibility of losing Lance.

With no further need to keep up appearances with Luisa, he grew thoughtful and made no attempt to match Lance's customary high spirits.

"I've been waiting to be alone with you," he said in explanation. "It's not always easy having her with us all the time."

"You're so wonderful with her. I know we can't go on like this indefinitely."

"Maybe we should talk about it some more. Let's wait till after dinner, sweetheart. We can talk all night if we want to."

"I can talk about anything with you forever. You're not feeling bad again, are you?"

"No, I'm fine."

"Good. Let's finish our drinks and get ourselves something to eat."

Robbie tried to achieve detachment so that he could say what had to be said calmly and without fearing the consequences, but Lance undermined his efforts. He was so sweetly beguiling, so winning, so charmingly seductive in every way that Robbie was tempted again to postpone the confrontation, run away from it, accept the perfect surface that Lance presented and try not to imagine what lay beneath it. He looked forward so much to the evenings without Luisa that he couldn't bear to spoil this one.

They ate and washed their few dishes. When they returned to the terrace, Lance curled upon the cot and looked up at Robbie expectantly. Robbie pulled a chair close to him but remained standing. Their eyes met. Lance saw a somber speculative look in Robbie's that warned him to be on his guard.

"You know how much I love you, don't you?" Robbie said unexpectedly.

The tenderness in his voice moved and disarmed Lance. If he wanted to talk about how much he loved him there was nothing to worry about. "I know how much I love you."

"I wonder. The point is, I can't help loving you even if you don't love me. I hate to cause any unpleasantness between us. Unfortunately, life is full of unpleasantness. We have to face it." He paused, breathing deeply to give his heart time to calm down. He could see apprehension settling over Lance's face. He plunged in. "Do you know somebody called José?"

"José?" Lance was so unprepared for it that the name was a shock. His mind raced, wondering how much he knew and how he'd learned it, but he managed a small smile. "Everybody here seems to be called José, if they're not Pedro or Juan."

"Oh, come on." The evasion stirred Robbie's anger and he welcomed it. It would help him stick to his purpose. "You either know who I'm talking about or you don't. The guy who raped you."

Lance gave a small nod of his head and then shook it helplessly. "I've wanted to tell you a hundred times but something always stopped me. It's so stupid. He came here one night. A Sunday, I guess. Luisa was with her family. I let him take me again. It was before anything had happened with us. You were still spending your evenings with Flip. You said you were in love with me. I was falling in love with you. I tried to fight it because José made me feel I wasn't good enough for you. He made me feel there were things in me that I didn't want you to know. He threatened me. He wanted to make money with me. He said he had important friends who would pay well for me. He was going to pimp for me. I didn't agree but I didn't dare turn him down flat."

"What kind of threats?"

"He said he'd make my life so miserable that I wouldn't want to stay. Considering what he'd already done, I believed him. I wanted to tell you so you could help me get him off my back. Then he went to the capital and stayed away quite a long time. Nothing's happened that I couldn't tell you about. That's what's so stupid."

364

"He didn't introduce you to Don Antonio?"

"No. I told you about that." He was on safe ground, breathing more easily. "He came to the shed and wanted to talk to me about something. I didn't know who he was."

Nervous tension had kept Robbie on his feet but he settled down now on the chair with a grateful sigh. He'd worked himself into a state about nothing. Lance had no great confession to make. He had no obligation to tell him about things that had happened before they were lovers. Even Filipe's malicious interpretation was based on enough facts to be pardonable. Lance did know José. José did pimp for boys. Interrogation wasn't Robbie's line. He wanted Lance to talk to him freely. He had saved himself in the nick of time from a hideous blunder.

"I don't blame you for not telling me about José, beloved. We were just getting started. It didn't have anything to do with what was happening with us. Still, you see how important it is to tell each other everything. I don't like people being able to make me suspicious of you."

"I wanted to tell you. I honestly did but I wasn't ready to admit even to myself that I was homosexual. Wanting him to take me seemed to leave no doubt about it. Are you going to tell me who's been talking about me?"

"Filipe, of course. He insisted on talking about you day before yesterday. He's a sneaky little creep. Naturally, I thought it was peculiar when he said you were friendly with the guy who raped you but it turns out he was right. You said Don Antonio's wife was with you at dinner the other night, didn't you?"

"I guess so. How else would you've known?"

"You're sure it was his wife?"

"I didn't ask her for her marriage license. Maybe it was some other lady he introduced as his wife for diplomatic purposes."

It was a clever explanation that never would have occurred to Robbie. It was too glib and contrived to have occurred to anybody who wasn't prepared to cover his tracks. All his suspicions burst into a blaze of doubt. "You don't know that José has been in the habit of procuring boys here for Don Antonio?" he asked evenly.

"How would I know that?"

"You know the people involved. He wanted to pimp for you. It's the sort of thing that was almost bound to come out."

Lance sat very still, feeling the storm gathering around him, helpless to divert it. He had paid so little attention to the nondescript houseboy that he hadn't thought of him as a threat. He had no way of knowing how vulnerable he was.

"Wouldn't it be easier to tell me everything Filipe has said?" he asked in a reluctant voice.

"I'm telling you. He said you were friendly with José. He said that Don Antonio's wife never comes here. He said that Don Antonio had always had young local boys until he met you. He said there was another man with you last time."

They looked at each other and both knew that in an instant they had become implacable antagonists, hunter and hunted. Lance couldn't stand it. He hated deceiving him. All his life, he had pretended to be something he wasn't. Robbie wanted to be deceived as a protection from being hurt. Lance wanted to live boldly and openly, without defenses, with the courage to accept the flaws they found in each other, offering each other tolerance and understanding. Robbie wanted to create a safe, sane, stable marriage; Lance wanted the heights and depths of passion.

"Are you going to say anything?" Robbie demanded.

"What do you want me to say?"

"I want you to tell me what you've been doing."

"Your informer seems to have brought you up to date."

It took Robbie's breath away. He had come up hard against a toughness that he hadn't known was in him. He didn't know how to handle it.

"For God's sake," he said, almost with a groan. "Don't you know what this means?"

Lance lifted his head, not defiantly but unflinchingly. "I know what I hope it means. I hope it means that you've found things in me that I didn't want you to know about but that you still love me and want to help me."

Robbie stared at him. His strength or his callousness was awesome. He was superb. This was what generations of ruling the world had bequeathed him. His pride

366

was invincible. "How can I help you if I don't know what you've done?"

"Can't you imagine it? Do I have to put it into words? I'm not the only person in the world with shameful sexual kinks—at least, most people think they're shameful. I don't necessarily. They're in me. I don't want to be ashamed of them."

"Are you talking about Don Antonio?"

"Don Antonio and others." The tone of his voice altered. There was an unmistakable undercurrent of excitement in it when he went on. "Why don't you beat me? I deserve it."

Robbie felt his response in his groin and hated himself for it. He lowered his eyes. He couldn't look at him when he was like this. The demons were stirring.

"I won't beat you. You want it. It absolves you of guilt. What did you do with Don Antonio?"

"I sold myself to him."

Robbie kept his eyes on the floor. "You took money from him?"

"He wasn't the first. I let myself be picked up at that bar on the port one afternoon. I told the guy I was a hustler. He paid me. He did something filthy with me. It was horrible and thrilling. Don't you understand? I'm not interested in pretty boys. Why should I be when I have the most beautiful guy in the world? I want to give myself to men who wouldn't ordinarily hope to have a luxury product like me. When something ugly happens to me, I feel as if I'm restoring the balance. Don Antonio uses me to have his revenge on the Vanderholdens. I want that too. We're in it together."

Robbie felt as if he'd opened Pandora's box. Lance's pride was the key to his capacity for self-abasement. There were no limits to which he might not go. Robbie had already heard more than he wanted to know but he had to hear it all to give himself the will to act. He felt a sickness creeping through his body, a sickness that was just beginning, the sickness of being without Lance. "You've sucked his cock," he said dully, driving himself on.

Lance remained silent as if he were trying to remember. "Yes," he said finally on a barely audible breath.

"He's fucked you?"

367

"Yes." Lance's voice rose. "He beat me and fucked me. I wanted it. It was a sort of charade of rape. The other guy was there to run the show. He tied me up. I did things at the doctor's party that I'm ashamed of because it was pure self-indulgence. I'd never before been wanted by a lot of guys all at once. The novelty of it made me lose my head. I didn't lie about being doped. I'll never do anything like that again but I'm still amazed that a guy can want me. I don't even feel desire in the usual sense of the word. It's knowing that I can enjoy things that are usually considered beyond the pale. I love sucking cock and having a guy put it in me. Any cock. You must understand. You've talked about the great urge downward. It hasn't got anything to do with us. You know I couldn't love anyone but you. It's all the rest of it I haven't got fitted together yet. I will if you'll help me. You've got to."

Robbie felt the sickness spreading through him. His mind reeled with everything Lance had said. Listening to him talk about sex had given him a shameful erection, vicarious and deceptive. He clamped it between his thighs, doubting that he would ever want him again. Self-respect demanded that he reject the temptation of a body that was so casually shared. He had to save himself. A future as the mate of a whore was beyond imagining. He couldn't think of anything to say that would stop short of unleashing all the revulsion he felt in him.

"I can't believe any of this," he said to fill the silence. "You've whored without even needing the money."

"I can use it. It's the only money that's really mine."

"The money you made with the pottery is yours."

"Not really. I couldn't've done it without you. But that's not all of it. It's so unbelievable being able to make money that way. A male whore, when I finally learned there was such a thing, always seemed to me the lowest form of humanity. I've been one. It's not as bad as all that if you can make somebody happy for a few minutes."

"Oh Christ." Robbie ground his teeth. "A whore with a heart of gold. What do you mean when you talk about my helping you? Do you reserve the right to go on with Don Antonio and all the other poor underprivileged bastards who've never fucked a Vanderholden?"

368

Lance pulled himself up straight on the cot, his muscles tensing. His lips parted as he took a quick breath. He was losing Robbie. He'd known he would lose him. There was nothing good enough in him to keep him but he was determined not to lose him for reasons he couldn't accept as valid.

Once he'd abandoned caution and decided to trust in truth, he had expected a crisis that might end in violence but would eventually bring them even closer together. He felt the distance between them widening. He had to bring him back to him. His eyes filled with appeal but Robbie wouldn't meet them.

"I reserve the right to love you and be myself the way you say I should be," he said. "I need you. I want you to help me the way you already have. I'm learning about fidelity. I'm not unfaithful to you with Don Antonio. The guys at the party didn't mean anything—just a momentary physical thrill—but I was unfaithful with Tracy. For a little while, I thought I wanted him as much as I'd ever wanted anybody. When I felt that, I should've cleared out or faced not coming back to you. I wanted it both ways. That's bad. Thoughts and feelings have more to do with fidelity than what you do with your body. I'm not sure it makes any sense for a guy to claim exclusive rights to another guy's body. We've talked about it. Have you ever felt, even for a minute, no matter what I've done, that I belonged to you any less?"

"No. You're very convincing. That makes it worse. I give all of myself to somebody who isn't there."

Robbie sounded as if he might be softening. Lance still hoped. "You haven't felt it because it isn't true. We can belong to each other completely without suffocating each other. The more air we breathe, the more we can grow into each other. I proved it to you with Michael. We were able to have him without being unfaithful to each other."

"I forced myself to accept him even though I knew it was bad for us. I've tried to adapt to your impulses. The more I give in to you, the more you take advantage. I've gone as far as I can go."

"That's because you won't accept what any of it means. Why do you think you have me? Because I'm queer. If I were a solid citizen, I wouldn't've let you

369

seduce me. I'm queer but it might not've led to anything if it hadn't been for you. You brought it all out. I may do things you hate but don't forget a lot of people would hate both of us just because of what we are. You reserve the right to be queer but you won't recognize it as a perversion. You want to be a respectable married man with a guy as a wife. I won't be unfaithful again—I've learned where to draw the line—but I'll go on being queer. If you don't know that that means there're urges and weaknesses in me that'll make me a difficult wife, you shouldn't've taken me in the first place. Please, darling. Allow us to love each other without keeping us under wraps. You want to shut us away somehow where we can't hurt each other. But if you'd accept the fact that all my love is yours, that I couldn't hurt you no matter what madness seizes me when I'm trying to fight my way out of the maze of my background, you wouldn't question me. You'd just want to help me."

"How convenient for you. Has it never occurred to you that I might need help, too?"

"Tell me how, darling. I'll do anything for you."

"Sure. You're going to be faithful to me. You're just going to let yourself be fucked by plain men instead of attractive ones. *And* get paid for it." He leaped to his feet with a roar. "God Almighty." His voice broke on a sob of rage.

Lance hadn't expressed a moment's remorse. Homosexuality absolved him from adopting any standards of decency. He placed responsibility for everything he had done squarely on Robbie. He strode to the parapet and looked out at nothing, getting a grip on himself.

For a moment he had been almost convinced that Lance was making a serious point. He could see in himself the qualities that Lance felt as irritants. His romantic view of love oversolemnized it in a way that was even a burden to himself. The high value he placed on fidelity *was* a form of self-protection. He was too vulnerable—too egotistical?—to adjust easily to the possibility that his lover might find somebody else equally desirable. He knew that a casual roll in the hay was no great sin against love and might be a useful release for two people who were totally engrossed with each other. He knew that Lance's search overlooked the obvious, such as conventional values. He knew that even after so much had been said that shocked him, he was still consumed by love for him. He had to remind himself of all this before he could face him with confidence.

He turned back and approached him. Lance was where he had left him, sitting very straight on the cot, his legs tucked under him. Robbie's eyes were dazed by his transfixing beauty. He seemed to be suspended in a profound inertia, waiting for him to speak again. Robbie stood by his chair, looking at him. "There's only one way I can help you," he said. "I have to go away."

Lance's face set with childlike stubbornness. "You can't."

"Why can't I?"

"Because you said you'd never leave me. You said I couldn't do anything that would make you not want to see me again."

Robbie's heart was wrenched by the childlike faith and trust in the words. It hurt him to shake it. "I haven't said I didn't want to see you again. I said I had to go away."

Lance felt as if all the blood were draining out of him. A chill was creeping up his legs and through his chest. His sense of touch seemed to be affected. His head felt light and insensible, as if it were in a vacuum. He thought this was the way he would feel if he were told that he was going to die, numb with incredulity. "For how long?" he asked in a normal voice that seemed to come from outside him.

"I don't know. I suppose that depends on you."

Robbie sank into a chair. He hoped that this was the way it would happen—quietly, as if they were discussing an everyday occurrence. He didn't trust himself to stand up to an emotional outburst of protest and entreaty. He went on cautiously.

"I realize our timing was all wrong. You should've had a chance to find out more about homosexuality before we fell in love with each other. I understand a lot of what you're saying and you're right in some ways. I don't think of us as perverts. I fought my sexual battles when I was so young that I forgot I was fighting for my right to be different. At first, I thought of myself as damned and acted accordingly. My father was eventually able to talk to me about being a decent homosexual. His making an effort at understanding made

371

me want his approval, and Maurice was a very decent man. We were accepted as a couple in respectable society. It's different in Europe. Class, who you know, counts for more than what you are. I began to forget there was anything special about me. I suppose it's made me straitlaced in the way that drives you so crazy."

Lance scarcely dared breathe as he began to hope again. Robbie couldn't be speaking like this about the end of everything they wanted and needed in each other. Yet, something in Lance was already resigned to it. Some voice in him told him that he had to be free to pursue his own destiny, a destiny that took from him everything he treasured most in life. But it was a fleeting voice, unable to quench hope.

"You're not straitlaced in bed," he said. "That's what makes me think you cover up a lot of your true feelings."

"Some of the things you do in bed shocked me at first. I love it, of course, but I suppose that's the depravity you talk about. Maybe you're naturally more depraved than I am but it's all a question of control. You've got to choose a course and not let anything throw you off it. If it's depravity you want, you don't need me. I'm going away so you can choose. You haven't had a chance to find out what you want with me here watching you and restraining you—not that I seem to have been all that much of a restraint."

"Where're you going?"

"I haven't thought about it. Back to France, maybe."

"No. You can't go home without me. It's too far away. Christmas is coming. We've got to have our first Christmas together."

"This isn't much of a place for Christmas. Anyway, it's more than a month away. Maybe I'll be back by then."

"What's supposed to become of me if you're not?"

"You'll be all right. Your work's going well. You have to look after Luisa. You have enough money for at least six months and the chess sets should make quite a lot more. Ah, yes! I keep forgetting you've found a way of solving any financial problems that might crop up. That's one of the things you've got to decide about. I won't ever come back if you go on with it. It's too disgusting for me to even talk about. You'll have the address of my dealer in New York. You can write me

372

if you find you need me. I mean, to live with as a re-spectable married man. That's all it amounts to. Whether you want a more or less normal life with me or have to go on until there's no ugliness left in life that you haven't exposed yourself to."

Robbie's matter-of-fact tone made his leaving sound like something that could happen. Lance still couldn't grasp it. His body felt like an empty shell. His heart beat in a void.

"I've told you. Nothing means anything if I'm not with you. Who cares if I'm a decent homosexual or a faggot for hire?"

"That's just it. *You've* got to care. Until you do, there's nothing I can do for you. You scare me. You don't seem to realize the dangers involved. Picking up men in the street. You read about sex crimes in the paper every day. You could be murdered."

"Then stay with me and help me."

"What's the point? You do what you do whether I'm here or not. I'm hoping you'll want me back enough so that you'll begin to think about staying within the lim-its that you know I can accept. That's all I'll want to hear—that you're ready to make a life with me with some consideration for my not very exaggerated de-mands."

"Shouldn't that work both ways? Don't I have the right to make demands?"

"Of course. I wish I knew what they were, aside from total devotion and dedication to you."

"Understanding. Flexibility. A willingness to exper-iment, at least for a while, like with Michael. Tolerance of my depravity. I know it's depraved to want to see you with other guys but I do. I haven't dared say it all but I will now. I wish I'd felt free to bring Tracy back to you. If I had, it wouldn't have gone as far as it did. I guess I'm learning that I'm a masochist. What do we do about that? It thrills me as much to see you with other guys as being beaten by you. I wouldn't't've gotten into all this other stuff if I'd felt I could let it all out with you. I know it would be good for you too, once you were sure it wasn't coming between us."

Robbie gave his head a little shake. "I can't complain if you tell the truth as you see it. All the more reason for me to go away. I told you I need help, too. I've got to find out if I need you enough to uproot all my deepest instincts about love."

"But don't you see how much I need you *now?* It's too soon. I suppose someday we might have to be apart, but not now."

Robbie's heart was wrenched again by the undisguised plea in his voice but he'd screwed himself up to the sticking point. If he backed down now, it would only be a postponement. Lance had said nothing that changed anything. He gave his head another shake. "I'm not ready for it. I've had all the shocks I can take. It's a miracle I'm still able to speak to you. If you throw any more at me, I'll begin to hate you."

Lance heard the cool finality in his voice and he suddenly felt his body again, knowing what it would feel like if Robbie weren't here to hold it. His stomach churned in a panic of loss.

"If you go away, I know you'll never come back. You'll just— If I were—" His voice failed.

Robbie saw his body stiffen. His face became a tortured grimace. A sob broke from him. Robbie felt as if his heart were being torn from his chest. He lunged out of his chair and they were in each other's arms. Lance clung to him, his body racked by sobs. Robbie's arms held him close, soothing him.

"Don't. Oh, please. Please don't, my beloved. We'll be all right. You'll see."

Tears welled in his eyes and spilled down his cheeks. He was making it more difficult for himself but he couldn't bear to see him suffer. His hands moved over his naked torso to comfort him and the sobs slowly subsided.

"I can't—I can't—" Lance gasped between long shuddering breaths.

"Don't try to talk yet." He hugged him to his chest and kissed the top of his golden head and wondered if he would ever know such piercing heartbreaking happiness again.

"Let me be yours," Lance moaned. "Oh, please. I belong to you. Keep me always. I'm nothing without you."

"You're everything to me. I can't help it. I want you to have a chance to find yourself. It's as important for

374

me as it is for you. You can let yourself go and discover what you really want. I hope it'll be me."

"It is. Oh God, it is. Take me, darling." Lance's chest heaved with a strangled sigh.

Robbie couldn't pretend that he didn't want him. He led him to bed and took him in his own way, with lingering, loving tenderness. They both had ecstatic tears in their eyes when they reached their climax.

When Robbie returned from the shower, Lance was asleep, an angelic smile on his lips. His golden hair was a halo around his head. Physically and emotionally drained, a whore had taken his place among the heavenly hosts. Robbie understood his readiness to give or sell himself to any taker. His beauty was one of the many gifts that had been lavished on him at birth, that he had never felt he deserved. His offering it prodigally diminished its value. Robbie was frightened by how close he was to forgiving him. He had to get away to find out if he had the strength to impose some control on him. They couldn't both succumb to depravity.

He snapped out the light and stretched out beside him, touching him lightly everywhere, but exerting no pressure that might disturb him. Robbie adjusted his breathing to his rhythm and wished that this was all he asked of life, feeling their union in their breathing and the light touch of their bodies against each other and his lover's peace.

Morning was coming. He knew what he would do if luck was with him. He sorted out the problems of travel—what he would take with him, how he would get where he wanted to go. He realized that he wasn't going to sleep and gave up trying to breathe with Lance. It was like a parting, and a great wave of anguish swept over him and threatened to drown him in tears. He clenched his jaws and waited for it to recede. This was going to be worse than anything he'd ever been through, much worse than learning to live without Maurice.

He sent loving messages to his dead lover, asking his forgiveness. They had had so much together but death left no decisions. Everything with Lance was going to require grueling decisions. He thought Maurice would approve the decisions he'd made so far. They had shared his initial infatuation with Lance and he would be amazed by how it had turned out. It comforted and amused him to think of Maurice watching over him. He was going to need him in the weeks to come.

Lance woke up in daylight and smiled as he moved to Robbie. He wasn't there. He shot up from the empty bed and ran out to the terrace. His heart was in his throat. He had only a tenuous control over his limbs. He careened along the terrace to where Luisa had set up her ironing outside the kitchen door. He was still dizzy with sleep. She looked up and her eyes widened.

"Where is Robbie?" he blurted out.

"He has gone away."

"You see him?"

"Very early. Just when I was coming home. He had a small suitcase. He said he had to go away. He said you would explain. He's coming back?"

"Yes. I tell you later."

He hurtled back along the terrace to the bedroom, driven by panic. He had to stop him. He had trouble getting into his clothes. He was shaking all over. He was aware of things missing from the makeshift closet but didn't stop to check what. Certainly not much. He tried to remember where Robbie kept his passport but hadn't seen it since the marriage. He wondered if he'd taken the car. He didn't see how he could go anywhere without it.

He ran back along the terrace. Luisa came out from behind her ironing to intercept him. "Are you going, too?" she asked with alarm in her eyes.

"Of course not. I will be back in a little while."

He leaped up the steps. The car was where it always was. He had a chance of catching up to him. He called as he ran through the citrus grove to the house. Filipe was waiting at the door when he reached it.

"He's not here," he said with a sly smirk on his face.

Lance wanted to kill him. "Where is he?"

"I do not know." He stepped back from the door to let Lance in. "He left a letter that he said I must be sure to give you."

Entering, Lance saw immediately that the nearly finished canvas was propped on the floor, the new one he'd just returned to still on the easel. Nothing had been disturbed on the work table. He couldn't have gone far or for very long if he'd left his work.

Lance took a deep, calming breath. Filipe approached, holding out an envelope. Lance took it and tore it open with an almost steady hand.

Beloved,
I didn't want a big farewell because we'd feel foolish if I come right back.

We didn't talk about whether we'd keep in touch regularly or let it go for the time being. I've never seen you write a letter so I don't know if you go in for it. I do but I don't want to overdo it. It would just be another way of trying to restrain you. I want you to pretend that I don't exist for a little while and see where it leads you. I guess that means we shouldn't write until we're ready to resolve matters one way or the other. I have your telephone number but I won't use it except in an emergency. It's too maddening trying to make sense on a bad connection. I'll send you a power of attorney from the capital in case you want to do business with Don Antonio.

The addresses are on the back. Use New York for now. I'll let you know later if I decide to go on to France. You can open my mail. Everything can stay here unless you think there's something I should have right away.

Please take care of yourself and be careful. I can't help worrying. I'll always think of you sleeping beside me the way you were last night.

I love you. R.

Lance moved hastily away from the boy beside him and folded the letter, his eyes blurred with tears. "When did he go?" he demanded, forcing his voice out with his back turned.

"I'm not sure. Over an hour ago."

"Did somebody come for him?"

"No. He walked. He had only a small suitcase."

He flung himself at the door and made a dash for the car. He still might stop him. The bus for the capital didn't leave till ten and rarely promptly. He might have gone down to wait for it in town just to get out of the house, away from Filipe. His note sounded halfhearted about going. If he found him and begged him to stay, he would win him back.

He drove recklessly through crowded streets to what passed for a bus station. It was more warehouse than a convenience for passengers, with a desk at the front where a man sold tickets. Lance had dealt with him for his shipments. Yes, he knew the *senor*'s friend, the tall dark foreigner. No, he hadn't been there.

Men were sitting around on the ground, nodding over bundles. Lance picked his way through them back to the car. He knew his way around well enough now so that he had no trouble learning that Robbie had found a man who was driving to the capital and had agreed to take him for a price. They had left an hour ago.

He sank back into the car behind the wheel, his body undergoing frightening, unbearable sensations. He couldn't feel his heart beating, just a knot in his chest making it difficult to breathe and an emptiness in his stomach that also felt knotted. His arms and legs were tense but without strength. A slick of sweat broke out on him. He couldn't stand feeling like this for long. He would have a breakdown, become a drunk, commit a crime. Anything to find relief from this strange unidentifiable alienation from his body.

He fixed his thoughts on Robbie's return. Of course he was coming back. He'd said so. He'd probably gone to the capital for a few days to be alone and straighten things out in his mind. He wasn't leaving him. There was nothing to break down about. A day to get there and a day to get back and a few days in between to get over his shock. They'd be apart for a week at the most.

His thoughts began to cure him. His body was returning to normal. If he didn't allow his faith in Robbie to be shaken, he would be all right. He'd warned him that he made no sense when they weren't together but maybe in a day or so when he got used to being without him, he'd be able to do what Robbie wanted him to do and straighten some things out for himself. He didn't see how he would go about it. Nothing had happened that made him feel that he belonged to him any less than he had at the beginning. He didn't want anything without Robbie.

He went to the shed and found his helpers firing the

pawns that he'd left for them yesterday. He couldn't bring himself to start anything new. He stayed for less than half an hour and drove home. It would help to be with Luisa. She was their family, as much Robbie's as his. She was, after all, the reason why he'd been able to stay here long enough to meet Robbie. He would always be grateful to her for that. She was the mother of his child. If for no other reason, Robbie had to come back to arrange things with her. She was his wife. Granted the marriage had been only a formality but he wouldn't have gone through with it if he hadn't been ready to undertake lifetime responsibilities. There was nothing to worry about. He'd be back.

She was putting her ironing away when he appeared. She put it aside and went to him, her expression gravely questioning. "Did you see him?" she asked.

"I not expect to see him. I go to know if he has found a car. He has gone."

"When will he be back?"

"Soon. He has business. His work and mine. He comes back when he finished."

Luisa looked at him, wondering why he looked so different. Robbie too had looked different this morning but she'd been so startled by his saying that he was going that she hadn't thought about it. Something bad had happened. She was deeply troubled. She wondered if it had something to do with a woman. She couldn't think of anything else that would make the brothers leave each other. "I don't understand why he didn't say anything last night before I went."

"We not know. We talk about it afterwards. We decide he must go. Very important but not for long."

"I am sorry. We will miss him."

"Yes. We will—" What he supposed was panic started to get a grip on him again and for a moment he felt incapable of combating it. It was a still, relentless panic on the edge of nervous breakdown. He felt that if he didn't control it he would go mad. He drew her to him and held her close. The swell of her belly against him diverted his thoughts.

This was life, stronger than the distractions and dissensions of everyday existence. This was the child that he and Robbie were going to bring up together. Robbie thought of the baby as partly his. That was something that couldn't be forgotten overnight. The ties between them were too strong to be broken easily. He hugged Luisa and was grateful to her for the comfort she offered. She had comforted him before. He would be all right with her.

"He will be back soon," he repeated against her ear, reassuring them both.

"I hope so." She felt his manhood stirring against her and she was frightened. Robbie had promised not to let him have other women. In her present condition, how could she hope to keep him without his help? She had to keep him. Robbie expected to find him here when he came back.

Lance had a vigorous swim, his eyes avoiding the path down to the rocks. It was too tempting to imagine Robbie making a miraculous appearance there. Unless his driver's car broke down, he couldn't possibly get back before tomorrow and he wouldn't allow himself to hope for him that soon. He climbed back to the house and had a couple of strong drinks before lunch. They made him feel so much better that he began to believe he would survive.

After lunch, he took Luisa to her room and undressed her and stretched her out on the bed. They lay naked together while Lance discovered the wonder of a pregnant woman. Pam had never let him see her naked after it had begun to show. Luisa's belly was a small smooth taut drum fitted snugly under her breasts. He stroked it with his fingertips and lay his head gently on it and felt the spasms of life in it. He had made this with her. It was something two men couldn't share. She played placidly with his erection and made him come with her mouth. They dozed together. He felt her contentment.

He had more drinks before dinner and decided that it wouldn't do anybody any harm if he stayed a little drunk until Robbie came back. It made the hours pass more easily. He had another drink before going to Robbie's bed. He wanted to be sure of sleeping.

He woke up early in the grip of one of his panicky seizures. He thought of Robbie sleeping alone in some hotel far away from him and his eyes filled with tears. He groaned to loosen the knots. He went over everything that had been said, everything Robbie had written, and slowly coaxed back his confidence that he would return soon. He hoped that work would help but he didn't see how he could work in this state. His hands were too stiff to do what he wanted them to do.

He thought of writing but there was nothing to say except that he wanted him, which he already knew. They had seemed to be making firm points with each other but their substance had crumbled and slipped away like a handful of powdered clay. Writing would mean thinking of his being in New York and he refused to believe he would go so far. There was no way of writing to him in the capital. Writing wasn't necessary. He would be back.

Luisa was ready to give him breakfast when he pulled himself out of bed. They sat together in silence. Robbie's absence made a hole in the house. Nothing would fit around it. They were like two orphaned children waiting for somebody to take charge and give them direction.

He went to work on the chess pieces. The pawns were finished but his fantastical vision of the other pieces had dimmed. It was plodding work. He supposed they would be all right when they were finished but they didn't fire his imagination. Nothing did without Robbie. Check and mate, he thought, wondering if he could put his helplessness into the figure of the king.

A day or two later, Don Antonio called. He had been busy with more important affairs and wouldn't have time for Lance's business for another couple of weeks. The connection crackled and faded.

"Have you been in touch with my mother?" Lance shouted.

"She refused my demands. We'll go ahead with my plans. I'll send a plane for you when everything is in order."

Having his prediction confirmed made him feel safe from his mother and he started to tell Don Antonio that he wouldn't be able to come to the capital after all. The connection went dead. It wasn't something he could explain under these conditions anyway.

He couldn't resolve anything with Don Antonio until he saw him. Nothing would be resolved as long as Robbie was away. Why didn't he understand that their being parted was a waste of time? Anger flared up in

381

him. He wished he could stay angry. It might push him into doing some of the things Robbie expected him to do. He was supposed to find out about himself but he didn't dare find out more about himself without Robbie; he was afraid to break the precious ties that bound them.

He kept himself going on drink and the routine of his uninspired work. The rains ended as abruptly as they had begun. He went by Robbie's house regularly to check his mail and added a letter or two every day to the little pile on his work table. The letters were all personal, mostly from Europe, but none of them looked urgent. It was the moment he liked best in the day because he was doing a job Robbie had entrusted to him. You didn't ask somebody you didn't expect to see again to read your mail.

Luisa asked him one evening if he wanted her to stay at home with him. Another Sunday had come.

"No. All fine. You go."

He had started his evening drinking already and wasn't afraid of being alone. He drank until he was almost asleep and fell into bed, the way he had done every night since Robbie left.

Lance had sunk into such a stupor of waiting that he was surprised by the spark of renewed interest he felt when Enrique appeared at the shed. He immediately put his work aside and went to meet him at the door. He realized that his smile of welcome was almost unforced. There was a connection between them.

Enrique looked him over slowly with desire in his eyes and put a hand on his shoulder. "Your friend has gone away," he said.

"Yes. For a little while."

"I think of you often. José wants to see you but I asked him to let me come instead."

"Why José wants to see me?"

"I will tell you. Will you come with me now?"

"I don't know. I—"

Robbie had told him to pretend that he didn't exist. He had questioned Robbie's exclusive rights to his body. He should probably find out if he'd meant it enough for it to affect their lives together. Perhaps this was the resolution they both seemed to be waiting for. Enrique's shaggy head was endearing. His big mouth was friendly

and inviting. If Robbie really didn't exist, the thought
of being held in his comforting arms would be irresistible.

"Where?"

"I have a friend who rents rooms. He will let me
have one. We can be alone. I'll tell you about José."

It was almost time to stop for the day. In an hour,
he would be well on the way to getting drunk. Living
in an alcoholic daze wasn't accomplishing anything for
either of them. "All right." He gave his waist a pat and
was rewarded by a grateful smile.

He told Big he was leaving. His helpers knew the
routine for putting things away for the night. He washed
his hands at the trough and took Enrique to the car.

Enrique's eyes were on him as he drove. A hand crept
up his neck and caressed his hair. The peaceful human
touch was so sweet after his empty days that it brought
tears to his eyes. Enrique shifted closer to him and
leaned over and kissed the side of his face while a hand
moved over the front of his shorts and gave him an
erection.

"You are a beautiful man," he said. "I like this part
of you. I like to put it in my mouth. I wanted to tell
you."

"I'm glad. Tell about José."

"It's about something he wants you to do with me. I
want it, too."

Lance drove through the somnolent shopping streets,
and following Enrique's directions, turned into a side
street lined with ramshackle two-story frame houses.
He stopped where he was told and they entered a house
with a board over the door announcing CAMERAS. Lance
began to come to life with a sense of adventure. He had
come to a sleazy rooming house to have sex with a good-
looking native.

They stood in a narrow lobby with a counter on one
side and a board with keys hanging on it behind it.
Enrique called toward a door at the back. A brief exchange followed with a man on the other side of it and
then Enrique leaned across the counter and picked a
key off the board. He turned to Lance with his gentle
smile and put an arm around him and led him up a
rough wooden staircase to a corridor of closed doors.

They stopped in front of one. Enrique let them in

and locked it behind them. They were in a dingy un-carpeted bedroom, bare and shabby but clean-looking, with an iron double bed. This was sex stripped to its essentials.

They pulled off their clothes. Their erections butted up against each other. Enrique's big sexy mouth was surprisingly uninhibited. Lance discovered the plea-sure he could find with a tall, well-made brown body. Holding it was a consolation that made his breath catch with relief. They fell onto the hard bed, their bodies welcoming their union. It had been almost two weeks since he'd had any sex; he hadn't realized how much he missed it.

Encouraging Enrique to discard his inhibitions and give himself to his excitement, Lance tried to remain detached in order to examine what being with him meant to him. He loved knowing that he was wanted by men. Learning how to please and satisfy them in unorthodox ways gave him the thrill of defying the world. It had nothing to do with love. He could control his urges, even suppress them, if he could find some reason why he should. Knowing that Robbie wanted him to should be enough but it seemed wrong to cut himself off from the spontaneous human contact that it had taken him so long to discover. For the moment, Enrique was helping him forget the agony of being without Robbie. Others could too. Maybe he wasn't made for an all-encom-passing exclusive love. That was what Robbie wanted him to find out.

Enrique finally banished thought. They took each other with their mouths and lay with their arms around each other. Their cocks stirred in their hands.

"I did not know I could love a man the way I love you," Enrique said. "I want you to be my partner. José says Don Antonio won't be back for several weeks. We could make money together."

"How?"

"The tourists. The season is beginning. José lets them enjoy him for money. I have been doing it too. He thinks you could make much money. I want us to do it together. They are often in pairs and ask me to bring a friend."

"You mean men?"

"A man cannot take money from a woman."

"You are right."

"We both need money. We can do it together or separately, depending on what the men want, but we would be working together. You could talk to them. Not many speak Spanish."

Lance liked his assuming that they both were motivated by need. Robbie had told him to let himself go and find out where it led him. If he was going to whore, it was more honest to do it in the streets and find out what it was really like as he had once before, rather than in the sheltered luxury of a rich man's villa. He wasn't signing a contract. He could stop when he wanted to.

"I go with you one night to see what is like."

"You have not done it before?"

"Yes, but I do not know where here."

"The bars where the foreigners go. I will show you. When I tell José you agree, I will ask him if there is anywhere we must not go."

"You have to ask him?"

"Yes. He decides such things. He could cause us both great trouble if he does not like what we do. We will have to pay him ten dollars a night. Everything else we can keep for ourselves."

"When we do it?"

"Tonight. Meet me at nine at the bar on the port." Enrique took Lance's hand and put it on his stiffening erection. "I want you very much, gringo."

"You are good man for me," Lance said as he squeezed his hard cock. "Make me your woman now."

When he got home, he felt no great need for a drink. He was finally doing something that might justify this separation. Superstitiously, he thought that making a move might break the stalemate and bring him home. It was hard for him to go on believing that he would spend all this time in the capital, but writing would be an acceptance of the probability that he'd moved on. In a few days he might have something clear and definite to say to him.

He told Luisa that he was going out.

"Will you stay out all night?"

She dreaded it but she wanted him to go out. He was looking almost like himself, brighter and more cheerful. It worried her for him to sit at home every evening

385

drinking alone. Her brothers were sure he hadn't found a woman. It was something they would know.

"No, not all night. I see some men. We drink. Not late." He gave her a reassuring kiss.

When he went to meet Enrique, he was astonished by the activity in the streets. Puerto Veragua apparently had a real tourist season. The foreigners looked as foreign to him as they undoubtedly did to the locals. Enrique told him that it looked as if there were going to be more of them than ever before.

They sat at a table with rum drinks and awaited developments. The bar was busy with an unpromising clientele of commonplace couples. Enrique said it was early for men to be on the prowl. After half an hour, he suggested moving on to the bars on the square. There, the bars were livelier and they were immediately picked up by two prosperous-looking middle-aged Belgians. They lost no time coming to the point and quickly settled on terms.

The Belgians had communicating rooms at the hotel. They liked watching Lance and Enrique together and participated only enough to get their kicks. Don Antonio had taught Enrique how to put on a good show and he made an extravagant display of Lance. They were content with each other's company and stayed long enough to come several times.

Back in the street, they agreed that they'd had enough for one night and returned to the port for a drink. They shared thirty dollars, having deducted ten for José. When they parted, they agreed to meet regularly. Lance was home before midnight.

The third week of Robbie's absence began and Lance finally resigned himself to the obvious fact that he hadn't waited in the capital but had gone on to New York.

Thinking of how intrigued he'd been by Michael, he shaved his armpits and trimmed his pubic hair to a minimum. It made his cock look strangely naked. He was a luxury item, artfully crafted. He bought lipstick and mascara at the new women's toiletries shop. The mascara made his eyes big and luminous. He used the lipstick as discreetly as he had with Don Antonio so that he didn't look made up but acquired a sexual ambiguity that he thought would attract customers. Enrique couldn't take his eyes off him.

386

After a few nights with his partner, he felt that he was becoming a real professional. He was prepared to accept any indignity or humiliation, but nothing very terrible happened. Their prey were unprepossessing middle-aged men and they took them on singly or in pairs. It wasn't likely that attractive young guys would be willing to pay; they could get all they wanted free.

He was surprised one night when two very good-looking young Californians accepted his terms after making a play for him. He was flattered to be wanted that much by this pair. He asked them if they wanted a fourth but they didn't. He spent several hours with them and they became very friendly. They'd been together for almost three years and considered themselves an old married couple. When they got restless, they allowed themselves some leeway but found that they avoided dissension by having their adventures together. Lance understood. He wasn't the only person in the world who thought that straying occasionally might be good for two lovers.

After two weeks of doing the rounds with Enrique, he was sure that letting himself go wasn't leading to anything except more of the same. He was proud of his ability to overcome disgust and there were other compensating satisfactions. He was toughening himself up. He even learned to steal. He took whatever was easy to pocket—watches, bits of jewelry, an occasional wallet—and passed them on to José.

Don Antonio called again and managed to convey over the crackling wire that with Christmas coming he had decided to postpone his business with Lance till after the holidays. That suited Lance. Now that his mother had eliminated herself from the picture, he hoped Don Antonio would fade away too.

When he thought of being parted from Robbie for Christmas he was seized again by the panic that made him feel as if he were losing a grip on his sanity. He couldn't bear to think of Robbie alone and struggled to convince himself that he wouldn't be. He had lots of friends who would be delighted to show off a distinguished young painter over the holiday season. Forlorn and incongruous Christmas decorations began to appear in the dusty streets. They would have laughed about them together. They plunged Lance into a sick suffocating paralysis of depression.

He knew that a crisis was coming, a moment when his courage would crumble and he would have had enough, when he would be able to write Robbie and ask him to come back on his own terms. Robbie had been right to go away. He had learned a lot that he'd needed to know. He knew that he could face anything in life without flinching. He knew he was oversusceptible to sexual novelty, but with Robbie to steady him he thought he would be able to keep it under control once he was satisfied that there were no more novelties for him. Robbie had known instinctively that he had needed time to sort things out for himself.

Luisa knew that he'd made friends with a man called Enrique. Her brothers referred to him as a "beach rogue," one of the floating population of young men without jobs who picked up petty cash from the tourists, but said that he wasn't as bad as some of them. She was surprised that Lance would bother with anybody like that but she had never tried to understand men's pleasures when they weren't after women.

One night at the port bar when Enrique had been taken off by a client, Lance's attention was caught by a woman at a nearby table. She was a bit drunk. Her movements were abrupt and uncontrolled. She gulped her drinks. Her long ash blond hair kept falling across one eye and she tossed her head frequently to get it out of the way.

He saw her light one cigarette from another. He heard snatches of a husky, raucous voice. She seemed to have modeled herself on Tallulah Bankhead. He could see that under carelessly applied makeup she was delicately pretty and unexpectedly young. She had the air of a performer and Lance began to think she looked familiar. She was wearing a long white cotton dress with some Spanish touches, like the dresses they'd bought for Luisa, but it wasn't very clean and looked as if it were about to fall off. Bewitching breasts were barely contained by it.

The man with her was a sleek Latin type who looked pained and alarmed by her. She spoke loud English and paid no attention to his replies, as if she didn't know what he was talking about. Her eyes roved the scene restlessly. She caught Lance's eyes on her and she gave him a long direct look that didn't leave him indifferent before she smiled slightly and took another gulp of her drink.

Lance finished his drink, remembering that he couldn't take money from a woman. He wasn't sure his standards were as fastidious as Enrique's but he could take the night off if it proved to be a problem. He rose and circled an intervening table and stopped in front of her.

"Will you buy me a drink?" he asked.

She looked up at him boldly. Close up, she looked absurdly young, as if her manner and appearance had been acquired for a high school performance of a loose woman. She quite clearly wasn't wearing a bra. It was the first time he'd seen a dressed woman without one. "I guess I can afford it if you can't," she said.

"I'm a hustler." He bowed politely to the man as he sat.

"Don't pay any attention to him. He doesn't understand a word you say."

"She say you no speak English," Lance said in his inelegant Spanish. The man shrugged.

"Hey, you speak the lingo," the woman said. "You can order me a drink, too."

Lance signaled the waiter, who knew him as a regular. He ordered another of the same for both of them. "My name's Van."

"Mine's Jill." Her husky voice filled it with innuendo.

His memory supplied her surname. Jill Longstreth. She looked familiar because he'd spent an evening with her at a party long ago. She had been so drunk that he didn't think there was any risk of her remembering him. She had had a brief celebrity at the end of the war as a "society" singer in nightclubs around town. She was the offspring of a distinguished Philadelphia family. He'd been deeply impressed by her because she'd dared to break away from her background. She'd been very young at the time, about five years younger than he. He looked at her breasts. They weren't big but beautifully firm and rounded, tantalizingly close to emerging from her dress. His hands were restless to find out

389

what they felt like. Maybe he wasn't as queer as he thought.

"What're you doing here?" he asked.

"I was working at a nightclub in the capital. This joker suggested driving down here. He thinks it gives him rights. Why don't we tell him to bug off?" She turned to the man. "Scram, buster."

"You work in nightclubs?" Lance said hastily to avoid a scene.

"Yeah, I'm a hustler like you."

"I'm a real one."

"I saw you eyeing the guys. Are you a faggot?"

"More or less but I could probably be saved by the love of a pure woman."

She laughed raucously. "You've come to the right guy, pal. If we're going to work on it why don't you tell this asshole to clear out?" She turned to the man again. "Take a powder, jerk."

"The lady is old friend," Lance explained politely. "She want to talk. She say you go and come back later."

The man shot them venomous glances and rose stiffly and stalked away.

"Hey, it worked," Jill crowed.

"How're you going to get back to the capital? It's a long bus ride."

"I won't get rid of him that easily. He'll be back."

"You better be careful. The people here don't like to be pushed around. You're apt to get killed. I almost got killed for getting smart with a guy on the beach."

"It's a tough life for faggots. I wish somebody would take the trouble to kill me."

"You don't mean that."

"It's all a crock. There's nothing worthwhile in life except being fucked."

"I know what you mean. Sometimes it's the only thing that makes you feel real."

"Hey, that's right. Who *are* you? You remind me of somebody. What did you say your name is?"

"I didn't. It's Lance Cosling."

"Never heard of you. You should go to Hollywood. A smart hustler can be a movie star. Look at Tyrone Power. I know a guy who kept him. Oh shit. I know who you are. You're Lance Vanderholden. What *is* this horseshit about a pansy hustler? You're God's gift to the working girl, if half of what they say is true."

"People change."

He looked at the girl. She'd be much prettier with less makeup. He looked at the gorgeous tits that were about to slip out of her dress. He wanted her. Why had he thought he'd never want a girl again? Robbie had expected him to go on being interested in them. That would provide variety. He didn't feel at all queer; everything was working the way it used to.

"I know who you are too," he said. "We met at a party about six years ago. I envied you because you'd broken away from your family. You were too drunk to remember."

"That hasn't changed. You really made it big. What're *you* doing here?"

"It's a long story. Accident, mostly. I've been here for over six months."

"I heard you'd been cut off by your family. I've been through that. Are you really hustling?"

"Sure."

She ran a hand up his thigh and found his erection. "As advertised. You don't feel like a faggot to me."

"You've cured me for the moment."

She uttered her raucous laughter. "Shall we see if we can make it stick?"

"That's what I have in mind. It's an emergency case." He lifted his hand for the waiter.

"Give me the bill," she said. "I said I'd buy you a drink."

"I can manage it."

"If you haven't been cured of being a hustler, the lady pays." She did so and he hurried her across the quay and into the side street where he'd left the car.

He opened the back door and they climbed in. His hands moved to her breasts as their open mouths met. She did something behind her back and hunched her shoulders and her dress fell to her waist. He drew back to look at her and ran his fingertips slowly over exquisite flesh. He'd forgotten how infinitely soft and smooth a woman's skin could be. He touched her hard nipples and drew her to him. They kissed again while she ripped his shirt open and ran her hands over his chest and abdomen.

391

She made quick work of his fly and her hands became active on his cock. She ran her tongue along it, while she pulled off his pants. She burrowed her nose in his crotch and sucked his balls. She was as aggressive as a man.

She was going to make him come if he didn't take charge. He held her shoulders, astonished by how slight they were, and lifted her, leaving her dress on the floor. He tilted her back against the window and struggled to his knees on the seat. She flung her legs around his hips and grabbed his cock and thrust it into her.

"Oh Christ. Oh Jesus, honey. Is all that cock? I don't believe it. Let me have it all. I've never felt anything like it."

Passersby glanced in at them and hurried on. He was disappointed. He'd thought a sex show would attract a nice little crowd. He lifted her in his arms and found his balance and made a final thrust into her. She flung herself about in his embrace and wailed like a cat.

He lifted her to him, got his legs out from under him and dropped onto the seat with her on his lap.

"There. You can do what you want with it."

She lowered her forehead to his shoulder and stroked his body while she rode slowly up and down on him, bearing down hard. It made his cock feel like an independent power, big and hard and deep in her. There was a lot to be said for women. Her lovely breasts swayed with her exertions. He lifted his hands under them and felt their exquisite caress on his palms. He stroked her thighs and the lips of her vagina working around his cock. Her movement accelerated and she shuddered and wailed again.

"God, it's the first good fuck in months," she gasped as she moved on him.

"I'm coming, Jilly. Oh God. This is going to be dynamite."

He shouted and his body jerked out of control. He threw his hands over his head and sprawled back in the seat, his body rocked by his spasms. She continued to move him in her and took the final throes of his orgasm. He pulled her down to him and sucked her nipples until he felt himself getting hard again.

"You better let me go, Jilly. I don't want it again here."

She lifted herself from him and he held her snuggled against him. She sighed. "I like this car. There's just room for me and your cock."

He slid the flat of his hand under it, palm down, and pushed it upright. "Look what you do to it. We're going to have trouble getting it into the hotel."

"You can hang your shirt on it." They laughed.

"Okay. Let's go."

He found his shorts on the floor. He wiped his cock with them and got into his slacks. She pulled her dress up over her legs like a man putting on trousers. They moved to the front seat and he started the car while she held his cock.

"If you're losing money on this, let me know," she said. "I can afford it. I never thought I'd buy myself a Vanderholden."

"You can give me ten dollars. That's what I have to give my pimp. I was supposed to be working tonight." He was pleased with himself. "From now on, I'm on vacation. How long are you staying?"

"I have to be in New York for Christmas."

"Well, that gives us about a week."

"We'll see. You're a body boy. I don't like body boys. I'll probably get tired of you. I always do."

"Just let me know."

He spent the night with Jill. They were making love when there was a pounding on the door.

"I told you I wouldn't get rid of him that easily," she whispered. There was a stream of Spanish curses and the pounding ceased. "He fucked me all the way down from the capital. What more does he want?"

"I guess he wants to fuck you again."

"I don't mind but I choose the time. I thought he was pretty good until you came along. Yes, honey, do that some more."

He got back to Luisa well before lunchtime and explained that he'd run into an old friend from New York and had stayed up all night talking to him. He added that he'd probably spend a lot of time with him for the next few days. He went back to the hotel after lunch to pick Jill up and encountered her man in the corridor.

393

He was in a visible rage, muttering to himself, and brushed past Lance without seeing him.

"You've had a visitor," he said when she let him in. She was beautifully naked and had obviously been drinking. She stripped him while they talked.

"You saw him? If you'd got here a little sooner, you could've watched him fuck me. It didn't seem to satisfy him. He doesn't understand me when I tell him to bug off but he gets angry anyway. If he doesn't kill me, I may kill him."

"Don't ask me to dispose of the body. I live here."

"I thought you were a friend. Come play with my tits and let me suck your cock. Then we'll get to know each other better."

They talked about their pasts. Jill had rebelled in much the same way he had, but much younger. Her foul language was part of her compulsion to shock, her sexual irregularities an effort to catch up to experiences denied her in the world she came from. He saw a lot of himself in her.

He told her about Robbie. "It's funny discovering you're a faggot. All our ideas about virility and pro-creation and the lot. I was behaving pretty badly and I wanted him to know it. I hoped he could help me straighten myself out. He left instead. I think he was right."

"How can we help behaving badly? We were taught we weren't human beings. We've had to find out. You better write him and tell him to come back."

"I'm going to. I'll wait until you go and then I'll write him that I think I can be good for him now. You could take a letter for me. He'd get it quicker. Will you call him for me and tell him I'm waiting? Don't tell him about the hustling but you can say anything you like about us."

If she could contact him in two or three days, Robbie would be back in less than a week. Lance felt it in his bones. The ghastly wait was over. He was ready. He knew now how to make things right with them. Jill had made him feel that there was nothing very daring about hustling. Her messy little sexual adventures made him see them as Robbie would—shabby and unre-warding. This was what letting himself go had led to.

"He sounds dreamy," she said. "Do you think he'll fuck me?"

"I doubt it. If he did, you'd love it. His cock is bigger than mine."

During the next few days Lance saw a great deal of Jill. He tried to go on with his work at the shed but found that he could only concentrate for a few hours each day. Sometimes he'd take her to deserted beaches where they could be naked and make love. At night, they would usually meet at the port bar and Jill would buy him dinner because they both liked the feeling that he was being kept. Then they would go back to her hotel and make love all night. Lance made it a rule that he be back home by dawn.

One night Lance looked at a handsome young man with an appraising professional eye and immediately scored. He came to the table and introduced himself as Bill and said he was a merchant seaman. He had a visible erection of adequate proportions. Jill offered him a drink and he sat with them. His determination to get Lance was so evident that she finally said, "Why don't we take him home and put him out of his misery? You want him, don't you?"

"Yes," Lance said to the sailor.

Jill drove to the hotel with Lance and Bill in the back seat locked in each other's arms. In the room she sucked Lance's cock while Bill fucked him. Later, Lance worked the sailor up to fucking her. When he was gone she stretched out with Lance's head on her breast.

"That was nice. You like being fucked as much as I do. Thanks for letting me have him too. I've always wanted to see guys doing it together. Did you wish his cock was bigger?"

"No. I don't care. It's the idea that counts."

"I didn't use to, but you've spoiled me."

"If you were in love with me would you've minded that?"

"Good heavens no. It made me wish I *were* in love with you. I like having you around. We could have guys together. That nice-looking room boy, for instance. Have you noticed him? He fucked me this morning. I was in bed naked and he came in and took his clothes off and fucked me. His cock was bigger than Bill's, but I liked it better just now with you here."

"You're not getting tired of me?"

"No. It's amazing. It can't be entirely because of your cock but that's a big part of it. A *very* big part of it. Especially right now."

"I'm going to fuck you. Maybe the room boy will come back."

Jill reported later that he'd turned up after Lance had left that morning. "I didn't appreciate him the first time. He was just getting warmed up. There were some real fireworks today. If we leave you out of it, his cock is fairly sensational. He made me come. I wish you'd been here."

"He probably watched for me to go. The people here have their own ideas about what's correct."

Her week was drawing to a close. There were only a couple of nights left unless she suddenly decided that she didn't have to get to New York for Christmas after all.

"I'm going to miss you, Jilly," he told her when they were lying naked on the beach. "A lot. I've got to write that letter for you to take. I'd better drive you to the capital. The bus is hell. It's only four or five hours. With time out for sex, call it an easy day's drive. I'll spend the night with you and take you to the plane."

"I wouldn't be surprised if Alfonso turns up again to do the honors."

"The hell with Alfonso, if that's his name. I want to take you. I ought to spend some time with Luisa so she won't feel abandoned. I'll have an early dinner with her this evening and meet you at the port at nine. I can have a glass of something and watch you eat."

"That's good. That'll give me some time for Mike."

"Who's Mike?"

"My room boy. I think he said his name is Miguel but I call him Mike. He said he wanted to see me late this afternoon. Something to do with his working hours. At least he speaks enough English for us to have a vague idea what we're saying. He's getting as bossy as Alfonso. The men here are spoiled rotten. They act as if women were put on earth to serve them. Mike comes in now and lies down and tells me to take his clothes off. I haven't refused but he looks as if he'd beat me up if I did. It's rather exciting. I like a little caveman stuff."

Lance told Luisa when they were eating that evening

that he might drive to the capital in the next day or two. His friend was leaving and had hated the bus coming down. He would go up one day and come back the next.

Luisa received the news in silence, her eyes round and unseeing, her face composed. She was devoured by fears. She knew his friend wasn't a man. If he went away with her, he would never come back. She had known she couldn't keep him without Robbie. She prayed for his sudden reappearance. Only Robbie could stop him from doing something terrible.

"What's the matter, little one?"

"Nothing. Do you know when Robbie is coming back?"

"Soon. In about a week, I think."

He had never known anything so wonderful as the rush of joy that swept through him at being able to say it. Robbie would get his letter the day after Christmas. He might need a few days to finish off whatever he was doing but he'd ask him to send a telegram so he'd have a date to cling to. Life was going to make sense again.

Luisa remained still and thoughtful for the rest of the meal. Fears gnawed at her. A week wasn't soon enough. She had to do something. If she pretended that there was something wrong with her he might not go. She could say that the baby was suddenly giving her strange pains. It might take a week for a doctor to decide that she was all right. She had to think.

Jill arrived half an hour late that evening, which she considered prompt. Her eyes were shining.

"I've had the most frightful row," she announced with satisfaction. "I told you Alfonso would turn up again. He came barging in when Mike was there. We were naked and poor Mike had a lovely hard-on. I think it drove Alfonso wild to see that it was bigger than his. It was pretty dumb of Mike not to lock the door. Alfonso managed to throw him out. He kept shouting *mañana* at me. I think he expects to take me away tomorrow."

"Did they hit each other?"

"Just sort of pushed each other around."

"They take that sort of thing seriously here. Somebody's honor has probably been sullied. Be careful. You better not have anything more to do with either of them. I'm taking you to the capital day after tomorrow. You don't have to bother with Alfonso."

"You're the boss, honey."

"I just don't want you to get hurt."

He left her earlier than usual, having agreed to take her to the beach during the day but to eat with Luisa again in the evening as part of his predeparture effort to make her feel cared for.

When he got home he found her room empty. He shrugged as he went on to his bed. She was probably upset by being left alone in the house at night so often but it wouldn't be for much longer. When Jill was off his hands, he would stay home with her until Robbie returned so that he would find a peaceful household to come home to.

He found her going about her chores in the morning. She looked normal, if slightly preoccupied and withdrawn. He didn't tell her that he was definitely going to the capital the next day but he referred to it again as a possibility. He said that he would decide with his friend that evening and warned her that he might stay out late for a last-night celebration. She nodded solemnly.

His date with Jill that evening was for nine o'clock and he'd told her on the beach that she could expect some caveman stuff from him if she kept him waiting again. She wasn't there. He sat alone with a drink and wondered if she was with Mike. A half hour passed and he thought of going to look for her at the hotel but was afraid of missing her in the streets. He decided to give her another half hour.

Jill didn't show up. It occurred to him that Alfonso might've come along and dragged her away with him. He felt unkind for almost hoping he had, but the drive to the capital didn't sound like fun. He'd rather stay at home and wait for Robbie's telegram. Then he remembered that there would be no telegram if Jill didn't take his letter. He had to find her.

He parked in front of the hotel. The bars on the square looked busy but he didn't expect to find her at one of them. He went into the bleak hotel lobby. He supposed she might have left a message for him but there was no one visible at the desk and he decided to find out as much as he could for himself. If she wasn't in her room he would at least see if her things were still there. He didn't trust the night clerk to provide reliable information about the guests. He'd been in and out of here dozens of times for the last few weeks without encountering any hotel staff. If she hadn't left her room, the clerk wouldn't know anything about her anyway. He suspected that a drinking bout was the most likely explanation for her failure to appear.

When he reached her door, he paused to make sure that there were no voices raised in anger, nor wails of passion issuing from within. Nothing. He knocked lightly. There was no reply. He tried the handle of the door. It opened. He pushed it open wider and looked in. Light from the hall fell across the foot of the bed. Her sleeping form was in shadow. It was as he'd expected. Passed out. He'd wake her enough to try to make her understand that he'd be back for her in the morning and then go home.

He entered the room and closed the door behind him. He waited for his eyes to get accustomed to the dark, then moved toward the bed. He made out what had to be her foot but he couldn't see whether or not she was naked. He leaned over and gave the foot a little shake. "Jilly," he said quietly.

She didn't move. He edged around the side of the bed and leaned forward, trying to find her shoulder to shake. It wasn't where he expected it to be. He lifted his knee to steady himself, but it slid moistly out from under him. He almost toppled over onto her. His hand struck motionless flesh. He struggled to recover his balance. He was on his feet again, rooted to the spot. His scalp tightened. A chill ran down his spine. He felt paralyzed but somehow wrenched the door open and hurtled silently down the corridor. His heart was leaping about erratically in his chest. He mustn't let himself be found here.

Quick images from the catastrophe with Scot flashed through his mind. The hospital. The police. He couldn't go through anything like that again. He slowed to a brisk walk as he reached the lobby. He shot a quick glance toward the desk. There was nobody in sight. He veered off toward the door. As soon as he was outside, he would be able to think. She might have had some sort of attack. She might need help.

Who would get help except him? His eye was caught by a dark stain on his trouserleg. It looked black in the muted light. His blood ran cold and he stopped abruptly. She needed help urgently. He turned slowly, knowing as he did so that life as he wanted to live it was over for him, and ran back to the desk calling, *"Señor! Señor!"* into the strangely wide-awake face of the clerk.

Lance sat across from Ramiriz at the desk in the police office. It had been going on for hours. Policemen in slovenly uniforms came and went. The phone rang constantly. Ramiriz took notes and made maddeningly laconic replies, so that Lance had no way of knowing what was going on. The chief wasn't in uniform. His battered hat was pushed onto the back of his head. Lance yawned. The shock was wearing off. There had been a few minutes of horror and then the endless grinding of official machinery had been set in motion. He hoped he'd be allowed to leave soon. He wanted to get home before Luisa heard about it. The telephone rang again.

Ramiriz hung up and sighed and kneaded the rolls of flesh under his chin. He moved papers around on the desk. He brought his hands down flat on them and looked at Lance.

"Very well. What have we? The autopsy is without surprises. The cause of death is obvious. You saw the body. It took place between eight and eight-thirty. She had intercourse shortly before."

"I've told you. I didn't see her after five. When you say shortly, do you mean just before?"

"The experts can tell us but I think it's of no great interest. A man does not kill a woman just after intercourse unless it is rape. You saw her. She looked astonished as the dead often do, but not frightened or angry. There were no signs of struggle. You say that she spoke of seeing only two men, the one you met called Alfonso and the employee of the hotel she called Mike. We have found Miguel. He claims to have had nothing to do with her, which is natural but rather foolish if the man called Alfonso confirms her story about his finding them naked together. People at the hotel say they saw her with a man who fits your description of Alfonso but it could be a description of half the men in the capital. I think we will not see Alfonso again unless somebody remembers something more helpful about him."

"Start at the nightclub where she was working," Lance suggested, trying to make his weary mind think. "Somebody there probably knows who brought her down here."

Ramiriz made a note and nodded at him. "You see why I need your help. You knew her. You think of her as more than just a body found in a hotel room. You may remember some chance remark that might throw some light on this unfortunate business."

"I thought of the nightclub because she said she'd met Alfonso with a friend who acted as her interpreter. Obviously, somebody who speaks English and Spanish."

"Excellent. We may find Alfonso easily but there remains the tiresome question of motive."

"You know better than I, but if two men are having the same woman wouldn't they feel that their honor was at stake?"

"Very possibly but in that case I would expect one of them to kill the other, not the woman. I know my people, as you say. If we look at it simply, there is only one person who has reason to wish Miss Longstreth dead. Your woman Luisa."

"Don't be ridiculous," Lance said, snapping upright in his chair.

"Oh, I do not mean that she did the thing herself. Killing is not woman's work. We have our own ways in such matters. She saw her family last night or the night before." He picked up a sheet of paper and dropped it with a shrug. "No matter. It is the family's obligation to protect a young woman's honor. You have seen a great deal of Miss Longstreth since she has been here."

"Luisa had no way of knowing that. I told her I was seeing a friend, a man."

"You are very innocent, friend. We all know everything we want to know about each other here but we interpret things in the simple ways we understand. Your woman knows that you are seeing Miss Longstreth and wishes her dead. That we can understand. At least two other men were enjoying her favors but that is no reason to kill her. We may enjoy loose women but we do not kill them. They are beneath our notice. You foreigners force us to look at things in ways we do not understand. Why, we must ask ourselves, would you kill Miss Longstreth?"

"That would be a hard question to answer," Lance said, accepting it as part of police routine. Everybody was a suspect. Even if he wasn't suspected by the police, he knew he'd be tried by the newspapers as soon as they had the story. "You'd also have to ask why I made myself so easy to catch. I found Miss Longstreth. I could've got out of the hotel without being seen. I knew there was something the matter with her but hoped something could be done for her. I immediately told the clerk to get a doctor and contact you."

"Immediately? The clerk says that he saw you coming in from the street."

"I've explained that. I was rattled. I didn't think where I was going until I saw the doors in front of me and realized I was going in the wrong direction. The fact remains, I told the clerk to do something."

"Considering the time she was killed it makes little sense for you to be there unless you had just discovered the body or wished us to believe you had."

Ramiriz nodded at his desk and heaved himself back in his chair. He lifted his hat and ran a hand through his thick black hair and put it on again. He gazed at some point above Lance's head.

"I've seen photographs of you taken in shameful circumstances. Do you know them?"

"Yes."

His cheeks were burning. He forced himself to keep his head up and his eyes on the policeman but his stomach contracted with guilt and self-disgust. He should have known it would all come out. At least the pictures were too bad for any newspaper to publish.

"For those who admire men's bodies, yours has much to admire. I know you sell it to male tourists," Ramiriz continued impersonally. "What will a court make of you and those photographs? I am not a lawyer but I can imagine. Here is a man who is capable of any sexual excess. A sex-obsessed woman loses her head over you. She makes demands you have no wish to satisfy. She taunts you for your lack of virility. No man can accept that easily. You kill her in a sexual rage. For lack of anybody with stronger motives, you are obviously guilty. You were there."

"When? When is this supposed to have happened?"

"Between eight and eight-thirty, when it did happen."

"But I wasn't there then. I didn't leave the house until almost nine. Luisa will tell you."

"Luisa lives with you. Her testimony will not be considered seriously. And how easy it is to make a mistake of half an hour."

"I was at the Bar del Puerto or whatever it's called from nine till I went to the hotel. About ten-thirty. The waiter can tell you. He knew I was waiting for Jill— Miss Longstreth."

"It is very clever. You kill her after you leave your house. You go show yourself and establish the fact with the waiter that you are waiting for a woman who is already dead. Somebody else might find her, which would be even better for you. After you have waited a reasonable time, you go look for her. An innocent man couldn't have a better alibi."

"It would've taken a hell of a lot of nerve. I could never've done it."

"Is—was Miss Longstreth very well known in your country?"

"After what's happened, the press will invent a lurid past for her to make a good story. A torrid torch singer. The daughter of a vastly wealthy and aristocratic family. Everything they like best, with me thrown in."

"Yes, I see. There have been many calls from news services. I think there will be a dozen or more reporters here tomorrow. Later today in fact. We must be ready for them." The telephone rang. Ramiriz answered with laconic phrases. He looked at Lance, nodded, and hung up. "You are accustomed to dealing with reporters," he said.

"I've told you how much I've tried to avoid publicity." Lance passed a hand over his eyes and rubbed his forehead. "Can't you help me? I knew what was going to happen the minute I found her. I knew I was done for. Do you have to bring me into it? If I'd known she was dead, I could've got away. That may sound cold-blooded but it would've been insane not to. There's a door in back. I couldn't leave her when I thought she could be

403

helped. Do I have to be punished for that? The only important fact is that she was killed. Does it matter who found her? She was found in the ordinary course of events. You're working on the case. What else does the press have to know? If you have to say who found her, can't you give the name I've used here, Cosling?"

Ramiriz sighed and crumpled up his face with his hands like a washcloth. He didn't understand the rich. Ramiriz had known the family was important but he was discovering for the first time tonight how overwhelmingly important it was. He had thought the rich were hard and overbearing but this young man was quite extraordinarily innocent. He expected to be believed simply because he said he was speaking the truth. He was in very serious trouble but he turned for help to the man least likely to offer it, asking him to collaborate on an absurd fiction.

"Your name had to be given when your embassy was notified. I think there are those who wish your name to figure very prominently. I could catch the murderer but even if I did in the next few days, which I think I can do—a week at the most—would it not be too late? Your involvement would be widely known. Why do you fear publicity so much?"

"You don't understand. It makes it impossible for me to live any sort of ordinary life. If the papers get going on this, I might as well have killed her. As far as everybody is concerned, I'll be a murderer. Before I came here, I was involved in an automobile accident and they made me look like a criminal for that. I'll have to go somewhere and start all over again. Can't you please use Cosling?"

"I will do what is permitted. I am waiting for a call with instructions. I am sorry. You are well liked by the people here. I do not think you are a bad man. But I remember thinking when you first came here that you might bring trouble with you."

"That's just it. I always do, just because I can't be what others expect me to be. I do things that lots of people would think are bad but that's not what causes the trouble: not being able to do ordinary things, like reporting an accident or, as it turned out, a murder to the police, without its becoming a major event that makes everything impossible. Unless you think I committed the murder, I don't see why you can't call me Cosling."

"What I think is unimportant. I tell you, it is impossible to use false names in official business. Tell your embassy to call you Cosling."

"Yes, I'm being foolish. Maybe for once they won't be interested in who found her. Will you call Don Antonio for me?"

"At this hour? Never mind. He is already dealing with the matter at the highest level."

"I see. Well, I've got to go. I've got to see Luisa. I want her to understand that I'm sorry and horrified about the girl, but that she wasn't of great importance to me."

"You have been very help—"

The telephone rang as Ramiriz finished the word. He picked it up, said *"si,"* and listened. He listened for a long time adding an occasional *si* while the silence gathered around them. He hung up and scrawled some notes on a sheet of paper. He kneaded the rolls of fat under his chin and leaned forward and banged on a bell like the bells on hotel counters used to summon bellboys.

"I must place you under arrest," he said.

Lance's hands clenched convulsively into fists. The muscles of his face seemed to set into a frozen mask. His heart stopped for a beat while he told himself that he would have to stay here till morning. Being arrested would be good for a headline but there was no shortage of material for those. He was finally locked into his name; he would no longer be able to dream of escaping it. It was all over. Making it as easy as possible for Luisa and her unborn child was his first responsibility now.

"Arrested for what?" Lance asked.

"For murder, of course," Ramiriz said without looking at him. A policeman slouched into the room, straightening his clothes. Ramiriz issued a rapid stream of orders.

To his surprise, Lance was more curious than anything else. What was going to happen to him now? Probably nothing he couldn't face. The newspapers would have a field day with him but he'd been resigned to that for the last few hours. He had come to the end of the road he had chosen to follow. He no longer had to drive himself; there was nowhere else for him to go. He stretched his legs out in front of him and looked at the stain on his trouserleg. It had turned a dirty dark brown.

"Will you please tell Luisa to come see me?"

Ramiriz glanced at his notes. "I will see her and tell her what you've said about her. I can't let her see you."

"What's that supposed to mean?"

Ramiriz contemplated the top of his scarred desk. He didn't like the way this case was developing. He was being thwarted from applying his professional skills to solving what he suspected was a very simple murder for revenge. He sighed and lifted his eyes to the young man opposite him. Lance's aloof calm was impressive. He supposed that the supremely rich couldn't feel threatened like ordinary mortals. This was turning into a rich man's game. Since he didn't know how to play it, he was going to have to be careful not to take his usual small initiatives to make the law work comfortably. He shrugged and looked at the ceiling.

"My orders are that you are to have no contact with anybody."

"What about messages, letters?"

"That too. No contact of any sort."

"A lawyer?"

"Presumably you will be allowed a lawyer when formal charges are made."

"I see. I'm just going to be put away without any formalities at all. It's a great little legal system you have here."

Ramiriz shrugged with embarrassment. "It has a certain amount of flexibility. You will be allowed to see the press."

"Why should I want to see the press? I refuse to see the press."

"You will be obliged to see the press. It's very important for you to be seen and photographed."

"Important to whom?"

"To those who are interested in your case. You probably understand their interest better than I do."

Lance thought of Don Antonio's plan to extort money from his mother. "What if I expose the way I'm being treated?"

"I do not think that will worry anybody. You may

speak freely. The censor will not pass anything that is damaging to the government."

"You have to get arrested to understand a country. Thanks for telling me how matters stand."

"You must be patient. If you are formally charged and tried, you will probably be heavily sentenced for appearances' sake, but quickly released and deported as soon as the case is forgotten. I think it is hoped that a trial can be avoided. I can tell you no more."

Lance had trouble swallowing; his mouth was dry. His attempt at bravado had failed. He felt utterly drained, his spirit suddenly broken, but some irrational unidentifiable ray of hope remained. He even found bleak comfort in knowing that they wouldn't tell him if Robbie was here. He could believe that he was, even if he weren't. When he was sure that he could speak, he said, "Do you know that Luisa is having my child?"

"Yes. It is unfortunate. It is easy to say that you should have thought of that before you became intimate with Miss Longstreth but young men cannot be expected to think of everything. Her husband will surely do everything necessary for her."

"I'm sure he will," Lance said listlessly but with conviction.

"You can go with this man now. I will be busy for the next few days. I will send for you when it is time for you to see the press. I will see Luisa and ask her to get some things you might need."

With an effort he felt hardly capable of, Lance pulled himself to his feet. The uniformed policeman moved in beside him and led him to the door. They went out into a guardroom where policemen were sprawled on wooden benches. Lance forced himself to carry his head high and didn't look at them. They went through another door into a corridor that led to a barred gate. The policeman banged on the bars with what Lance saw was a pair of handcuffs. If they had been meant for him, Ramiriz had spared him.

A hulk of a man shambled toward them, wearing the usual local pajama costume. He unlocked the gate, motioned for Lance to enter, and locked the gate behind him. The two men exchanged a few words and the guard who was now in charge of him took his arm and headed him along a wider corridor, into another part of the building. The floor was stone, worn and uneven. It was dimly lighted and smelled of wet rock and urine. They passed empty cells with open barred gates. They came to a right-angle turn that led to a dead end ahead of them. As if waiting to be out of sight, the guard moved in behind him and squeezed his buttocks and ran his fingers between them. Lance looked at the guard. He leered at him with a mouth full of broken and discolored teeth. Maybe he was a friend of José.

Everything had a sort of ghastly logic. He had wanted to come to grips with all the harsh and ugly aspects of life. He had become the property of the state. The state's servants probably had the right to handle him. Maybe this was what life was going to be like for the next year or longer. He might as well adjust to it as quickly as possible.

At the end of the corridor, the guard pushed him through a doorway and pulled a barred gate closed behind them and locked it. They were in a big cell with three-tiered tubular frames holding bunks against two walls. A barred opening framed a square of sky high up on a third wall. A dim bulb hung from the ceiling. It was suffocatingly hot. It felt as if the heat of centuries had been imprisoned here.

"Take your clothes off," the guard ordered him. A hand was moving over the front of his loose pants, shaping his erection.

Lance obeyed. Despite his exhaustion, his own erection sprang out when he uncovered it. It helped, being a pro; he knew by now that it excited him to strip for anybody who wanted him. He went to a lower bunk and lay down on his stomach. The guard climbed over him and entered him. He smelled of stale sweat and sour breath. Lance was able to lift his hips sufficiently to jerk himself off over the edge of the bunk. He hoped it would help him sleep. When the guard was finished he pulled out of him without a word. Lance had been assigned a role in prison life.

He heard the rusty grating of the lock, the creak of the hinges as the gate swung open and clanged shut. The lock grated again and the shuffling footsteps receded. He was too tired to move. He didn't want to think. He lay on the rough pallet in a gathering pool of sweat and tried to sleep.

* * *

He was awakened by the clang of the gate. He supposed he hadn't been sleeping heavily because he didn't have an agreeable moment of confusion about where he was; he was immediately confronted with the leaden reality. A guard locked himself into the cell with him. He looked less forbidding than the other one, more ordinary and considerably younger. Lance rolled over onto his stomach to hide his morning erection. The guard took it as an invitation. Lance heard the scraping of metal on stone and then the guard drove into him. He took more notice of him than the other one had. He felt his body with interest and seemed to measure his cock with his hand. He jerked him off while he fucked him. In a moment, the guard slid out of him. He was a new convenience that had been added to the prison's minimal facilities. He sat up and dropped his feet onto the floor. The guard brought him a metal mug of thin tepid bean soup.

"The toilet?" Lance asked.

The guard carried a bucket of water across the cell and put it down beside a hole in the floor under the window. He turned to Lance.

"You shout if you want anything." He bunched up the front of his pants in his hand and laughed. "Maybe you'll want this." He locked Lance in and went off along the corridor.

Lance looked up at the window and drank his watery soup. He could see the tattered fronds of a palm tree and, above, a vulture slowly circling in the sky. This was what it was like to hit bottom—boring and uncomfortable but not frightening. He looked at the bucket sitting beside the hole in the floor and wondered how long it had been since a Vanderholden had had to squat.

A few months ago, he wouldn't have been able to look at Jill to identify her without collapsing. Granted, he'd barely glanced at her for only a second but that had been horrifying enough. It was sad that she'd faded so quickly into a nightmare moment but he couldn't let himself dwell on the pleasure she'd given him for a week. He was still alive and in bad trouble because of her. He had to concentrate on whether there was any way of getting out of it.

Concentrating led nowhere. He could do nothing to

409

affect the outcome and knew that no decisions would be made until Don Antonio and his colleagues at "the highest level" had had time to mount their campaign to derive some profit from his plight, a campaign doubtless to involve his mother.

He splashed himself with water from time to time. He considered using the hole in the floor, then realized that something was missing. He went to the bars and shouted. Eventually, he heard the slap of footsteps and the guard appeared. He asked for paper, pointing at the hole. The guard looked blank and then a light of comprehension dawned. After some time, he returned with a few pieces of torn newspaper.

He didn't know how many hours had passed when Ramiriz arrived. He let himself in and didn't bother to close the gate behind him. He was carrying a suitcase that Lance recognized as one of Robbie's. He was in uniform, his bulky body looking as unkempt as usual. "The reporters have arrived," he announced, putting down the suitcase with a sigh.

"What time is it?"

"Not yet noon. They must have started very early. More than a dozen of them."

"Have you found the murderer?"

"Possibly, but I do not think anybody is interested. Here are your clothes."

He hadn't been able to bring himself to put the stained slacks on again and it was too hot to bother anyway. He put the suitcase on one of the bunks and opened it. He was pleased to find a sarong on the top. He saw a couple of towels, his toilet case, and some toilet paper. Ramiriz must have given Luisa an idea about his accommodations. He wrapped the sarong around himself.

"Is there any news?"

"They were anxious in the capital to get the reporters here. They were going to be flown down but the plane wasn't ready and they didn't want to wait. A plane is on the way now to take them back, as many as it will hold. I have told them they will see you in about half an hour. There were other people they wanted to see."

"Can you get me some hot water to shave with? That's all. Wait a minute. Can you get me a bottle of rum? I need a drink."

"If you keep it out of sight and don't let my men have

410

any. I'll let you know when the press people come back."
He went, locking the gate after him.

The guard was back quite quickly with a mug of hot
water and a plate of beans. Lance polished off the beans
and shaved. He wanted to make a good impression.
Photographers could make anybody look like a criminal
if you weren't careful how you carried yourself. He
wanted to minimize his importance in the case so that
the papers might be careful about how they handled it.

He threw the sarong onto a bunk and poured water
from the bucket over himself, using the soap Luisa had
sent. Ramiriz returned while he was drying himself,
carrying a bottle wrapped in newspaper. Lance hitched
the towel around himself. He thanked the chief for the
bottle and pulled out the drawn cork and took a generous swig from it. He shook his head and felt the glow
of it spread through him. He didn't need it for the reporters. He needed it to get him through the rest of the
day. He offered it to Ramiriz.

"Thanks. I'm not used to seeing newspapermen." He
drank and wiped the mouth of the bottle on his sleeve
before returning it. "Some of them are back. They say
the others will be here in five or ten minutes. We can
go when you are dressed."

Lance took another drink and wrapped it in his soiled
shirt and tucked it into the bottom of the suitcase. He
threw the stained slacks into a corner of the cell and
put on a fresh shirt and cotton trousers. He combed his
hair and was ready. Ramiriz nodded and they left the
cell together.

A policeman was waiting to let them out the outer
gate. There was a stir as they entered the guardroom.
Flashbulbs popped. Everybody began to talk at once.
Lance was careful to keep his head up and stood for a
minute in a relaxed position while cameras clicked
around him. Ramiriz kept his hands off him and remained a few feet from him. It was clear that he was
under no restraints.

The chief led him to a platform at one side of the
room with a desk on it. It looked like an informal mag-
istrate's dais where the day's bag of troublemakers might
be heard. Ramiriz seated himself behind the desk and
signaled to Lance to join him. He advanced through the
little knot of jostling men with a slight smile, spotting

411

a few compatriots but seeing that most of them were Latins. He saw a film camera pointing at him. He stepped up onto the low platform and stood facing them. Flashbulbs popped again. He heard the film camera whirring. He'd be a film star yet. A microphone was thrust into his hands. Quiet settled over the room.

"How does it feel to be arrested so soon after the last time? Are you beginning to wonder if there's something wrong with the way you live?" It was one of the Americans. Lance recognized the tone of mocking hostility. It was the way they'd spoken to him before.

"I've never been arrested," he said reasonably. "If you're referring to the car crash last spring, you can check your files. I was questioned by the police to establish the facts and that was the end of my involvement except for a strictly personal one. I'm not sure I've been arrested this time. Being held pending further investigation. I've sure as hell been locked up without any legal procedure. They say I can have a lawyer if and when I'm formally charged but I don't have a lawyer now. That's a point you might make when you're writing your stories."

The questions began in earnest. They wanted to know about Jill and his relationship with her and why he'd been in her hotel room last night.

"I assume you know about her career," he said. "I knew her slightly in New York several years ago. I naturally saw quite a lot of her when we ran into each other here. I had a date with her last night. When she didn't show up, I went to look for her. In New York, I'd have called her hotel and asked for her but things don't work like that here. For one thing, the hotel clerk is usually asleep. Her door was unlocked. The light was off but I could see her lying on the bed. When I spoke to her she didn't answer so I thought she might be sick and ran to get a doctor. That's all there was to it."

"You didn't think she was asleep? Did you speak loud enough to wake her up?"

"Yes. I went quite close to her. There was something about her that worried me. She was too quiet. Something was wrong." He didn't want to arouse his memory. If he did, it might affect him in ways that the photographers could make something of.

"I understand she had some very nasty knife wounds. Didn't you—"

"I'm not going to talk about that," Lance broke in. "The police can tell you anything you want to know. I didn't see anything in the dark."

Mercifully, the questioning moved on. The Americans had done their homework. They wanted to know about Robbie and Luisa and his pottery works. They knew about the success of his gollies in the States. His cover as Lance Cosling was blown. He told them that he and Robbie were business partners and reminded them that Robbie was the distinguished painter Robi. His friend had taken a house where he worked but he liked a change of scene at night. Luisa and he had offered to let him stay with them.

"Would you call it *ménage à trois?*" one of the Americans asked.

Lance could see where this was leading. "Strictly speaking, I suppose three people living in the same house is a *ménage à trois* but if you and your wife had a friend come stay with you, I suppose you'd say you had a friend staying with you."

"Did you refer to this girl as your wife? She's pregnant. Are you married?"

"If you know as much about me as you seem to, you know we're not. I have a wife and two children in New York. We're separated but not divorced, because she doesn't want it. She's a Catholic and devout. If you left your wife and couldn't get a divorce, what would you do?"

"I guess I'd settle that before I left her. We can't all do whatever we feel like doing. Where's Mr. Cosling?"

"What's he got to do with it? He left for New York on business about a month ago. If you want to see him, I can't stop you. He may be out of town for Christmas but he shouldn't be difficult to find." Why should Robbie let himself get mixed up in this sort of thing? He'd had a month to get used to being without him. After this, he'd probably be thanking his lucky stars that he'd left. Even if a sense of obligation brought him back, he should tell him to forget him. He'd always brought trouble to everybody who cared about him and always would.

"Did you kill Miss Longstreth?" one of the Latins

413

asked. The room exploded with laughter. Lance couldn't help joining in. Flashbulbs popped.

Lance sobered with an effort. "I'm sorry. We shouldn't be laughing. I guess that's the only question that's really to the point. The answer is no. I don't think anybody seriously thinks I did. I can account for my movements last night down to within minutes. I couldn't've killed her even if I'd had some reason. She became a dear friend while she was here. You can imagine how I feel. I'm doing everything possible to cooperate with the police. Is there anything else I can tell you?"

There was a murmur of consultation and one of the Americans asked a final question. "Have you been in touch with your mother about this?"

"My mother? Why should I be? My mother and I disagree about almost everything. She wouldn't like my being involved in a murder any more than I do but she'd probably think I was guilty." He couldn't resist the flippant note. He hoped he'd be quoted and that his mother would see it. It might help her make up her mind against intervening on his behalf. If he wasn't allowed to get through this on his own, he'd be neutralized for the rest of his life.

The reporters began milling about, talking among themselves. One of them relieved Lance of the microphone. Lance stepped down from the platform and pushed his way past the little crowd and went to the outer gate. His guard was waiting on the other side of it. A policeman opened it and he went through, headed back to his cell with the guard at his heels.

He wanted a drink. He wanted several drinks. It hadn't been too bad, but when he thought of the tone of the questions and what would be made of the story, his stomach churned with outrage and despair. The newspapers weren't finished with him; they would stay with him to the end. If Robbie were here, he'd be soiled by them too. He was too decent, his talent too important to be subjected to the sort of squalid publicity that might be focused on a Vanderholden at any moment, no matter where he was. Robbie had almost convinced him that they could lead reasonable lives dedicated to each other but he'd been wrong. A great love was a luxury that could be bought only with privacy. It had no place in the real world he had to learn to live in.

414

The guard opened the gate for him and locked him in. Lance pulled off his clothes, retaining only his jockey shorts, and threw them onto a bunk. He doubted if it was even one o'clock yet. Time was the enemy. He counted on rum as his familiar ally. He eyed the bottle. Enough to put him to sleep.

He was awakened by somebody taking him. The dim bulb was burning overhead so he supposed it was night. He saw his jockey shorts on the floor. It was exciting to think of being stripped and taken while he slept. The rocking rhythm of copulation plunged him into unconsciousness again.

When he was awake, he put on his jockey shorts and shouted for the guard. A plate of beans was on the floor. He ate the tepid mess and heard the slap of approaching footsteps. He handed the guard his empty plate and asked him to tell Ramiriz that he wanted to see him. His bottle was empty.

He sat on the floor with his back to the flaking wall and studied how his foot worked. He could stretch and wiggle his toes in all sorts of interesting ways. His mother always maintained that a shapely foot was a sign of breeding. He supposed his was quite shapely as feet went. He heard Ramiriz's heavy tread approaching from what seemed a great distance. When the chief finally lumbered into the cell, Lance pulled himself to his feet.

"Any news?" he asked.

"Nothing."

"Have you any idea how long it'll take the highest levels to make up their minds?" He went to his suitcase for the empty bottle.

"I believe they are very well pleased with the results of your talk with the reporters yesterday. I am told there are big headlines and photographs in all the North American newspapers. Here too, of course, but the others are the ones that count."

"What do the headlines say?"

"That you have been arrested for murder. You are more famous in North America than anybody knew."

"Even more so now, I guess. Aren't you going to have to make a formal charge?"

"I think it will be a few more days before a decision is made."

"What if I insist on my rights? I should think the embassy would have to take steps."

"With a case that the press is watching we must be careful of legality, of course. Some of the reporters have stayed. The law permits us to wait a week."

"A week? Well, that gives us a time limit, anyway." He handed Ramiriz the bottle. "You might as well bring several. I won't give the guards any."

"I will inform you whenever I know anything of interest to you." Ramiriz locked the gate behind him. Within minutes, Lance heard his footsteps returning. The police chief handed him two bottles through the bars. "I'll bring more tomorrow," he said.

The matter-of-fact way in which he said it made Lance feel as if he would be here forever. It was up to him to make tomorrow come. He poured a hefty drink into the mug and took a long swallow. His stomach turned over but he knew the second swallow would start the slide into oblivion. He took off his shorts. He was more comfortable without them and it would save the guards the trouble of taking them off. He wondered if any of them had had him while he was asleep. He sat on the edge of the bunk and tried not to watch the circling vulture. Round and round. Watching it made every minute an eternity. So far, he knew that they were only playing at his being a prisoner. If he were sentenced and really imprisoned, he wouldn't be given a cell all to himself. He wouldn't have a friendly police chief to bring him rum.

He conjured up all the guys he'd had sex with, starting with the masseur. Not counting the ones who'd paid, who were mostly faceless, he couldn't get up to twenty. He tried to recreate the particular sensations he'd experienced with each one of them but they all blended into Robbie except Jim the masseur, the first one, who remained memorable for having been so unexpected. He could still feel the skillful professional hands on him working seductively toward their goal. His drinks were beginning to make his mind blur but thinking of Jim gave him an erection. It filled his hand reassuringly. He lay back on the bunk, propped up on one elbow, and shouted for the guard. He began to masturbate slowly.

The guard appeared, the one who liked to feel his

body. He entered the cell and locked himself in. Lance rolled over onto his stomach, filled with defiant satisfaction at exposing himself so blatantly and making no attempt to disguise his contemptible desires. This was the gutter. He wasn't exactly wallowing in it; it was his natural habitat.

He woke up with the light on and ate the plate of rice with bits of fish that he found on the floor just inside the bars. He almost fell over trying to pick it up. He spilled rum into his mug and wandered around the cell, bumping into the walls and trying to remember how long he'd been there. He used the hole in the floor, amazed at how much more comfortable it was than more civilized arrangements. He had a feeling that he ought to be thinking about something but he didn't know what.

He awoke again lying on the floor with the sound of church bells pealing in his ears. He struggled to his feet, every joint aching, and stumbled to the rank of bunks where he'd left the almost empty bottle. The full one was still comfortingly in his suitcase. Robbie's suitcase. He ran a hand over it and was shocked to find tears misting his eyes. He was tough. He wasn't supposed to feel anything anymore. Sobriety led to despair.

With a drink and the mug of bean soup that had been left at the door, he managed to get himself functioning again. As the pealing of the bells continued, it slowly dawned on him that it was Christmas. Tidings of comfort and joy. Merry Christmas to all. He had another drink to celebrate and decided to try to bribe the guard when he appeared with a plate of rice.

"Do you know where I live?" he asked.

"Everybody knows now."

"Go there. See my woman. Ask if our friend is here. Our friend. He lives with us. Will you do that?" He emptied the pockets of the slacks that had been lying in the corner for several days and showed him a generous present. The guard looked at it for a long moment and pocketed it quickly.

"I will let you know," he said.

He woke up with the light on, in daylight. He heard Ramiriz approaching and wrapped the sarong around himself. He was shy with the chief because of the doctor's photographs.

417

"It is not good to bribe the guards," he said, looking over Lance's shoulder. "They will take your money but come to me. They will tell you whatever you wish them to tell you but it will not be the truth. They have all been warned that they will lose their jobs if they disobey me. They think I have eyes in the back of my head."

"What difference does it make for me to know whether or not my friend has come back?"

"It has been decided that you must not have contact with the outside. I told you. I will tell you whatever I wish you to know. If you make trouble, I will have to be more strict with you."

"All right. Forget it. It doesn't matter. Nothing matters."

Despair gripped him. The longing to know if Robbie was here was a momentary weakness. He should be hoping for him not to come, not clutching at the straw of comfort that his being here would represent. He could adjust to anything bad that happened to him. It was only the good things that threw him off balance.

The bottles were his calendar. He had a rough idea that he was drinking a little less than one a day. When he started on his fifth, he knew that the week must be almost over. He stank. He was going to have to shave soon simply because it was too hot to grow a beard.

Ramiriz paid him one of his regular visits, bringing another bottle. Maybe the week was over. He left the gate open and stood under the window looking at some partially obliterated graffiti that had been scratched on the flaking whitewash of the wall. He turned to Lance, thinking how shockingly he had disintegrated. He had turned into an animal. The rich had no strength to resist adversity. "Your mother is coming," he announced, wondering if it would help him to pull himself together.

Lance slowly finished tucking the bottle out of sight in the suitcase. He didn't feel much of anything. Some slight relief at something happening, anything that would break the endless crushing monotony of waiting. He'd known that she was responsible for his being held. He wasn't afraid of anything else she might do.

"Here?" he asked.

"Yes. She is in the capital. She will fly down here tomorrow. She has her own plane."

"Are you going to let her see me?"

"Of course. That is why she is coming. It is hoped that you will come to some arrangement with her so that you can leave with her. She has reached an agreement with the government. I believe she is prepared to pay a very large sum for you to be released in her custody. That is, as long as you're in this country, you will not be allowed to go anywhere without her."

"That sounds almost worse than staying here."

"It is no concern of mine. I follow orders. I have known that somebody expected to make a great deal of money with you. I wish to remind you of the alternative if you do not go with your mother. A case has been prepared against you along the lines I suggested to you. If your mother leaves without you, formal charges will be made against you. You will be tried and convicted. You will be released after a few years and deported. Your mother is prepared to pay for that too, but less."

Lance poured himself a drink. He had almost two bottles. He could get roaring drunk before she got here. If he looked like a hopeless case, maybe she'd give the whole thing up and go home. Left to his own devices there was a chance that he might not be convicted. No matter how they rigged it, there was no real case against him. "Have you found somebody to replace me if I go?" he asked.

"No. I know who it must be, but nobody will speak up against him. That is usual in such cases. The people here unite against the police. I will arrest somebody for a few days. If you go, I think the newspapers will get bored. Do you want me to bring you more clothes?"

"What for?"

"Do you know what you look like? You surely want to look right for your mother."

"Why? This is the way I am. I want to see Luisa."

"That is still impossible. If you stay and are charged, you will be allowed visitors like any prisoner, at fixed hours in the visitors' room in the presence of guards."

"Don't you have bail here?"

"That is decided by a judge. In your case, it will not be allowed. It rarely is with foreigners."

That was the end of Luisa. If they had their way, he would never know their child. His mother's arrival seemed less and less important. It didn't matter what

419

he decided. He was being stripped of everything that was his own. He was doomed to remain a Vanderholden.

The rest of the day was like any other. He slept. He woke up. He drank. He slept again. He knew a new day had started when the guard brought him a mug of bean soup. His mother was coming. She could take him away, but once out of the country what further hold would she have on him? He would probably be barred from this country as long as the present government was in place. If she cared, she could probably see to it that Luisa was never allowed to leave. She could end his life here but nothing more. He hoped he had strength enough to let Robbie go if given the choice, but he couldn't prevent them from deciding about that for themselves.

He had a couple of light drinks as the morning advanced but agreed with Ramiriz that he should remain reasonably sober for her. Eventually the chief appeared in uniform and told him that she was on her way and would be here in an hour. Lance was wearing his sarong. He didn't intend to make any other preparations for her.

He sat on the edge of the bunk with what was left of his last bottle and had a few more drinks while his heart thudded heavily, reminding him that he'd still be alive when this was over. He kept his mind a blank. There was only one person in the world he wanted to think about and he no longer had the right to think about him. The long blank stretch of time ended with the purr of motors growing louder and the wail of sirens. The motors came to a halt nearby and the sirens growled into silence. His mother had arrived.

He stood and secured his sarong with his back turned to the barred gate. There was a hum in the air of voices and movement indistinctly heard. Doors slammed and he heard several disconnected words shouted. He held himself taut, unaware of his own breathing, existence suspended. He heard the scuff of feet approaching along the corridor, a small army of them dominated by the brisk click of heels. The volume altered as they reached the right-angle turn. He heard the rasp of the key in the lock and the creak of the hinges. He turned with a faint smile fixed on his lips.

"Hello, Mother," he said.

She was planted on her stocky legs just inside the

420

cell, dressed like Queen May for Ascot in a pale mauve silk dress with a matching toque planted on her white hair. She was propped on a matching furled parasol. She looked older than he'd expected but as indomitable as ever. She remained without moving, her sharp eyes darting over him. Somebody brought a straight chair. The crowd in the hall faded away in silence.

"Come in," he said. The last time he'd seen her she'd said she no longer considered him her son so he didn't think a kiss would be appropriate, "Have you ever been in a jail before?"

"Why are you in this disgusting state, Marcus?" she demanded. "Don't they allow you to bathe?"

"We don't dress for dinner here. I thought you'd like to see what's become of me." He moved the chair closer to the tier of bunks and made a little gesture to it.

She waved a gloved hand in front of her face. "You have a very disagreeable odor."

"Some of it's me. Some of it's the place. I'll keep my distance. Sit down. You must've had a tiring trip."

She looked at the chair with distaste before sitting heavily, her hands folded on the ivory knob of the parasol. "Thank you for your concern. I must say I find the heat exhausting." She slipped a small handbag off her wrist and withdrew a lace handkerchief and dabbed her upper lip.

"I can't imagine why you've come although I'm sure it's very kind of you." He sat on the bunk in front of her.

"You're my son, Marcus, even though you've behaved like an unnatural one. The family could hardly stand by and see our name dragged in the gutter. Have you any idea of the publicity? Your brother and sister wanted me to wash my hands of you but I prefer to think that there's some hope of saving you."

"Are you sure there is? I mean, it all depends on what you mean by saving. I haven't seen the papers but I couldn't help knowing a girl who had the misfortune of getting murdered. She was very well connected, as you'd put it."

"She was perhaps socially acceptable although you never know with these Philadelphia families. You also couldn't help knowing a black woman who almost got killed in a car crash. Your choice of friends has been

421

unfortunate. That's part of what I mean by saving you. I hope these experiences have taught you some wisdom."

"The world is changing, Mother. Even the socially acceptable get murdered these days. I suppose the papers have made it look as if I did it. I didn't."

"I haven't supposed that you'd murdered anybody, Marcus. The fact remains that you've been charged with it."

"No, not yet. I gather I won't be if you say so."

"It's a good deal more than saying. It's paying. A price has been put on your freedom. A small fortune, I might add. It's shocking the corruption one encounters here. I don't see how you could choose to live in such a place."

"I don't seem to choose my places much better than my friends. I take it I'd be saved if I used better judgment."

"You'd have saved us all a great deal of heartache and embarrassment if you'd accepted my guidance from the beginning. I was right about the theater, as I think you'd be obliged to admit. I would like to see you come back and take the place in life that your birth entitles you to. It's shocking to see a person of your breeding and background going to seed in a place like this. I have nothing against colored people but they don't belong to our world. If you would accept the responsibilities of your name I'd be prepared to offer you all the help I've offered in the past."

"I guess that would mean not going places or seeing people you don't approve of."

"It would mean making a genuine effort to learn what is fitting for a person with your station in life."

"I understand we own a large part of this place. What did we want with it if it's so dreadful?"

"We've had substantial interests here but your brother is divesting us of many of them. He feels the situation is too unstable for them to be sound investments. After what I've seen here, I'll urge him to proceed as rapidly as possible."

"Well, that takes care of this country. What exactly do you propose doing with me if you're not going to divest yourself of me?" He noted the words she used and the slightly vulgar stateliness of her phrasing and felt the well-remembered sense of suffocation creeping over him. Having learned how to breathe, he couldn't fit himself back into his "station in life" without dying of asphyxiation.

"I'm being asked to make a considerable investment in your future. It wouldn't be fair to your brother and sister to take money they properly think of as theirs unless you can persuade me that it will be money well spent. I wish you to come home. Pamela has been waiting faithfully for you since you left her."

"She left me, Mother."

"A gentleman never speaks of his wife having left him, Marcus."

"Okay. She just stepped out for an errand two years ago, taking my child with her."

"Nothing has happened that you can't put right."

"Quite a lot has happened. I have a girl here who's going to have my child."

"You won't be allowed to stay here so we needn't discuss it."

"Only because you're making an investment in having me thrown out." In the interest of creating some air, he decided to shock her. "There's another thing. I've developed an unexpected interest in men."

"I've heard hints of it, Marcus," she said imperturbably. "I'm not surprised. It runs in the family. Your Uncle Charles. Cousin Osbert. I've always thought of it as an aristocratic affliction but it appears to be growing quite common in the worst sense of the word. I'm sure Pamela would be understanding. Her brother Fredrick shares your inclinations. A most attractive young man. He's been staying with us for Christmas."

She brought her parasol down on the stone floor with a decisive tap. "These things can be handled with discretion. I'm prepared to give you the same generous allowance you had before. When you've had time to straighten yourself out, you can have your own establishment again. If you wish to have a separate little place where you can lead a private life behind closed doors, you'll be able to afford it. I believe your Uncle Charles has some such arrangement. There's been a friend in the background for some years. Naturally, he's not inflicted on the family."

Closed doors. Back into the closet. She absorbed even

his unorthodox sexuality into the family tradition. She made his rebellion look ridiculous. He could have gone about his business without attracting attention to himself. Apparently only being an actor was beyond the pale. He could have discreet girl friends or boyfriends, as it struck his fancy, so long as he didn't inflict them on the family. He'd probably go mad but there was doubtless room for that in the family tradition. He would always be a Vanderholden. He couldn't go on fighting it. There was nothing to fight for except a passionate engagement in life that always ended in being destructive to others. He'd go home and fuck his very pretty brother-in-law. That shouldn't ruffle the smooth surface of life.

"I've had some small success making pottery. I'm told you know about that. I think I want to go on with it," he said.

"That seems to me a harmless hobby. Why shouldn't you?"

"Thanks. What's to prevent me from just walking away when we get to New York?"

"With no money? You're not a fool. However, I expect you to give me your word of honor that you accept my proposals before I have you released."

"My word of honor? I'd forgotten I had one. All right. If I understand you correctly, your proposals are that I accept your money and don't do anything Uncle Charles wouldn't do. I must talk to him. I've always liked him. Am I to be undisinherited?"

"All in good time, Marcus. It all depends on your behavior. I have great faith in your breeding. We'll discuss it in a year."

"Okay. You're in charge again, Mother. I told you you needn't've come. Did you expect me to put up more of a fight?"

"They've told me what to expect if you don't come with me. I had to be here to settle the terms. I don't regret it. We'll have a happy New Year's. The last few years have been a sad trial for me."

"You should've tried to accept my acting ambitions, but I don't have any regrets either. Being thrown out by you was the best thing that ever happened to me. I'm sorry you didn't see the show."

"I saw it, Marcus. You were thrilling. It was one of

the most terrible evenings of my life. I thought you were lost forever. I couldn't believe you'd give up something you did so well."

"Well, well, well."

He passed a hand over his eyes and sprang up and took a turn around the cell. He was touched by her. He didn't want to be touched by anything. The thought of the old woman going through an evening she must have hated for the sake of participating in his galling success brought tears to his eyes. Maybe it was possible to be a good Vanderholden, as Robbie had said. He returned to the bunk and sat facing his mother. "Thanks for telling me. What's the program?"

"The ambassador has arranged for me to use a house here. People have been very helpful. The Silvertons lent me their plane. I want a bite of lunch and a rest. I'll be back for you in two hours. Needless to say, you'll go nowhere with me unless you make yourself presentable."

"Won't I need my passport? I'm not sure where it is."

"Don't worry. It's been given to me." She stood with the help of her parasol and took a step back from him, waving a hand in front of her face. "I assume you have some clothes." She turned and stumped out of the cell. The click of her heels was joined by the sound of numerous footsteps as she and her retinue marched down the corridor.

The guard entered and picked up the chair and started out with it. Lance smelled himself and decided that he didn't want to stink anymore. He'd made his point.

"Wait," he said. "I want water. Hot water to shave and many buckets to wash. Please tell Ramiriz I want to see him quick."

The guard nodded and closed the gate on him and locked it. Lance heard motors, cars, and motorcycles roar into life. Sirens wailed and the noisy procession rapidly receded into the distance. His mother's arrivals and departures weren't exactly discreet. He had made himself powerless and intended to remain so, no matter what riches she heaped on him. He couldn't seriously believe that she would succeed in restoring him to his "station in life." He'd let her get him out of here and then make his decisions. He could do nobody any good sitting here and rotting, waiting to be tried.

425

His word of honor. He'd promised to go home with her and take her money. Taking her money didn't commit him to anything. If he gave it all away, she'd stop giving it to him. Home was New York. It was a big city, big enough for Robbie. Now that the future was becoming imaginable again, Robbie was moving back into the center of his consciousness. He mustn't think about him yet.

The guard let himself in with two buckets of water. "I'll bring more," he said. "I'm heating the water for shaving."

He went out, leaving the gate open, and Lance heard Ramiriz's footsteps approaching. He came in and lifted his arms in an expansive shrug. "It is settled. I'm glad for you. You have made the only reasonable decision."

"I want to see Luisa now. You must send for her quickly. I have only two hours."

Ramiriz shrugged again, less happily. "I have much regret. That is still not possible. Your mother wishes you to see no one. She mentioned Luisa in particular. Great sums of money depend on nothing happening to displease her."

"But for the love of God, this is the last chance I'll have to see her. She's having my baby, for God's sake."

"You will probably be allowed to come back in time when all this is forgotten. Maybe as soon as six months or a year when everyone is sure they can collect no more money from your mother."

"Listen. You can get her in without anybody knowing. We're leaving. What difference can it make?"

"There are many reporters out there. It is impossible to do anything without their knowing. There is somebody else who wants to see you. I do not understand it but he seems to be with your mother's party. I might be able to let him in without notice."

"Who?"

"Your friend. The painter."

Lance felt as if he'd been lifted off the floor. He put a hand out and gripped the policeman's arm to steady himself. "Señor Robbie? He's here?" He was barely able to get the words out before his throat closed to suppress a sob.

"Yes. He tried before to see you but I could not permit it. He came while your mother was with you. I will wait

426

to hear that she has made no change in her plans and then I'll send for him. He is at your house. You will see him when you go in any case. It can do no harm."

Lance didn't listen to him or try to make sense of what he was saying. Robbie was here. Robbie was his. He would make him his forever. He wasn't aware of Ramiriz leaving. He scarcely noticed the guard when he brought more water. Robbie was here. Despite all the public harassment and indignities he was letting himself in for, he hadn't been able to stay away. Lance had never doubted his devotion. He would see to it that he never left him again. From now on, they would help each other through the bad times.

He began to shave, hacking at the stubborn growth and going over his face a second time. He dropped the sarong and poured a bucket of water over himself and soaped himself from head to foot with the bar that had been in the suitcase but that he hadn't bothered to use for a week. He poured water over himself to rinse and started all over again, taking more care. It was the most satisfying wash of his life. Being deprived made you appreciate things. That was something his mother would never know.

An almost unused towel was on a bunk and he dried himself lightly so as not to lose the cool freshness on his damp skin. He heard sounds in the distance, the clang of metal and muffled movement. In a moment, he distinguished footsteps, the shuffle of the guard and the light assured step that he knew so well.

He whirled around to face the wall and began to tremble so violently that he was afraid he wasn't going to be able to stand. He clenched his fists. His heart felt as if it were going to leap out of his chest. His mouth stretched open in a silent howl of thanksgiving. He drummed his fists lightly on the wall and his cock lifted into erection. It grew more rigid with every approaching footstep. He wasn't going to break down. He was going to raise hell with him for leaving him. He wasn't going to let him forget that he was the most desirable guy he'd ever seen.

He heard the familiar sound pattern of the key turning and the gate opening. He swung around and their eyes met. "Oh God," Lance sobbed and flung himself into his arms, relinquishing all rights. He didn't care

427

whether Robbie had decided to do without him or not. He was his. He was going to keep him. Their mouths offered each other a ravenous welcome. Lance accepted what he was wearing as normal—dark trousers and shirt with some sort of epaulettes on the shoulders. He wanted him to be naked. He opened them all down the front and shivered with excitement as his big erection soared up superbly from them. Robbie helped him dispose of them. Their naked bodies writhed and wrestled together. Their breathing grew labored.

"Oh God. God damn you. You shit," Lance panted. "You don't know what you've put me through." He began to laugh at himself. Robbie joined in.

They were laughing uncontrollably as they wrestled each other to their knees. Lance soaped his cock and ran a soapy hand between Robbie's buttocks while their mirthful bodies played a game of provocation and evasion. They suddenly jostled each other into position and Lance entered him. Their laughter died abruptly. They whimpered ecstatically together while he completed his possession of him. He was joining them. He was making them belong to each other. He was assuming his responsibility for his lover. He would cherish and protect him and keep him always. Making love with him bore no relationship to having sex with anybody else. It was a consecration of love transcending desire, an ecstasy of union. They reached a triumphant climax together and lay on the floor in the shuddering aftermath of consummation.

Lance stirred finally and withdrew and washed himself again. He emptied a bucket of water over Robbie. "It feels good to be wet here," he said, dropping to his knees beside him.

"You don't know what that did for me," Robbie said without stirring. He was stunned by Lance, as usual. It was evident that Lance finally felt right in his own skin, as the French said. He belonged to himself. The toughness Robbie had felt in him before was no longer directed against himself but was a safeguard for both of them. "I've wanted it so much—your wanting me enough to take charge of me, feeling the man in you. I can accept you now, everything about you. I don't want to change you anymore. I just want to be yours. You're Lance, my life."

428

Lance stroked his back. His tan had faded somewhat. His romantic good looks were more striking when he looked less of an outdoor man. "Jill was leaving for New York. She was supposed to take you a letter. I was going to tell you I wanted you to come back no matter what the conditions. It probably wouldn't've been true. It's silly trying to turn yourself into a cipher for somebody, no matter how much you want to. So much gets in the way. Oh God, you're here, darling. We're together. That really is all that matters." He looked down at Robbie's magnificent bottom and stroked it, marveling that he'd taken him at last.

Robbie lay motionless, glorying in the gentleness of the hand that caressed him, waiting for Lance to put together all the broken pieces in any way that he wanted them. "I don't care if they keep us locked up together forever," he said.

"No, don't think like that anymore, darling. I hope I'm never locked up again. I want us to be free and together." He spoke passionately but without the edge of torment that Robbie was so accustomed to. "You think of us as man and wife but we're two men. You don't want us to take risks but we can't help taking risks. It's a risky business, two men trying to make a life together as if we were married. Everything's different, starting with sex. We belong to each other with our minds and our feelings more than maybe we ever can with our bodies, even though that's tremendous too. I discovered with Jill that I still like women. You expected it but I didn't. That may be something you'll have to accept."

Robbie sat up and put a hand on his neck. He drew him closer and kissed him tenderly on the mouth. "I told you, I accept everything about you. I've changed too. A lot of you has rubbed off on me. I pay more attention to people. It seems to make me attractive in a way I haven't been before. That's not surprising either. If you respond to people, they like you. If they like you, you respond to them more, sometimes more than you think you should. That's the way you don't want me to think. I understand that now. Funnily enough, I met your brother-in-law a week or two before all this happened."

"Freddy?"

429

"Yes. Actually, it was no great coincidence. Everybody in gay circles in New York seems to know everybody else. It's like a circulating library. Everybody ends up borrowing the same book. I met him at a party. When I realized who he was I paid a great deal of attention to him. We had a little affair. That is, we went to bed together more than once. We didn't want it desperately but we were pleasantly attracted to each other. It happened with a couple of others too. It wouldn't have if you'd been there but I didn't feel I was being unfaithful to you. If it had happened that often in a few weeks when I was with Maurice I'd've felt I ought to slit my wrists. I owe Freddy a lot. He called me about you before it hit the papers."

"How long have you been here?"

"I got here on Christmas."

"We had Christmas together after all." They reached for each other's hands and held them. "How much do you know about what's going on?"

"Just about everything. Probably more than you do. Freddy told me that he thought your mother was planning to take over. I got here two days ahead of her. I saw all the people she saw later, including Don Antonio. I tried to make a deal. I thought you'd rather not have your mother get into it. I went as high as a hundred thousand dollars before I realized I didn't stand a chance against her."

"A hundred thousand dollars for me? My mother's paying more?"

"A good deal more but she's making a lot of demands. I couldn't go higher without selling the house in France and that would've taken time. I gave up and rushed down here to try to see you. I wanted to get back to the capital while your mother was negotiating. It turned out to be important. Fortunately the papers have reported her movements so I couldn't lose her."

"You know they won't let me see Luisa? What're we going to do about her?"

"Nothing."

They looked at each other and pulled themselves to their feet. Lance led him to the tier of bunks he hadn't used and they stretched out on the lower one.

Lance ran his hands through his dark hair and sucked

430

on the seductive fullness of his upper lip. "Nothing?" he repeated.

"I've been with her, naturally. I don't understand her anymore. She's reverted to what I suppose she was before, a real primitive. She's thinking with her blood. She's glad Jill was killed. She says she deserved to die. I've warned her that you won't be allowed to stay but she's convinced that you'll be back. Fate or something. I've promised that I will be when the baby's born. I've arranged with the lawyer to represent us and keep in touch. It hasn't occurred to her to hope that you'd take her with you. I don't think she believes anywhere exists except here. The fact remains that she's my wife and therefore an American citizen. The embassy agrees but they say that if this government makes difficulties, it could take some time to regularize her status. Your mother has seen to it that there'll be plenty of difficulties. It looks like something we'll have to think about later. There's so much to talk about and so little time, but I don't think we need feel bad about her. She wouldn't fit in anywhere else and we're neither of us made to take on a permanent female attachment. She's better off than she was before. She says if you go, she wants her family to move in with her. Her family has suddenly become important to her. I can see her turning into a sort of matriarchal figure and forgetting that we ever existed."

"I don't want to forget the child, 'specially if he's a boy. I'm sure he will be. I was looking forward to him so much."

"I know, my beloved. So was I. We'll be able to think about it when we get out of this."

"We're more or less out of it, aren't we? You know Mother expects me to go home and become a good little rich boy again? I gave her my word of honor that I'd go through the motions. I guess we won't see each other for the next day or two but I'm going to need you in New York. Can you get there as soon as I do?"

"Probably sooner if I want to."

"What do you mean?"

"I don't think you're going to feel that you have to take your word of honor very seriously. Did she tell you where she's taking you?"

"New York, I guess. She said home. Where else?"

431

"I'll tell you but don't get upset. I have to explain a few things first."

"For God's sake, tell me. What is it?" His heart began to pound but Robbie was looking at him so lovingly and reassuringly that his momentary alarm was dispelled.

"Didn't you notice the clothes I was wearing?"

"Vaguely but I was so anxious to get you out of them that I didn't pay much attention. You looked a bit peculiar. Is it some kind of uniform?"

"Yes, my steward's uniform. I came down on the plane with your mother."

Laughter swelled in Lance's throat. "How marvelous," he crowed. "How did you manage that?"

"It's funny up to a point but not so funny why I did it. I couldn't understand why a woman like your mother would go to so much trouble and part with so much money if she just planned to take you back to New York and let you go about your wicked ways. I thought she must want more than that. Freddy gave me the clue. I called him from the capital to find out if there were any developments. He told me that your mother was leaving and if all went well he was going to join her in Palm Springs for New Year's. He's mad for you. When I told him you'd discovered that you weren't entirely indifferent to guys, he couldn't stop talking about you. He may've hinted to your mother that he'd make a more suitable companion for you than his sister while you were adjusting to a new life. Anyway, he said he was hoping to see you. The rest I had to find out for myself."

"I suppose you know you're turning me prematurely gray. For God's sake what's this leading up to?"

"It's leading up to the fact that your mother doesn't hand out her money for nothing. I got back to the capital after your mother arrived. It wasn't difficult to find her pilot. His name is Tom. There're only two or three good hotels where everybody stays. I picked him up in the bar of my hotel. I was in luck. He's queer and damned attractive. I knew the minute we looked at each other that I was all set. We've spent a couple of very pleasant nights together and he told me all I wanted to know. He's taking you to Palm Springs. The Silvertons—the newspaper people who've lent your mother the plane—they have one of those huge, high-security places that the rich go in for in the States, with electrified wire

432

fences and trained dogs and armed guards. Once she gets
you there, you won't get out till she's ready. Tommy's
heard all sorts of rumors. He thought you were off your
rocker, as he put it. She's going to have a doctor waiting
for you. I thought I'd better make the flight with you.
I was in luck again. The regular steward has a girl in
the capital. He was delighted to have an extra day or
two with her. He'll catch up to Tommy quickly enough
for nobody to notice anything. I paid for his ticket to
Palm Springs with enough extra cash for a wild night
on the town. Everybody's happy, particularly Tommy
with his new steward."

Lance imagined what it would have been like to discover all this as he went along, alone with his mother,
learning that they weren't going to New York, that he
wasn't going to be reunited with Robbie. He'd have torn
the plane apart with frustrated rage. Robbie had saved
him as he'd known he would. He pressed his lightly
sweating body against the splendor of Robbie's.

"You wouldn't look so pleased if you didn't have it
all figured out. Have you worked out a way of getting
into this place with me?"

"God no. I don't want either of us to see the inside
of it. What's the doctor for? Why did Tommy get the
impression that you were nuts? We don't have to let
our imaginations run wild with mad scientists turning
you into a vegetable but there're all sorts of drugs these
days you can use to manipulate the personality. Everybody in New York talks about quacks who do the
damnedest things. She may want to get you hooked on
some kind of tranquilizer to make you manageable.
Freddy will be there for a little light entertainment.
Tommy knows she's planning to stay in Palm Springs
at least a month."

"Son of a bitch. I was actually touched by her. I
should've known better. She dragged Freddy into it in
a way that seemed sort of peculiar. God damn her."

"She probably has Him where she wants Him but
there's still the U. S. Government. She can't detain you
by force until she has you where you can't do anything
about it. When we get there we could probably just get
off the plane and walk away but Tommy wants us to
put on a little show to cover him. We'll be landing at
the Silvertons' private air strip. Since he's worked for

433

them he's gotten some of his friends ground jobs. He's arranging for one of them to meet us in a car. He'll taxi in close to it. I'll open the door. I've had instant training as a steward. When I've got it open you'll jump up and knock me out of the way and go. You push the door closed after you. I'll help by pulling. I'll close it and pretend it's jammed. When he sees you're in the clear, Tommy will come back and show his dumb steward how to open it. You'll be driven to some club. We'll join you there as soon as we've escaped your mother's wrath. She may bash us both over the head with her parasol but there's not much else she can do. End of plot."

"You're incredible. She has my passport. Does that matter?"

"She won't have your passport long. Tommy will collect all the passports before we leave the country tomorrow. He'll give yours back to you before we land in the States."

"I'm going to get a new one anyway. It's easy to have your name changed legally. I'll get a new passport in the name of Lance Cosling. Are you sure you want to spend the rest of your life with a guy who has to go through all this to get away from his mother?"

"It's quite fascinating so long as we *do* get away from her. You know you could never go back to her, even drugged, don't you?"

"Of course, but I wasn't sure of anything until you walked in. I thought it might be the only solution. I thought maybe I should give you up for your sake. I wasn't even sure you'd want me back. Nothing can go wrong with your plot, can it?"

"Tommy says it could be tricky changing personnel in a foreign country but the Silvertons are big shots. Nobody checks him very carefully. He's not worried. I don't think I've forgotten anything here. I've packed our clothes. Our bags are on the plane. I packed all my heavy stuff and had it shipped. I've taken everything out of our account and left enough money with Luisa to take care of her for the time being. I gave your Juans a couple of months wages. They were pleased. I think that's it."

"I'll stop worrying. I never thought I'd be happy again. I'll never forget what you've done. It'll make me think twice before I do anything too appalling but I'll try not

434

to let it reform me completely. Being too happy is frightening. I want to keep us on our toes."

He felt Robbie's cock swelling against him. His own felt wonderfully restless. His hands grew active in the places where Robbie was sensitive. Robbie's began to do the things he loved him to do. Their bodies were instruments that they played like virtuosos. They purred with laughter.

"Where do we go from Palm Springs?" Lance asked.

"France. I want to find out if you like it."

"It's where you belong. I'll love it. We have time, don't we?"

"Ramiriz is going to let me know fifteen minutes before your mother comes for you. I don't want her to see me here. Tommy will be outside. We'll be on the plane when you get there. You won't know me, of course. We can make friends on the flight."

"I'm not sure I'll want to fraternize with the hired hands. I'm very ready to fraternize now. Shall we fraternize, brother?" He rolled off of Robbie and sprang to his feet. His cock sprang up into full erection as he did so. Robbie sat up and reached for it. Lance took a step closer and put his hands on his hips and swung himself slowly back and forth to enjoy the loose grip of Robbie's hand. "Tell me I have the most beautiful cock in the world," he demanded.

"Amazingly enough, you have."

"Is it any wonder I want to show it to everybody?"

Robbie laughed. He was adorably outrageous when he made fun of himself. "I think it's your duty."

"When you put it like that, you make it sound less tempting. It's like something my mother might say. Maybe I'll do it less often." They laughed together and Lance backed up, drawing Robbie to his feet with him. He pulled the pallets off two of the bunks and dropped them on the floor. "Let's go down there where there's room to maneuver," he suggested. He sprawled out on the pallets with his head on Robbie's thigh, holding his erection in front of his face where he could reach it with his tongue. "This is really the most beautiful cock in the world. I may start showing it to everybody. You're obviously beginning to enjoy it yourself."

"Maybe."

"Well, don't count on it. I might—to somebody who's

435

after you—just to show him it's mine. I'm going to keep you for myself. Every part of you was made for me."

He twined himself around him and made love to his body with wet lascivious lips. He was going to make himself his loose woman and his demanding husband. Their mouths met and hungrily possessed each other once more. Lance drew back.

"I hope you don't think my mighty display of masculinity was supposed to establish a pattern. I want to be had by a handsome guy with a big cock. Put some soap on it."

Robbie did so, still stunned by the transformation that had taken place in him. They were going to be all right. He didn't mind being kept on his toes; his big effort of adaptation was behind him. He had found the flexibility in himself. Lance was running out of experiments. They would soon be living like any other two people in love—for each other.

"Are you going to keep track?" Robbie asked with a chuckle while they were lying together recovering their breath. "Next time, you take me. Actually, I should have accrued credit for the last six months."

"I better get a notebook to keep it all straight."

They laughed together and splashed water on each other and washed. They heard Ramiriz approaching while they were drying. They kept their backs to the gate when he appeared. "It's time," he said.

"I'm just getting dressed," Robbie replied.

"I'll be back in a few minutes."

Lance hitched a towel around himself while Robbie put on his uniform. "I left the cap that goes with it on the plane," he said. "It's frightfully chic."

"I can't wait to see it. We'll be together again in half an hour. It's too wonderful to be believed. I don't care what you had to do to arrange it."

They stood facing each other, holding each other's biceps, and looked deep into each other's eyes for a long, loving moment. Their eyes withheld nothing from each other, accepting each other. "We'll have to be apart tonight," Robbie reminded him. "You and your mother will be with the ambassador. I'll be with Tommy to make sure nothing happens without me. That'll be the end of it."

"Is Tommy fucking you?"

"No. Just peaceful cocksucking."

"That's all right. We'll keep our asses for each other. Our cocks are sort of public anyway. There's too much of them to pretend they're not standing up if they are. Maybe mine will learn to behave itself."

"There's a cabin on the plane for you. We can make love all the way to Palm Springs."

"We can make love all the way to the end of our lives."

They gave each other a little shake and squeezed their arms as Ramiriz reappeared. Their lips touched and the gate swung open. Robbie was gone. Lance looked after him and laughed from deep in his throat, the muscles of his neck swelling. All the nightmares were over. He and Robbie had emerged into the broad sane light of day.

"Come in," Lance called expansively to the policeman who had planted himself at the bars. "I won't try to seduce you." He flung his towel aside and began to pull clothes out of the suitcase that lay open on the bunk.

Ramiriz came lumbering into the cell. The policeman looked at him and gave his head a little shake. The rich were astonishing. He had watched this young man sink lower than the meanest peasant, a pitiful human wreck. A few buckets of water had transformed him into a young god, blazing with health and high spirits. The body that he gave to men with such prodigal carelessness was more beautiful than any woman's he had ever seen. He watched a new personality being assembled as Lance dressed quickly, remembering him as he had been when he had first come here—a pale, moody youth carrying his shoes in his hands. The rich could afford to be eccentric.

Feeling that he had already escaped her, Lance had decided to put on a good show for his mother to make her regret her loss. Luisa had packed one of his good summer suits. It was made of some soft magical material that didn't crease. He shook it out and found a sumptuous Madras silk shirt. A pair of sandals had been polished to a high gloss. Luisa must have thought he'd be leading an elegant social life in prison.

"Are there a lot of newspapermen still outside?" he asked over his shoulder.

"More than when you saw them before. My men are waiting to escort you to your mother's car. You go first. I'm tired of being questioned."

Lance ran a comb through his hair. Clothes were an unfamiliar confinement. If he didn't melt in the meantime, he'd get out of them at the first opportunity and back into Robbie's arms. He was going to have sex on a plane again. He chuckled to himself as he pushed things back into the suitcase, closed it, and dropped it to the floor. He straightened and faced Ramiriz. The policeman gave his head another little shake as his eyes traveled slowly over the resplendent figure. The distant wail of sirens drifted into the cell. Lance glanced up at the window for a last look at the vulture. They hadn't got him this time. With Robbie at his side, they never would.

"She will be here soon," Ramiriz said.

Lance looked at him and held out his hand. It was taken in a friendly grip. "You'll be hearing from me," he said. "Thanks for the rum. Thanks for letting me see my friend. He's my lover, you know," he added proudly. He would never deny Robbie again.

"I know," Ramiriz said. His grip remained firm and friendly.

Lance was suddenly moved by departure. This man had been kind to him. He had found himself and much human warmth and sweetness here. He thought of Luisa and pulled away, his eyes stinging and his jaws tightly clenched. He snatched up the bag hastily and started out.

Ramiriz followed slowly. His golden hair against the light, his graceful body in the expensive white suit, Lance seemed to cast a radiance on the dingy row of cells. The young man strode down the corridor as if he owned it. He turned the corner and disappeared.

Ramiriz shrugged heavily as he lumbered after him. He doubted if he would ever know anybody like him again. Puerto Veragua would be dull without him.